CW01099801

Fool's Gold

Jae Malone

For Sonny and Beau
Best wishes
Jae Malone.
xx

Published by New Generation Publishing in 2015

Copyright © Jae Malone 2015

First Edition

The author asserts the moral right under the Copyright, Designs and Patents Act 1988 to be identified as the author of this work.

All Rights reserved. No part of this publication may be reproduced, stored in a retrieval system or transmitted, in any form or by any means without the prior consent of the author, nor be otherwise circulated in any form of binding or cover other than that which it is published and without a similar condition being imposed on the subsequent purchaser.

www.newgeneration-publishing.com

New Generation Publishing

For Cathy and Dad

Chapter One

'Papa! Papa Gabriel!'

The old priest had dozed off over his newspaper and woke with a start at the shout and the urgent loud knocking on his window. The newspaper slid to the floor as he stiffly rose from the comfort of the armchair and opened the slats of the window blind to find nine-year old Marisol Vasquez, clearly distressed and waving frantically at him. He had never seen her in such a state, her red-rimmed eyes pleaded with him for help and, having secured his attention, she rushed off towards his front door.

'Is there no peace?' he grumbled, forcing his creaky knees to move. 'I've been sitting far too long.' He shuffled slowly along the dim hallway as Marisol called and hammered incessantly on the door.

'Alright, alright child!' he shouted. 'Have patience!'

On opening the door, the sunlight dazzled his eyes, blinding him momentarily. Before he could see what was happening Marisol pounced forward and grabbed his hand. 'Come, Papa Gabriel! Mama needs you!'

He pulled away. 'What is this? What is the matter with you?'

But the girl was insistent. 'No time, Papa. Mama sent me.' She wiped away her tears with dirty fingers. 'She needs you. Now!'

'Wait, wait, Marisol, I must get my sandals.'

'No! There's no time for that, Papa Gabriel. Bare feet do not hurt.' She pointed to her own small dirty, unshod feet. With a resigned grunt, he reluctantly allowed the child to drag him along, cursing under his breath as he tripped on the hem of his robe scraping his toes on the stony dirt road. The sun reflected on the whitewashed walls of the one-storey houses, it hurt his eyes, his head began to throb and perspiration ran down his face. He hated the early afternoon heat and avoided going out until the cooler evening if he could. He thought resentfully of the sheltered comfort of his home situated as it was behind the church and in constant shadow but, once

again, the Vasquez family were in trouble. There was always one or more of them in some kind of mess. Life was hard for Raul and Inêz Vasquez with a family of ten children, but then life was hard for many families in this backwater village. He shaded his eyes with his free hand.

Marisol, unusually unkempt and agitated, let go of his hand and ran along ahead of him, urging him to hurry when he stopped to get his breath. She ran back to him and reached out. 'Don't stop, Papa Gabriel. Come on!'

He pulled away from her grasp. 'Marisol. What is this? Why does your mama need me?'

'No time Papa Gabriel,' she urged. 'Come, come,' she pleaded again and clutched at the sleeve of his robe, tugging frantically. He gave in grudgingly and allowed himself to be pulled along by this determined child. Doors opened and sleepy-eyed villagers, disturbed from their siestas by the noise, began milling about in the street. Even black-garbed Rosa, snoring in her rocking chair in her doorway, managed to get to her feet.

Father Gabriel shouted at them to return to their homes. 'There's nothing to see. What do you want here? Go home!' he shouted but to no avail as the mob refused to budge. Soon a column of curious villagers had formed behind pursuing them through the narrow winding streets.

The Vasquez' home was at the end of an alley which afforded some shade from the intense sunlight in the shadow of its walls and Father Gabriel was able to stop squinting. The door opened and little Dolores Vasquez tearfully ran to join her sister. They grasped each other's hands tightly. The sight of a second crying child made the old priest wonder if he should have taken the time to fetch his Bible. Once inside the tumbledown house he closed the door shutting out the nosy villagers and found Inéz Vasquez carrying six month old Alejandra, pacing back and forth across the wide, square area that served as a kitchen, living room and bedroom for the older boys. She turned as he entered the room with the two little girls. Her face drawn, her eyes puffy and red, she appeared defeated, beaten. 'Father Gabriel, thank you for coming,' she said quietly without ceasing her pacing.

'My child, what's happened? The children didn't tell me.'

'It's Elêna, Father. She has vanished.' Alejandra, far too young to comprehend what was happening, tugged at her mother's hair. Inéz gently released the baby's grip and, with one hand, threw a bundle of brightly patterned tourist-aimed shawls piled on the bench to the floor, so that the old priest could rest while his heart rate slowed and his lungs could breathe

2

easily again. Father Gabriel grabbed her hand and pulled her down on to the bench beside him.

'When?' Apart for the little girls, she was alone. 'Where is Raul? He should be here with you.'

'He and the older boys are out searching for her. Sandro and Hector are with my sister, Juana.'

Through the open window, the sound of the ever increasing crowd grew more raucous. A few were whispering but most were talking loudly, too loudly; their speculation causing added suffering. He heard a few sympathetic comments but some were obviously enjoying a good gossip, theorizing on what could have happened to the Vasquez family this time. It was distracting and his head throbbed painfully. He went to the window and closed it, ignoring the inquisitive eyes and craned necks as the curious neighbours tried to get a better view. The noise lessened a little. Inéz cradled the gurgling baby, her eyes glazed and staring at the door while Dolores clung to her and Marisol stood behind, her arm resting on her mother's shoulder in a mature and loving gesture of comfort.

'What happened, Inéz?'

'We don't know, Father. She went to collect wild papaya…and cucumber from the lower hills early this morning…she should have been back after an hour or so,' she gulped as tears brimmed. 'Father…what am I to do…my girl has not returned?'

'Could she be at the ruins?' He knew Elêna spent as much time as she could spare in the ancient temple.

'No Father, Raul has already been there. There was no sign.' She looked down at her youngest child and tears dropped onto the baby's face. 'He and the boys have gone to look in the places where she usually goes to find fruit for us.' Inêz fell silent.

Father Gabriel stood up and groaned. He flexed his knees until they stopped creaking before he went to the window and pulled down the raffia blind shutting out the prying eyes.

Fourteen year old Elêna was his prize pupil at the village school, where he was the only teacher. She was not his favourite, she was too distant, too cold, but she was keen to learn, extraordinarily keen, and soaked up any knowledge he wanted to impart. She never forgot anything and always did as she was told without fuss or comment. Her intelligence and ability to absorb set her aside from the other pupils; intelligence and the most remarkable eyes he had ever seen. They reminded him of ice cold emeralds.

3

Green eyes these days were virtually unknown but, in this area, there were many people with Aztec blood and, if the stories he read were true, green eyes although unusual, were not rare and Elêna had been fortunate for that gene to show up again in her. She certainly showed an interest in legends of the Ancients. He realised that the only time he ever saw any genuine animation in her face was in their shared interest in local mythology and archaeology. Like many others who heard the calling to the Church he had been fascinated with the old deities, indeed this had been his first love although now he served God. But Elêna's absorption in the subject was almost an obsession. Few people called her friend and she showed little emotional attachment to her siblings or parents.

A shout outside caught Father Gabriel's attention. He lifted the blind and saw the crowd part as Raul and the four older Vasquez boys elbowed their way through. Inêz extricated herself from Dolores and handed Alejandra to Marisol. The baby had fallen asleep and she whimpered at being disturbed. Inêz ran hopefully to the door as Raul, her husband and their sons Pedro, Jorge, Esteban and Emilio, their ages ranging between 13 and 10 years old, entered the room. Raul's hands were hidden behind his back. Jorge, Luis and Emilio stayed close to their father, their sorrowful faces clear evidence of misery, only Pedro stayed in the doorway. There was something almost like relief in his eyes. He saw the priest watching him and lowered his eyes hastily.

'Thank you for coming Father,' Raul's right hand gripped the priest's, the left stayed behind his back.

'Raul?' Inêz looked into his eyes, her question plain to see.

He shook his head sorrowfully. In his left hand he held a dirty, badly torn wicker basket with what appeared to be dried blood stains. Elêna had tied a number of ribbons to the handle some weeks before but now only a few tattered shreds remained.

'It must have been a jaguar or a stray wolf,' he struggled to speak, his voice grated harshly.

'*No!*' Inêz screamed and clung to her husband as he and the priest stared at one another in shared grief over her head. Father Gabriel broke eye contact first, miserably aware of how inadequate he was to help this despairing family, he laid an unacknowledged hand on Inêz' shoulder in an effort to console her, her heartbroken sobs pierced his soul. The girls wept with their mother while the boys stood in wide-eyed silence, attempting to hide their emotions. Grown men did not cry. Their self-control was agonizing to watch, except for Pedro who showed no emotion.

Inêz screamed. 'Father, she is dead. My Elêna is dead!' and she

4

collapsed at his feet. The old priest lowered himself painfully to kneel with her, took her hands in his and prayed.

Chapter Two

The wind whistled through the gaps in the rotting window frame and, where the rain lashed against the single-glazed panes, water seeped in where old putty had dried and fallen out. What had been a small damp stain on the landing carpet became a puddle as water trickled over the ledge and onto the floor adding to previous storm damage.

On the darkened landing, a girl stood at the closed door of the first dormitory, listening for movement inside. Her ear pressed tightly against the door for a few moments but the only sound from within was a soft snoring.

From the next room, the second dormitory, came a faint and pitiful sobbing. Elêna knew it would be the mouse-like Catalina who cried at every loud noise; thunder terrified her. She pictured the scrawny girl, huddled in her bedclothes, hiding under her bed, far too terrified to leave that sanctuary. Hearing no other sounds, she also judged that it would be unlikely any of the other girls would be brave enough to leave their beds; they would be too scared of Mother Ignacia and being beaten by her. Elêna had no such worry; she was protected and could not be discovered.

At the fire escape, one last look confirmed she was completely alone. She touched the gold, black and turquoise amulet that hung on a gold chain around her neck for luck. It was warm and comforting; she felt Tlaloc's power flow through her. He would see her safely through this night and beyond. A brilliant flash of lightning lit up the landing followed by a quickly shushed scream from the second dormitory. She held her breath half expecting a door to open at any time, but no-one came. The longer she waited, the more chance there was of being discovered. Hurriedly, she slipped through the door to the windowless fire escape and into inky darkness where no lightning broke through to illuminate the staircase. She felt her way along the short landing to the banister, counting her footsteps

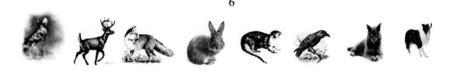

to the top stair. She had taken every possible opportunity over the past few weeks to practise going up and down the stairs with her eyes closed, familiarising herself with the landing, stairs and banisters and the effort had paid off.

Unworried by the darkness, she negotiated each step to the first landing, turned to the left, took six steps forward and turned left again before descending the final flight to the bottom of the stairs where she ran her hand along the wall until she felt the back door and located the lock. She fished in her pocket for the key she had stolen earlier that evening from Mother Superior's desk and slid it into the metal lock. It clicked loudly, the sound echoing around the hushed lobby. She hesitated, deciding almost as an afterthought, to check just one last time no-one was about. The door on the upper floor remained closed and the convent was quiet apart from the annoyingly loud tick of the hallway grandfather clock.

She had no fear of being caught leaving the convent at night without permission, or of any subsequent punishment by Mother Superior. It just did not fit into her plans; she was so close to achieving her dream, discovery would mean failure and that was unthinkable. In just a few days she would be free but until then she had to remain alert.

At the back door, she stepped out into the alleyway leading to the street and the welcome hammering rain, firmly closing the door behind her. A long flash of lightning lit up the sky and she smiled as the amulet grew warm. Tlaloc was with her; his storm was her protection.

She glanced up at the dormitory windows. Inside the girls were tucked up in bed or hiding underneath and on the other side of the building, Sisters Teréze and Mary Margaret would be in the hospital wing tending the patients, well Sister Teréze would be doing all the nursing. Sister Mary Margaret did crosswords and ate chocolate with her feet up all night leaving Sister Teréze to carry out the night shift, but they would both be on duty until dawn.

Her thoughts turned scornfully to Mother Superior who would probably be on her second bottle of wine or nodding off to sleep over her celebrity magazines. Not that any of this was part of Elêna's life any more. Soon she would escape to a new life far away with enough money to enjoy the freedom from boredom, poverty and drudgery. Tlaloc had arranged the storm to ensure no-one would see her leave, her business would be done and she would be back within two hours. That was all the time she needed to accomplish her mission.

Away from the shelter of the alley walls, the storm unleashed its rage as the rain hit her full on. Sheet lightning followed forked lightning with little

let up in the crashing thunder aftermath. Night-time on the streets of Alvarez City could be dangerous but a storm of this force would keep most people at home. In this vicinity only the rats and the criminal fraternity ventured out at night; the good and godly preferred to ignore its existence. Lightning split the sky again followed by another roll of thunder.

She opened her mouth to drink in the rain as a car passed by sending a crescent of muddy water across the crumbling pavement. The driver had not noticed her as he drove by and the tail-lights faded as the car quickly disappeared into the distance. Under a weak street lamp she tried to check her watch but another lightning bolt gave her all the light she needed. She held her hand over the watch to keep off the rain. Her destination was still fifteen minutes away on foot. Lightning flashed and she laughed. Even the rats hid on nights such as this. The wind blew her hood back but instead of gripping it tighter to her head, she cackled again as her dark shoulder-length hair clung to her head in sopping clumps, but she was unconcerned by the downpour. Being alone at night in one of the worst storms she had ever experienced should have been terrifying, but all she felt was exhilaration. With her head held high against the teeming rain and torrents gushing from the roofs and gutters above, she strode through the puddles without a care. None of this was important; soaked clothes and wet hair were of little consequence.

A narrow alleyway opened up on her left. She entered the dark, deserted high walled corridor between tenement buildings without hesitation and soon her eyes became accustomed to the inky blackness. In this narrow place, there were no street lights at all, only the reflected light from a few of the apartments above. She stayed close to the wall avoiding the rush of displaced water overflowing from the swamped drains that could no longer cope with the deluge that raced down the central gully and striding through the torrent, she kept up a steady pace, excited and eager to get her business over and done with.

Sheet lightning tore the sky, the first flash followed by another and another, the tall white buildings revealed in stark ghostly contrast to the red-black sky. Thunder roared, rolling on and on answering the lightning. The storm was magnificent, charged with electricity; she thrilled at its glorious force.

The narrow alleyway snaked between ramshackle tenements where few lights burned. Within, grown men were hiding under beds praying to whichever deity they worshipped, for the storm to pass them by. Contemptuous of their superstitions she chuckled at the absurd image. The storm was her ally.

The maze of interconnecting alleyways criss-crossed the district of El Lugar de Tres Perros (The Place of Three Dogs) and, in this sector of the city a person walked with danger after dark. Her coat felt heavy but it was not the rain that weighed it down, the full bottle of Tequila in her right inside pocket and a bulky envelope in the left, dragged it down at the front. They felt heavy against her ribs but were less obvious inside her coat, a bag would have invited trouble and she had no time for unnecessary interruptions. Nothing would be permitted to interfere and, although she was scared of no-one, it would be stupid to attract attention.

She quickened her pace, sloshing through the swollen puddles. A cat, far too wet for its colour to be determined, glared miserably at her from its hiding place under a communal rubbish bin. It skulked away from her, ears flattened and spat at her before slipping out of sight under the bin. Animals always behaved that way when she wore the amulet but their reactions were not her concern.

The rain ricocheted off the ground and ran into her boots as she hurried along the narrow alley; she could hear little over its constant drumming. She glanced again at the luminescent face of her watch. She would be late, but *he* would not complain; he had too much to gain. Or so he thought.

The rain eased a little and she brushed the wet hair from her forehead. Lightning flashed again provoking an even louder crescendo of thunder and a scream from one of the shabby two-room apartments nearby. She gave a snort of derisive laughter, cut short as a dog appeared from nowhere, its wet coat clinging to its skeletal frame. It sidled up to her apparently seeking comfort from the storm; its eyes wide with terror, but it only took a second to realise he had found the wrong person to go to for reassurance. Their eyes locked, his hackles stood on end and more terrified of her than the storm he slunk away, low to the ground desperately seeking a place to hide. Further up the lane it squeezed underneath a burnt out car, where it shivered and whined until she passed by before sloping away, still whimpering, into the darkness.

Having encountered no-one apart from two terrified animals which suited her very well, she thought with disgust of the man she was to meet. Having met him twice previously, she was pleased that after this last time their business would be done. She would not need him again. He was a fine craftsman and she appreciated his skill. For now he was a necessary evil, but his greasy, unwashed hair, soiled fingernails and smell of stale body odour disgusted her. She shuddered at the thought of him.

At a crossing in the alleyways she walked straight ahead. There was just a half mile to go. The hair on the back of her neck crawled and she

felt, rather than heard, a presence behind her. Someone wanted to play games. Her hand went to the amulet. Warmth spread along her arm sending a fiery strength into her veins. She was ready. A nicotine smelling hand tugged her head backwards, clamping her mouth shut. The other held a knife to her throat.

'Buenos noches, Sênorita,' a harsh voice whispered. Bad breath assailed her nostrils, stubble scratched her scalp. 'Give me your money!' His left hand lowered to hold her neck tightly in a strangling grip.

Her voice hoarse from the force of his hand on her windpipe, she hissed at him through clenched teeth, 'If you want my money you'll have to lower the knife while you search me.' She tried to wriggle free from his strong grasp but he held her more tightly. She was not beaten, or afraid. 'That means you take a risk.' She twisted, loosening his grip, 'I might fight back or,' she squirmed her head away from the smell of his stinking breath, 'you keep the knife pointed at me and let me get to my pockets,' she replied calmly.

'Or I kill you first and take your money when you're dead. You did not think of that Sênorita?'

'Of course I did…but you won't do that.'

'No? I will not? Why would I not? There is no-one to see us. There will be no witnesses to your death. No-one will hear you scream over the storm and, if they did, in this place, no-one would help,' his mouth twisted into a sneer.

'True but…' Talking to him had put him off guard and her retaliation had not occurred to him. There never did come a time at any point in his life when he worked out how she had taken the advantage but suddenly her thumb pressed unbelievably hard into his left palm with one hand while, with her right forefinger and thumb, she yanked his little finger away from his hand at right-angles. He howled in startled pain and staggered back as she spun around to face him. Angered at being taken by surprise so easily and pride wounded at being outdone by a woman, especially one so small and who still showed no fear, his mood changed to one of vengeful resentment. With the knife pointed directly at her, he moved in for the kill, his thick lips sadistically contorted into a vicious snarl exposing his missing teeth.

'You will not do that!' she commanded in a quiet, dangerous voice.

At least twice her width and several inches taller, he still believed he had the advantage and continued forward, the knife raised and ready to strike. It was at least seven inches long with a wide blade that glinted in the weak street lights. He looked down at his victim, murder in his eyes. She

locked her eyes into his. Someone screamed. Images of the fires of Hell surged through his brain while a shock of white-hot pain seared his soul. It had been he who screamed! He backed away, desperately trying to avoid her stare that bored into his soul. The knife plopped harmlessly into a puddle. In the dim light his face was ashen, terrified. 'What are you?' he croaked, cradling the hand that had held the knife with the other. It hurt terribly, almost as if he had been burned.

'You don't need to know.'

He shrank away. Her eyes held him.

'GO!' she commanded.

'Si. Graçias Sênorita…I go. La Madre del Dios, me ayuda.' Tripping over his feet, he ran as if all the demons from Hell were chasing him, mumbling prayers and rattling his rosary beads.

Typical, she thought, laughing out loud. Even street criminals needed the comfort of religion. But it was getting late and she moved on, he had been nothing more than an annoying interruption and she was almost at her destination. She put him from her mind as she arrived at the flaking brown painted door that banged open and shut with the force of the wind just as the rain began to ease. From two streets away the bell at the little chapel of Santa Maria del Cruz struck midnight.

She reached for the light switch on the wall inside the door. A faded Chinese paper lantern depicting a red dragon chasing its tail swung from side to side in the draught, its shadow shifting from wall to wall. The eye-holes of the dragon had been cut out and she casually wondered who had been having fun with scissors.

The short reprieve from the driving rain had not lasted long; she could hear it drumming deafeningly on the pavement again bringing with it more lightning. One, one thousand, two, one thousand, three, one thousand, she counted. Thunder rumbled, increased in volume and ended in an explosive crash. The storm was immediately overhead.

She took off her wet coat and shook the excess rain drops off it in the entrance hall. Not bothering to close the door, she strode the length of the rundown hallway brushing the dripping rain from her face and hair, unconcerned by her damp clothes. Like others in this area, this house would once have been an elegant family home and there were still signs of long-gone affluence, but years of neglect had allowed blackened damp spores to spread and the wallpaper and paintwork to peel. No-one had cared enough to mend the broken wooden banisters. None of the residents on the four floors of bed-sitting rooms had enough money to do anything about the property and even less interest in it. A rancid smell wafted up at

11

her. With the door unsecured any stray cat could get in. When her business was done, she would never be wet or hungry, never poor as her uneducated parents had been and never have to see anywhere like this house again. A life of luxury awaited her as long as she stayed focused.

Loud music blared from a room on the left. She remembered the old woman who lived there. Probably terrified of the storm she was trying to drown out the crashing thunder. At the far end of the hall a door opened; *he* waited for her. She took a few good deep breaths to brace herself before going in, not from fear, but from disgust. Steeling herself, she walked towards his leering grin. She had no fear of people, she had no fear of the Law, but smells turned her stomach. She had to hide her revulsion at the yellow teeth, yellow eyes, unshaven face and lank greasy hair and, as usual, his dirty blue shirt was open revealing a torn string vest stretched tight across his vast hairy belly.

'I'm sorry,' she forced a smile, 'I'll probably drip on your floor,' she thought it was probably the only time the grimy cracked linoleum would get a wash.

'Come in Sênorita. Mi casa es tu casa,' he leered. It could not be called a smile by anyone's standard. 'A few drops of rain do not matter.'

Holding her breath for as long as she could, she entered the shabby room illuminated only by a powerful table-lamp on the battered wooden desk on the far side and a feeble coal fire in the grate. Thin wisps of smoke floated into the room from the chimney with each gust of wind that came through the narrowly open window. Even with the draught of fresh air, the room was filled with an offensive combination of stale alcohol, cigars, body odour, and quite definitely, tom-cat, which assailed her nostrils and she struggled not to gag. A thin mangy tabby licked his paws on an old unmade bed in the corner of the room, its torn striped mattress showed under the blankets. Hearing voices the cat looked up. It saw her, yowled furiously and darted for the open window where it hesitated on the ledge for a moment to hiss at her before fleeing for the shelter of the lower steps of the outside fire escape; terrified to stay in the room but too scared of the storm to run off into the night.

'Gato estúpido!' the man spat as she edged by him into the dingy room.

'Are they ready?' she asked, ignoring his comment and trying to hurry things along.

'Si,' he replied with a yellow grin. 'Pardon, Sênorita. Yes, of course they are complete. I show you.'

Her hand cupped over her mouth, she followed him to the untidy desk where two passports lay open at the back page; her photograph was in both.

Beside them a slightly damaged photograph of another girl, approximately the same age and with similar green eyes and raven-black hair, looked back at her. She looked away. This girl had almost become a friend but there was no time for sentiment. She had died and her death had become a convenience. Returning to the passports, she picked up his magnifying glass and examined the details with meticulous care. One was in the name of Tanith Randolph-Sanchez; her birthplace, Boston, Massachusetts and her date of birth 28th August, 1985. The other showed the same birthdate, but bore the name Angelina Mattiolli from Rome. Unable to resist, her eyes were drawn back to the crumpled photograph. No, she would not forget this girl; it was thanks to her that her own future was assured. But *he* was standing close, too close, his breath stinking, waiting for her to comment but he could wait until she was ready. Eventually, her emerald eyes gleamed with approval, she smiled, ignoring his rank stench.

'You have done well Senor Ortega,' she forced a smile.

'You have the money, Sênorita?'

She nodded, patting the inside pocket of her raincoat.

'Yes, I have the money...but...first, by way of celebration; you would like to have a drink with me?' She reached into her pocket and produced a bottle of tequila.

His eyes lit up. 'We need cups.' He headed to the draining board where several chipped cups were placed upside down.

She unscrewed the cap and filled both cups half full, then pulled out the chair from behind the desk and sat down while Senor Ortega plonked himself down on the bed making the worn springs groan. He took a long swig from his cup, then a second and drained his cup.

'Here's to your expertise Senor.' She raised her cup but did not drink.

'Let me refill your cup Senor Ortega,' she smiled sweetly. 'This is a celebration. Think of how much money you'll have. You can leave this place and move to the coast. That is your dream, is it not?'

'Si Sênorita. I was born in a small house on the Yucatan Peninsula. My father earned a living by fishing,' he replied, his eyes filling with tears.

'Really? I had assumed you were from the city.' She kept up the conversation. 'I, too, was born outside of the city and I can understand why you would want to return. Childhood memories always haunt us.' She looked away, a wistful expression in her eyes and picked up the passports from the desk.

Ortega drank again, taking huge gulps of the warming tequila.

'You have a great skill Senor Ortega, the passports are perfect.' She looked at her watch. 'But I must go.' Reaching into the inside pocket of her coat she produced the thick envelope.

'Here is your money. Five thousand American Dollars as we agreed. I presume you still have the first instalment?' She handed him the envelope.

He nodded towards the desk and gave a throaty chuckle. 'Si. Of course I do. In there.'

He tried to get up to show her but his legs were unsteady, he lost his balance and flopped back on the bed. The tequila was working.

She pointed to the drawer. 'In here?'

'Si!'

'Good. Look after it. You won't get your dream without it. Trust no-one and take my advice, leave here quickly. If word spreads you have money you won't keep it long. Your life will be worth nothing.'

She picked up the passports and headed towards the door. 'We shall not meet again Senor Ortega but thank you for the service you have done me.'

'Adios, Sênorita,' he slurred. He tried to stand but dizziness overcame him and he fell on to the bed.

'It's alright. I'll see myself out. I'll leave you to get some well deserved rest.'

Leaving the door slightly ajar, she hid in the shadow of the staircase. The storm still raged and no-one was about. She heard a grunt from inside the room and moved closer to the door. Not yet. A chair scraped along the floor, followed by a loud groan and a heavy thud; then breaking crockery. She looked at her watch; the digitalis had worked faster than she had expected.

Ortega lay on the floor, blood oozing from a nasty gash on his head where he had hit the corner of the desk as he fell, the desk lamp lay on its side and papers had been dragged onto the floor beside him. She held a small mirror close to the blue lips. He was not breathing. She locked the door; she could not afford to make a mistake now and be caught. Stepping over the body, she opened the desk drawer and removed an envelope. It was full of American Dollars, her Dollars. She washed both cups at the cracked, grimy sink before wiping them thoroughly and leaving them on the wooden draining board careful not to touch either of them again. Then she poured the remaining tequila down the sink with the tap full on, rinsed out the bottle and put it in her still very damp raincoat pocket. She turned off the tap and wiped it with a cloth. Lastly, she put both envelopes into her inside pockets, picked up the old photograph and rifled through the other documents on the desk, making sure she had retrieved anything that

14

could link her to him. Satisfied there was nothing left she headed for the door where she stopped and thought carefully about her movements since she arrived. Had she touched anything else? No, she was certain she had not. She stared down at the body. It was unlikely he would be found soon and she would be out of the country in twenty-four hours. From what she knew of him, there was probably no one to miss him.

She laughed out loud. 'I said you should trust no-one didn't I? Nunca hacer el negocio con el Diablo! No, never do business with the Devil!'

Delighted with how little time had been wasted, she slipped back into the street and dumped the empty bottle at the first rubbish bin she passed. She had chosen her victim well, his counterfeiting skills were incomparable, but his weight, constant drinking and smoking had affected his health. He had obvious signs of heart problems. The digitalis had just sped up the inevitable and stopped his heart. His over-indulgence was no fault of hers. It had been his own greed that had killed him. Now he would never talk and there was nothing left in the room to show she had ever been there.

Chapter Three

As the sun rose over the Mendip Hills in Somerset it spread a golden pink glow over the treetops casting a glorious colour that swept gently down the slopes and over the village of Winterne. The dawn chorus announced the start of day and, in the elves cavern, Primola began preparations for breakfast. Feeding the hungry clan was no small task and she needed help, especially on this day when scores of visitors would be arriving.

'Saldor! Saldor, it's time to get up, dear,' she called cheerfully through the interconnecting communication tube.

'M'ready up,' Saldor yawned as he checked his reflection in the bedroom mirror. He wanted to be particularly well-turned-out this morning and made some last minute checks on his appearance. Clean, green leather boots, freshly laundered white cotton shirt, yellow woolly jerkin, grey breeches, yes, he told himself, everything spotless and correct for the day. 'Wassed n dessed...be...be down soon,' he stammered hardly able to contain his excitement. It was going to be a wonderful day with many old friends arriving from other clans across the country.

That terrible night when Jossamel had carried the semi-conscious Saldor back to the clan cavern home several years before was now a distant memory for everyone except Saldor who could remember nothing of it at all. He had been missing for several hours and the search party sent to look for him had roamed the wood, tunnels and caves long after the moon had risen. Finally, in the early hours the following morning, Jossamel and Lommie had found him swaying and wild-eyed in a narrow dead end tunnel where the elves rarely went.

Unable to recognise his old friends, he screamed in fear, shrinking away and calling them demons. Jossamel had called his name softly, reassuringly, talking of their elfling escapades hoping to break through into Saldor's subconscious memories, but nothing worked. Instead Saldor

shrieks grew louder and his terror increased with each step they took towards him. Frantic, he huddled against the rock wall in a tight ball to protect himself from the imagined harm they were about to inflict and lashed out at them in a violent struggle before fainting away in an imagined terror.

Although frightening for his rescuers, this was also something of a relief as it allowed them to carry him home where the clan quickly formed a protective group to watch over and nurse him.

During the long weeks of recovery he was unaware of being moved from his small alcove to new quarters above the kitchen. Being a little larger, more comfortably furnished and closer to the kitchen and bathrooms provided his carers with two benefits. The first was the warmth from the hot water piping that ran through his new room to the bathrooms, and the second was that the close proximity to the hot water outlets made it much easier for them to nurse him. The increased space also eased the congestion for his numerous visitors, many of whom turned up at the same time and eventually the numbers had to be restricted to four at a time.

But they also had an additional worry to deal with. Jossamel's reaction to Saldor's condition became a real concern for the clan. Clearly distressed by his friend's situation he angrily paced the cavern corridors unable to find release for his feelings of helplessness and frustration in not knowing what happened or why. At times, he shut himself away from everyone and when he was amongst them, he snapped and snarled more often than not until eventually, to give him something positive to do, Rondo suggested they excavate two small tunnels through the earthen wall to install a pair of narrow arched window to allow in natural light and fresh air. Everyone was delighted with the result except Saldor of course, who remained totally oblivious to everything.

Ellien and Primola, also eager to do something, hit on the idea of brightening the room by making curtains and a matching counterpane in a sunshine yellow to brighten the grey-brown cave wall, convinced that bright, cheerful décor would speed Saldor's recovery. Flowers and gifts arrived with every visitor and Charlie, knowing how much Saldor loved watching wild birds hung five colourful bird pictures in a line on the wall where he could see them easily from his pillow and a metre long gilt framed mirror leant against the wall, donated by Piggybait and Clap-trap.

Halmar had his own contribution to make. Unable to help in any other way, he used his skill to create a beautifully carved wooden chest which he placed at the foot of Saldor's bed which was used to store his clothes. A few weeks later he gave the convalescing patient an equally ornate carved

rocking chair where Saldor sat by the window as his health improved delighted to watch the wood wildlife go by.

There were very few mirrors within the elves cavern home and this was by far the largest. Some of the young female elves were a little jealous that it had been given to Saldor, especially when he was unable to make use of it but they never uttered their jealousy out loud. Piggybait and Clap-trap had found the mirror attached to an old wardrobe someone had fly-tipped in the wood and after a struggle detaching it from its base, had dragged it back to Saldor's new room. Whoever had dumped it could never have imagined it ending up in the sleeping quarters of a sick middle-aged elf.

After the initial shock where no-one knew quite what to do other than make Saldor well and happy again, Jimander had begun asking questions reasoning that someone must know something about what had happened but to no avail. It seemed no-one had any idea what had happened to him, so together with Jerrill he set up a formal investigation to get to the bottom of Saldor's sudden illness.

Jossamel and Lommie went over what they knew again and again trying to recall whether there was anything they had missed. Tarryn and Tildor, the twins, who had been visiting at the time, eventually admitted having been in that area at the time, told the Council of Elders that they had seen Saldor wandering off with a group of ten or so pixies led by the much disliked Garrak, known for his risky and sometimes downright criminal behaviour.

They said they thought that some of the pixies appeared to be chewing what looked like shredded herbs and offering them to Saldor. They said they caught up with Saldor and had tried to persuade him to return to the cave with them but he had laughingly refused and walked away with the pixies.

When Jimander asked why it had taken them so long to explain what they knew, they tearfully explained that Garrak had threatened them shortly after Saldor had been found and said that what had happened to him would happen to them if they spoke up.

Although Jimander and Jerrill considered it strange Saldor would have spent time with the pixies when he knew how dangerous they could be, there was no evidence to contradict the twins statements. He and Jerrill hoped that when Saldor recovered they would discover the truth but, until then there was nothing more to be done. Shortly after that the twins returned to their own clan and did not return.

Saldor did recover but it soon became obvious he would never regain his former health, in body or in mind and, other than a few fragments of distorted memories he seemed content with his life.

On emerging from his coma he remembered nothing and recognised no-one, but slowly accepted that his constant visitors knew him well. Confused and terribly weak, he lay on his bed drifting in and out of sleep and was never left alone, not even for a minute, as his companions nursed, cajoled and bullied him back to health. All his waking hours were filled with someone talking to him, feeding him, bathing him or simply being there to care for him but no-one ever told him what had happened, avoiding the questions in his eyes by talking about anything else other than his condition.

Sometimes in his dreams he thought he caught snatches of hushed conversation or raised, angry voices and the name 'Garrak', although he had no idea what that meant. But by far the most terrible time came when he tried to speak. As he struggled to form coherent speech, his constant companions, Piggybait, Clap-trap and Primola, encouraged him, soothed his disappointments and simply loved him. Even the elves power of healing could not heal whatever afflicted Saldor.

The Chief spent many hours sitting on the floor (they had not brought up his enormous chair) talking about the wood and the wildlife, just talking for the sake of it. Saldor later remembered his voice echoing through his dreams, but it was a while before he remembered who the huge man was.

Piggybait and Clap-trap talked to him of the clan and piece by difficult piece he began remembering who everyone was but still they avoided telling him how he came to be so unwell. After several months he rejoined the clan at mealtimes, helped in the kitchen and did whatever he could to participate in clan life spending as much time as his simple duties would allow, accompanying Piggybait and the others on night patrols or on other excursions from the cave.

Primola, in particular, nursed him, almost adopting him as one of her own offspring to which Rondo and Rondina made no objection. When Saldor was ready to get out of bed he had to learn how to walk again and with Rondo on one side of him and Rondina on the other, he soon gained enough strength to walk unaided.

Primola's husband, Rondalas, also took Saldor under his wing and worked with him for hours each day until Saldor was able to form his words clearly enough to be understood although his speech never fully recovered its previous clarity and he often struggled to remember vocabulary.

Saldor and Rondalas became great friends and, although close to Piggybait and Clap-trap and Primola's family, when Rondalas died it was a terrible blow to the recuperating elf, setting his recovery back by months. Halmar, taking pity on Saldor's grief and his struggle back to health, encouraged him to get out more, took him to the stables, farm and the lake where he could watch the humans from the trees without being seen.

Daylight, sunshine and fresh air gave him the stimulation he needed and soon he was looking forward to his daily trips above ground, dressed and ready to go no matter what the weather, at least an hour before Halmar came to collect him. But still no-one answered his questions. And so life continued for Saldor.

There was just one elf who made Saldor feel uncomfortable to be around and that was Jerrill. Unlike the others, Jerrill rarely smiled and kept his distance most of the time. On the odd occasion when they did find themselves in the same space, Jerrill would seldom speak; his usual acknowledgement being a curt nod before going on his way. Many times when he mentioned Jerrill's attitude to Primola she would only say that it was just his manner and he should not worry, but worry he did.

Other than that, life was generally good apart from one sorrowful episode. When Jimander died, he grieved for him. Jimander had become his much-loved protector and father-figure and always would but, again life moved on and Primola kept him busy with catering for the wedding of Ellien and Halmar and he was thoroughly enjoying the responsibility.

That morning, his fingers shook so much he found it difficult to hook the loops over the toggles on his jerkin. In fact his excitement had awoken him early making sleep impossible once the dawn chorus began streaming in through his open windows at daybreak. Before getting up he thought about all the guests who were due to arrive that day and how much help Primola would need from him. He had bristled with pride when she said she could rely on him far more than the headstrong Rondina who would probably let her down by disappearing just when she was most needed. Looking up from struggling with his jerkin fasteners, his eyes looked back at him in the mirror. He could still not remember when he began to look so old. Thin wispy grey hair above grey streaked brows and tired grey deep set eyes in dark hollows stared back from his gaunt pallid face. He had occasional flashes of memory of someone with thick chestnut coloured hair, a wide smile and cheerful disposition, but they floated away before he could grasp them and he was unsure who this ethereal being was. His puzzling dreams, many of them terrible nightmares, had lessened over the

years but there was still the odd night when he woke in fear desperately trying to deal with some spectre of the past he could not understand.

Physically he appeared so much older than his contemporaries, Piggybait, Clap-trap, Jossamel and Lommie but eventually realised it was futile to try and change what could not be changed and he became resigned to life the way it was. The fact that he was once a handsome, sociable and somewhat flirtatious character, much sought after by female elves, was in the past. Settling for life the way it was brought contentment and he gave up chasing the shadows of his past.

After smoothing down his thin unruly hair, he headed happily down the stairs to help Primola in the kitchen. He puckered up his lips in another attempt at whistling but only succeeded in making a terrible squeaking noise. For weeks he had been attempting to copy Sam who had had seen whistling in the wood on one of his visits and had practised over and over again much to the irritation of his friends but still could only manage a shrill sharp screech.

By the time he reached the kitchen, there was already a bustle of activity. Primola was barking orders at a group of noisy elflings who were getting under her feet and she sighed with relief as he helped her scuttle them out of the room. He guessed she would have little time for elflings with all she had to do that day even though he had been looking forward to it. This was the day the guests were to begin arriving for the pre-wedding celebrations.

Chapter Four

Charlie had a wonderful life; protecting and maintaining the woods and being close to the wildlife was his greatest joy apart from his duties at Christmas, of course, and being with the love of life, his wife, Cathy.

His Christmas activities meant he lived in parallel worlds which he had managed very successfully to keep apart. Naturally there was the odd overlap. Sam, his nephew, had managed to cross into both of Charlie's realms, so too had Armistice Jenks, which was evidence of just how much he trusted them.

He had been at work since early that morning and his stomach told him it was time for lunch. He laid his ancient and faded khaki-coloured army jacket on the riverbank, sat down on it and took a plastic box from his bag. Inside were four thickly cut wholemeal bread sandwiches of cheese and pickle, an apple, and his favourite chocolate bar, king-sized, of course.

Brilliant turquoise dragon flies hovered in the waterside rushes, their colour matched by the busy kingfishers as they dived into the crystal blue water of the stream as it flowed to join the wide River Axe.

Here he could breathe; here he was at one with the Earth. After all the rain of late, working deep in the wood had been suffocating; the trapped humidity made it far too uncomfortable to work for long but on the grassy riverbank, the air moved freely and he wanted to stay for a while. He leaned back, resting on his elbows feeling his shoulder-length grey hair sticking damply to his temples as he breathed in the cooler air. His beard felt hot and itchy and for a fleeting moment he contemplated shaving it off, but thought better of it; these high temperatures would not last forever. Perhaps he could allow himself a little time off by using the time to observe the wildlife around the river.

On the opposite bank, two small hinds stepped uncertainly down to drink, their eyes flicking from left to right, their bodies prepared for flight

at any sign of danger. Kingfishers, their small nests built into in the riverbank dived into the water looking for fish or snatched insects in the air, their bodies a breathtaking blur of blue and orange.

Charlie loved the riverbank whatever the season, but summer brought a particular beauty when everything came alive; fish jumped, insects buzzed, birds sang, and he was always rewarded by the company of the wildlife that came to drink. Most of them knew him well and were not unduly concerned by his presence. He thought, ruefully, that these wonders were disappearing from the modern world in favour of housing and industrial developments and felt a pang of sorrow that there may be little left of the natural beauty of this world for people to enjoy in the future. The pressures of modern life and continual demands for land and building space would leave humanity lacking the miracles of nature.

The air hummed with bees and hoverflies flitting from one wildflower to another, a water vole splashed into the water and swam slowly upstream, dragonflies flitted amongst water reeds that slowly swayed in the soft breeze. With the scenic, busy riverbank life swarming Earth should be treasured but more often than not, money was more important and the beauty of nature was forced into second place.

'Charlie! Charlie!' Peace shattered, the deer scurried off into the sanctuary of the trees and the kingfishers darted into their nests as Armistice Jenks ran towards him excitedly waving a piece of white paper. Fond as he was of her, Charlie could not help feeling a pang of annoyance at Armistice having shattered his idyll but managed to conceal it as she approached with Merlin and Bandit running alongside. He stood up to join her leaving his half-eaten apple on the grass for the birds and insects to finish. Had it been any other type of litter he would have taken it with him; leaving rubbish in the countryside was not on his agenda. He had seen too many animals die getting their heads caught in plastic bags or bottles and knew that any rubbish could cause damage.

He wiped his hands on his dark green cargo trousers and looked back across the river before clambering up the bank to meet her. The deer had disappeared completely so had the kingfishers; peace and harmony gone.

He sighed, 'Whassup, Armie?'

'Oh Charlie, it's fantastic! It's wonderful! It's such exciting news!' Merlin jumped up to greet the big man and as Charlie leaned down to stroke the loveable dog, Bandit leapt onto his back then up onto his shoulder where he spread himself out purring loudly nestling against his thick neck. Armistice was so breathless she could hardly speak. Excitement temporarily robbing her of speech, her eyes shone a little too

brilliantly as she waved the paper in front of him; her hand shaking uncontrollably.

'Good news is it?'

'It's the best,' she panted, finally able to get her words out. 'It's wonderful Charlie. All this time I believed I had no family left but this letter changes everything. It arrived this morning and I just had to find you. Read it. Read it! It's wonderful.' Her hand shook as she passed him the letter.

Charlie scanned the paper while an excited Armistice paced up and down, delight and anticipation flashing in her deep blue eyes.

'Well? What do you think?' She searched his face for a reaction. 'Of course I telephoned her at the number they gave as soon as I got the letter and it's all in hand.'

'What's in hand?'

'It's all arranged. She's going to come and live with me.'

'I can see why your so het up. It's pretty amazing. This would be your great-niece?'

'Great-niece. She's my sister Artemis' granddaughter,' Armistice explained. 'You remember. Artemis had a daughter, Lilith. Lilith married that American doctor, Roscoe Forbes Randolph and they moved to Salem in Massachusetts. Their daughter Tabitha was born there. When she grew up she went into nursing and met Luis Sanchez, he was a young Mexican doctor training at the hospital. They went back to Mexico and worked in the poorer villages there. Tabitha followed the family line in being a natural healer; family genes you know. You remember, Edward and I paid them a visit when Tanith was about two years old...such a pretty child.'

Charlie nodded, waiting until Armistice had finished before trying to get a word in.

'Well anyway, I heard the gift of healing passed into her and she showed a remarkable understanding of herbal medicine from a very early age. Five or six, so I heard.'

'But weren't they all killed in the floods a few years ago?'

'Yes, well that's what we were told but...isn't it wonderful...Tanith survived. No-one quite knows how. Their home and the clinic were swept away and they found Luis and Tabitha's bodies a few days later. We thought Tanith was dead too but, now of course, I understand why her body was never found. As you can see from the letter, she was taken to a convent where she was nursed by the nuns.'

'It says she was suffering from amnesia,' Charlie added looking down at the letter again.

24

'That's right,' Armistice cut in, 'but goes on to say that after a couple of years working in the convent hospital, things slowly started coming back to her and now she has remembered who she is. The nuns helped her to trace her family and found me, as her only living relative.'

Armistice was so exhilarated she did not notice Charlie's look of concern.

'It'll be good for me to have company, Charlie. I'm starting to feel my age…'

'Don' believe you,' Charlie butted in.

Armistice shot him a knowing look.

'Flatterer! But seriously Charlie, I'm beginning to feel my age and look closely, the signs of age are beginning to show. Sometimes my memory fails me and my joints are beginning to ache. It'll do me good to have someone to care and keep me company.'

'Are you sure she's prepared to do that?'

'I've spoken to her and yes, she will. She's just so pleased to have someone of her own family to live with that I'm sure we'll get on splendidly. Oh, Charlie, she leaves Alvarez City tomorrow, flies out from Mexico City on Sunday and, bearing in mind the time difference, she'll be here Friday, late afternoon.'

Although a little calmer, Armistice was still shaking. Merlin, having picked up her mood, ran around her legs, barking. But Charlie looked down at the letter again. An involuntary shiver ran down his back that had nothing to do with the cat sprawled across his shoulders.

Chapter Five

From the opening of the Wookey Hole Caves for public tours that morning, Piggybait had been baffling the tour guides by appearing behind the groups of visitors for a split second when only the guides could see him and then vanishing again. By the time they were aware of him, he had ducked behind the rocks or slipped down a small tunnel, known to the elves, only to pop up somewhere else and drive the poor guides to distraction in the belief they were hallucinating.

At one point he even lay down in the Witch's Kitchen cave, beside the stone reputed to be her dog, and confused a young newly appointed female guide by pretending to be a second dog. He found it a little less amusing when she ran off in floods of tears, leaving her party abandoned in the cave known as the Great Hall. Feeling a little guilty, he scuttled away to the wood hoping that he had not upset her too much.

It was only on his way back home by way of the river that he remembered guests would soon be arriving for Ellien and Halmar's wedding. His favourite oak tree was just a few metres ahead; the perfect place to spy on the first guests arriving.

Ellien, the only child of their previous leader, Jimander, was much cherished by the Winterne Clan and almost as well loved was Halmar, son of Jerrill, one of the clan Elders. He, together with Piggybait and Clap-trap currently led the Winterne elves. It was therefore with great excitement the entire clan were preparing for the celebrations.

Having settled on a comfortable branch, it was only a short while before Piggybait saw a group of elves approaching. He leaned forward as the newcomers approached his unseen vantage point and was surprised to see the dark blond twins Tarryn and Tildor. Piggybait scowled. So they were back! He had hoped never to see them again, their appearance usually meant trouble.

Born into the Winterne Clan, the twins had become increasingly unmanageable as the years had gone by. Stealing, as opposed to the more acceptable elven 'borrowing' or 'finding', their bullying and fighting, together with the suspicion of the involvement in what happened to Saldor, led eventually, to their expulsion from the clan at the command of Jimander. For years the clan heard nothing of them until, a few months ago when word reached Jerrill that they had been with the Pennine families for some time and, by all accounts, quite peacefully.

Having put them out of his thoughts for years, just seeing them again made Piggybait shudder but now here they were and, for Ellien's sake, he would have to be polite.

The twins were tall; Tildor, being the larger of the two, were easily the tallest elves Piggybait had seen and still, as had always been their custom, the now middle aged twins were dressed alike. Piggybait suppressed a chuckle, thinking they looked a little silly still dressing in identical jerkins and leggings at their age. Unaware of the amusement they had caused, Tarryn and Tildor strode along the riverbank followed by, as Piggybait later discovered their combined brood of seven young elflings and, in single file, following behind them, were three females. Judging by their ages, he guessed the leading two were wives of the twins.

The first had dark hair, greying at the temples, tied back in plaits, secured by a band of the same dull leaf-green material as her gown. She walked with a determined stride after her menfolk, shoulders back and head held high; something about her made Piggybait feel an instant dislike.

The second female, was somewhat slimmer and less matronly in appearance than the first. She had a softer expression and hummed a cheerful tune as she took in the sights and sounds of Winterne Wood. Her deep blue eyes scanned the world around her and, for a brief moment, her gaze seemed to settle on his hiding place but she turned away when Tildor spoke. If she had seen Piggybait, she did not let on and his attention shifted to the third female in the group.

Dressed in a flowing primrose yellow robe, her features hidden by a mane of long dark hair that fell straight and glossy to her waist, she gave an impression of great sorrow. Piggybait felt that if he could just see her smile, she would be very pretty but her bearing was so downcast he wondered if she ever did. Loneliness flowed from her as she trailed behind the leading group, every step portrayed her dejection.

He looked away; to continue watching her would be an intrusion into her melancholy. A few paces behind the despondent female, were four stern-faced males he did not recognise and a much older male.

The young female temporarily forgotten, Piggybait's sharp eyes examined this particular male closely. There was something very familiar about him; the way his grey hair curled down onto his shoulders, the way he held his head and the confident stride, but try as he might, Piggybait could not place him.

Tarryn held out his hand to help the two more mature females down the embankment to the rough path. No-one assisted the doleful female but she did not look for help and fended for herself very well.

One by one the group followed the path alongside the river until they disappeared, single file, beneath a cascade of thick trailing ivy concealing one of a number of narrow caves carved into the limestone hillsides by the force of the river.

He had counted seventeen in the party. Was that all that were coming from the Pennines? That was not nearly enough to show respect; the Pennine clan was one of the largest, comprising a number of established families; Piggybait had expected a much larger contingent. This turnout was very disappointing and he wondered whether the others had opted to stay at home but it occurred to him that this may just be an advance party with more arriving later. There was still time after all.

The afternoon sun blazed down on what was the first hot day in a number of rainy weeks encouraging the wood plant-life into rapid and lush growth advantageous to the nosy elf and his people as it helped veil their increased activity from human eyes.

A rustling behind Piggybait heralded his friend Clap-trap's arrival.

'You're late!' Piggybait carped without looking round.

'So?' said his silver-haired friend. 'Is that a problem?'

'No, just stating a fact.'

'Anyone worth watching?'

'Mmm. A handful from the Pennines are here, not as many as I'd have thought would turn up though and you'll never guess who's with them.'

'Tarryn and Tildor?'

'How did you know?'

'I guessed. It would have to be someone we didn't expect or like for you to comment.'

'Huh,' Piggybait sulked. 'Everyone's a Sherlock Holmes!' For a few moments the only sound was the movement of the river and bird song until the peace was broken when Piggybait spoke again.

'Not only are the twins here but there was someone else with them. I'm sure I recognised him but…can't think who he is.'

'Description?' Clap-trap settled himself comfortably on the branch.

'Longish grey hair, medium height, normal stuff for an Elder, but...I don't know, there's something about him...the way he walks, his...his posture...it just reminds of...oh, I don't know but you'll see what I mean when you see him.' He looked towards the ivy covered cave.

'And...um...there was someone else, a female...young, pretty, very sad. She intrigued me.'

'Oh yes,' Clap-trap grinned.

'Don't say 'oh yes' like that,' Piggybait said, huffily. 'I just felt sorry for her that's all.'

'Oh yes.'

'*Yes*!' Piggybait protested. 'She had long dark hair and looked lonely and sorrowful.'

Clap-trap held out his slim hand and examined his long fingernails. 'That'll be Aerynne.'

'Who?' Piggybait looked blankly at his friend. 'How come you know who she is?'

'What's the matter with your memory? Too much acorn wine perhaps?' Clap-trap tutted impatiently. 'She's Rynnor and Aellsa's daughter, remember? They died during Rynnor's brother's wedding in Bavaria...around thirty years ago...the avalanche!'

Piggybait looked at him blankly. Clap-trap stared at him, astounded that he was unable to recall the tragedy. How could he have forgotten such a disaster when so many clans had suffered casualties?

Slowly the memory came back to Piggybait. 'Oh yes, I remember. Rynnor's brother's entire clan were wiped out,' Piggybait recalled. 'Didn't Aerynne predict it? A dream?'

Clap-trap nodded. 'Now you've got it. As I heard it she warned them but Rynnor felt duty bound to go and ignored her. Aellsa, in turn, felt it was her duty to go with her husband but she made him agree to leave little Aerynne behind with the clan. Young though Aerynne was, many of her predictions had proved correct and Aellsa's instinct made her leave her daughter behind with her mother's clan, just in case anything did happen. And, of course, it did. They say the poor little thing has lived with the guilt of not stopping them.'

'Isn't she the one with rain-cloud coloured eyes?'

'That's her,' replied Clap-trap. 'She's renowned for the colour of her eyes, her exceptional gift of The Sight and her sorrow.' Clap-trap got to his feet. 'Come along, Piggy. It's time we paid our respects to our guests before the evening festivities, whether we like them or not and, don't forget we're on night patrol tonight.'

'Thanks for reminding me!'

Chapter Six

There was little movement in the dusty schoolyard of St Merriott's Comprehensive; only insects found enough energy to buzz around in the blistering thirty degree heat. Usually the yard would be thronged with students playing football, standing in groups talking or, with the school Prom arranged for next week, practising dance steps. But on this particular Friday the grounds were almost deserted as most of the students had stayed within the cooler environment of the solid brick school.

At some time in the past someone had made the mistake of planting a circle of ash trees far too close together. Having matured over the years, they now formed a thick border around the school creating a sun-trap where the temperature rose to uncomfortable levels. It had only taken a day or two without rain for the effect to show in the yellowy-brown patches of grass.

Although nearly everyone was inside, there were a few brave souls resolutely making the most of their breaks from lessons and a handful of scattered groups lazed against the wall or sat on the cool ground within the shade, talking, playing cards or looking at magazines.

In view of the conditions, Mr Davies, the Head Teacher, had relaxed the rules on school uniform; there were no school ties to be seen anywhere, sleeves were rolled up, top buttons on shirts and blouses undone, and boy's shirts were hanging loosely outside of trousers instead of being tucked in. All this informality was received with snotty-nosed disapproval by the school secretary, Miss Earnshaw, who continued to wear her jacketed suits buttoned-up. But the dampness of her dragged back hair, her flushed appearance and shiny nose, betrayed her stubbornly strait-laced discomfort.

Sitting on the steps of the main door, shaded by the portico above, two girls with rolled up sleeves and rolled down socks, had somehow summoned up enough enthusiasm, or possibly panic, to catch up with notes

they should have taken in class. A small group of four other girls were talking 'Prom' dresses, hairstyles and make-up and a few of the boys were discussing, cricket, the lack of football, girls and bands but there was little movement anywhere.

At the back of the building, three wide concrete steps led up to a set of double doors, where sweltering, even within the shade of the building, a group of friends preferred to spend their leisure time talking in private. It was not that they had anything to hide but, with everything they had been through in the last few months, they felt more comfortable together than with anyone else. One of the boys, with dark blond spiky hair had tied his school tie around his head, the ends hanging down at the back. His girlfriend gave it a tug.

'Oi!' he gripped her hand.

'Jason thinks he looks cool like that,' Sue, joked as Jason struggled to keep the tie in place.

'Don't!' he laughed, making a good-natured protest.

Jenny Richards, her pale blonde hair tied back off her neck in a ponytail, fanned herself with her Geography notebook while looking down at her bare feet and wondering whether she could bring herself to put her sandals back on for the afternoon lessons.

'Have you sorted your dress out for the Prom yet?' Sue asked. Having red hair and very pale freckly skin, Sue had to be very careful in the sun and was making sure she stayed in the shade.

'I had that sorted out a couple of weeks ago,' Jenny replied, rubbing dust off her instep.

'Well, what's it like?'

Jenny grinned. 'You'll have to wait and see.'

Having listened to Sue describing in great detail the dark green dress she planned to wear, Jenny teased by giving nothing away, refusing to let Sue wheedle it out of her.

'She won't tell you,' Sam Johnson grinned, throwing a wink at Sue whose freckled cheeks took on an even rosier hue. 'I've been trying to find out for weeks now and I'm taking her.' He was sitting on the step below Jenny and she gave him a little push with her foot.

When Sam first arrived in the village Sue had developed a huge crush on him and there was a time when Jenny would have been jealous of his wink. At one time there had even been animosity between the girls, but now Sue was happily going out with Jason, friendship was restored.

'If it wasn't so bloody hot I'd get her to tell me.' Jonah Atkins said from the top step where he was lying on his back, his head resting on his school

bag; his left arm flopped across his eyes. As he had not spoken for a while they had assumed he was asleep.

'Oh you think so? And just how would you manage that Jonah Atkins?' Jenny challenged.

Jonah did not move. 'You've got ticklish feet, remember?'

'You wouldn't dare.'

'Whatever you do, Ms Richards, don't dare me. You may be sorry.'

Sam listened to their banter recalling a time when things had not been so pleasant. Jonah had been known for his vicious and brutal behaviour and when Sam moved into the village, his first few weeks had been pretty miserable because of Jonah. But all that changed when Sam saved Jonah's life during a cave-in underground at Christmas. Since then he and Jonah had become good friends and even Jonah's previous victims had eventually forgiven him, even though many would never forget. Then, over the Easter school holidays, Jonah had been grateful for Sam and Jason's help when his family had been caught up in an attempted diamond theft during the Easter holidays. Together they had caught the crook and rescued his family.

Since then, life had settled down and their main source of excitement had been getting involved with the excavation of the dungeons at Jonah's home, Winterne Manor. Experts had carried out DNA tests and other examinations on the skeleton and torture instruments the boys found at Easter and the family were still awaiting the final results. Fortunately, a good friend of Jonah's mother, Harriet, was supervising the excavations and had agreed to keep quiet about the secret tunnel from the wood into the Manor and the boys never mentioned Jonah having found an old ring inside the skeleton to anyone. It was still hidden in his room and would remain under wraps until he found out more about it.

With the mock GCSEs over, they were looking forward to a relaxing summer holiday and Sam had plans to visit Nottingham to catch up with his old school friends. His best friend, Dave Russell would be returning with him for a short stay in Winterne which worried Sam a little, giving him nightmares about Piggybait and Clap-trap turning up at awkward moments which they often did just to embarrass him.

'Hey, Sam!' Richie Bishop was rushing towards them looking very agitated.

'Wonder what he wants,' Jenny said as Sam dragged himself from the step and walked over to meet Richie. Jonah half sat up, opened one eye and squinted into the sunlight to see what was going on before laying back

down again, apparently uninterested. 'I dunno,' he replied, 'you'll find out soon enough.'

Jenny and Sue tried to make out what Sam and Richie were talking about but it was only a couple of minutes before they saw Sam nod his head enthusiastically and Richie sloped off looking very relieved. Sam was on his way back to them when the bell sounding the end of the lunch break rang. Jason picked up Sam's bag and reluctantly got to his feet before the others moved.

'I'm not looking forward to being stuck in that portakabin for an hour,' Jenny scowled forcing her sandals back on to her slightly swollen feet. They hated the portakabins the school used as temporary classrooms; they were too hot in the summer and freezing in the winter. 'I could always make out I'm sick and go home,' she grinned as Sam joined them. Jason handed him his bag.

'What did he want?' Jenny asked, her curiosity getting the better of her.

'Tell you later.'

'Sam's keeping secrets,' Jonah teased Jenny as he dragged himself up from the cool step. 'Not a good sign Richards. He's keeping things from you already. Just think what it'll be like when you're married.'

'Oh, shut up, Jonah! Stop stirring it!' Jenny snapped, blushing.

'I hope Shep'll let us have the door open,' Sam changed the subject.

'Knowing him, he won't even have the windows open,' Jason grumbled screwing the top off a bottle of water. 'You know what he's like about bugs flying in. Yeuk! This is warm.' Giving the bottle a look of disgust, he threw it in a nearby bin.

'Pity we didn't think to bring the 'fridge out here, eh, Jen?' Sue giggled. 'And your skirt's dusty,' she said, pulling at the back of her skirt to check her own.

Jenny brushed off her skirt and linked arms with Sue as the girls walked a short way ahead of the three boys. As they turned the corner heading for the four portakabins the girls stopped.

'Sam! Look at this!' Jenny whispered, signalling him to hurry.

Hidden from the main yard, a small Year Seven boy cowered, arms raised over his head and face, as a much older boy, towered over him pinning him to the wall with a thick shovel-like hand against his shoulder. A second boy, appearing to be nothing more than a spectator, sniggered at the younger boy's obvious terror. Sam recognised them both. Alan Hallett, a Year Ten pupil with a large ego and matching frame, and his friend, Martin Brooks, Ian's brother. Neither boy seemed aware they were

being watched as Hallett puffed out his chest threateningly, took a step backwards to savour the smaller boys terror-stricken expression.

'Stand back. This is a job for Atkinsman!' Jonah exaggeratedly rolled his sleeves up and pushed by the girls. Jenny looked at Sam who shrugged his shoulders, while Sue grabbed Jason's hand.

'...an' Oi'll 'ave tha' phone off yer an' all,' Hallett cracked his knuckles. Brooks sniggered again as the younger boy blanched. He turned his terrified face away from the imminent beating and seeing Jonah approaching and the group of friends following, he threw them a pleading look.

'Hallett! Hey, Hallett, don't you know anything? You're doing it all wrong,' Jonah smirked. Hallett and Brooks looked shaken. 'You need help from the expert. Watch and learn fans.'

'Oh, for Heaven's sake!' Jenny barked, pushing past Jonah.

'Jenny, Jen...what you doing?' Having been watching Jonah, Sam had missed seeing Jenny move forward to interfere in the potentially dangerous situation. She ignored him. He tried to pull her back but Sue grabbed his arm, her face a picture of smug satisfaction.

'Leave her alone,' Sue whispered. 'She knows what she's doing.'

'Stay out of this Richards,' Jonah ordered, not taking his eyes away from Hallett while a gormless Martin Brooks looked from Hallett to Jonah and back again, not knowing what to do.

Ignoring all of them, Jenny gently took hold of the younger boy's hand and pulled him away from the wall, walking with him between the two bullies, while Jonah looked on in admiration.

'What's your name?' she asked the bemused boy.

'D...Digby...J...Jonathan Digby,' he stuttered, gazing up at her adoringly.

'Well, J...Jonathan D...Digby,' Jenny teased kindly, 'get along to your class and don't worry about these lumps here, we'll sort them out. They won't bother you again.'

'Wha...whaddya mean, sort us out?' Suspicion and fear mingled with bravado in Hallett's eyes. 'Wot's an ickle girlie like you gunna do?' Losing face in front of an audience, especially to a girl, would make him look stupid.

'Try me!' Jenny said quietly, turning back to Hallett as Sue moved Jonathan away from trouble and urged him to leave. The atmosphere was tense. Brooks tittered, nervously keeping an eye on Jonah and Sam. Jonathan seemed reluctant to go and held back at the corner to watch.

'Jenny! No!' Sam yelled. He could not believe how stupid she was being.

'Let me deal with it, Jen,' Jonah begged, shooting Sam an anxious look. Jason had gone very pale. Only Sue seemed unconcerned.

Hallett was still trying to brazen it out, but Brooks looked scared and started backing away, very unsure of himself. To Sam's surprise, Jenny showed so little fear he thought she was behaving like a complete idiot. She was between Hallett and his escape route into the schoolyard. Jason moved forward to stand beside Sam.

'How about we stop all this, eh, Jen? Hallett?' Jonah said forcing a laugh, trying to make light of the situation, but Hallett was having none of it. He could not be seen to be 'bested' by a girl; it would make him look bad and anyway, getting past her would be easier than going through Atkins or his mates. Jenny dropped her bag and faced him. Hallett smirked, obviously thinking he was in for an easy time of it.

'Jenny! Look out!' Sam yelled, moving forward to get between her and Hallett.

'No! Sam, stay back!' Jenny yelled, not taking her eyes off the thug in front of her.

Hallett swung at her, his right hand closed in a tight fist. Throwing her left arm out as he lunged, Jenny blocked his punch and forced his right arm away from her. Even before Hallett could register his surprise at being thwarted, Jenny followed up her block with a swift, breath-taking punch to the solar plexus, ripping the air from his lungs and landing him, dazed and not a little embarrassed, on his large backside in the dust. It was all over in a split second. Gawping, open-mouthed, at his friend for no more than two seconds, Martin Brooks abandoned him and tore off around the corner. Jenny stood firm, legs slightly spread, fists clenched and positioned ready to fight off retaliation, silently daring Hallett to come back at her. Sue gave a whooping cheer and Jason breathed again. Only Jonah burst out laughing. 'Bully boy Hallett, floored by a girl. Now I've seen everything.' He clapped a hand to Jenny's shoulder. 'Well done, Richards,' Jonah grinned. 'I didn't know you had it in you.' He walked over to Hallett who still sat on the hot tarmac ground. 'Respect the girlies, Hallett,' Jonah smirked. 'I'd scarper tough guy, before we let her loose on you again.'

Sue walked up to Sam. 'See, I said there was nothing to worry about. She knew what she was doing.'

'Yeah, but how…when…?'

Hallett ran off as fast as he could and Jenny, coolly acting as if nothing had happened, picked up her bag and linked her arm through Sam's as they walked on. 'Close your mouth Sam, there's a tractor coming.'

Sam stopped. 'What just happened there?'

'OK, OK,' Jenny began. 'You know those dance classes I've been going to on Wednesdays and Saturday mornings?'

Sam nodded. Jenny pulled him along again. 'They're not dance classes. They're Karate classes,' she grinned wryly. 'Come on, we'll be late.'

Sam allowed himself to be led along. 'Karate!'

'Er...yeah, Karate,'

Behind them, Jonah was still chuckling and Sue, obviously very proud of her friend was grinning from ear to ear. Only Jason was still too gobsmacked to speak.

'But why didn't you say anything?' Sam asked, not a little surprised.

Jenny looked behind to see how close Jonah was. 'After what Jonah did,' she leaned in close to him, 'and how you sorted him out, I decided no-one would ever bully me again and talked to dad about it...he's training too.'

'But why didn't you tell me?' Sam repeated his question.

'I wanted to get through a couple of gradings before I told you.'

Sam stopped walking. Jonah, Sue and Jason followed suit.

'What?' Jenny asked. 'Why have you stopped? Are you annoyed with me?'

Sam took her hand. 'No, I'm proud of you but you scared me witless. I thought he'd hurt you.'

Jenny smiled and gave him a quick kiss on the cheek. 'You're sweet,' she said.

'Just don't go scaring me again like that, alright. I'll get mardy and you won't like me when I get mardy,' he grinned.

'Mardy? What's that?' Jenny asked him.

'It doesn't matter,' Sam grinned taking her arm again. 'Come on you lot, we'll be late for Shep.'

'Erm...excuse me,' a small voice called from behind them. It was Jonathan Digby; he had followed as they walked away. 'Thank you. I think you're very brave,' he mumbled shyly up at her.

'That's OK. Don't worry about it.'

'My dad bought me that phone and he'd 'ave killed me if it got stolen,' the boy went on.

36

'You know mobiles aren't really allowed in schools, Jonathan,' Jenny began.

'They tempt thieves and bullies,' Sam added. 'Keep it out of sight for today and tell your dad they're not allowed. The teachers'd probably confiscate it if they knew about it. It's to stop kids like you getting into trouble with people like Hallett.'

Jonathan nodded.

Jonah stepped forward. 'Whatever happens from now on you've got your very own protection squad. Any problems give us a shout. But since Hallett's been floored by an ickle girlie, as he called her, he'll stay away. We'll make sure everyone knows. He won't know where to hide after this.'

The boy gave Jenny a shy smile. 'Thanks again. I'd better get along now.'

They watched him run off before heading for portakabin. Somehow Sue, Jenny and Jason had moved a few paces ahead of Sam and Jonah.

'What did Rich want?' Jonah asked.

'I'll tell you later, but I need you to do me favour,' Sam said keeping his voice low. Jenny was waiting at the top of the portakabin steps for them.

The windows were closed just as Jason predicted but as their teacher had still not turned up he and Jonah opened all the windows which allowed some air to flow through.

'Why can't we have a fan in here?' someone grumbled.

'Or go into the school,' Sue added.

'The rooms are all full,' Jenny replied.

'But there's always the hall. We…'

She was cut off as they heard a noise on the steps. 'Shep' had arrived.

From the desk behind her Jenny heard Jonah whisper, 'Proud of you Richards.'

'No more talking!' Mr Shepherd said closing the door behind him. 'And why are the windows open?'

Chapter Seven

'Primola!' Jossamel shouted as he struggled down the stairs hampered by several large earthenware jugs he was struggling to carry in each hand. Saldor watched from the doorway with no thought of helping even though the jugs looked heavy.

'What's the matter with him now?' Primola wiped her floury hands on her apron as she went to stand beside Saldor at the door wondering what the excitement was about. Having finally got to the bottom of the stairs with no mishaps, Jossamel used his shoulders to push through the throng towards them.

'Get out of my way, will you?' he grumbled at a group of elves who were blocking his way and too busy talking to notice his predicament. 'If you're not going to move at least give a hand.' The group parted but none of them offered to help.

'What've you got there, Joss?' Primola took two of the jugs and prompted Saldor to do the same.

'Thank you. At last,' he flexed his stiffened fingers. 'Wait till you see what I've got here. I've done really well this time.' He certainly appeared delighted with his haul. 'By Alfheim, it's hot in here.'

'What d'you expect with all this baking, icicles?' Primola snapped. 'Come on let's see what's in these?' Primola put the jugs down on the stone floor, Saldor followed suit.

'There,' Jossamel put two jugs on the heavily scrubbed wooden table pulled the stopper out of one of them. 'Have a sniff of that.' The grin was wider than ever.

'It's cider! Joss, you old rogue!' Primola laughed. 'Where under earth did that come from?'

'Above earth you mean,' he retorted with a grin.

Saldor watched, open-mouthed and beaming but not really understanding what all the fuss was about.

'Ben Bragg's barn.' Jossamel smirked, 'and there're plenty more where they came from. I lost count of the number of jugs he's got in there. Stacked to the rafters they are, so he won't miss a few. I think this one's mead.' He took the stopper out, sniffed. 'Ahh, yes.' He closed his eyes, savouring the sweet aroma of the mead, an appreciative smile on his lips.

'With the number of people coming for the wedding I'll have whatever you can get hold of,' Primola said, putting the stopper back in the first jug. 'But don't get yourself in trouble and stay away from that shotgun.'

Saldor blanched.

Primola leaned closer to Jossamel, took his arm and led him away from Saldor. 'I would've suggested you take Saldor along for the outing, if it was anyone else's farm,' she whispered.

Jossamel nodded, understanding. 'No, he's not quick enough on his feet. Rondo's quick and cunning, no offence,' he added seeing the injured look on her face.

'None taken,' she fibbed. That was her son he was talking about.

'A few jugs of mead and cider aren't worth any of you getting hurt but, if you promise to be careful and you're quick…and you wait until dark, then alright. You can take Rondo. Why not see if Clap-trap will go with you. And please watch out for those dogs.'

Jossamel gave her a reassuring smile. 'We'll be fine. I know what I'm doing but I haven't seen Clap-trap for a while. Is he about?' A thought occurred to him. 'I know what you're up to, you're pretending this all about our safety but you're thinking the more of us there are, the more jugs we bring back, eh?'

Primola threw him a look of hurt innocence. 'Joss dear, whatever do you think of me?'

Jossamel winked at Saldor who had been following the conversation even if he missed the point of their banter. 'Do you want me to take Piggy too?' he asked her.

'No. He's out spying on the arriving guests. He got all excited, just like a human child at Christmas, bless him and now I come to think about it, I haven't seen Clap-trap for a while either. I bet they're together. No, better forget them both. Just see if you can round up three or four young, fast moving, sharp eyed elves.' She paused. 'What about Corporal? I think he's finished in the transit cave for today and he doesn't get out much. I'm sure he'd love to join a raiding party for a change.'

Jossamel made a deep mocking bow to her before leaving the kitchen whistling cheerfully. An affectionate smile played around Primola's mouth as she watched him head through the ever growing number of guests, greeting newcomers and old friends as he looked for Rondo, Corporal and a few of the more cunning elves. She was fond of Joss; he was almost like a son to her and just cheeky enough to have been one of hers.

'Right, come on, Saldor my lad, it's time we got on. Look at all those mouths to feed.' Primola brushed back her greying hair, secured it with an ornamental comb that Rondina had 'found' in the village. She lifted several pure white tablecloths down from a shelf and handed them to Saldor.

'Put these out on the tables for me will you, my dear, while I get some more from the backroom.'

The massive cavern the elves called home had been split into different areas for the festivities and the tables set out for the feast were located in an area to one side of the long staircase that extended to the far end of the cave where it was deserted and quiet for the moment; the mass of elves were congregating way off at the far end or talking in the smaller chambers that led off it.

Saldor had just laid out the last of the tablecloths when someone tapped him on the shoulder. Behind him two middle aged elves leant against each other staring at him. One of them smiled coldly. Saldor looked from one to the other. Pictures flashed through his mind; memories too fluid to grasp but they frightened him.

'Saldor old friend,' the smiling one said, moving towards him. 'Good to see him again isn't it, Tildor?' The other one nodded but did not speak. Saldor was not quick on the uptake but something warned him these two meant him no good.

'Oo are you?' They seemed to know him and he felt there was something familiar about them. He looked around for someone from his clan. He wanted a friend, someone who would help him but there was no-one in sight. He looked hopefully towards the kitchen door; perhaps Primola would come out. But neither she nor anyone else appeared. He was alone and scared.

'Ha! Would you believe it, Tildor? Our old friend Saldor doesn't recognise us.'

'Come on Tarryn, leave him alone,' the one called Tildor said, not meeting Saldor's eyes. He made an attempt to pull his brother away but Tarryn snatched his arm away from his brother's hand.

'Now, now, Tildor, where's your manners? We need to re-acquaint ourselves with old friends and Saldor's definitely an old friend.' His voice was steely. Tildor shuffled his feet and looked around the room then back to Saldor.

'We'll talk later, Saldor. On you go, you must have things to do,' he said, moving aside to give Saldor the chance to escape, but Tarryn blocked the way.

'Alright, brother, you win,' he said never removing his menacing stare from Saldor who squirmed with fear. Saldor tried to push past but Tarryn grabbed his arm and held on, very tightly.

A memory, their faces, much younger, blazed through his mind but the recollection brought no comfort. Something had happened, something bad. He raised his eyes to look at Tarryn seeing a momentary flicker of surprise and then it was gone replaced by the pleasure of instilling fear in another. Saldor wanted to get away but Tarryn still blocked his path. He turned to Tildor who had sounded kinder but he just averted his eyes. Tarryn moved closer, his manner threatening. He looked around to ensure they were not being observed then pushed Saldor roughly against the cave wall hurting his back. Tildor did nothing. Saldor wept, terrified of the brutal assault.

'I'd have thought that after we were so good to him, he'd have been pleased to see us again, wouldn't you Tildor? After all we were such good friends.'

Tildor gave his twin a 'don't bring me into it' look and shrugged, lowering himself onto a nearby bench as if distancing himself from his brother's bullying behaviour.

'Don' push…d…d…don' like it,' Saldor pleaded, turning his face away from Tarryn.

'Poor Saldor don't like it. He can't even talk right. But what's he going to do about it?'

'Nothing. He's going to do nothing at all,' a voice said from behind them. 'But I will.' Halmar had been at the top of the stairs taking a few quiet moments away from the hub-bub when he saw the twins approach Saldor in this deserted part of the cavern. At first he saw nothing wrong and looked away over the crowd gathering in the larger chamber for recognisable faces when something drew his attention back to the trio. The posture of one of them was no longer amiable and Saldor looked terrified. It was time to investigate.

Tarryn backed away from Saldor at Halmar's approach. 'Just a little playful fun amongst old friends,' he said looking at his brother for support. 'Isn't that right Tildor?' Tildor turned away.

41

Halmar moved nearer to Saldor. 'Prim needs you in the kitchen, Saldor? I'd head off if I were you. You know she can't manage without you.'

Saldor, quaking, was delighted to get away from the twins and rushed off. 'Than's 'Almar.'

Chapter Eight

Having decided to escape her dull life in the village in such a way she could never return, Elêna decided that her death by a wild animal attack would be believable. Would she miss her family? She doubted it. Would she miss the shabby village? Definitely not.

She had mulled over the idea of heading directly to the bright lights and bustle of Mexico City but opted instead for Alvarez City. With a population of a few thousand less people than Mexico City, it was smaller but equally busy and a hundred or so miles nearer. Also, having been there twice before, she knew something of the layout.

For the first few miles of her journey, on foot, she followed the road closely until she felt she was far enough away from anyone who would recognise her to allow herself the luxury of catching the bus to Alvarez. It was in the early hours of the morning when she arrived and found a quiet corner of the bus station to settle down for a few hours sleep until she was awoken by a cleaner who took pity on her, gave her a welcome cup of coffee and chunk of bread from her own packed lunch; they saw plenty of runaways at the bus station.

Thanking her benefactor, she found the ladies toilets, splashed her face with cold water from the creaking tap that produced a thin trickle of water, brushed her hair with her fingers, tied it back in a ribbon, smoothed down her crumpled skirt and headed out into the brightly sunlit metropolis to look for accommodation and work.

Hours later, after trudging the streets unproductively looking for work as a waitress, cook or cleaner, her adventurous spirit began to fail. Each time she asked for work she received the same shake of the head; she looked too young, had no permanent address, had no experience or she was simply unsuitable; nothing went the way she had planned.

Unable to get a job, the little money she had soon ran out and she begged, stole food from restaurant kitchens or clothes and blankets from shops whenever she could and shared a disused garage with another girl and her brother who were also homeless.

It was on one of her food raids she noticed a number of nuns near to her makeshift home and followed them back to their convent. She waited on the steps outside the main door until she saw two more nuns approaching and, with an Oscar winning performance, began weeping silent tears and rocking back and forth in clear distress. Playing on their good nature, she managed to persuade them she was an orphan in need of their help. The Convent of the Order of Santa Marisa was a hospital, residential school for girls and home for destitute young women.

Putting her to work in the hospital wing, the nuns quickly saw Elêna's intelligence and speed of thought. Her lack of formal education was soon made up for by Sisters Mary Victoria from London, England and Eithne from Athlone in Ireland from whom she learned about Europe and she practised their accents in private surprising herself with her talent for mimicry. She explored the convent until she knew every nook, assisted Sisters Téreze and Maria Consuela in the hospital and cleaned Mother Superior's office three times a week learning the management routines as she went along.

Mother Superior eventually began paying her a little money for her work and, not having anything to spend it on she had soon built up a tidy sum which she kept hidden at the back of an unused cupboard in the Pharmacy.

Sister Teréze, in particular, saw how quickly she learned nursing skills and noted her interest in conventional medicine and the healing powers of herbs. When nights were quiet on the hospital wing, she encouraged Elêna by spending hours teaching her anything she wanted to know about medicine and herbs. Once again, Elêna soaked up as much knowledge as the kindly nun wanted to pass on. It was on a cloudy November day she heard they were to expect an emergency patient being helicoptered in from the flooded areas up country. A little over two hours later, a survivor of the floods, injured, very ill and suffering with amnesia was stretchered in to the convent and taken to a small single room where she was watched twenty four hours a day.

Although Alvarez City was too far from the flood area to be actually affected by it, the city populace were very well aware of the devastation and every day victims were brought in to the already overcrowded city hospitals.

Casualties were legion with the mortality rate increasing by hundreds with each day that passed. Their unidentified patient had been found as the

weather eased and the flood water levels lowered, delirious and alone on a muddy riverbank not far from the remains of a virtually destroyed village. There being no nearer clinic since the flooding, dehydrated and terribly ill she was airlifted by the emergency helicopter service to the convent of the Order of Santa Marisa.

Two weeks later, as the emergency passed and the nuns had more time, Sister Téreze set about tracing the background of their new patient, convinced they would eventually discover who she was, and took on her care personally, enlisting Elêna's help. Sometimes their patient lay quietly asleep but there were times when in her delirium she whispered and moaned or cried out for her parents. Night after night Elêna sat patiently by her bed barely catching the jumbled chatter but piecing together some of what she said, Elêna was able to make out 'clinic' and 'Rio Toro'.

These snippets of information aided Sister Téreze's investigation but she was appalled to discover that not only had the village been all but destroyed by the flood, but among those who had died were the doctor, Luis Sanchez and his American healer wife Tabitha. Full details of the disaster filtered back to them together with a description of the dead couple's missing daughter that confirmed their unidentified patient was indeed Tanith Randolph-Sanchez who had been on the list of missing persons since the clinic hospital wing had been flattened by a mud slide and swept away into the river.

Satisfied their un-named patient was the missing girl, Sister Téreze sent for identifying papers. When the passport arrived, the photograph confirmed her identity and the supporting documents gave details of her parents and extended family. After informing the authorities that Tanith had survived, Mother Superior safely locked away the papers in her office safe until the time came when she would need them. On the down side though, the doctor diagnosed Tanith as suffering with Malaria. She was extremely ill for some weeks but eventually showed signs of recovery and was occasionally allowed out into the convent garden in a wheelchair, usually pushed by Elêna who volunteered to accompany her.

Even though Tanith was still very ill and weak, Elêna was struck by the similarity of their appearance. Both had thick shoulder length very black hair, both were green eyed and of similar height and age, in fact the nuns sometimes referred to them as 'the twins' and soon the girls developed a strong bond.

Tanith gained in physical strength as the weeks went by but she could remember nothing of the floods, her family or her past; she did not even know her own name. Whether it was shock or injury that caused it, the

doctor was unsure, but even when her personal documents were shown to her, Tanith could remember nothing for some time.

But the day came when hearing Sister Helen, from Boston, talking to two girls about a visit to Salem something sparked in Tanith's memory. Hesitantly at first, the clouds in her mind cleared and within a few days she recalled her mother's home in Salem, Massachusetts and her village in the mountains. From that time, piece by piece, the jigsaw puzzle that was Tanith's memory was slowly and painstakingly put together until she remembered everything, at times causing her terrible pain.

Elêna comforted her as best she could and was an extremely good listener to Tanith's recollection of growing up with her parents and the stories they had told her of their family background; some true and some more likely than not legends and rumours. She was with her when Mother Superior told Tanith they had managed to track down a distant relative of hers in Britain, a certain Mrs Armistice Jenks who lived somewhere in a place called Somerset. Of course, Sister Mary Victoria knew the area vaguely and offered to get in touch with Tanith's great, great aunt for her, but Tanith asked her to wait until she felt well enough to make contact herself. Mother Superior tried to persuade her otherwise but Tanith was adamant; she wanted to wait until she felt ready. But that day had never arrived.

As the months went by Tanith endured many malarial episodes, each one leaving her a little weaker than before. Elêna spent as much time as her duties allowed tending the deteriorating Tanith, partly from genuine friendship but more from the use her memories could be in the future. Then, on one rainy night while Elêna was reading to her, Tanith asked for Mother Superior. Elêna ran to her rooms only to find the senior nun so drunk she could barely stand. By the time Elêna had located Sister Téreze and returned to her bedside, Tanith was dead.

For the next couple of weeks, Elêna's head reeled with mixed emotions. On one hand Tanith had given her a future; life held more possibilities than she had ever envisaged before, even with Tlaloc's aid, and for that she was grateful. Tanith's death had given her so much to hope and plan for, it could only be an advantage but, on the other hand, she missed her, missed their talks and the time they spent together. Tanith had been the closest she ever had to a real friend.

Elêna's mind jumped to the day soon after Tanith's funeral when she had been cleaning Mother Superior's office. Having knocked on the door and received no response, she had supposed the office to be empty but was surprised to find Mother Superior standing with her wide back to the door

closing the door of a safe which was securely hidden behind the back wall of the bookshelf. Still unaware of Elêna's presence, the senior nun slid closed a panel over the safe, replaced the books in front of the panel, then slid a piece of paper into the leaves of an encyclopaedia before returning it to the shelf above. Elêna had seen it all. Mother Superior turned to her left and Elêna realised why she had not been heard. Mother Superior was listening to music from an MP3 player and had earpieces in both ears. She loved to listen to loud choral music.

Retracing her steps, Elêna slipped back through the door and knocked again, more loudly this time, slowly opening the door at the same time. Mother Superior saw her and invited her in to carry out her cleaning duties. After exchanging polite greetings the nun left the room leaving Elêna alone.

Standing at the door listening to Mother Superior's retreating footsteps, Elêna waited until she was sure she would not be disturbed before reaching for the encyclopaedia. Soon afterwards she was looking into the safe and staring open-mouthed at thousands of American Dollars. Later that night she tossed and turned in her dormitory bed, unable to sleep, wondering why the convent would have so much money and how could she get her share of it?

The money, escape and a new life were in sight; all she needed was to plan carefully, very carefully.

Dawn was breaking by the time she finally fell into an exhausted asleep. Sister Maria Consuela had been concerned about her at breakfast, asking if she felt unwell and continually touching Elêna's forehead to see if she had a temperature; the mildest fever, in this part of the world, could turn out to be a symptom of something more sinister.

Elêna thought of her parents. She had not seen them since she was twelve years old. They were very poor and, as the eldest of ten children, four sisters and six brothers, she was expected to cook, clean and work to help support the family. Her mother had been unwell since the birth of her last brother and her father was of little help, spending most of the time playing dice in the Cantina with his friends. It suited her very well that her family believed she was dead and the nuns that she was an orphan; she had closed all the doors behind her except for this one at the Convent but that would change very soon. At just seventeen, her life held the promise of a wonderful future as long as she remained strong enough to take each step towards her goals and Tlaloc would help her all along the way.

Chapter Nine

The sun had just slipped behind the Mendip Hills in a glorious red and gold streaked sky, when Clap-trap and Piggybait returned to the home cavern. Having taken a short cut through the tree root camouflaged window under an enormous oak, they descended the wooden steps to the next level down where the sleeping and bathing quarters were situated. Making way for an optically-challenged, twitchy-nosed mole, they descended again to the next level which led them to the earthen tunnel sloping down to the main staircase. The sound of laugher and cheerful conversation became increasingly loud as they approached, as did the clean fragrance of newly laid herbs and rushes and the welcoming aroma of freshly baked bread and pies.

At the top of the main staircase they looked down on more elves gathered in one place than they had ever seen before. Some had obviously arrived, unseen, having taken other routes, much to the chagrin of Piggybait, who for once was lost for words.

Clap-trap slapped him on the back. 'I told you they wouldn't all come in the same way, didn't I? But, then, you knew better,' he smirked.

Piggybait shot his friend a filthy look but refrained from adding to the insult by retorting. Clap-trap leaned against the tunnel wall as they surveyed the crowd below them. There must have been, by his estimate, at least four hundred elves, and picking out recognisable faces from that many, from this distance, would be almost impossible, or so he thought. Piggybait nudged him and nodded towards a group of some forty or so elves who had collected around the happy couple.

'The New Wood Clan is here already. See, there's Radocas,' Piggybait pointed to a dark haired elf, wearing a sandy coloured shirt. 'He likes catching me out. He'd have known I'd be waiting for him and sneaked in through the south tunnel.'

'It looks like he's brought the entire clan with him,' Clap-trap added. 'At least they are showing the right level of respect. Come on, let's go down.' As they descended the stone staircase, Jossamel and Rondo waved them a greeting. 'Jerrill's over there,' he pointed. Piggybait followed the direction and saw Jerrill talking to an elf couple he knew well.

'Look who Jerrill's talking to, it's Kaellec and Zarianne from Sherwood. Come on, let's say hello.'

They pushed their way through the crowd recognising members of clans from the New Forest, Forest of Dean, Epping and some from Cresswell Crags in Derbyshire. Although they knew invitations had been sent to the Crags, there were usually very few visits between the groups because of the distance involved. Piggybait nudged Clap-trap again, pointing to the food tables. At the far end of the vast cavern, twenty four tables, seating twenty elves at each, were set out in six rows of four ready for the feast.

Clap-trap nodded. 'It looks like Primola's lost none of her skill,' he said appreciatively looking at the food laden tables. It must have taken her ages.'

'It did, she's been planning this for weeks. Everything to the last 'T',' Piggybait agreed.

The Great Chamber was festooned with garlands of summer woodland flowers; white yarrow and sweet cicely, red campions, deep pink musk mallows and herb Robert, yellow meadow buttercups, cowslips and birds-foot trefoil and the soft blues of speedwell and comfrey. The air was freshened with rushes newly scattered on the floor together with lemon balm, mint, sage and rosemary. Firefly lanterns hung from leafy vines stretched above them and torches in wall sconces blazed brightly adding to the festive mood. 'Let's have a quick look,' he said to Clap-trap.

The tables heaved under the weight of tureens, bowls, plates and goblets. The saliva-inducing aromas were tempting. Huge bowls of steaming barley broth and vegetable soup, pots of fragrant herby dumplings, fried beans with wild onions and garlic, jacket potatoes, fish, wild mushrooms, carrots, beans and cauliflowers, stood on metal plates above candles keeping them warm. Large silver platters containing a variety of cold food, breads, red and pale cream coloured cheeses made with herbs and honey, cakes, pies and salads and fruit preserved from the previous autumn, apples, plums, pears, cherries, nuts, pine nuts, gingerbread, sweet pastries and, Piggybait's favourite, almond tartlets. Pewter and wooden plates and goblets were set out at each placing and several jugs of cider, acorn wine, dandelion beer, crystal clear water and honey ale were available for all.

'Ouch!' Piggybait, his full attention given to investigating what was on offer, did not see Ellien break away from the group and come up behind him. He had been about to help himself to an almond tartlet, when she playfully slapped his hand. He spun round expecting to see Clap-trap and discovered Ellien. Clap-trap had vanished into the crowd.

'Hungry Piggy? Can you not wait until the feast?' she smiled at him. Dressed in lilac, an unusual colour for her to wear, her pale gold hair parted in the middle and dressed in long plaits entwined with lilac blossom, she was almost ethereal, delicate and enchanting. He had watched her grow from a quiet, adorable elfling into a serene and beautiful adult and his only regret was that Jimander was not here to see her marry.

'Your father was proud of you, Ellien. He should have been here to see this day.'

Ellien hugged him. 'Thank you, Piggy. He and my mother are here, I can feel their spirits.'

'Should I be jealous?' Halmar had joined them, a beaming smile on his handsome young face.

'Probably,' Ellien joked. 'After you, Piggs would be my choice,' she said lowering her arms from around his shoulders and tucking one arm through his and the other through Halmar's.

'Do you remember my uncle Avaroc, Piggybait?'

Avaroc! Of course, that's who it was, thought Piggybait. Jimander's brother! Jimander hated him; never trusted him. What was he doing here? They had not seen him for years.

Avaroc, Tarryn and Tildor were huddled close together, talking quietly at the bottom of the long staircase and Piggybait was sure he saw Avaroc shake his head slightly as they approached. They stopped talking.

'Later,' Piggybait heard Avaroc whisper to the twins.

'Uncle, I've brought someone to meet you,' Ellien said sweetly.

Tarryn compressed his lips and looked angry as he and Tildor moved aside.

'This is Piggybait, Uncle. Together with Halmar's father, Piggybait is one of our three leaders. You still have to meet Clap-trap but I can't see him around at the moment. I'll introduce you later.'

Avaroc refused Piggybait's outstretched hand but gave an overly elaborate bow. 'Good to meet you…'er Piggybait?' As he raised his head, there was no sign friendship in his cold expression, no emotion at all.

Although he knew he was being mocked, Piggybait allowed the humiliation to pass for Ellien's sake and forced himself not to react to the cynical smile Avaroc gave Tarryn. Ellien, looking at Halmar missed it but

Halmar, however, intercepted the smirk and shot Piggybait an almost imperceptible look that betrayed his own distrust and dislike of Ellien's uncle and his companions. It was not difficult to understand why Jimander had loathed and mistrusted his half-brother.

'The name's Baymar,' Piggybait said, indignantly pulling himself up to his full height. 'Piggybait's a nickname.'

'And it suits you,' Tarryn sneered.

Piggybait ignored the jibe. 'You are very like your brother, Avaroc,' Piggybait struggled to be polite but this meeting was not going well, the atmosphere crackled with animosity.

Avaroc smiled sardonically. 'Yes, so I have been told but alas, bearing in mind that we were only half-brothers and the age gap between us, I knew very little of him.'

Piggybait held his tongue as Avaroc went on. 'His mother died and our father re-married after his departure from Winterne. He settled in the Pennines where he met my mother and we lived very happily. Although Jimander spent a few years with our clan, he returned here and we lost touch. He and our father were never particularly close.' Ellien blanched.

Piggybait knew that was a lie. Jimander had told him of the heartbreak Avaroc had caused their father and how often Jimander had covered up the trouble he caused. After their father died Avaroc left the Pennine clan and headed for Europe. Jimander had never heard anything more of him from that time on but from the conversations they had had, Piggybait knew he had always hoped Avaroc would change his ways. Having met him, he took back his wish that Jimander could have been there. In fact, he felt relieved he could not see Avaroc now. He would have been disappointed and possibly even worried. This was still a dangerous elf.

'Changing the subject,' Avaroc went on, 'I understand your other, um…colleague is called…what was it again, Tarryn?'

'Clap-trap,' Tarryn smirked.

'Oh yes, Clap…trap,' Avaroc said mockingly. 'Classy name.'

Piggbyait controlled his rising anger. He did not want Ellien to notice this mood of distrust and deceit and was glad she had missed this exchange while talking to Halmar. She seemed delighted to have her uncle by her side and Piggybait did not want her upset so close to her wedding; she deserved better. Being a trusting soul, she had no doubts about her uncle. Having seen portraits of him amongst her late father's belongings, his identity was not in doubt; just his character.

'Oh but you'll get to know each other very quickly, I'm sure,' Ellien said, smiling. 'But come and see the arch, Piggy. Halmar's finished

51

it…it's beautiful.' He allowed himself to be led off to inspect the wedding arch by the ecstatically happy Ellien, while keeping one eye on Avaroc who walked away with Tarryn and Tildor to a table at the far end of the cavern. There they huddled together again in hushed conversation, guardedly watching and changing their subject when anyone came close.

Ellien continued to chatter merrily away to the half-listening Piggybait but his attention was far more focused on what Avaroc and the twins were up to.

Chapter Ten

Having arranged to meet Jenny after dinner, Sam walked home with Jonah.

'What was all that with Jenny today? She was fantastic. Amazing. Brilliant!' Jonah gushed as they approached the gates of Winterne Manor. He pushed the lever and the gates swung open. 'I never knew she had it in her.'

'Yeah,' Sam replied thoughtfully as the gates swung shut behind them. 'She never said anything about taking Karate lessons, but she's done well.'

'But she must have had injuries or bruises. It's a rough sport, she's got to have been thrown around?'

'Yeah, she did, but she told me she got them dancing,' Sam shrugged. 'How was I to know?'

'Well yeah, I suppose you wouldn't have guessed, after all, it's not like her is it? What made her take it up?' he asked innocently.

'Not a clue,' Sam lied.

Jonah started chuckling.

'What's so funny?' Sam's puzzled look made Jonah laugh all the more.

'It's like I said before, who'd've thought she be so sneaky?'

Sam said nothing.

They were glad of the shade afforded by the trees; it was a long walk up the drive and, although the overhanging branches gave them some respite from the sunlight, they were both sweating from the exertion of walking from the village and soon Jonah too fell silent. At the fork in the lane they said goodbye and Jonah turned away towards the Manor. He had only gone a short way when Sam called out to him.

'Hey, Jonah!' Jonah stopped and the boys walked towards each other. 'Do me a favour, will you?'

Later, as the temperature became more comfortable, Jenny persuaded Sam to join her on a three mile bike ride to Godney to visit her mother's

school friend, Helen Miller and she borrowed her brother Simon's bike for him. Helen and her husband, Ted, lived in a beautiful farm house where they ran a Bed and Breakfast guest house. Jenny had often promised to take Sam there, praising Helen's baking, but somehow it had never happened before.

They met very little traffic on the narrow tree-lined roads, but twice drivers waved to them as they drove by; Sam recognised one of them as Dr Brownlow. Even though the temperature had dropped slightly, the sun still blazed through gaps in the canopy of branches as they cycled by wide fields of parched yellowing grass, where cows twitched their tails to keep the irritating summer flies away as they, and the sheep, sought the shade of tall hedges and trees. The shallow streams that usually flowed on either side of the road were little more than muddy rivulets. One more day of the searing heat would see them completely dry. The only creatures that seemed unaffected by the soaring temperature were a family of magpies that hopped about in the branches above Sam's head.

'They don't seem to care how hot it is,' he looked over his shoulder to see if Jenny was watching the playful birds and almost collided with a pheasant that appeared from nowhere probably disturbed by their presence. He felt its tail brush his nose.

'*What goes on here*?' He slammed on the brakes. 'It's more dangerous here than in the city!'

The pheasant had shot out of the hedge so quickly there had been no time for Jenny to shout a warning but, with no harm done, she burst out laughing which upset Sam all the more. Jenny found his reaction so comical she was doubled-up with laughter but Sam, unfortunately, was not amused.

'Yeah, thanks for that!' he bellowed, failing to see the joke. 'I never had any problems in Nottingham,' he glowered. 'Everything here wants to kill me!'

The magpies above him in the branches made a 'chacker-chacker' sound.

'And you can shut up too!'

That was too much for Jenny who laughed until she cried.

'You think that's funny! That…that,' he could not remember the name of the bird, 'thing could've killed me!'

'It'll…teach you…to keep your eyes on the road!' she giggled. Pedalling her bike around the very peeved Sam, she moved off still chuckling leaving him no choice but to follow muttering under his breath. But as a naturally good-natured person, Sam soon regained his usual

humour and by the time they reached Godney, he could clearly see the funny side of the incident.

On the edge of the village he rode side by side with Jenny over a small bridge that crossed the bordering stream. The pretty village of Godney comprised two rows of spread out cottages facing open fields with the range of Mendip Hills on the horizon. One row followed the line of the road while the other, smaller row, was on the other side of the weeping-willow edged stream, accessed by two small bridges. Unused to so much cycling, Sam's legs began to ache.

'How much further?' he shouted at Jenny who was now speeding ahead.

'Almost there,' she shouted back without turning round. Sure enough, soon they pulled off the road into the farm driveway and walked the bikes round to the back garden. Two large pale golden coloured Labradors lazed in the shade of an enormous copper beech tree. They raised their heads and wagged their tails at the new arrivals but were too hot to bother getting up.

'Hi Jenny. It's about time you visited.' Helen Miller, was sitting at a table, reading a book under a huge garden parasol, a large glass of iced orange juice beside her. As they approached, she stood to greet them and held out a hand to Sam.

'You must be Sam. I've been looking forward to meeting you. I've heard all about you from Sarah.'

'Oh, right. Er, yes…nice to meet you Mrs Miller.' Sam felt a bit awkward and thought it probably showed but Helen seemed unaware of it.

'It's Helen. Not Mrs Miller, Sam. Come on in both of you,' she urged as a long haired tabby brushed by them swishing her tail irritably.

'Oh never mind Jess, she's in a bit of a mood, it's probably the heat.'

Helen shepherded them into the kitchen.

'I'll get you a drink. You must be parched after coming all this way in this weather. Piece of cake both of you?'

Sam looked towards Jenny who answered for both of them.

'Yeah, thanks Helen.' She turned to Sam. 'You'll love Helen's sponge, Sam. You think mum's good? Helen's cakes are brilliant.'

'Don't you let your mum hear you say that,' Helen laughed, 'or I'll never hear the last of it. You both make yourselves comfortable outside and I'll bring it out to you.'

Fifteen minutes later, with the sponge finished, Sam and Jenny sat on the circular seat built around the trunk of the copper beech tree, stroking two very happy Labradors.

'See the Tor?' Jenny pointed out the hill and tower in the distance.

55

Sam nodded. He had been a bit quiet since Helen had gone back into the house.

'What's the matter? You've not said much for a while.'

Sam hesitated. 'Nothing's wrong. It's nice here…a bit quiet though,' he smiled. Paddy, one of the Labradors, nudged his hand to remind Sam he had stopped stroking him.

'Then what's up?'

Sam struggled to find the right words and his dithering worried her.

'Well? Are you trying to dump me?' she asked.

'What? No, of course not!' He seemed genuinely surprised she had even thought of that possibility.

'Well then?'

He looked a bit uncertain. What he had thought was a good idea earlier on might not be so good after all. 'I'm not sure whether you'll like this or not,' he began.

'Try me,' Jenny said with a slightly sour expression.

'You know Richie Bishop came over to talk to me earlier?'

'Yeah,' Jenny answered calmly. Sam sensed this was not going to go well.

'He wants me to stand in for Jamie, playing drums at the Prom.' Sam looked at his feet.

'But that's great.' She looked relieved but then the smile faded. 'OK, why so worried?'

'We'll be playing for the first hour of the Prom…before the disco,' he replied, still not looking up.

'And?'

He raised his eyes to watch her reaction.

'I've asked Jonah if he'd take you to the Prom and look after you while I'm on stage.'

'You've done what?'

'I thought it'd be alright to begin with, but…when I thought more about it…I thought you might not like it.'

'*Might not*?'

'You don't then…I was right,' Sam whispered.

Jenny was furious. 'Did you think that one up all by yourself? Why didn't you talk to me about it? I'd have waited till you were finished. Did you not think I could look after myself?'

'I was…I was just trying to help,' he said lamely. 'I didn't want you to be on your own.'

'First of all, I can look after myself, second of all...,' she stopped; speechless with rage.

For a few minutes they sat in angry, awkward silence.

'I'm sorry,' Sam said. 'I was just trying to help. I thought I was doing the best for you.'

Jenny, arms folded and legs crossed stared out across the fields towards the Tor, furiously speechless. Then she turned on him.

'You...you didn't think at all! You had no right to ask Jonah to *look after* me. It's embarrassing. It's humiliating! And...and after everything he did, you had to ask him...of all people!'

'But that's in the past; we're all mates aren't we? He's sorry for that and...'

'Yeah! Maybe! But what's he going to think? That I don't have any other friends to hang out with while you're playing?'

Both dogs stood up and sloped away into the house at the sound of the raised voices.

'He's...' Sam began, but Jenny would not be interrupted.

'And...and what if he wanted to take someone else. Now he's stuck with me?'

'But it's...'

'I know it's only for a while, but what girl is going to want to go with him when he's stuck with me for part of the evening? Did you think of that? No, I can see you didn't.'

'I...'

'No! You didn't think at all!'

'I'm sorry. I was only trying to help. I didn't think you'd be so upset. I thought it was a good idea to have you kept company while I was busy. Jonah didn't mind, he agreed right off...I don't think he'd asked anyone anyway. Look, I'm sorry if I got it wrong, but I was only thinking of you and trying to do you a favour...'

'*You* were doing *me* a FAVOUR?' Jenny had calmed a little but that remark had her boiling again. 'I'm going home! You know your way back.'

She ran to the backdoor of the house.

'Helen, I've just realised how late it is and I'm off now. Thanks for the cake. I'll see you again soon.' Grabbing her bike she headed for the gate. Sam heard Helen's voice. 'Bye dears, see you again soon,' Helen called from the kitchen assuming they were leaving together.

Sam got up and followed dejectedly as Jenny disappeared. When he got to the road, he could see her pedalling away at high speed. He thought

about nothing else on his lonely way home. It was her he had been thinking of, surely she could see that. Humiliated she had said! Embarrassed! Why? He would never understand how a girls mind worked. Jonah hadn't minded. He'd been pleased to help in fact. Jonah wouldn't want her humiliated; he was trying to make up for the past; that was all.

Feeling sorry for himself, Sam's thoughts turned to righteous indignation and anger as he convinced himself he was right and Jenny had taken everything wrongly. Pedalling angrily, his stomach twisted into knots, the argument played and replayed in his head as he tried to fathom out why she couldn't see that he meant well and was only trying to do Richie a favour and make sure she was OK at the same time? What else was he supposed to do? How were they going to play without a drummer? He couldn't let them down? Why did girls have to be so difficult? After all, he'd be free for the Disco. It would only be an hour and he'd have been with her so she wouldn't have to be with Jonah for long! Girls!

'Whoa!' Sam foot shot to the ground. He had just turned into the Wells Road, and not really concentrating on what he was doing, he almost collided with a taxi heading towards Winterne.

Without stopping the driver gave him a contemptuous glance and shook his head. Angry with himself for his stupidity but blaming the driver, Sam was about to make a very rude gesture but was startled by two remarkably green eyes watching him from the back window as the car passed by. He forgot his anger at Jenny and the taxi driver. Caught up in the moment, he was unable to think clearly as the taxi disappeared around a corner and he came to his senses. Getting back on the bike, he cycled on towards the village but had no wish to go home; he needed somewhere quiet to think.

The tree-lined road cut through Winterne Wood where he knew his way around very well. Getting off the bike, he wheeled it off the road and clambered down the roadside bank and into the woods looking for somewhere to leave it safely. After struggling with it over rough, pitted ground, he found a place to hide the bike, watched only by a pair of collared doves. Their puzzled expressions made him smile.

Leaves rustled as small animals ran for cover and insects, disturbed as he waded through the long grass and ferns rose into the air. He waved his arms to keep them away. Shafts of sunlight broke through the canopy the rays beamed down through the trees highlighting specks of dust and small buzzing flies.

After a while, he lost all sense of time and found himself much further into the wood than he had intended. Here, where the trees grew closer together and the undergrowth more dense, the earth was still damp. A low

lying mist created a ghostly atmosphere which Sam had encountered just once before but that had been in winter; this was different, it felt unexplainably weird.

His anger dissolved and, for a moment his isolation scared him, then he remembered, he would never be alone in this wood. All the same, he thought, it must be time to head back. He hoped he would be able to find the way back to his bike again.

As he retraced his steps, he saw, ahead of him, the rise where Piggybait and Clap-trap had shown him the secret entrance into Winterne Manor. Broken sunlight streamed down onto the slope and it seemed to Sam like an oasis, a haven of security from the ghostly mood of the wood floor. After a few minutes he was sitting at the top of the rise, his arms wrapped around his knees. It was warm and relatively dry at the top where the sun's rays bathed the grassy slope in brilliant sunlight and he gazed down at the misty lower level.

His recent uneasiness having eased, his thoughts returned to Jenny and his bad mood returned. With his head lowered to rest on his knees he plucked tetchily at the grass throwing aside the torn clumps.

'Sam?' Charlie's booming voice broke through the wood sounds.

Sam did not reply.

'Oh, there you are!' Charlie strode up the hill towards him.

Sam answered without moving. 'How did you find me?' He tossed aside more tufts of grass.

'Are you kidding?' Charlie chuckled. 'Take a look around.' He waved a shovel sized hand in the direction of the trees at the bottom of the slope. On one of the lower branches of an oak, Piggybait saluted. Two branches higher up Clap-trap swung his feet and, at the bottom of the next tree, peeking out from a hollowed out niche in the trunk, Saldor waved his cap energetically, a wide smile showing the gaps in his teeth. 'There's nothing goes on in these woods they don't know about.'

'Yeah, I know.'

Unfortunately, even Saldor's gappy grin did nothing to alter Sam's disposition and he lowered his head onto his knees and began tearing at the grass again.

'Wha's up, Sam?'

'Nothing.'

Charlie lowered his huge frame to sit some way off from Sam but did not look at him. Neither of them spoke for a while until Sam broke the silence.

'I know I'm late. I suppose Mum phoned?' he asked flatly watching the ferns at the bottom of the rise moving as two fat wood pigeons rooted around under the fronds.

Charlie turned towards Sam. 'She phoned Jenny then Jenny came over asking if I'd seen you.'

'Oh.'

'She's worried about you. Said you'd argued.'

'Did she tell you what it was about?'

'No.' Charlie stroked his long beard.

'I'm fed up, Charlie.'

Charlie turned to face his miserable nephew. 'Do you want to talk about it?'

'I was doing her a favour,' Sam replied sullenly. 'I asked Jonah to take her to the Prom while I stood in for the drummer for the first bit, but she knows I'd have been with her afterwards. So does Jonah.'

'Oh.'

Sam turned to face Charlie. 'Why? What?' Sam glowered. 'Jonah's happy enough to help out. Why can't she see I was just trying to make sure she wasn't on her own?' He picked up a broken stick that had been lying on the ground beside him and toyed with it.

Charlie gave a faint smile. 'Did you discuss it with her before you asked Jonah?'

Sam paused. 'Er, no.' Sam looked down at his feet.

'Don't you think you should have? Girls like to be consulted. And have you thought that it might not be such a good idea to throw them together.'

Sam did not answer. He took a deep breath and looked around him. Clap-trap, Piggybait and Saldor were nowhere to be seen.

'They've gone then?'

'They left a few minutes ago. They were only waiting till I got here.'

Squirrels chattered and chased each other from branch to branch while birds sang as they flew between the trees, but Sam noticed none of this. The air was fresher than earlier and the strength of the sun had lessened a little. Having been preoccupied with his own thoughts, Sam suddenly became aware that he was actually feeling a little chilly.

'I s'pose it's time to go home,' he said giving Charlie a half smile.

'Just waiting for you to say the word, m'boy. You got any idea what you're going to do about Jenny?'

'Apologise, I guess,' Sam said throwing the broken stick into a bush. 'Come on Charlie. I'll go and see her tomorrow and sort it out.'

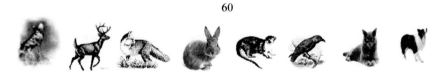

'Remember Sam, there are ways of treating women no matter what age they are. They don't like to have decisions made for them; they're perfectly capable of deciding things for themselves.'

Deep in thought Sam spoke little as they headed back to the road and Charlie did not press him.

Charlie looked at his watch, it was nine-fifteen and still light but evening clouds were beginning to gather. Even so, as the trees thinned and the remaining sunlight broke through, the air was alive with bees and butterflies, some species of which Sam had never seen before. The wood rang with birdsong and harsh caws of rooks returning to their colony of nests high up at the top of the trees. The wood teemed with life and Sam suddenly woke up to the beautiful world he was living in.

'I think I'll still ask Jonah to look after Jenny and take her to the Prom. I can't really go back on that now, but I'll apologise to her and I'll talk to her properly about it. I guess I took it for granted she wouldn't mind.'

'I guess you did,' Charlie smiled. 'Now you're getting the idea.'

By luck or more likely Charlie's unerring sense of direction, they found the spot where Sam had left Simon's bike and wheeled it back to the road. Charlie lifted it easily to put it in the back of the jeep.

On their way back to the village, Sam used his mobile phone to call his mother to let her know he was on his way home. He had expected her to be angry with him but, thankfully, she was just relieved he was alright.

'I'll see Jenny tomorrow, Charlie. It's a bit late now.'

'You could give her a call.'

'Hmmm, no I'll wait till tomorrow,' Sam grinned. 'I don't think I'm brave enough tonight.'

At the outskirts of the village Sam remembered something. 'I nearly got knocked down by a taxi earlier. He swung round the corner really fast.'

'Lots of drivers speed on these roads, especially outsiders. They think they won't meet other traffic on these country roads. There's far too many accidents around here. Good job you're OK.'

'Yeah, but that's not all. There was a girl in the back. She had the most enormous green eyes.'

'That'll probably be Armistice's great-niece or whatever she is. She was supposed to be arriving this afternoon but her plane got delayed and she was a couple of hours late getting in.'

Sam was curious. 'Flown in? Where from?'

'Somewhere in Mexico I think.'

'*Mexico?*'

'Yeah. Armie's properly excited about it. She thought she had no family left. Seems this girl's family were killed in floods and she was found some months back, delirious and sick with Malaria. She had amnesia too. Got taken to a convent where the nuns looked after her. Bit by bit her memory came back and they eventually traced Armistice. There's only the two of them left as the rest of the family have all gone now. Armie thought she was alone now apart from her friends but at least she found she has one relative.'

Sam had been looking around the village square in case Jenny or Jonah were about but something in Charlie's voice made Sam look him look around.

'You don't seem too happy about it.'

'Oh, I don't know, m'boy. It's just that something doesn't sit right. It's just a little too convenient for my liking. But it's probably just me being suspicious.' He looked thoughtful, then his usual smile re-appeared. 'Take no notice of me. I'm sure it'll be fine.'

Chapter Eleven

As Jenny sped angrily away from Godney, Jonah sat at the long wooden table in the spacious kitchen of Winterne Manor. Its tall fireplace and cosy armchairs made it the place where the family most liked to relax, and was probably the most lived in room in the Manor. His chin rested on his cupped hand and he stared out of the window. He had been quiet for so long that once she had popped the apple pie she had just made into the oven, Marjorie Seymour, sat down at a chair at the other end of the table and wondered how long it would take before he noticed she was watching him; his glassy-eyed expression showed he was actually miles away.

'Penny for 'em,' she said, after waiting a good ten minutes for him to come back from wherever he was. He was so wrapped up in his thoughts, when Dorothy Renwick, his mother's cousin and the family housekeeper came in through the backdoor, her arrival went unnoticed until a few moments later when he became aware of being stared at.

'Oh, hiya Marj,' Jonah replied without turning.

'That's Mrs Seymour to you, my lad,' Dorothy barked.

'Oh, yeah. Sorry, Marj,' he said, still obviously preoccupied.

The two women exchanged looks. Dorothy pulled out a chair and sat down beside him.

'Alright, what's up?'

'Nothing,' he said distantly, before seeming to snap out of his daydream. 'When did you come in?'

'Must be a girl, Marjorie,' Dorothy winked at the older woman.

'No. It's not!' Jonah protested, finally taking notice. 'It's just Jenny!'

Dorothy tried to keep a straight face while Marjorie stood up, went to the sink unit and began wiping up the cups draining upside down on the rack, trying to hide her amusement.

'Marjorie, do me a favour will you? Next time that very pretty Jenny Richards comes over, remind me she's not a girl please,' Dorothy said seriously.

'Oh, come on, Dorothy. Give me a break,' Jonah pleaded. 'You know what I mean. I can't...don't think of her that way. She's...she's just a...just a friend, that's all.'

'Are you sure? It doesn't sound like she's just a friend to me.'

Marjorie looked on, sympathetically quiet. Over the years she had worked for the Atkins family she had detested Jonah; his behaviour had been impossible to tolerate, even if she had tried to make allowances for how difficult things had been for him as he grew up, but that was all in the past.

Since Christmas the change in him had been nothing short of remarkable. He had matured into a much nicer boy and was more popular than he realised. It upset her to see him so confused.

'Well she has to be, Sam's my friend and...she doesn't like me much anyway.'

'But you like her.' Dorothy thought of an image of Jonah at around eight years old and she became aware of his innocence and vulnerability.

He didn't answer that question. 'And now Sam's asked me to escort her to the school Prom next week.'

'Why on earth does he want you to take *his* girlfriend to the Prom?'

'It's only for the first hour or so. Richie needed someone to take over from Jamie on drums 'cos he can't make it now. His folks booked their holiday ages ago, so they'll be away.'

'But if you're taking Jenny, that means you can't ask anyone else,' Dorothy observed. 'That's hardly fair, is it Marjie?' Marjorie shook her head.

'It's OK. I don't mind that. At least I'll be doing something for Jenny for a change and helping Sam out. I'm OK with it...honestly.'

Dorothy stood up. 'Anyone want a cuppa?'

'What was that about a cuppa?' Harriet had come into the room unnoticed. She walked over to Jonah and ruffled his hair.

'What's all this about Jenny and the Prom?'

Jonah went over everything again avoiding the complication of his relationship with Jenny, which she already knew about. But Harriet was shrewd enough to detect something was wrong. 'And?'

Jonah changed the subject. 'Mum could we have Stuart take us to the Prom in the Jag?'

'I don't see why not…or better still…I have an idea. Leave it with me.' She started off towards the swing door. 'I'll be back for that tea in a minute, Dorothy.' She rushed out of the room.

'Wonder what she's up to?' Dorothy said watching the doors swing in Harriet's wake.

A few minutes later Harriet returned. 'Well that's all settled.'

'What is?'

Harriet sat on the table close to Jonah's chair. 'You shall go to the ball, my son,' she was grinning from ear to ear, 'but not in the Jag. I've just been on to Theo Hardy…'

'The car hire bloke?' Jonah interrupted.

Harriet nodded. 'Uh…huh. You've got a white Rolls Royce for the event.'

Jonah was stunned. 'Oh no! Mum, that's way too flashy. Stuart and the Jag will be fine.'

'But you want to do this properly don't you?'

'It's a pity it's not for something worthwhile,' Dorothy muttered under her breath to Marjorie, 'like taking a girlfriend of his own.'

'Yes, I do,' Jonah controlled his rising resentment, 'but not to show up everyone else.'

'But that means I'll have to cancel it and I've only just sorted out it.'

'Fine, just do that, please, Mum. It's way over the top,' he protested. 'And I wish you'd asked me first. It would have saved you bothering Theo.'

'You're so ungrateful, Jonah. Your mum just wants the best for you…'

'Don't keep on Dorothy. It is worthwhile to me,' Jonah interrupted impatiently.

Harriet poured herself a cup of tea. 'So you're taking Jenny,' she said changing the subject from cars.

Dorothy tutted. Marjorie said nothing.

'No mum, I'm not taking her. I'm just picking her up and staying with her until Sam's finished.'

'And I take it you still want to make it special even for that short amount of time?'

Jonah nodded.

'Have you thought about a corsage?'

'A what? What's one of those?'

'A flower, or something like that. Girls either wear them on their wrist or waist or on the lapel area. It's traditional.'

'Perhaps Sam should get that for her. I'm not really her date, he is. I'm just her…her *escort* for an hour or so.'

'I would think all the other girls will be wearing them, or probably will. Normally the corsage is given to the girl when her date collects her. Sam won't be collecting Jenny, you will, so it should be you who presents it. After all we Atkins's like to do things properly.'

Jonah thought about it. 'So what do you suggest?' He was a lot calmer now.

Dorothy answered. 'As you're just friends, you need to be careful about the type of flower you give her. Do you know what her dress is like?'

Jonah smiled. 'Nope. She won't tell anyone.'

'Ahh, well that helps!' Dorothy griped.

'Not even the colour?' Harriet asked.

'Nope. Not even that. She's been dead sneaky lately. Seems she been taking Karate classes too.'

'Yes, I know,' Harriet said. 'Sarah told me. Then she remembered Jenny didn't want anyone to know and swore me to secrecy?'

'See what I mean?'

'Back to this corsage,' Dorothy said as Marjorie cleared away Harriet's empty cup.

'I think as Jenny isn't Jonah's 'date' for the evening, he needs to be even more careful about what flowers he gives her,' Harriet added.

'Orchids are nice,' Marjorie put in.

Jonah looked horrified.

'Yes, but they'd be wrong in the circumstances. Too romantic and far too adult for a young girl,' Dorothy argued.

Jonah bristled as the three women talked, wondering if they had forgotten he was there.

'Gardenias or Camellias are too…grown up as well,' Harriet said.

'White roses?' suggested Marjorie.

'How about…?' Jonah tried to get a word in.

The back door opened and Meredith, Jonah's sister entered. Her Dalmatian dog, Wilmot, bounded up to Jonah and licked his face.

'What's going on?' Meredith asked as she swung her legs over the arm of the big green armchair.

'Jonah's taking Jenny to the Prom and we were just deciding what flowers we wanted to make up her corsage,' Harriet told her.

'But why's Jonah taking her? What's happened to Sam?'

'Nothing's happened…,' Jonah began.

'Jonah's a stand-in,' Dorothy broke in unaware Jonah had clamped his lips together in fury. They were all just taking over, ignoring him altogether. He might just as well not have been there.

'A stand-in! Why? Why hasn't he got his own date?'

'Oh, just you carry on and talk about me like I'm not here!'

'Oh yes,' Meredith grinned. 'Hi Bro.' How's it going?'

Jonah looked up at her through lowered eyelids. 'Well, it was going alright...up until this lot took over,' he snapped.

'Oh Jonah, don't fuss,' Harriet said, dismissively. 'We're only trying to help.'

'That's what I wanted. A bit of *help*. Not a bloody take-over.' His voice was calm but inside he was seething. 'I know you all mean well and thanks for the offer of the car Mum *but*...' He looked around the room at the four women. 'Will you please listen to me? I want to keep this a little more low key. Jenny doesn't need showy fancy flowers. She's clever, brave and likes things simple. Giving her a corsage is fine but it needs to be something fresh, uncomplicated... simple.'

Marjorie slipped away to her larder and Dorothy looked slightly uncomfortable. Harriet on the other hand was looking at her son as if she was seeing him as a grown-up for the first time and Meredith was just enjoying the whole episode.

Jonah pulled at his ear-ring. 'I don't want shop bought flowers for Jenny. I've got a bracelet upstairs I bought for her for Christmas but didn't get round to giving it to her. It's like silver netting.'

'Filigree,' Harriet corrected.

'Yeah, filigree...whatever. Garden flowers would be better. Something that smells nice.'

'There's white jasmine in the conservatory, how about that?' Harriet suggested. 'It's small, pretty and fragrant.'

Jonah looked grateful for the suggestion. 'I'd forgotten about that. Mix it with something else and it'll be fine.'

'Choose what you want, Jonah. I'll help twine them into the bracelet,' Meredith volunteered.

'Thanks Sis.' He moved towards the back door. 'You know, just because we can afford to do things in style, doesn't mean we have to.' He went out to the garden.

'He really cares about her, Mum,' Meredith said.

'I know but I think it's too late for that...there was too much damage done and some things can't be forgiven even she manages to put them to the back of her mind.'

Chapter Twelve

Throughout the evening, guests continued to swell the numbers in the cavern even though there were still a few days to go to the wedding. Piggybait enjoyed catching up with old friends but could not shake off a feeling of unease; something made his scalp crawl, a feeling that he had learned to trust over the years. It always meant trouble.

Circulating amongst the clan and the newly arrived guests, feasting and dancing with pretty female elves in a cavern that rang with laughter and cheer, Piggybait tried over and over to forget his troubles by focusing on Ellien's happiness. Her gaiety radiated throughout the cavern spreading joy among the growing company of elves and creating an atmosphere of celebration, song and laughter aided of course by dandelion beer, acorn wine and lots and lots of good food.

Ellien's adoring gaze never strayed far from Halmar and her happiness brought it home to Piggybait just how lonely he was. He had his friends of course, and his duties, but he had no-one to really care for or to care for him and he now felt that more acutely than ever before.

Ellien's laughter rang out dragging him from his musing. She was radiant, her eyes and skin glowed and, with her naturally cheerful disposition, she had no premonition of the trouble Piggybait was convinced would come. Nor would he have wanted her to.

He nudged Clap-trap and nodded in Halmar's direction. Clap-trap followed his gaze. Halmar was studying Avaroc from a distance. So he has his doubts too, thought Piggybait.

Avaroc had dressed sumptuously for the feast. His pure white linen shirt worn under a soft, sleeveless velvet jerkin in a deep russet colour, embroidered in gold thread around the collar and paired with matching breeches and soft light brown leather boots, gave the impression of

prosperity. The slim beige scarf draped loosely around his neck conveyed a casual elegance.

Clap-trap watched Avaroc as his sharp-eyed gaze roamed across the gathering, unsmiling and coldly settling fleetingly on one elf, then moving on to another as if summing them up. Lounging back in the comfortable chair he swung one long leg over the arm and took a swig from his goblet, then his stare fixed on someone. His eyes narrowed.

Clap-trap craned his neck to see who had been unlucky enough to warrant this venomous glare. It was Tildor. Was there a falling out among them? Clap-trap tapped Piggybait on the arm but just as his friend looked around, Clap-trap became aware that the observer was being observed. Tarryn was glowering at them.

'The watchers are being watched, old friend,' Piggybait said in an undertone.

Tildor sat beside his brother but, although his eyes flickered in their direction occasionally, there was no animosity from him. It was Tarryn's unblinking stare that unnerved Piggybait.

'Come on, let's go,' he urged Clap-trap. 'Prim's made some cakes and I need cheering up.'

They pushed their way through the crowd and became separated by the sheer number of elves who wanted to talk to them both. Piggybait eventually saw Lommie who was handing out some of Primola's home made cakes and made a bee-line for him. It was then he saw, behind Lommie, that Clap-trap had found Aerynne and they were deep in conversation. She had looked so melancholy before that the warm smile she bestowed on Clap-trap caused Piggybait conflicting emotions. It was wonderful to see her smile and it cheered him but it also stung him. Why couldn't it have been him to whom she gave her smile?

Unreasonably irritated, and with the intention of breaking up their cosy conversation, Piggybait pushed his way through the crowd and reached them just as Jerrill's voice rang out.

'Would everyone please take their places at the tables,' he called above the din.

Aerynne said goodbye and Piggybait stared regretfully after her as she returned to the Pennine clan table while Clap-trap, not noticing Piggybait's frown, pulled him towards the top table they would share with Jerrill, Halmar and Ellien.

But someone was missing.

'Where's Saldor?' Piggbyait asked Clap-trap.

'Don't know. He's probably at one of the other tables.' Clap-trap looked around trying to spot their missing friend. 'Thinking about it, I don't actually think I've seen him for a while, but he must be around. He won't miss out on this feast.' They settled onto a bench beside Jerrill and thought no more of the missing Saldor.

From somewhere unseen a harp played a musical accompaniment during the lively feast but it was hardly audible over the din of laughter and shouting, which went on for many hours with Primola nervously hovering about asking everyone if the food was to their taste and if they were enjoying themselves.

Eventually Rondo took her by the shoulders, guided her to his table, forced her onto the bench beside him and handed her a large goblet of honey mead. From then on she began to relax and enjoy herself, allowing her children and friends to make a fuss over her as a reward for all her efforts.

It was very late when the elflings were finally put to bed that night. Many of them had to be carried, already fast asleep, up the stairs by their parents. It was then that the older elves settled comfortably into soft chairs and settees to talk. Soon some, like the elflings, were asleep and softly snoring.

During a lull in the conversation Avaroc stood up, looked down his long nose at the assembly and casually strode to the second step on the long staircase where he leaned against the wall and cast a disdainful look at the weary and sated elves remaining.

At first, few of the elves noticed him or his contemptuous glower, until the four young male elves who had accompanied him from the Pennines, but had remained aloof and silent during the entire evening, went to stand on the step below him. Clap-trap and Piggybait murmured quietly to each other. Avaroc nodded to Tarryn and Tildor who rose from their seats to join him.

But Tildor hesitated. Piggybait sensed reluctance, as Tildor held back a little. His wife, Yarenni, clutched nervously at his hand; she seemed fearful. 'I have to do this,' he whispered to her, before Tarryn pulled him away, pushing him in front, giving him no room for manoeuvre.

Avaroc's eyes narrowed as the subdued Tildor approached to stand on his left. Tarryn stood to his right and gave his wife, Feystra, a triumphant smile. She, in turn, gave Yarenni a scornful sneer before returning her husband's smile with a look of pride.

Now, more of the Winterne elves and other guests were waking up to the fact that something was about to happen. Piggybait was already one

jump ahead of them. He had a very good idea of what Avaroc was about to do.

'I'd like your attention please,' Avaroc's voice rang out, but not everyone stopped their chatter.

Ellien looked up at her uncle fondly. Halmar glanced quickly at Piggybait, suspicion in his eyes.

'Here it comes,' Piggybait whispered to Clap-trap.

'What?'

'The real reason he's here.'

'My friends,' Avaroc began. Ellien smiled. Halmar took her hand protectively; she was so trusting. 'We have not met before, but we are related and most of you will be aware that I am Jimander's brother…his only brother. You have a strong leadership here in Jerrill, and his foolishly-named colleagues.' He looked directly to where Piggybait and Clap-trap were sitting. Ellien's smile vanished. Halmar, still looking at Piggybait and Clap-trap seemed to trying to read their thoughts.

Avaroc turned away and waited for the expected angry reaction of the affronted elves to calm down. Some were on their feet shaking their fists, some were shouting, but others were open mouthed unable to believe what they had heard. No-one had disrespected their friends like that before.

'*Quiet!*' he roared, casting a glaring eye over the clan and their assembled guests. Eventually everyone quietened.

'It is not my intention to insult or to anger. I will continue. Yes, you have strong leadership but it is not strong enough!' He waited until the following murmured response had died down.

Tarryn and Tildor had not moved. Their expressions were stony. Piggybait looked for Aerynne at the Pennine clan table. Her eyes were downcast.

'Look at them,' Piggybait whispered to Clap-trap indicating the twins and their four companions. 'They're not wedding guests, their hench-elves. They're not here to celebrate.'

Clap-trap nodded in agreement. 'Let's see how far he goes.'

As they were talking Jerrill got to his feet and approached Avaroc. 'You have come here to celebrate a wedding. Your niece's wedding. How *dare* you do this?'

Tarryn ordered him to be silent and pushed him away. Two of Avaroc's younger elves took his arms and forced him back in to his seat. There was uproar. Rondo, Lommie and Jossamel moved forward to defend Jerrill but were pushed aside by Avaroc's bodyguard. Halmar got to his feet and led a shocked Ellien away from the table.

'I will not be silent!' Jerrill's fury was evident. 'How dare...' But again he was forced back down into his chair by a third member of Avaroc's young bodyguard who, unnoticed in the pandemonium, had moved to stand behind Jerrill's chair. The Winterne clan, stunned by these new developments, had no time to react.

'I'll continue if I may, *without* interruption,' Avaroc bellowed.

'I'm sorry are we intruding?' a deep voice boomed across the hall. Charlie and Sam, having arrived a few moments before, had witnessed the beginning of Avaroc's speech. At first Charlie had intended to wait to see how things developed, but seeing the strong arm tactics being employed, he felt it was time to make his presence known.

A very relieved Jerrill pushed past Avaroc's hench-elf to join Charlie and Sam. Avaroc now appeared to lose some of his confidence as his furious expression changed to one of apprehension as they approached; he was clearly shaken by the Chief's unexpected, and definitely unwelcome, arrival.

Piggybait and Clap-trap silently left their chairs and joined Sam and Charlie, mirroring Tarryn and Tildor's stance on either side of their Leader.

'Sorry we're a bit late,' Charlie said, pleasantly, 'but Sam and I got held up. Still we're here now to join the festivities.' He approached Ellien who smiled gratefully at him, and bowed. There was no sign of Halmar. He had slipped away during the distraction of Charlie and Sam's arrival.

'Do go on, Avaroc,' Charlie said, politely. 'This is my nephew, Sam, by the way. Sorry, I'm interrupting again. Oh, don't mind us. Go on with what you were saying.' Sam detected a hard edge to Charlie's usually more amiable voice.

Ellien looked around for Halmar, seeking his comforting presence.

Tarryn and Tildor took a few steps back leaving Avaroc isolated. There was a heavy silence.

'Um...yes. Right. I'll continue,' Avaroc faltered, no longer displaying the arrogance or assurance he had shown before. 'As I was saying...um...with my blood tie to your previous and very...er...worthy leader,' his voice grew stronger, 'no one has a better claim to be Lord of the Winterne Clan than I and I now claim that right!'

Once again a roar erupted around the chamber. Chairs were turned over as elves sprang to their feet. Primola fainted and Rondina ran to fan her with a dock leaf. Jossamel and Rondo, having tried to rush at Avaroc, were restrained by two of his gang.

'Can he do this?' whispered Sam to Charlie.

'I don't believe so,' Charlie replied calmly. 'I think Jimander may still have a part to play.' He winked at Sam. 'This is not finished.'

'Tarryn! Tildor! You know what…,' but Avaroc was prevented from saying anything further.

'Avaroc!' Halmar shouted his name from halfway up the long staircase. 'I challenge your claim on behalf of another!' Ellien rushed up the stairs to him. The elves fell silent and, as one, they turned to him. A hush fell over the crowd. 'Avaroc. This shall not be!' Halmar's clear strong voice rang out again, his eyes almost black with rage. 'There is only one who has a claim to rule and that leadership is not solely for Winterne.'

There were whispered responses and surprised expressions all around the cavern.

Avaroc blanched. 'Rule? No! You lie! I do not believe this.'

Halmar put his arm around Ellien and they began descending the stairs.

'Just one person here has a true blood-line to the ancient Lords of Alfheim and I can prove it,' Halmar continued.

Avaroc's face was pale, his fists clenched in rage.

'Sir,' Halmar approached Charlie, 'I understand you know something of this already.'

Charlie nodded. Sam looked from one to the other, trying to understand what was going on.

'Then I would appreciate it if you, sir,' he said to Charlie, 'and you, Sam, Piggybait, Clap-trap and you Father,' he said to Jerrill, 'Ellien, Avaroc and two others of our clan,' he ran his eyes over the crowd, 'Jossamel and maybe…Aelfrar,' he indicated an elderly elf who shuffled slowly to his feet, 'would come with me. I have something to show you.'

Avaroc glowered. He appeared to be about to refuse to go with them but soon realised he had no choice. 'Tarryn, Tildor, with me. Now'

'You already know what this is all about, don't you Charlie?' Sam asked.

'Why do you think I wanted you here, this late on a school night, Sam.' Charlie winked. 'You're about to witness a revelation.'

Chapter Thirteen

While Sam and Jenny had been arguing and Jonah lost in thought in the family kitchen, Armistice Jenks nervously paced the kitchen floor unable to sit down for more than a few minutes. This pattern was only broken to pay frequent visits to her small front room to peer through the net curtain.

After an hour and half of this unrelenting repetition, she walked to the front gate, looked up and down the road and, not seeing what she hoped to see, walked briskly back inside muttering to herself, repeating the entire process every ten minutes or so.

When she first began this strange behaviour, Bandit tried to keep up with her but after getting his paws trodden on, being accidentally kicked and scolded for getting under her feet, he gave up and stayed on the table well out of the way.

For what must have been the umpteenth time, Mrs Jenks looked at the mantelpiece clock and again headed for the front door. Merlin, unimpressed by all the activity, snored under the table and soon a very bored Bandit spotted the large black hairy spider, whose web still hung from the curtain pole, was lowering itself to the window ledge. Now he had something to do.

Arching his back, he stretched his legs and yawned widely exposing very sharp pointed teeth and, in no hurry, dropped onto a chair before springing lazily onto the sink worktop. The spider, tantalisingly, was now just a few centimetres above the window ledge. It froze as a slight breeze drifted in through the open window. Bandit edged closer. The spider moved again, descending centimetre by centimetre, completely unaware of being observed. Bandit licked his lips. Dropping to the ledge the spider hesitated. Bandit stretched out a paw and lightly touched the spider, toying with it. It sped away from the touch, its quick movement even more attractive to the tormenting cat that bided his time. The spider made a dash towards the open window. Bandit sprang, but he was too late. With a blue-

black flash of feathers, wings and a very long beak, Mélusine, with a look of triumph in her eyes and a beak full of twitching hairy legs, flew away making a 'chuck-chuck' sound as Bandit hissed menacingly at her.

The disturbance awoke Merlin who jumped up at the sink-unit and barked at the bird as she made her getaway. Mrs Jenks rushed back inside.

'What's going on in here?'

Merlin darted under the table but Bandit, being a little more courageous decided to brave it out and stood his ground on the window ledge, but eventually under the scolding, joined Merlin in hiding.

Mrs Jenks was usually in a good mood but today her nervousness made her intolerant. Bandit had lost count of the number of times she had straightened the curtains, fussed with papers or checked her appearance in the mirror. Unfortunately, the room remained in its normal disorderly state in spite of the number of times she had 'tidied up'.

There was a knock at the front door. Mrs Jenks took a deep breath, checked her appearance in the mirror yet again, took another deep breath and, shoulders back, walked sedately to the front door.

Merlin sat up, so did Bandit, both wondering what was going on. But they did not have to wait long. The door opened and Mrs Jenks reappeared carrying a holdall and there was someone with her. The girl had long black hair and glittering green eyes and Bandit hated her on sight. Spitting and hissing, his fur bristling, he backed away. Likewise, Merlin bared his teeth; his lips curled backwards, his neck hair ridged upwards. The girl made no response to their reaction but Mrs Jenks was horrified.

'Please, just ignore them, Tanith. They'll settle down soon. It's just that we don't see many visitors in here and they're not really used to having people around.'

She put the holdall down and took a step towards Bandit. 'Now come on, you silly thing. This is Tanith. Tanith's family, you'll soon get to know her.' As she went to lift him up he twisted out of her reach, scratching her hand with his claws and sprang onto the worktop. With one last defiant hiss at Tanith, he disappeared through the window and vanished.

'Well! I've never seen him act like that before,' Armistice declared to the girl. 'I'm so sorry. I'm sure he'll come round soon. But this is Merlin. Merlin's a big softie, aren't you?' She had obviously forgotten he too had shown his displeasure on seeing her visitor. She reached out to stroke him and he backed away, never taking his eyes off the newcomer; his neck hair rigid.

75

'Oh Merlin! Not you too,' Mrs Jenks pleaded. 'Tanith is a friend, you'll like her.'

But Merlin was having none of it and backed away under the red chenille tablecloth until all that could be seen were his curled lips and bared teeth.

'I don't know what's got into them, dear. As I said, they're not usually like this.' But 'Tanith' was not concerned by the behaviour of the animals. Instead she was staring in fascination at the astrological charts on the walls.

'This is wonderful, Aunt Armistice,' she gushed, her voice girly and soft.

Armistice reached out to put a hand on her shoulder but pulled it back wondering if it was too soon for signs of affection. It was enough for now that after so long, she had found a relative when she thought she was alone. They had plenty of time.

'I'll make some tea,' Armistice volunteered, 'while you take a look around. If there's anything you want to know, just ask. We'll take your bags upstairs later and there's plenty of books for you too look through in the study.' She knew she was talking too much but her nerves had got the better of her.

'I'm fine, thank you, Aunt Armistice, but could I have coffee please. Black and no sugar, thank you.'

'You don't have to call me by that awfully formal title, dear. Armistice will do, or better still some of my friends just call me Armie. Why don't you?'

'Very well, I'd be delighted to,' the girl smiled sweetly. This was going to be so easy.

Armistice filled the kettle and took a quick look to see if Bandit was anywhere to be seen in the garden but there was no sign of him which upset her. She loved her clever cat and hated to see him upset

With Armistice's back to her, Tanith moved towards the table. Merlin shifted further back but not far back enough. With a swift movement, Tanith stepped on his paw. He howled in pain.

'Oh, I'm so sorry,' Tanith seemed genuinely upset.

'What happened?' Armistice rushed to him.

'I didn't notice his paw was sticking out and stepped on him accidentally. I'm so sorry.'

Armistice shook her head. 'No, no my dear, it was obviously an accident. Don't worry he'll be fine.'

'But I feel so bad. I've only just got here and he hates me already. So does your cat.' Her eyes filled with tears making Armistice feel sorry for her; Merlin's injury already forgotten.

'You come and sit down and we'll talk. We have so much to catch up on and I want to know so much about you. Maybe later, I'll take you to the pub for a meal tonight. I feel like celebrating. After all it's not every day you find a lost relative.'

Tanith sat on the rocking chair in front of the fireplace and took another good look around the room. What a mess! Papers, books, charts, plants and spider webs! Everything she had done to get here had led her to this mad old woman and her stupid animals.

Armistice handed her a mug of coffee. 'I'll tell you about all of this,' she nodded towards the charts, 'as time goes on and there's so much to tell you about the family history, what I do and this village.'

Tanith stifled a yawn and hoped Tlaloc would arrange things so that she could get out of this place soon. If he didn't, she had the means to move things along in a plastic bag in her case.

'If it's no trouble,' the imposter asked, 'can I take my things to my room? I kinda feel like I'd like to freshen up.'

Armistice looked mortified. 'Oh my dear, I should have thought of that myself. Of course you can. Your room's ready for you. It's at the top of the stairs and turn left. Can I help with your holdall?'

'No, no thank you, Au…Armie. I can manage for myself. I'll be down soon.' She smiled sweetly and left the room. Armistice, observant as always, noticed Elêna's smile did not reach her eyes but dismissed it as jet lag.

As the sound of footsteps moved up the stairs, Merlin's nose emerged from under the tablecloth.

'Well I don't know what's got into you two, but you've both been very rude,' Armistice scolded. Whimpering, he slunk back to his hiding place and lay down with his chin on his front paws.

Having struggled with the bulky holdall to the top of the narrow stairs where the air was considerably warmer, Elêna paused to get her breath and take a look around. The stairs ended in the middle of a wide, white painted landing with a sage green carpet. In comparison with downstairs, everything was very clean and uncluttered but even though all three long narrow windows on the facing wall were open, as were the doors, the lack of breeze coming in from outside, made the landing stuffy.

There were several doors situated on either side of the landing and she could not resist investigating. The first door on the right was open. The

77

sage green and white décor was repeated in what was obviously Armistice's bedroom, giving it the same clean but rather tired look. Against the wall opposite the window stood a magnificent pine carved wardrobe with a matching chest of drawers on either side. The bed too was made of polished pine and covered with a brightly coloured crocheted counterpane. Surprisingly there were no mirrors or personal items on display other than several framed photographs; one showed the same smiling man in the picture downstairs. Another showed Armistice cuddling a little girl, probably about two or three years old. From the similarity in features Elêna supposed the child was Armistice's daughter, but then recalled that she had no children.

The happy photograph unexpectedly made her eyes prickle and she turned away. Back on the landing, she tried another door, but this was nothing more than an airing cupboard with shelves of neatly folded bedding and towels and a number of brown paper bags, tied with string and hung on hooks that released a powerful herbal aroma of mint and rosemary. Next door was an all white bathroom with a bath and modern shower cabinet, white wall tiles, laminated wooden flooring and several fluffy white towels on chrome rails. The entire effect was pleasingly simple but comfortable and even luxurious. This house was full of surprises.

At the far end of the landing, was what she took to be an office or study with a heavy dark wood desk and chair, an old armchair and several book cases, all of them heavily laden. The last door was the spare bedroom. This was obviously to be her own during her brief stay. It would do.

A slight breeze ruffled the curtains and brought with it a sweet, floral fragrance that captivated her. Still on the landing she pulled back a curtain and settled comfortably on the window seat overlooking a well tended front garden of lawn and beds of roses in an assortment of colours, bordered by a neatly trimmed hedge. The roses explained the perfume in the air.

She leaned out and looked up and down the road; her first real look at the village. A tired looking man in a grey suit approached the front gate on a bicycle. He stopped, pulled a white handkerchief from the back pocket of his trousers and wiped his forehead and the side of his neck. His round white collar identified him as a clergyman. A Priest! Could she not escape them even here? She watched as he removed his jacket, revealing sweat patches under the arms of his shirt, and laid it carefully on the handlebars before cycling off around the corner.

Almost immediately, from that same bend, came a loud rattling sound that turned out to be an old battered jeep. It juddered to a halt as a beautiful chestnut horse trotted up from the opposite direction. The female rider

78

waved and called out something to the driver, a man with long grey hair and a thick beard. They stopped to talk. Elêna could hear the girl was talking but was too far away to hear anything clearly. But the man's voice was so loud it carried plainly to her as she gazed down in admiration at the tall, dignified horse with the glossy coat. She had never seen such a beautiful animal. At home the horses were thin and scrawny, beasts of burden or used for other work, they were not sleek and beautifully muscled like this one.

As the rider turned slightly to wave to a woman and child as they passed by on the other side of the road, Elêna saw something written on the back of the girl's pale blue tee-shirt but at that angle was unable make out what it said until the rider leaned forward to pat the horse's neck. 'Winterne Riding School and Livery Stable'. She wondered if all the horses there looked as good as this one.

'Oi don' s'pose you've seen anythin' of Sam, 'ave you, Meredith?'

The girl shook her head and said something but, again, from that distance she could not hear the reply.

'No, daft lad's gone missin.' The man scratched his head. 'Oi dunno. Seems 'e 'ad a row wi' young Jenny and stormed orf. Course me an' Cathy 'ave 'ad 'is mum on the phone an' Oi'm orf ter look fer 'im.' He started up the rattling engine. The horse shied in alarm, obviously troubled at the noise but his rider held the reins firmly and leaned forward to pat his neck.

'Sorry, Meredith.' The man switched the engine off and the horse quietened. 'Oi'll wait till you've gone on. Shoulda known Angelo'd react loike that so close to the jeep. My fault. Prob'ly not concentratin', all this nonsense wi' Sam an all.'

The girl said something to him and he gave a rough chuckle. 'Yeah, well you get orf then an' take care. Say 'allo ter yer mum for me.'

The girl and horse trotted off while the man waited a few seconds before driving in the opposite direction. She fleetingly wondered who the missing Sam was but then put him from her mind as being of no importance.

Tired of watching the village inhabitants, she picked up her holdall and went to her room. Again, in contrast with the chaotic mess of the ground floor, the room was plain but beautifully furnished. Decorated in pink and cream, with pine furniture the room was a delight that needed further exploration so she dumped her holdall by the window to unpack later.

The dormer window overlooked the back garden and she could see a round wooden and steel constructed tower, with six hexagonal shaped legs and a metal ladder reaching skywards to end on a ledge surrounding what looked like an enclosed metal tank. What is was she had no idea, but she

would ask. Beyond the hedge, was the wood with its closely-packed trees of so many varieties it took her breath away. Although Tanith had never seen her great aunt's home, her portrayal had been uncannily accurate, but even her description had not prepared Elêna for the incredible beauty of the English countryside. Alvarez City had been a bleak place of concrete and crime and her home village, San Pablo, had been nothing more than a dust bowl inhabitation, but this was another world.

The minutes ticked by as she stared at the dense wood and the hillside backdrop. There was definitely something unnerving about someone who was supposed to have been born so long ago yet looked so much younger; something mystical perhaps, and the paraphernalia downstairs was definitely weird but, for all that, Elêna discovered she actually quite liked Armistice Jenks. Maybe, if things had been different…another time, another place…maybe? No! Her plans were made and she would stick to them, her conscience she would deal with later, if it ever bothered her.

With the money she had in both her bank accounts it would be easy to disappear whenever she wanted, especially now she was in Europe. She could go wherever she wanted. No-one in Mexico would know where she had gone. All she needed now was to decide what her next move would be and she was in no hurry, although her 'aunt' clearly expected her to stay indefinitely. Well, that was not going to happen. She would leave when she was ready and only then when she had found what she came for.

She lay down on the bed her hands behind her head, her ankles crossed, and congratulated herself on how well her plans had worked out. It was then she remembered the reaction from the cat and dog. She smiled. If they gave her too much trouble they would be dealt with but something else began nagging at her; something was wrong or out of place but she could not think what it was. She was still trying to figure it out when Armistice called up the stairs.

'Tanith? Tanith, dear?' Deep in thought, Elêna forgot her new identity and did not answer.

'Tanith? Are you alright?' Armistice called again.

'Yes, yes, thanks.' She jumped off the bed and headed downstairs attempting to get back in character. 'I just took a look around the village. It's so green. I am not used to this lush greenery.'

'It's usually greener than this but we've had so little rain in the last few weeks,' Armistice said. 'You should see when we've had a real downpour. By the way, I've booked a table at the pub for seven-thirty this evening, dear, so we've got about three quarters of an hour. If we go the long way

around I can show you some more of the village. It's a beautiful evening, just right for a walk. How soon will you be ready?'

'I'm happy to go now, if you want.' Elêna's pretence in being interested convinced Armistice.

'Right my dear. It'll make a nice change for me to go out.' Armistice found she was actually looking forward to being around other people. Bandit and Merlin's reaction to Tanith had surprised and upset her. It was not like them and they only reacted that way when they were frightened of something. But why would they be frightened of her great-niece? Perhaps it was just that they were so used to living alone together, having someone else about had disturbed them. Maybe they only needed some time to get to know each other and everything would settle down quickly. She certainly hoped so. But she had not seen Bandit for hours.

Chapter Fourteen

With the company of elves watching, Rondo ran to the ledge where the lanterns were stored and lifted out six. He blew softly into each one and handed them out to the group as they followed Halmar, with Ellien clinging anxiously to his arm, into the tunnel. She whispered to him asking where they were going and what he was going to show them, but Halmar gently hushed her.

'It will soon become clear,' he soothed. His blue eyes gazed lovingly into hers which had now darkened to deep green pools of misgiving. 'Do not worry. I will not let anyone do anything to hurt you. Trust me *and* your father.' Holding her small, cool hand, he led her and the others, including an extremely surly Avaroc, for what seemed to Sam like several kilometres, along dry and dusty tunnels with Charlie the last in line. As always, the tunnels expanded to accommodate his great size before shrinking back to normal behind him.

After what felt like an hours (Sam was convinced it must be about two o'clock in the morning), they arrived at the Transit cave. Four quad bikes stood idle in corner and the conveyor belts were not in use yet; it would be another couple of months before the Christmas preparations began but Corporal and two other elves Sam did not recognise were busily oiling cogs and testing some of the machinery. Corporal was still wearing his knitted woolly hat pulled down to just above his eyes covering his flat ears. He saw the group walking single file along the ledge and looked up.

'Evening Chief, Sam,' he called, standing up to watch them go by. 'Everything alright?' His two companions stopped what they were doing and they too stood to watch the party with their eyes. They were unused to seeing anyone so late; Jossamel, Phaeron and Pernia had returned from the night patrol some time ago.

Charlie and Sam waved back to Corporal. 'Evening, Corporal,' Charlie boomed, his voice reverberating around the vast, cathedral roofed cavern. 'Everything's fine, thank you. Belts OK?'

'Yes, sir, they'll be fine,' Corporal called back slightly disappointed. His curiosity about what was going on would not be answered just yet. 'There was a slight tear in one of them, but nothing that can't be mended.'

After circling the cavern, they took the second tunnel on the left and for a while Sam wondered if they were heading towards the reindeer but soon, Halmar stopped. The company halted and watched in fascination as he ran his hand slowly over a piece of overhanging rock and then downward.

'In the name of Alfheim, what is all this nonsense?' Avaroc grumbled but Charlie silenced him with a cutting look. Avaroc had a poor opinion of humans in general, but the Chief was different. He was worthy of respect and admiration.

'Listen!' Ellien said in a hushed voice that echoed softly around them.

A rumbling, scraping sound came from inside the rock wall. Avaroc appeared shaken as from the floor upwards the wall began to rise slowly revealing a double metal door. Halmar raised his hand and the door slid effortlessly open.

Sam lifted his lantern and gasped. A room, the size of a standard two-storey house, filled with row upon row of large pigeon-holed shelves, opened up before them and in the middle of the floor stood a heavy wooden table. Every one of the square openings surrounding the room was filled with gold-ribbon bound scrolls; there were more in neat piles on the floor. Ellien stood rooted to the spot.

'Halmar, what is this place?'

Charlie moved to stand beside her. 'Your father and I created this room, Ellien.' He took her hand and led her further in. 'This room contains the entire history of your people,' he told her, watching her eyes widen with wonder, 'right back to the beginning of time.'

Ellien's gaze roamed around the room and she wandered alone between the shelves, her hand lightly alighting on one yellowing scroll then on to the next while she listened to Charlie's story. Halmar walked on Charlie's other side watching Ellien as she marvelled at the extraordinary history the room contained and wondered what it meant to her future.

'Let's have some more light in here,' Halmar suggested brushing the dust off the large lanterns standing on the table.

'Your father showed Halmar this room shortly before he died,' Charlie explained.

Halmar smiled at her puzzled expression and gently blew into one of the lanterns. It took a few seconds for the light to flicker into life but soon it blazed more fiercely than any of the lanterns Sam had seen the elves use before. Halmar repeated the process with a second and third and hung each one from brackets on the wall. Their powerful light made their own lanterns redundant and they blew them out.

'But why did my father never mention this to me?' Ellien asked looking this way and that, turning slowly to absorb the spectacle.

'He brought Halmar here when he realised his time was growing short,' Charlie explained. 'He knew this time might come and wanted to ensure his people were guided safely, they were protected.'

'Protected? Protected from what?' Avaroc spat.

'Protected from you or someone like you,' Charlie answered matter-of-factly without looking at him.

Sam had caught up with Halmar. 'What are we looking for, Halmar?'

'I don't need to look, Sam. I know precisely where the scroll I need is. Jimander showed me where he had stowed it securely.' Sam followed him to the back of the room where Halmar pressed a small dark area on the wall that Sam would never have noticed.

Again a scraping, rumbling sound followed and a partition slid aside to reveal a solid wooden door behind. Opening the door, Halmar removed a deep red wooden chest with gold key escutcheon and carried it back to the table. The others crowded around.

'Do I want to see this?' Ellien asked nervously looking at Halmar for reassurance; her eyes a deep green earlier were now a brilliant emerald in the flickering light of the lanterns.

'Don't worry, Ellien. I'm here and I'm staying by your side.'

'We all are,' added Aelfrar, who up to that point had stayed quiet throughout the venture. Piggybait nodded in solemn agreement.

'Are you going to open that chest or are we just going to stand here looking at it?' Avaroc demanded.

'Go ahead, Halmar,' Jerrill said. Charlie nodded. Sam held his breath. Piggybait and Clap-trap exchanged uneasy looks.

Inside the chest was another scroll, this one tied with a purple silk ribbon but as Halmar lifted it out something glinted underneath.

'What's that?' Ellien asked.

'You need to see the scroll first,' Halmar said putting the chest on the floor under the table. He unrolled the scroll and laid it out on the table, asking Piggybait to hold the top corners as they automatically tried to roll

back. He asked Sam to do the same at the bottom end. The group crowded around the table.

'But...but this can't be genuine!' Avaroc protested as his dreams faded. Sam was unable to make out the inscription on the scroll but guessed it might have been some form of runic lettering, completely indecipherable to him but the others seemed to understand its meaning.

'I can assure you, it's absolutely genuine,' Charlie told him, with a smile. 'This scroll charts the royal lineage of all British Elfdom from the beginning of time.' He pointed to the last name on the chart. 'Malliena, Ellien's mother was the last of the House of Alfheirex. Ellien's blood is pure and true and she is the indisputable Queen of Alfheim!'

Jerrill, Piggybait, Clap-trap and Jossamel fell to their knees. Aelfrar tried to follow suit but his stiff knees prevented it so he made a simple bow. Sam too kneeled, feeling it was the right thing to do. Only Avaroc, Halmar and Charlie remained standing. Ellien looked at these friends who now made obeisance to her, not knowing how to react. 'Please, no, don't kneel. Please get up,' she said tearfully reaching for the support of Halmar's hand.

'The Lords of Alfheim!' Ellien said, with an overwhelmed sigh, 'No, no this is wrong! You're my friends, please, please get up.' She turned to Halmar in wide-eyed appeal. 'Tell them to get up, Halmar.'

He shook his head. 'This is how it was meant to be, Ellien.'

'But I don't understand,' she cried. 'Why did I not know? Why did my father not tell me?' Halmar stood behind her, one hand under her right elbow the other on her left shoulder in a gesture of support.

Charlie took her hand, he spoke softly. 'Jimander always hoped you would never have to know,' Charlie went on. 'He trusted Jerrill, Piggy and Clap-trap, with Halmar by your side and me to watch over you, that you would be allowed to continue leading a simple, uncomplicated life, but...' he glowered at Avaroc, '...this challenge changes things.' He lifted her chin gently with his shovel-like hand. 'Avaroc is just one who may challenge the leadership here. Some of the other clans are in disarray, disputes and power struggles are beginning to upset the natural order of Elfdom and they need a true leader, someone who can unite and guide. You are that person Ellien,' he ended sympathetically.

Ellien gripped Halmar's hand tightly. 'But what if I don't want this, Sir?' Her voice shook.

'You have no choice my child. You are loved and respected by your clan and by any who know you. You are just, knowledgeable, gifted and...yes, even shrewd. The only thing you lack is confidence, confidence in your abilities...'

'*This is nonsense!*' Avaroc shrieked. Charlie ignored him but Piggybait gave him a shove and he fell to his knees beside the others, grumbling under his breath.

'Quiet!' Piggybait hissed. 'Or we'll leave you in the dark somewhere on the way back. It'll take years to find your way out.'

Ellien was pacing up and down, clearly shaken. Then she stopped. 'Halmar, there was something else inside that chest. What was it?' She turned to her companions. 'Oh please get up. I feel so uncomfortable with you on your knees.'

They stood, all apart from an indignant Avaroc who was prevented from rising by Piggybait and Clap-trap leaning on his shoulders. Aelfrar took a moment or two to straighten up. 'Thank you my Lady.'

Halmar reached for the chest and laid it on the table. Lifting back the lid, he reached inside. Ellien gasped as he produced a pale gold circlet; a small crown. The narrow shimmering band of ancient Elven gold widened at the front to a downward point that, when worn, would rest in the middle of the forehead. Engraved in the centre of this point was an image of an oak tree with three gemstones, one above the other in the trunk; at the top, a diamond, below it an emerald and, at the bottom, a ruby.

'These stones represent eternity, the earth and the blood of our people,' Halmar told her. 'This is your crown Ellien. Your father hoped you would never have to wear it but knew that, if the day came, you would wear it well.'

Avaroc cursed and Piggybait, looking in the other direction, silenced him with a quick slap to the back of his head. Charlie took the crown from Halmar and placed it gently on Ellien's head. Sam was still surprised at what a light touch this huge bear of a man could have. Ellien had no need to adjust the circlet, it fitted her perfectly and, once it was in place, she straightened her shoulders, lifted her head and declared, 'I will wear this crown proudly in the name of the Lords of Alfheim and pray I will do it justice.' As she reached for Halmar's hand, Jerrill realised that from this time he must defer to his son; something he had never anticipated.

'Sir,' she began.

Charlie broke in. 'You will never call me Sir again. Instead it is I who should call you My Lady or Ma'am or even Your Majesty. Which would you prefer?'

'How about Ellien?' she smiled. 'And you'll be Klaus…if I can remember to use that name after all this time.'

'Come, My Lady,' Halmar said, 'our people will be waiting to find out what all this is about,' he rolled up the scroll and put it inside his shirt.

Leaving Piggybait and Clap-trap together, with Aelfrar, to return the room to normal, Halmar led the way back through the tunnels. Avaroc found he had no choice but to follow Ellien and Halmar, with Charlie, Sam and Jerrill behind him, back to the clan, his thoughts awhirl with hatred, disappointment and defeat.

On reaching the Transit Cave, Corporal and his two colleagues stopped their work and looked up. Seeing Ellien wearing the Crown of Alfheim, they too fell to their knees but she smilingly told them to stand. 'Follow us to the Great Chamber and everything will be explained.' Although she did not appear to be shouting, her crystal voice resonated across the cavern sounding stronger and more clear than ever before.

'That'll be the crown,' Charlie told Sam. 'The simplest way to explain it is that it acts a little like a microphone. While she's wearing it any speech Ellien makes, no matter how many people are there, will be clearly heard without her raising her voice.'

'Cool,' replied Sam, 'but isn't it time we got going? I don't want to stop the party or anything but I've got school tomorrow and I've got to sort things out with Jenny and it must be about four in the morning.'

Charlie's white beard parted in a smile. 'You're probably right Sam, but don't forget, we can 'tweak' time a little. It'll only be about ten o'clock last night when we get back and we really do need to get this finished tonight.'

As they reached the Great Chamber, Ellien stopped, she was trembling. 'Our people know me well, Halmar. I have no doubt that they will believe, but what about the others...the New Forest, Cresswell Crags...,'

'Don't worry,' Halmar reassured her. 'I have the scroll. They will believe this.'

Holding herself erect, Ellien took the lead into the cavern. Primola had recovered her senses but was dozing in an armchair and Rondina, to allow her mother to rest, was busily chivvying a team of elves into clearing up the debris from the feast. Spotting the crown, she shook her mother awake and called to Halmia, Halmar's twin sister. Halmia moved to the front of the gathering group. Ellien gripped Halmar's sleeve.

'Elves of Winterne! Guests!' Halmar called out over the chatter that had sprung up. 'Behold your Queen.'

Her eyes sparkling with emotion, Ellien stepped ahead of him. The Winterne elves moved forward as Ellien began to speak, her eyes sparkling with emotional tears. 'I promise you, I knew nothing of this until tonight and I have no intention of changing my relationship with you. I shall be here to support and help and, hopefully, in the time of need, help provide

strength. I will only use whatever powers are granted to me for the welfare of all of my people.'

Halmia was the first to drop to her knees in respect of their newly named Queen. She had always been fond of Ellien and had no reason to doubt the veracity of her claim, particularly as the Chief, her father and her brother were supporting her. Rondina followed suit as, one by one, did the other Winterne elves.

Radocas' keen eyes scanned the crowd for Avaroc and found him, just as Piggybait, Clap-trap and Aelfrar arrived. Avaroc was skulking at the far end of the cavern talking to Tarryn and Tildor. He had his back to everyone but from his posture and clenched fists, his fury was apparent. Radocas had never liked Avaroc and was glad to see him brought low. If Ellien's claim was true he would serve her with his life if necessary, but he was not to be persuaded without proof. This revelation could just be a ploy to block her uncle's claim.

'How do we know this is true?' he called from the back of the crowd. Kaellec and Zarianne nodded. Elves from the other clans were not so easily swayed as Halmia, although they too felt that her supporters would hardly lie.

Piggybait, Clap-trap and Aelfrar moved closer to join Charlie, Sam and Jerrill as they gathered around Ellien. Halmar ascended the stairs, two at a time and stopped halfway up. He unfurled the scroll for all to see.

'This scroll is undeniable proof of Ellien's bloodline. It shows that, until her birth, her mother, Malliena, was the last of the Alfheirex Line.' Several elves began talking at once. Halmar called for quiet. 'When she married Jimander and settled here at Winterne, Malliena sought a simple life and kept her bloodline a secret. The clans were at peace, there was no need for her ever to reveal her authority. Her life here with Jimander, who was not of royal blood, was one of contentment and she put thoughts of monarchy aside. Jimander told me of this shortly before he died convinced as he was that a time would come when the clans would be threatened. That time has come and Ellien will unite us.'

'May I see the scroll?' Radocas asked.

'Of course, Radocas. You will all have an opportunity to see it for yourselves. There is no deception.' Halmar finished his speech and descended the stairs to rejoin Ellien. He handed Radocas the scroll when they met at the bottom step. Kaellec joined Radocas and together they scrutinised the document in silence.

Radocas looked up at the silent mass of hopeful faces. Halmar and Kaellec stood either side of him. Ellien's bottom lip trembled. 'The scroll

is genuine,' he said loudly. Then he and Kaellec walked to Ellien and bowed in obeisance. At their signal all the elves from their clans formed a procession of two long lines as two by two they moved forward and kneeled before their Queen. Holding her head high, but smiling lovingly at every member of the united clans, no longer simply Jimander's daughter, but now their Queen. Charlie felt a lump in his throat.

'I'm not sure this is the time for sentimentality, Klaus,' Jerrill appeared beside him. 'Avaroc has vanished.'

'I see Tarryn and Tildor are still here,' Charlie saw the twins were back with their families. Tildor's wife was talking to him. Her eyes flickering anxious looks at Tarryn who, involved in deep conversation with his own wife, had not noticed.

'I'll be glad when they've gone,' Jerrill sighed.

Chapter Fifteen

On leaving the front garden, Elêna remarked on how green Armistice's lawn was in comparison to the other gardens that were mottled with large patches of brown, dried grass.

'Green fingers, they call it, my dear,' Armistice smiled, 'and possibly, luck. It became very hot very suddenly and although we have had plenty of rain earlier this summer, everything is drying out quickly with the temperature being so high.'

A woman, pushing a child's buggy walked towards them. The younger child slept peacefully but her older sister dragged her feet and tugged at her wrist rein, wailing in ear-splitting screams of temper. Busy remonstrating with her unruly toddler, she only became aware of the two women when they were just a couple of metres or so from her. Grabbing her unruly daughter very tightly by the wrist, she swerved off the pavement and crossed the road to walk by on the other side casting quick anxious looks at Armistice. Elêna thought her behaviour very peculiar but as Armistice ignored it she made no comment and they continued their walk with Armistice showing 'Tanith' where various people lived, Dr Brownlow's surgery and giving her information about village life in general.

'S'cuse us.'

Two boys in school football strips, one of them dripping with sweat and bouncing a football, wanted to pass by the two dawdling women, obviously expecting them to move aside to let them pass on the narrow pavement. But, on seeing Armistice, he elbowed his friend and they instantly stepped into the road to circuit the women and sped off giving Armistice sideways looks.

This time Elêna expected some reaction from Armistice but received none, so again she made no comment and they continued their slow walk to the Pub without seeing anyone else. Elêna did mention that she would have

expected to see more people about but Armistice explained that, not only was this generally the time of the evening meal, many people preferred to stay inside out of the heat. Having come from a hot climate, Elêna found that a little hard to understand. Where she came from, the cool of the early evening would be the time when people would arise from their siestas and populate the streets, but she accepted things were done differently in other parts of the world.

The pub was full. 'So this is where everyone is,' Armistice remarked as they entered the lounge bar area. Elêna could see through to the back garden where laughing children played on swings and climbing frames while parents sat at tables talking to other adults.

Half a dozen or so people sat on tall stools by the bar while groups sat round numerous square tables, their conversation loud and hearty until Armistice and Elêna were spotted, then the chatter died very abruptly.

Behind the bar a red-faced plump man was returning clean glasses to the shelves when he noticed the sudden lull in conversation. He had been laughing over a joke told by one of his customers but on seeing Armistice the smile faded for a moment only to be replaced by a phoney expression of welcome as he walked around the bar and came forward to greet them. Dressed in a formal white shirt and navy blue polka dot bow tie that looked a little too tight, he wiped perspiration from his forehead and his chubby neck with a tea-towel he had had tucked into his trouser belt.

'Evenin' Mrs Jenks,' he frowned. 'Not often we gets the…pleasure of your comp'ny.'

'No, Bill. As you know, I don't go out much, but this is a special occasion.' She took Elêna by the arm. 'This is my great-great niece, Tanith. She's come to stay with me, isn't that wonderful?' Armistice looked so happy, Elêna almost felt guilty.

Nearby patrons stared. They were unused to being in such close proximity to Armistice Jenks. Aware of their reaction and the ensuing whispering, Bill Pope prayed her presence would do no harm to his business; diners usually stayed on and bought a drink or two after their meal while others just enjoyed a few drinks, maybe a game of darts or skittles in the barn at the back. The weather brought good trade to the pub and he could not afford to have people leave. But she was here now and he had to deal with it He made a note to tell Pauline, his waitress, not to take any bookings from Mrs Jenks in future; they would be full at all times.

'Tanith, this is our landlord and host, Bill Pope.'

Pope! Again the Church! What was this? Elêna's left hand dived into her pocket and she gripped the amulet which she had taken off earlier

preferring to keep it hidden. 'I'm so pleased to meet you, Mr Pope.' She shook his hand.

'Yer American then,' Bill said, his legs turning to jelly as he drowned in the depths of those wide green eyes. 'We…umm…er… don' get many American visitors in 'ere,' he stuttered, trying to regain control. 'Most welcome, m'dear…both of you, that is…o' course,' he lied, while Armistice raised a cynical eyebrow. His displeasure at having Armistice mingle with his patrons and having to be polite to her went completely out of his head as a pink sheen crept up his neck.

'Erm, follow me…ladies,' he would normally have asked Pauline to take patrons to their tables, but he was glad of the excuse to turn his flushed face away as he led them to a table laid out for four people overlooking the garden. The other diners turned away as they approached and whispered or pulled faces as they past by.

Bill held Elêna's chair out for her. 'Pauline'll be with you in a moment or two to take your order.' He appeared to be in a great hurry to get away and headed off towards the bar trying to remember what instruction it was that he meant to give Pauline.

Elêna wondered at the whispering and the looking away whenever people saw she had noticed them staring; it all seemed to be directed at Armistice.

'See the effect you're having,' Armistice told her as they sat at a table by the window overlooking the garden, but Elêna was convinced Armistice was the cause. She needed to know more.

A waitress came to take their order and while they were waiting Armistice talked of the family and listened while Elêna recounted Tanith's story as if it were her own. Many questions Armistice asked Elêna was able to answer fully but others were more difficult and she wriggled out of answering by blaming her injuries and subsequent ill health for the gaps in her memory. At one point Elêna mentioned the photograph with Armistice and the child, and asked who it was. Armistice looked at her in surprise.

'Why, that's you my dear. I came to visit when you were around two years old. I suppose you wouldn't remember.' Elêna thought quickly.

'I'm sorry, there are still so many things I've forgotten. The amnesia, you know.'

Armistice said she understood and offered to help with filling in the missing details as time went on but only as and when Tanith felt up to it.

The meal of cold chicken and salad washed down by a glass of white wine was fairly mediocre and the vaguely unpleasant feeling of being watched while she ate made Elêna uncomfortable. She was relieved when

Armistice suggested it was time to go home. At the bar Armistice paid the bill and they left, again watched by the patrons.

'Are people around here always so unfriendly?' she asked as they crossed the village green.

'Take no notice, dear,' Armistice took her arm. 'Not everyone's like it. I do have some very good friends. I'll introduce you to them once you've settled in. You'll like them but I warn you, they're quite unusual.'

They waited at the edge of the village green to let a dark blue jaguar go past. The driver turned to look in their direction and almost swerved as he caught sight of Elêna. Armistice chuckled. 'See, I said it was you everyone was looking at. I don't think they've ever seen anyone quite so exotic.'

'Who was that?' Elêna asked staring after the car as it disappeared up the road.

'That's Stuart Seymour. His mother's the cook at Winterne Manor.'

'Winterne Manor?'

'Yes, it's the local big house. Stables, lake, secret dungeons, you know the kind of thing. They've had problems over the last few months. One thing after another…murders, criminals, all sorts of things going on and never a dull moment.'

'It sounds fascinating. Can I take a look at the place sometime?'

'Oh, I expect so dear but, let's get you settled in first, there's plenty of time for exploration.'

Elêna wasn't so sure. She wanted to get away from the area as soon as she had everything she needed.

Chapter Sixteen

Instead of taking their usual route through the wood which would take them close to Charlie's cottage, Sam and his uncle took the long way round towards Winterne Manor. Although this would take longer, it meant they would be closer to Sam's home. It took a few minutes for Sam's eyes to become accustomed to the darkness after the bright lights of the cavern, but as he and Charlie stuck to the wider paths he managed not to trip over upraised roots or other obstacles. Charlie, however, had perfect night vision and avoided all hazards.

Winterne Wood spread across many acres and, even though Sam spent a great deal of time visiting the elves or exploring, he was astonished at how quickly it transformed into unfamiliar territory with the varying seasons or something as simple as a change in the light. A fallen tree could render a section of the wood completely unrecognisable.

In daytime, the usual sounds were birds and buzzing insects and, of course during the summer months, the incessant background hum of holiday traffic. But by night, with the diurnal birds at roost and most of the insects waiting for sun up, the wood teemed with life from another world.

Ferns and tall grasses rustled, unseen animals crept and slithered through trees, bats emerged from hollow tree roosts, foxes yipped out barks, owls hooted and, in spring, 'Baron' the stag could be heard bellowing his warning to other male deer to stay away. Sam was never quite sure whether he enjoyed being in the wood at night and it was always more comfortable having Charlie for company.

'See, Sam,' Charlie pointed upwards. Red lights flickered on and off as planes flew thousands of feet above through the night and the moon shone directly overhead.

'It's just as I said. It's only ten o'clock. The sun starts coming up at about four-thirty so if it was as late as you thought, the moon would be a lot

lower, dawn would be just tipping over the trees and birds would be singing the Dawn Chorus. You really should trust me, you know.'

But Sam was not impressed. Charlie was not going to pull the wool over his eyes again. 'Then why am I so tired?' he griped. 'It feels like I've been up all night.'

'Just an illusion, old son. It's all in the mind.'

'So, what happens now, Charlie?'

'Happens? Happens about what?' Charlie looked lost.

'Well, Ellien's Queen, Halmar will be a fine king, or consort, but what about Piggy, Clap-trap and Jerrill. Will they carry on as Elders...and what about Avaroc? The way he and that other two sloped off like that, it can't be a good...whassat?'

There was a sudden and loud rustling above them. Charlie pulled a torch from his pocket and directed its beam upwards into the branches. Two big yellow eyes blinked down at them.

'It's OK it's Barney, Sam, nothing to worry about.' The barn owl's wings made a whumping sound as he disappeared into the darkness away from the ill-mannered humans who disturbed his nocturnal hunt.

'He's annoyed with us again.'

'What do you mean, annoyed with *us* again?' Charlie bellowed. 'It's not me who annoyed him before, it was you, remember?'

'Oh yeah, forgot about that,' Sam replied, recalling a certain night just before Christmas and another at Easter. 'But going back to what we were saying, Charlie. What about Piggy and the others and Avaroc. What do you think will happen?'

It was too dark to see Charlie's lined forehead, but his silence gave Sam the impression he was trying to think of an easy answer and having difficulty trying to come up with one.

'To be honest Sam I really don't know...I wish I did.'

'Gut feeling?'

'My gut feeling is that Avaroc has had his nose put out of joint...for the moment. Whatever Tarryn and Tildor have been involved in they always caused disruption and the three of them together will spell big trouble. Tarryn's the older twin and never let Tildor forget it as they were growing up. Tarryn's power-hungry and seems to think Avaroc's the way to get it and I'm not sure how far he'll go either. I don't believe anything will happen yet as I'm convinced Avaroc will lick his wounds for a while. But both he and Tarryn are ambitious and he's made his intentions clear...thrown down the gauntlet so to speak.'

'But now Ellien's Queen of all the British elves surely he can't do anything to contest it,' Sam protested, alarmed at the thought of any harm being done to Ellien.

'Ahh, now that may be so but I wouldn't put it past him...or those blasted twins. No, Avaroc and Tarryn will keep stirring each other on towards power. They'll push, bully...anything to move themselves into a superior position.'

'You didn't mention Tildor.'

'No. Alone, Tildor is no threat. On his own he would be fine but Tarryn leads him by the nose. I'd bet he would like to settle somewhere like Winterne, if he had the choice but he's led by Tarryn. Tarryn's the strong one, the one who starts trouble. Tildor can't or won't stand up to him. Alfheim help him if he ever follows his conscience and rebels, especially now Tarryn's being influenced by Avaroc.'

Sam walked along in silence his mind working overtime.

'No. You mark my words, Sam. Avaroc will go into hiding, lick his wounds of humiliated pride and wait until the time is right to plan a coup. I believe with Tarryn's help and the submissive Tildor in tow, Avaroc will look for the loners, the unhappy, the misfits and keep chipping away at anyone who wants to listen, until they have a strong enough force to attempt an uprising.'

'What! You're kidding right?' Sam could not believe what he was hearing. He thought of Ellien and how kind and loved she was even by the other clans. He had witnessed their devotion; how easily they accepted her as their monarch. Avaroc plotting against her and Halmar was unthinkable.

'I wish I was...but don't worry, it won't happen yet. If Avaroc had enough followers he would have brought them with him and there were just a handful this time. I suppose you saw the others in his group sneak away.'

Sam nodded, 'Yeah, I saw them...but that girl stayed behind.'

'Aerynne?'

'Er...yeah, I think that's her name. How come she didn't go back with them?'

'She didn't want to. In fact she was quite stubborn about it. When Tarryn's wife...um...Feystra, tried to drag her away, she clung on to Claptrap and Piggy...said she was staying. They didn't seem too upset about it.'

'But you really do believe there'll be trouble?' Sam yawned. Even news of this importance did not prevent tiredness. Trudging home and making conversation at the same time, this late at night was getting harder to manage. All he really wanted was to crawl into bed.

'Oh yes.' Charlie seemed unaware of Sam's fatigue. 'Yes, I certainly do, but that's in the future. We have a couple of worries closer to home to sort out first.'

Now they were in the lane, Sam could see his cottage in the distance and his legs grew heavier still, it was a real effort to maintain interest. Whatever Charlie was worried about could surely wait?

'I've got enough to face apologising to Jenny in the morning.'

Charlie gave a short laugh. 'That's what happens when you grow up Sam. You have to take the flak when you do something daft. But that's not what I'm talking about. I'm still not convinced about this visitor of Armistice's. Something's not right. And did you notice anyone missing tonight?'

Sam thought for a moment then shook his head. 'No, I don't think so. Why?'

They were at Sam's front door. 'Did you see Saldor at all this evening?'

'No, no I didn't, now you come to mention it. I...don't remember seeing him at all.'

'And you don't think that's strange?'

'I never thought about it. There was so much going on.' Sam fell silent for a second then added. 'I feel bad now.'

'Don't,' Charlie reassured him. 'I didn't realise either. I think everyone thought he was with someone else. It wasn't until we got back from the Scroll Room that Piggy asked me if I'd seen him. He and a few of the others had a look around...there was no sign.'

'He usually hangs about with Halmar...since Jimander died,' Sam rightly observed.

'Yes, but Halmar was busy with his guests, keeping an eye on Avaroc and then talking to everyone about the scroll. He had too much on his mind tonight to worry about Saldor and he too would have assumed he was with someone else.'

'So what happens now?'

Charlie's eyes twinkled in the moonlight. He rubbed his beard thoughtfully. 'Well you go to bed and I go home,' Charlie replied. 'There's nothing we can do tonight. Piggybait's getting a search party together to try and find him. I'll get along there early in the morning and see if anything's happened or if they've found any clues, but if Piggy hears anything tonight he'll let me know.'

Sam tried to stifle a yawn but it was too strong.

Charlie grinned. 'Go on, lad, you get some sleep. You just get Jenny back on side tomorrow and that'll be one worry out of the way. I'm sure Saldor will be OK, we just have to find him.'

As Charlie headed home under the starlit sky he thought about Sam, Jenny, Armistice, the mysterious relative and everything that had happened around the village during the last very long twenty-four hours. He felt drained. Emerging from the trees he saw a light on in the back bedroom of his cottage. Cathy was probably still reading, waiting for him to come home. He would have to find some excuse for being so late. Poachers? Yes, that would do. She never questioned him, but that just made him feel duty bound to offer an explanation when he came home later than he had intended. While he rummaged in his pocket for his key, Frida appeared from the darkness and rubbed her head around his ankles asking to come indoors.

'What's all this then? It's not like you, Miss Frida. You don't usually want to come in at night. Not hunting this evening?' Bjorn and Benny barked as he opened the back door and ran barking loudly to greet him, jumping up and making so much noise that Frida ran up the stairs where she snootily observed the overexcited dogs from between the banisters on the sixth and seventh steps on the staircase until they calmed down and padded off to their beds. Charlie pulled up a chair and tugged off his boots. He yawned and stretched, thought about making himself a cup of tea and thought better of it. His elbows on the table and his bearded chin resting on his cupped palms, Charlie's thoughts went into overdrive as images of Armistice, Avaroc and a jumble of faces and thoughts spun around his head.

Frida jumped on his lap. 'You know something's up, don't you girl?' She purred as he stroked her arched back. 'That's why you're staying in tonight.'

'That you, Charlie?' Cathy called from the bedroom.

'No. Father Christmas. Who d'you think it is?' he laughed as he got up to turn out the kitchen light.

Chapter Seventeen

Over the next couple of days, Piggybait and Clap-trap organised a number of search parties to look for Saldor investigating all the tunnels and caves they thought were likely haunts.

Rondo had convinced Primola they would find Saldor very soon and promised her that wherever he was, Saldor was still well. Jossamel seconded this argument by adding that, with his close friendship with Saldor, he would know instinctively if anything untoward had befallen him.

Individually they were all conscious of the fact that something awful could have happened to their friend but no-one wanted to voice their concern.

Piggybait and his team searched the northern caves. Clap-trap took the southern side while Jossamel and Rondo formed two teams to search the wood for any sign of Saldor.

Charlie spent as much time as he could spare from his duties and his home without Cathy becoming too suspicious and even brought the dogs with him to see if they could pick up his scent. But nothing helped. There were no clues, no signs, Saldor had simply vanished.

The only consolation they had was that he had obviously meant to leave. Primola and Rondina had searched his room and discovered some of his clothes were missing together with a blanket and a pair of boots.

'Well it looks as if he planned it,' Jossamel said, scratching his head, 'but I can't fathom out why.'

'Maybe I can,' Halmar joined them. 'I think Tarryn and Tildor are involved.'

'Oh no, not them again,' Jossamel said, shaking his head. 'What've they done this time?'

Halmar explained how he had stopped the twins intimidating Saldor. 'It was that same night he left. I should've thought of it before, but got so caught up in everything, it slipped my mind. Sorry.'

'He's gone into hiding,' Primola cried. 'Poor little thing.' Piggybait put his arms around her trembling shoulders.

'We'll find him. Don't worry. Why don't you check the larder and see if anything's gone,' he said urging her back to the kitchen. With the amount of food and drink consumed over the last few days it would be hard to judge if anything had gone but he wanted to give her something to do. He waited while she made her inspection of the cold store and larders.

Soon she returned to where he was waiting at the doorway, her reddened eyes lit up in a beaming smile. 'Piggy you're a genius,' she planted a sloppy kiss on his cheek. 'There's a piece of cheese I kept aside specially for him. That's gone and some bread and apples…a seed cake and even a jug of dandelion beer. They were all kept aside from the provisions used for the guests and banquet,' she laughed. 'Isn't it good? They've gone.'

'Did you hear that?' Piggybait shouted to the others. 'Saldor's got food. He won't starve.'

'As long as we find him soon,' Clap-trap whispered to Halmar.

Chapter Eighteen

Armistice fed Merlin and left a dish of food out for Bandit who had still not returned. She was beginning to worry. She had never known him stay away so long and in her concern over Bandit it took her a while to realise that Merlin too was off his food.

'Well what's the matter with you? Don't you play me up as well,' she said with false cheeriness. Merlin slowly sidled over to her, his tail between his legs. 'Oh, my little lad, what's wrong?'

At that point, Elêna returned to the kitchen from upstairs. Merlin bristled.

'He doesn't like me. That's what's wrong with him.'

Mrs Jenks watched the unhappy dog as he skulked towards the backdoor, scratching fretfully, asking to be let out. She sighed and shook her head. 'It certainly seems like that but I can't understand why. He's normally so friendly.'

'I'm a stranger, that's all.' Elêna tried to make it sound as if she cared.

'Yes, perhaps it'll just take him a little while longer to get to know you. Perhaps it'll be better tomorrow.'

'I think I'll turn in now, if you don't mind. It's been a long day with all the travelling and I'm exhausted.'

Lying on her comfortable bed watching the sun go down on what had been a very strange day, Elêna turned the amulet over in her hand. The face of the goggle-eyed god worshipped long before the Aztecs adopted him stared back at her. His jaguar teeth and snake like fangs apparently had made the Aztecs liken him to the jaguar, the most powerful feline they knew.

She thought back to some of Father Gabriel's stories of the ancient ones, they always enthralled her. It took her away from her poverty and drudgery. Helping her mother to look after the house and family with nothing more to look forward to than more of the same was not enough.

She wanted so much more. She wanted money, travel, a new life. Tlaloc understood her; he would reward her devotion to him. He would help her get her new life.

The light in her room began to fade as night finally fell. Was dusk always so late here? She closed her curtains, turned on the bedside lamp and lay back in the bed still fully clothed. The stairs creaked and she heard footsteps on the landing.

'Goodnight, Tanith,' Armistice called.

Pretending to be asleep she did not answer. She refused to be distracted from her memories. Owls hooted in the trees outside and a dog barked somewhere in the night. In Alvarez city there had been shouting, car noises, drunks singing, fighting or the cries of patients in the hospital wing of the convent. It was so quiet here.

Contented and relieved at having made her escape from Alvarez with the money and passports, she thought of Ortega and wondered if his body had been discovered yet but it was not her concern anymore. She was safe in her new guise and could not be traced now she was Tanith Randolph-Sanchez. Security was good, life was good and the future would be better.

She closed her eyes and soon she was climbing the stone stairs to the temple. It was late and almost dark. The sun was still in the sky but the moon also showed. Father Gabriel's face swam into her mind and floated up to the temple ruins with her. His voice intoned another story of the ancient ones but she could not understand its meaning. She was holding something and looked down at her hands. She held a basket full of mangoes and papaya, more than she had ever found in one trip before but she did not need them in the temple and left the basket on a step.

She no longer climbed but somehow hovered above the steps until she reached the top level where the temple, darkened and lonely, awaited her. Father Gabriel had gone. Whispering voices called. They called to her to enter. She was not afraid; Tlaloc would not harm a believer. The Ancient Ones would not desert her. She had listened so intently to the old priest's stories that soon she felt she knew them personally, especially Tlaloc, the Rain God. He could create life with gentle rain, destroy it with floods or, if he withheld his favour, death would follow from famine; life or death was within his control.

She had explored the temple a hundred times before but somehow she felt this day was different. Something waited for her inside the empty chambers. Her eyes became accustomed to the dim light and the gods watched her as she entered their world; she knew they were waiting for her and became a little afraid but it was worth the fear. Voices whispered and

the breeze whistled through cracks in the walls, the sound was eerie, the atmosphere intense.

She was drawn to a dark corner of the temple where a low narrow alcove, she had never noticed before caught her eye. Nearby a large square stone lay upended on the floor, its shape and size a perfect fit to cover the now exposed recess; some force had moved it. On her knees she examined the niche, running her hands gently over the gaps between the stones.

Taking her fruit cutting knife she scratched away the soft dry dirt and managed to prise up one of the stones. Through the dust a glint of something glittered in the gloom. She reached down and lifted out a fine gold chain attached to an amulet. She recognised the image immediately. Tlaloc! Why did he want her to find this? And why at this time?

Her hand throbbed with a life force emanating through the amulet and into her fingers. A light glimmered from the eyes; it grew stronger, brighter, hurting her eyes. She wanted to look away but it would not let her. A terrible pain filled her head, the temple walls began to spin and everything went dark.

When she woke, her eyes no longer hurt, neither did her head. She stood up. She felt fine, in fact she felt better, stronger than she had in a long time. The amulet was still in her hand, the eyes no longer shone. Slipping it into her pocket she almost flew down the long stone staircase, and remembered to collect the basket of fruit before running all the way home, expecting a scolding from her mother for being late. It would not be the first time and normally she could not have cared less what her mother thought but tonight she wanted to be left with her thoughts.

To her delight on returning home, her mother so delighted at how full her basket was, forgot to chastise her over the time she had been away. Later, when the meal of maize, beans and tortillas followed by papaya, was over, Elêna found it difficult to relax. With her father at the cantina playing dice, her mother busy making shawls to sell to tourists and the younger children asleep, she left the house to walk and think. As she turned a corner by the church, her brother Pedro caught up with her.

'Where were you today? You were gone so long, mama was worried.' It was an enquiry not an accusation, but it angered her. She grabbed him by the shoulder and pushed him against the wall. Pedro was smaller than her by at least two inches and skinny; she was much stronger. He cowered against the wall and turned to look at her, a look of terror in his eyes.

'Your eyes! Your eyes! Madre Mia!' He tore away from her and ran, crossing himself.

Her eyes! What was the matter with her eyes? She felt no different. What had he seen? Running back into the church, she made straight for the room where Father Gabriel kept his ceremonial robes. She stood in front of the mirror, her eyes closed frightened to open them. One, two, three. She opened her eyes.

Her face was her own but instead of her rounded pupils they were now long and vertical. Catlike. No! She was imagining it. She closed her eyes again and shook her head. But Pedro had seen it too. She gripped the amulet and begged Tlaloc for help. One, two, three. She opened them again. Her eyes had returned to their usual shape.

Gradually her breathing returned to normal and her legs regained their strength. Thankfully Father Gabriel had not seen her enter the church and she met no-one on her way home. She was not in the mood for conversation. Her mother had gone to bed, her father was still out and Pedro was nowhere to be seen. It was easy to slip into the bed she shared with Marisol but she could not sleep. Unable to move for fear of waking her sister, she lay still contemplating what to do, the amulet under her pillow. She could not, would not stay in this village, but how to go was the difficulty. It would need careful planning. Once she left there would be no coming back.

When she woke it was very late and she was enveloped in overwhelming darkness. The night-time silence surrounded her and she felt a fleeting moment of panic, wondering where she was. Then she remembered. She was safe. She was where she wanted to be. Her new life had begun and would only get better. The old lady was easily fooled and clearly believed she was Tanith. Keeping up the pretence would not be for long. Soon she would take everything she wanted from this house, from this old woman and would be on her way without ever thinking about her or this miserable village again.

Chapter Nineteen

Slipping quietly away early the next morning, Tarryn and Tildor left their families sleeping in their rooms on the upper floor. Tarryn lifted a lantern from the hooks and they made their way along a deep, root veined tunnel. After the failure of Avaroc's declaration and his resulting humiliation, Tarryn had suggested he and Tildor find somewhere private to discuss their future plans.

'I'm not sure being in league with Avaroc is good for our health, brother. Maybe you're right about him.' Tarryn smiled affectionately at his twin. 'You were always the more civilized one, trying to stop my more extreme deeds, shall we say. I know just the place where we can talk freely away from other ears.'

'Yes, yes, I'd like that.' Tildor looked very relieved. 'But where are we going?'

'You'll know it as soon as we get there. Come on,' Tarryn urged. Encountering nothing other than a couple of nervous rabbits and a muddy nosed mole, they trailed along the tunnels in silence until they found a place where it widened into a small circular chamber.

'Here we are,' Tarryn said cheerfully, holding the lantern high. Tildor was relieved at the change in his brother's mood. Tarryn was usually angry and taciturn. The cavity, half way up the rocky face, was wide enough for two elves to crawl along side by side, a dim light showed at the far end. Tarryn handed Tildor the lantern and hauled himself up into the opening. Tildor blew out the lantern plunging them into near darkness, handed it back to his twin and climbed up beside him. His eyes quickly adjusted to the gloom. Tildor saw Tarryn's gleaming white teeth as his lips parted in a wide grin.

'Remember this place and the times we hid from mother here?' he chuckled. 'Come on, let's see if it's still the same.'

At the far end of what was little more than a wide burrow, they dropped onto a wide ledge and looked downwards to a fast flowing river that vanished under the rock wall. Narrow chimneys created by rock movement over thousands of years allowed sunlight to filter through and illuminate the creamy pillars of stalactites and stalagmites formed over thousands of years of constantly dripping limestone laden water. It was one of Nature's most beautiful creations but few people knew of its existence.

'It's just the same,' Tildor said, clambering over the edge, he dropped to the floor.

'Not quite,' Tarryn landed beside him and nodded to a pile of newspapers, carrier bags and what looked like an old sleeping bag crumpled up in the corner of the ledge. 'Humans have been here,' he added.

'One anyway,' Tildor agreed. He sat down, legs hanging over the ledge. 'Human occupation or not, Tarryn, this is still a beautiful place.'

Tarryn sat beside him. 'It's certainly a good place for a talk. No curious ears to hear and…no prying eyes to see.' Tildor missed noticing the slight break in Tarryn's voice. 'As I was saying, you were always my conscience, Tildor. Always tried to stop what you considered to be my excesses.' Tarryn turned his cold cobalt blue eyes away from his larger but kinder twin. 'You know I didn't think those seeds would affect Saldor like that,' he sounded genuinely remorseful.

'Neither did I,' Tildor agreed. 'If I had I'd have tried harder to stop you.'

'I know. You'd like me to confess to Jerrill or Ellien wouldn't you? She is our Queen after all.'

Not the quickest to pick up on alternative meanings, Tildor missed the tone in his brother's voice.

'I think if you did, if *we* went together to confess, we'd both feel better. Saldor's so terrified of us he's gone into hiding. Perhaps if he realised we weren't a threat anymore, he'd come back.'

'You always did what I wanted no matter how you really felt, didn't you?'

Tildor looked down at the river. 'You were always stronger than me. I had to go along with you.'

'But not now?' Tarryn asked. 'That conscience of yours has finally had enough, eh?'

Tildor nodded.

'You know Avaroc's leaving?'

Tildor looked down at his feet. Tarryn continued.

'I get the feeling you want to stay here at Winterne?'

106

'Yes, I do,' Tildor looked up into his brother's face and answered in a small voice. 'Yarenni and I both want to stay. Winterne was my home and I'd like my elflings to grow up here. It was yours too,' he said with an optimistic look at Tarryn.

'That won't happen. You know I'm leaving with Avaroc?'

Tildor gave Tarryn a sad smile and nodded. 'Yes. I knew you would but I hoped you wouldn't. Can't I persuade you to stay?' he pleaded, anguished by the idea of separation from his twin. Although they were poles apart in character, Tildor loved his brother. 'Why not do as I'm going to, confess to Jerrill...do penance if necessary but then we can put it all behi...'

'You were right Tarryn,' a dark voice said from behind them. 'He is a coward.'

'Avaroc!' Tildor began. He scrambled to his feet. Tarryn walked over to Avaroc without looking back at his brother.

'That's Lord Avaroc to you, Weakling!'

Tildor's terrified eyes flew from his brother to this menacing elf who called himself Lord.

'Tarryn? What's happening? I thought...'

'You thought, Tildor. That's part of the trouble, you think too much. You listen to that little voice in your head. It nags at you when you've done something wrong.'

'But...'

'Do you know how boring that's become?' Tarryn yawned exaggeratedly. Avaroc's lips curled in what could hardly be called a smile.

'Tildor, let me explain. Tarryn's tired of your whining and I don't need you. You're a liability, surplus to our requirements, redundant.' He moved closer, his eyes narrow with cruelty.

Tildor saw his fate in Avaroc's merciless expression. He looked to his left. If he could he just make it down the slope to the cavern floor. That was his only chance of escape. Tarryn read his thoughts and barred the way.

'Tarryn! Don't do this,' he pleaded. 'Let me go. I'll take Yarenni and our family and we'll go away. Epping...or...Dean. You won't see me again.'

Tarryn stepped towards him and drew a small knife from his jerkin pocket.

'No! Tarryn, please, I won't go to Jerrill. I won't say anything! No!'

'Oh yes,' Avaroc answered. They closed in.

'Tarryn doesn't want to hurt you, Tildor. It's just that you're a weak link. You can't be trusted.' He grabbed Tildor by the chin. 'I have plans. I don't care what her new *Highness* says. I don't care that she has blue blood, royal blood and I don't. I don't care if her blood is sky blue pink. It means nothing!' His breath reeked of mead. 'My time will come and your brother will be with me. We'll raise an army, destroy this *pretty* little haven. Tarryn will be my second-in-command.' He grabbed Tildor brutally by the neck, his fingers pressing tighter and tighter on his throat until his eyes bulged.

'You could have worked with us, had a position of authority,' he spat, his eyes flashing venomously, 'but you're spineless…pitiful. Not like your brother. I can't think how you came from the same mother!' He threw Tildor to the ground and stood over him as Tildor gasped for breath, rubbing his throbbing neck.

'I'm not…weak,' he groaned. 'I'm just not…like Tarryn. I don't like hurting people.'

'Then you're no good to me!' Avaroc sneered, looking pitilessly down at the gasping, terrified elf. Avaroc turned away to look over the ledge. 'It is beautiful here. You're right. It's a fitting place to meet your end. Tarryn! Finish it!' he commanded.

Realisation of just how perilous his position was, finally dawned on Tildor. He scrambled backwards in terror until the rock wall blocked his way then struggled to his feet, desperately seeking a way out of his nightmare. Tarryn moved closer, his hand tightly gripping the knife.

'But what will you tell Yarenni?' he screamed. 'She'll want to know what's happened to me.'

Tarryn looked questioningly at Avaroc who drummed his fingers on the wall.

'In the name of Alfheim, get on with it,' he said sounding bored. 'There's no more time for thought.'

'She'll be fine, Tildor,' Tarryn hissed. 'Don't worry about Yarenni or the children. They'll eventually get over the terrible accident that befell you. You never know she might even marry again. What do you think, *Lord* Avaroc?'

'No! Tarryn! You can't do this!' Tildor's scream echoed around the cavern. Tarryn ignored the plea.

'Tarryn! No, please…please…Ughhhh!'

As the knife sliced into Tildor's chest, the last thing he heard was Avaroc's terrible prediction.

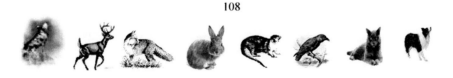

'Yes, she might very well marry again, Tarryn. I must make sure to help you look after your brother's pretty widow. But let's deal with this,' he kicked Tildor's lifeless body. 'Throw earth over the blood, scrape it up and toss it into the river. There must be no sign of blood. It has to look as if he fell.'

Together they heaved Tildor's body over the edge and watched it bounce down the rock face into the river where they saw rather than heard the splash. Tarryn had not expected the conflicting emotions churning through him as his twin's body was taken below the surface of the fast, freezing water and under the rock wall.

'I'm going.' Avaroc checked his shirt cuffs for bloodstains. There were none. 'Those fools all think I've gone already so I'll leave you to clear up here. Follow as soon as you can.'

Tarryn nodded. 'I'll have Yarenni, Feystra and the elflings ready to leave in the next day or so when it appears more in keeping with our terrible tragedy. After Tildor's *accident* we have a good excuse not to stay for the wedding.'

They gripped hands. 'Well done, Tarryn,' Avaroc's almost black eyes did not reflect the smile that twisted his thin lips. 'After this I cannot doubt your loyalty. My time will come and you will stand alongside me. It may take a while but my plans are already in preparation. Ellien's succession is merely a stumbling block, not an end. We will return with an army and I *will* prevail.'

It was around thirty minutes later that Tarryn, sobbing hysterically, ran into the cavern and fell to his knees in front of Yarenni to break the news to the elves of his brother's terrible accident.

'We were climbing, just climbing...he slipped. I don't know how it happened...I tried to grab him but he was too heavy. The river...the river just took him away. It was all so quick. There was nothing I could do, Yarenni. I'm so sorry,' he sobbed.

Piggybait almost applauded. Tarryn's acting was so convincing. But there was nothing he could do. With no evidence to the contrary, there was nothing he could do for now but the truth always did surface at some time and he would do all he could to help it.

109

Chapter Twenty

Although still concerned about Saldor's disappearance, the wedding preparations were so advanced they could not be cancelled. Yarenni had insisted that the tragedy should not stop the celebrations. And so, with just two days before the wedding, a group of elves supervised by Piggybait were busy working on the cavern decorations.

Still wondering what had become of Saldor, but intent on trimming the festive cavern as ostentatiously as possible, Piggybait lay on his stomach halfway up the staircase, leaning precariously over the edge, with Kaylin and Aygelin, Jossamel's elfling sons holding on to his feet to stop him sliding over and crashing to the floor on his head. Having stretched down to attach silver and crystal chains to the lantern hooks on the wall he struggled not to over-reach himself.

But Saldor was paramount in his thoughts. He had decided that if Saldor had not shown up by supper-time, he was going out to look for him again.

Clap-trap, on the other hand, leaned nonchalantly against the wall observing Piggybait's efforts with a great deal of amusement. He briefly considered offering his help but was having far too much fun watching and wondering how long it would be before his friend plunged headlong onto the rush-covered floor.

He too, found his thoughts turning to Saldor, but after all they had done to find him, wondered if maybe Saldor did not want to be found. He would talk to Piggybait and Jerrill later if their missing friend did not show up, but now he was going to have some fun.

Jerrill was at one end of the cavern examining the wedding arch, but as he was not known for his sense of humour, Clap-trap decided to find someone else to share a joke at Piggybait's expense.

In a recess close to the kitchen, Rondo was practising dart throwing (using the ears of dried grasses of course). Perfect, thought Clap-trap.

'Hey Rondo. What odds will you give me that Piggybait manages to stay up there and not fall on his head within the next five minutes?'

Rondo put down his darts and walked over to Clap-trap with a broad grin on his young, handsome face. 'I think probably evens, 50-50,' he laughed. 'But at least it won't hurt if he lands on his head.'

'Don't you dare make bets on me!' Piggybait yelled, swinging himself around to look at his friends. Being very young and small, Kaylin and Aygelin struggled to hold on to his wriggling legs until Kaylin had the bright idea of sitting on him, much to Piggybait's fury.

'Get off, get off!' Piggybait squealed while Lommie wandered over to Clap-trap and Rondo to join in the teasing. Clap-trap leaned on the younger elf's shoulder.

'I'd stay there if I were you Kaylin, my boy. Piggybait's life is hanging by a thread and only you can save him.'

Jerrill, at the far end of the cavern, ignored the boisterous antics of his Council of Elders colleagues. He was used to their shenanigans. He had been admiring Halmar's skilful crafting of their wedding arch and slowly ran his hand over the intricately carved images of flowers and animals, and realised just how much he had underestimated his son. He was also acutely aware that Halmar had always known it.

Hallane, the mother of his twins, Halmar and Halmia, had died soon after they were born and, for some inexplicable reason, Jerrill had blamed Halmar, the last to be born, for their mother's death. He had always been fond of Halmia but had never allowed Halmar to get too close. Nor had he ever admitted to himself that it was his own failing which caused the divide between them. But as he observed the skill and artistry that had gone into building the arch he resolved to change that. As soon as an opportunity presented itself, he would talk to Halmar and make amends for his failure as a father. Engrossed as he was in his own thoughts, he did not notice a soft movement close behind him until a low growl spun him around. Wolf!

'No...no...we're not having you here!' Jerrill barked. 'Piggybait,' he shouted, 'come and deal with this animal of yours!'

Then everything happened at once. Primola, carrying a huge bundle of clean tablecloths she could barely see over the top of, tripped over two excited elflings who ran to see the wolf, fell over the legs of a chair and landed in a heap on top of the linen.

Kaylin and Aygelin, never having seen the wolf before either, jumped up, forgetting their respective holds on Piggybait who overbalanced, slid over the side of the staircase just as Clap-trap and Rondo, having realised what was about to happen, threw themselves forward, breaking Piggybait's

fall and leaving the three elves in pile on the rush strewn floor, with Piggybait still hanging on to a string of now broken crystal lanterns.

Jerrill, almost cracked a smile, but his sense of humour was buried far too deep for it to develop into a laugh.

Wolf padded over to them. 'When you can tear yourself away from your friends, Piggy,' Wolf said dryly, 'there's something you need to sort out.'

Piggybait brushed some stray rushes off his jerkin, straightened his hat and stood up. Clap-trap first rubbed his bruised knee, then his shoulder and Rondo, hobbling, hurried off to help his mother up from the floor muttering something about letting Piggybait fall next time.

'What are you doing here?' Piggybait went over to the waiting predator with his grinning open jaws. 'You don't normally like it here.'

Wolf sniffed the air. 'I smell sausages.'

'No you don't. You know we don't eat meat.'

'Can't blame me for trying,' Wolf hissed, looking round at a particularly small elfling tot who had snuck up behind him and was fearlessly playing with his tail.

'Come on, you're making me nervous. Let's go for a walk and you can tell me all about it.'

Jerrill watched with obvious relief as Wolf and Piggybait made their way to the cavern exit but was horrified to see Ellien and Halmar meet them on their way out. The four stopped to talk for a moment and Wolf allowed himself to be petted by Ellien who stroked his ears affectionately.

Jerrill was taken aback to see the normally aloof wolf actually wagging his tail. They ended their conversation, said their goodbyes and Ellien and Halmar headed towards Jerrill, who saw real adoration in the wolf's eyes as he turned back to watch their Queen.

Inside the tunnel, Piggybait took down one of the lanterns, blew in it until the flame grew, and as they headed back to the cave Wolf shared with the reindeer he began explaining the problem.

'Donner's very upset. Since Nimbus arrived to take over from her she feels left out and jealous. She's bitten Nimbus, told the others to ignore her, even got Rudolph to kick her this morning.'

'But can't you sort it out?'

'Piggy…these…um…problems with the ladies are all yours. My job is to protect them, not make them behave.'

'I feel sorry for Donner. It's not her fault she's got arthritis. I know Armie's herbal cures help but being so close to the river and living in hiding underground seem to make her worse.'

'Perhaps she should retire,' the wolf suggested.

'Perhaps she should but I'm not going to be the one to tell her, she won't hear of it. The Chief tried suggesting it too but she gave him, yes even *him,* a mouthful.'

'You'll have to think of…'

'Wolf! Get back here and leave that poor rabbit alone!'

Reluctantly Wolf, unable to resist his natural instincts, forced himself to give up chasing the terrified rabbit that had inadvertently blundered into the same tunnel.

'No more of that, you hear me!' Piggybait scolded. 'They have a right to live as well and you get fed well enough.'

'I needed the exercise,' Wolf sulked.

'Now then, back to Donner,' Piggybait said, changing the subject. 'Have you got any ideas?'

Wolf shook his thick neck hair. 'Me, no. That's your province.'

A few minutes later, they had arrived at the Transit cave and Wolf's curiosity got the better of him. 'What's that down there,' he asked pointing a huge hairy paw at the two long conveyor belts.

Piggybait urged him on but explained the processes of the transit cave as they walked, although distracted by the reindeer problem, he lacked his usual concentration and Wolf had to prompt him back to the point every now and then.

'I've got it!' Piggybait yelled.

'What? What are you going to do?'

'Nothing. I'm just going to tell Donner that from now on she is to train the others, that she's the boss. Make her feel special. Think that'll work?'

'It might but what about Nimbus? How's she going to feel?'

'She'll be fine when I tell her it'll mean she won't get bitten or kicked any more…and, because Donner will have been given a supervisory role, that puts the others on the same level as Nimbus so perhaps they'll include her more.'

'It might work. Will the Chief go for it?'

'Why wouldn't he? Especially if it means a quiet life.'

Chapter Twenty One

Even though the sun was setting, the air was still very warm when Stuart Seymour left the cinema and shuffled miserably along the crowded alleyway, busy with patrons returning to their cars or parking them before going in.

Children, up later than he thought was good for them, demanded popcorn or ice-creams while parents either ignored their pleas or shouted at them to wait until they got inside. Everywhere, cinema, alley and car park bustled with couples and families. Only he was alone and his loneliness weighed heavily.

The film was good, but then he had expected it to be. Robert Downey Jr had long been one of his favourite actors and Stuart usually enjoyed his films, but even that failed to lift his mood. The couple sitting next to him had annoyed him with their canoodling and giggling. He moved away to sit in an almost empty row. Even in the car park, couples held hands or walked with arms around each other, fuelling his isolation.

Slouching, hands in his pocket, he headed for the street lamp under which he had parked his car. He always made a point of looking for a space near a lamp; thieves were more likely to attempt stealing a car in a badly lit area. He fished in his pocket for his keys, opened the door and waited a few moments for the air inside to cool before he climbed into the driver's seat, leaving the door open.

He put the key in the ignition but left it dangling, the house keys tapped against each other, as they swung back and forth. Reaching across to the glove compartment he rifled through the CDs, found an Aerosmith album and, slid it into the player but did not turn it on. The keys had stopped swaying, rattling.

Cars moved slowly in and out of the car park and, although he watched, lost in his thoughts, he did not really see them. He rested both arms against the steering wheel and leaned his forehead against his hands. Why had he

come back to Somerset? Because there was nowhere else to go, he answered his own question.

Pretty hazel-eyed Donna floated into his reverie. They had been together for almost a year before he had been posted to Basra but she soon found someone else after he left. He remembered his friends, Tom, Duke and Staffo, getting him drunk to try and cheer him up when he got Donna's letter but it didn't work, it just made him feel worse and hungover.

Basra, under gunfire and with a hangover, not the best place to be when you felt that bad, but over there friends looked out for each other, watched each other's backs, depended for their lives on each other…and he let them down. His eyes filled with hot tears and he thumped the steering wheel over and over again until the palms of his hands were red and bruised. He had let them down. He ran. He saw again as he had so many times before, the mangled jeep, Staffo's dead eyes staring up at him and the smoke, he could still smell the acrid smoke billowing up from the burning vehicle.

Tom was shouting, Duke throwing up. The street had been empty but from nowhere people ran at them, dozens of people, they were shouting, screaming in a language he did not understand. There were angry threats, fist shaking. One man picked up a brick and threw it at him; he missed. His mates were backing away. He was isolated. The mob was between him and the rest of his squad. He heard the sound of an approaching helicopter engine and hoped he would be rescued but the mob was closer. He was alone. Dust blew into his eyes, into his mouth. Then s*he* came up behind him. She tugged at his sleeve. It wasn't his fault. He wasn't to know she was trying to help. She shouted at him but he didn't understand. He pushed her away but he had been too rough. She bounced back against a wall and fell to her knees in the sandy earth. Furious but strangely disembodied he raised his gun, looked through the sights and almost fired. Then he saw she was pregnant. How brutal had he become?

Someone shouted. It was the captain. The mob had backed off as the helicopter hovered overhead, guns ready. There was free space between him and the squad. Then he was running to the nearest truck and throwing himself onto the duckboard. He looked back. She was still there clutching her stomach and groaning. An old woman, dressed all in black, as so many elderly women did in the Middle East, was trying to help her to her feet. She raised a fist and gesticulated angrily at him, cursing loudly as his truck drove away. His last memory of the scene was the Medics, protected by a second squad, lifting Staffo's body into the ambulance.

A week later he had arrived at Winterne Manor with only vague memories of how he got there. His mother had asked no questions, had not

115

pressed him, but left him alone until he eventually confessed he was absent without leave, on the run from the Army and could not face the thought of going back.

The story Marjorie put out was that between them they had bought him out of his contract and Harriet, unaware she was harbouring an absconder, allowed him to stay at Winterne Manor and employed him as a chauffeur and handyman. He had hidden when the Military Police came to look for him. As luck would have it Harriet had been away at the time, visiting relatives in Bristol. His mother had deserved an Oscar for her performance in convincing the 'Redcaps' that she had neither heard nor seen him and how much they had worried her by letting her know he was missing. He hated putting her in that position, but he could not face going back. She either protected him there or he would have to leave. She chose to protect him.

He straightened up, pushed the CD player button, turned on the engine and with the music blasting, slowly drove out of the car park and out onto the main road. The music and the rush of warm air blew away his grim memories. The Jaguar purred along the quiet, twilit backroads on which he knew there would be little traffic, especially at this time of the evening.

He thought of the Manor. It was where he lived, but it was not his home. One day, he would have his own home but for now, Winterne Manor was a good sanctuary. He could relax there most of the time. There had been that scare when the Police Chief thought he'd recognised him. Nothing had come of it that time, but how much longer could he keep getting away with it?

He turned off the Wells Road and into Winterne just at the time when evening visibility was at its worst, the street lights had not yet come on but dusk had fallen. Turning at a blind corner, he slammed on the brakes almost too late. Someone, in the beam of his headlights, it looked like a woman, was prancing about in the middle of the unlit road just yard in front of the car. It was that weird woman, Mrs Jenks!

'What the Hell?' Stuart wound down the window. 'Hey! Do you want to get yourself killed?'

But Mrs Jenks did not see him. She did not even hear him. She ran from one side of the road to the other, crying like a baby, her arms flapping about her head as if she was swatting a swarm of bees, but in the beam of the headlights Stuart could see there was nothing there. He turned off the ignition, got out of the car and slowly moved closer to the distressed woman, not knowing how she would react.

'Help me! Get them off me!' she screamed before slumping into his arms.

'Great!' he said looking around to see if there was anyone about who could help, but the road was deserted. Mrs Jenks weighed heavily against his shoulder.

'Never anyone about when you need them!'

Half carrying, half dragging the tall woman to the car, Stuart almost overbalanced as he settled her into the passenger seat and wrestled with the seat belt, leaning over her insensible body to secure it into place. She opened her eyes and stared, not at him but through him at some point beyond.

'Mrs Jenks. Mrs Jenks? It's Stuart, Stuart Seymour. I'm taking you home,' he told her slowly and calmly but her eyes remained fixed on whatever it was she was seeing and she remained silent.

A few minutes later they pulled up outside her cottage. Leaving the wax-like and lifeless woman in the car he approached the front door. There was music playing. His knock was answered by a dog barking. The music stopped. He realised he was quite excited at the prospect of seeing the girl with the beautiful green eyes again. Get a hold of yourself, man. This is not the right time to chat up a girl. The door opened and there she was, this unusually beautiful girl with the most extraordinary green eyes he had ever seen. His knees trembled. He forced them backwards to control his shaking.

'Yes?'

'My name's Stuart Seymour. I live near here at Winterne Manor.' He pointed to the car. 'I...I have your...aunt, is it? She was walking in the road and acting a little...strange.'

Her eyes flashed and for a brief moment, Stuart thought they looked cat-like, but then it was gone. It must have been his imagination; a trick of the light.

'You've found her! Oh, thank you. I've been so worried. Oh!' she exclaimed as a black and white collie darted out of the door and ran off down the road for all he worth. 'Merlin! Merlin! Come back here!' she shouted, but he had already vanished into the darkness.

'You're not having a good evening are you?' Stuart grinned.

'I'll worry about him later.' He found her soft American accent very attractive. He found everything about her very attractive. She smiled sweetly as she took his arm and hurried him to the car. 'My name's Tanith and I'm so relieved you've found Auntie. I was so worried about her. Thank you for bringing her home. I've been searching the village and the

back roads for hours but I still don't really know my way about. I was at my wits end and about to phone the Police. I've only just got back,' she gushed.

'Does she do this often?' he asked as they reached the car.

'I can't say, not having been here all that long, but she's not been…right, you know,' she pointed to her head, 'for the last few days.'

'Right, well let's get her inside,' Stuart said lifting the semi-conscious Mrs Jenks out of the car. Between them they bundled her to the door.

'It's alright, I can manage from here,' Tanith said at the doorstep.

'No, you can't,' Stuart replied taking Mrs Jenks' weight. 'A little thing like you, you wouldn't be able to cope with her. It's alright, I'll take her in,' he insisted.

Elêna opened her mouth to protest but Stuart, thinking she was just being considerate ignored her, lifted Mrs Jenks into his arms and carried her like a baby along the hallway and into the sitting room.

'Just lay her on the sofa,' Tanith ordered abruptly, 'and then you can leave her to me.'

Her attitude had changed. He got the distinct impression she was trying to get rid of him. Stuart did as he was told and lowered Mrs Jenks onto the sofa. A half full glass of wine was placed beside an open magazine on the small coffee table beside the sofa. The magazine looked as though it had been thrown there hurriedly. He said nothing and without lifting his head made a show of making Mrs Jenks comfortable while he took a look around. His eyes took in the CD player on the hearth. Through the clear Perspex top he could see the CD still spinning. How, if she was so busy out looking for her aunt and so worried, did she have time to read magazines and drink wine? Something was wrong here.

'I think you'd better go now.' Tanith's green eyes were as cold as cut diamonds.

Stuart walked towards the door. 'Yeah, I'll leave her in your care. But I think you'd better get the doctor in,' he replied frostily. 'And I'll call in a couple of days to see how she's doing.'

'Er…no, don't do that,' Elêna answered, hastily ushering him towards the front door. 'If she's well again by then, we don't want to remind her about this evening do we? It might upset her to know that she wandered off. Too unsettling, if you understand me.'

He hesitated at the door. 'Has she seen Doc Brownlow?'

'Who? Oh, yes, the doctor. Yes, yes of course she has,' she answered just a little too quickly, obviously keen for him to go. 'Thank you for

bringing her back. But I must go back to her now. You do understand?'
And she virtually pushed him out of the door.

'If I find the dog I'll bring him back,' Stuart said but the door had
already closed behind him. He started up the car then stopped to look back
at the cottage before driving off. A twitch of the curtains convinced him
she was still watching, waiting for him to drive away. She was a lovely girl
alright but something was wrong inside that cottage, not that it was any of
his business. He didn't know Mrs Jenks other than by sight, had never
spoken to her before and if things had continued as before, he supposed he
never would, but her condition tonight worried him. She was an elderly
lady and more vulnerable than he would have thought.

He wondered if he should talk it over with his mother but decided better
of it. Why bring her into it? Maybe this Tanith was just a bit shy. She
hadn't been in the village very long after all and must be worried that her
aunt, who she'd only just met, was a bit 'doolally'. That could explain her
attitude.

With a last look back at the cottage, he waved towards the window and
drove away having convinced himself that everything was fine and Tanith
would make sure Mrs Jenks was seen by Doc Brownlow again. It was
good that she had someone to care for her. There was nothing to worry
about.

119

Chapter Twenty Two

'*Hi Sam, how's it going?*' Dave answered his mobile. Sam thought he sounded very down.

'Fine, yeah things are good at the moment. How about you?'

'*School's a pain. Gibbo's driving everyone round the bend. He still hasn't retired although we're all hoping this is his last term. Apart from that, you know same old thing.*'

'Has he still got that long hair poking out his nose?' Sam laughed.

'*Yeah mate, two of them now and they're longer and greyer than ever.*'

'You don't sound good, Dave? What's going off?' Sam asked.

'*Forest got beaten again and another Coach has left! Can you believe it?*'

'Is that all?' Sam couldn't believe Dave was so down about it. He liked football himself. He'd supported Chelsea but it did not rule his life. There was so much more. Dave sounded very depressed. 'Yeah but he's got a right to move if he wants.'

'*Whaddya mean, is that all? Isn't it enough? Dunno what the Reds are going to do next season.*'

Sam thought about all the things that had happened to him in the short time he had been in Winterne. It looked as though his experiences had made him see life differently to Dave.

'So what else is going off?' he decided to change the subject.

'*Not much. I'm not going out with Joanne any more. Wouldn't admit it to anyone else but she dumped me. Still don't know why.*'

Sam thought he could guess. 'So what are we doing about me coming up? It'll be good to see everyone again.'

'*Ooh, yeah...don't know if we can do it this summer, mate. Mum's not too well and with Bethany only being three months old, she needs me to help out with Megan.*'

Sam was taken aback. They had planned this visit ever since he had left Nottingham. Now Dave seemed to be putting him off. 'But what about your dad? Isn't he there?' he asked. 'And what about you coming down here like we'd planned?'

'Yeah, well that's part of the problem. Dad's got a job lorry driving. Sometimes he goes to Europe and is away for days at a time. When he gets home he's a bit mardy for a few days...needs a bit of space. Might not be a good idea for you to come up while things are like this.'

Sam felt uncomfortable at the way the conversation was going, things were definitely not as easy as they usually were between them. They had been friends since primary school and grown up together but Dave seemed different, a bit distant and difficult to talk to but, strangely Sam found he was not as disappointed as he thought he would be at not meeting up after all. This was not the Dave he knew so well.

'Yeah', Dave went on, *'and he never knows until the day before where he might be going and that don't give mum much warning.'*

'Well forget me coming up then, but surely you can get down here for a week. I've told everyone you're coming. Jenny and Jonah are looking forward to meeting you.'

'Yeah, well, I dunno if I wanna meet this Jonah. Sounds like a bit of a prat to me,' Dave said.

Sam thought about it for a moment. 'Yeah, he was but he's OK now. We've been through some stuff and we're pretty cool now and I thought you wanted to meet Jen anyway.'

'I do. That was a cool photo you sent. I've kept it on my phone and showed Daz. He thinks she looks hot.'

Sam was uncertain how he wanted to react to that one. 'So maybe I can come up later, half term or something?'

'Yeah, maybe. We'll talk about it later but I don't think it'll be happening during this summer. Think we're gunna have to leave it for now. And anyway, I'll be going camping with Darren and his folks later when dad gets some time off, so I'll get away then.'

So that was it. Dave had put the barrier up. Sam struggled for something to say wanting to change the subject. 'How'd the exams go?'

'Lousy. Awful. Not expecting much for my grades next year. What about you?'

'Yeah. Fine, I think.' Sam wanted to get off the telephone. It was becoming more and more difficult to think of something to say. 'Yeah, OK, Mum, I'm just coming,' he shouted turning away from the mouthpiece.

'Is that your mum? Say hiya for me and mum says hello too.'

'I'll tell her. Yeah, dinner's ready so I've got to go. We'll talk soon, yeah?'

'Yeah, catchya later.'

Sam sat on the stairs, a little confused but relieved to have ended the conversation with his one-time best friend. He did though feel a bit guilty as Dave not visiting after all made things far easier for him. It meant he wouldn't have to find time or excuses for shaking Dave off when he visited the elves. Jenny popped into his thoughts. That was something else. The way Dave had said she was 'hot' had annoyed him. At least now he did not have to worry about Dave actually meeting her and he was thankful for that. Still it felt odd that, for the first time ever there was little common ground between them and after so many years and so much time spent together, their friendship had faltered.

He heard the clatter of dinner plates and returned to the kitchen. His mother was mashing potatoes in the saucepan while his father was setting the table. An older version of Sam, he still bore the scars from the car accident at the end of last year and although his shattered leg had healed well, he still walked with a slight limp. Only Sam and Charlie knew that Steve's remarkably fast recovery from his injuries was due to a little elven healing.

'What's up Sam, you look fed up?'

Sam pulled out a chair and sat at the table. 'No, I'm not fed up. I'm not going to Nottingham and Dave's not coming down this summer after all though.'

'And you're not upset about that?' Jane asked scooping mashed potato onto the plates.

'No. I feel I should be but I'm not. He's my best friend but it doesn't feel like that anymore 'cos it was really hard to talk to him just now. We didn't really have anything to talk about. I think I'm relieved it's not happening but I feel bad about not feeling bad, if you get me.'

Steve put Sam's dinner on the table in front of him, then his own and sat down beside him. 'Things change Sam. So do people. Dave has stayed as he is. Nothing has changed in his life except you moving away and a new baby sister. Although him having a new baby sister is special, when you compare that with everything that's happened to you over these last months, you've grown up more.'

'That's right,' Jane agreed. 'Nearly dying in that tunnel explosion and helping to catch an armed diamond thief...'

'…and standing up to knife wielding bullies,' Steve added, 'don't forget that.'

'It's not Dave that's changed, Sam, it's you. You've experienced more and matured faster than Dave has,' Jane explained.

And there's the rest that they don't know about, thought Sam.

'Everything that happens to us leaves us a little more able to cope with what's to come in life but can separate us from those who haven't gone through the same things. Life experiences change people and you'll probably find that as time goes by you and Dave will just drift further apart,' Steve said. 'The only thing that stays the same is that everything changes.'

Chapter Twenty Three

The Great Chamber rang with joyous laughter, bustle and music. Lanterns and torches blazed brightly and the rich smell of baking filtered through the tunnels. Elfings were light-heartedly told to go and play or make themselves useful instead of getting under the feet of their elders and even Avaroc's declaration and subsequent disappearance had done little to dispel the party atmosphere that spread through the entire clan. There were only two days to go before the marriage of Queen Ellien and her betrothed Halmar.

Matronly Primola, having selected a team to help her (and no-one escaped if she wanted them), slaved over the festive menu while Piggybait organised groups into working on the decorations. From time to time Ellien made an appearance to check on how things were progressing but, in general, was happy to leave the arrangements to her trusted team while she and Halmar examined the ancient scrolls listing her ancestors back to the Kings and Queens of Alfheim. The names unfamiliar but unexpectedly comforting, completing as they did her previously unknown ancestry.

'Why did he never tell me about this before?' she asked Halmar as she ran a long, elegant finger down the family tree. The names and dates of those listed were traced in gold and a few, including Malliena, had pictorial images shown. Malliena's serene beauty looked back at the daughter she had never witnessed growing up. Of course there was no mention of Jimander, Ellien's father. He had not been of royal blood.

'Life was so simple yesterday,' she said wistfully.

Halmar sat on a stool in front of her, his expression, solemn and compassionate. 'He wanted you to live a normal life, to be happy, to marry, have children and be free of the burden and responsibilities that go with kingship. Your mother did too. She had seen too many of our people

become greedy with power.' He stood up and walked behind her, his hand gently resting on her shoulder.

'A thousand years ago, before your father was born, war between two brothers who both claimed the throne ended the lives of hundreds of our kind. You can see one of them, Phaeras, named on the scroll. He was the rightful king but his younger brother, Naeron, planned an ambush in the caves at Cheddar and Phaeras was killed.'

'What happened to Naeron, do you know?'

'Your father told me the story as he knew it. Naeron died on being crowned. The crown has the power to judge the heart of those who wear it. Only those of Alfheim's royal blood can wear it...'

'...just as I did today.'

'Just as you did today, my love.' He kissed the top of her head.

A thought occurred to her. 'Then Avaroc cannot rule our kingdom. He is not of true royal blood.'

'Well, of course that is true...and not true.'

'I'm sorry...but you just said...,' Ellien frowned.

Halmar kneeled in front her and took her hands. 'No...he cannot wear the crown...but...if he raises a large enough army, he could rule through force without ever actually wearing it.'

'And so avoid its retribution.'

'Exactly.'

Ellien lowered the scroll onto the table and paced the sitting-room styled cave. The only sound was the rustling of the floor rushes as she walked over them, enveloping her in the smell of Lavender. Halmar watched in silence as she reflected.

She stopped in front of him. 'Do you honestly believe Avaroc is capable of such horror?'

'Yes,' he answered solemnly putting his arms around her as if trying to shield her from any harm. 'Yes, my dear, I do. It won't be yet, but he will gather an army and there will be bloodshed.'

She nestled against his chest drawing strength from him for a couple of heartbeats then pulled away.

'Well, if it is not imminent, we will put it from our minds,' she smiled and brushed away the tears. 'We have a wedding and a party for our guests to attend to, so for now we will carry on as normal.'

He smiled at her in admiration. She was not going to let this future threat ruin their plans. They would deal with Avaroc when the time came and, she was right, their wedding and the celebrations must come first.

'Of course, Ellien, there's one thing we have that Avaroc doesn't, apart from the love and respect of our clan that is.'

'What's that?'

'The Chief.'

Shoulders back, head held high Ellien walked ahead of Halmar, determined not to let her people see any sign of fear.

Chapter Twenty Four

The day of the Prom finally arrived and, as their homes were on the way, Jonah asked Stuart to stop the Jaguar to pick up Jason and Sue before collecting Jenny. Like everyone else, Stuart thoroughly disliked Jonah previously and stayed out of his way as much as possible. But that was in the past, and these days they got on very well so Jonah noticed when Stuart seemed quite withdrawn as they got into the car. He was definitely not his usual self.

'What's up, Stuart? You're pretty quiet,' Jonah asked.

'No, no, I'm alright,' Stuart replied as he pressed the button on the remote control to open the gates. 'I've just got some stuff to think about, that's all. No big deal.' From then on he made an effort to be more sociable.

Jason was ready when they stopped outside his house and ran out to the car as soon as they pulled up. By that time Stuart's mood had lifted so well that when they called at Sue's house, he opened the car door and saluted her as she joined Jason in the back of the car.

Jonah thought Sue's long deep green gown was a bit too old and fussy for her but was too polite to say so even though it would have looked better on her grandmother. A year ago he would have told her exactly what he thought and probably would have been quite insulting but now he was not so unkind. He understood that to tell her would be hurtful.

Jason scratched his neck and ran his finger under the stiff collar of his shirt. 'Can I undo my tie?' he pleaded with Sue.

'No you can't, not yet. You'll have to wait until the disco starts, then Mrs Wilkinson said it can be jackets off and ties undone.'

'But it's so uncomfortable,' he whinged. 'It don't seem to bother you if you look like a penguin,' he said to Jonah who had been looking pensively out of the window as the car wound it's way up the lane towards Jenny's

cottage. Jonah, wearing a tuxedo, crisp white shirt and a red silk bow tie, was incredibly smart but very at ease in his formal outfit.

'Used to it. Any time dad had business people at the house, he wanted us to make an impression, you know, look smart.' He turned around to face them. 'Couldn't be bothered to talk to us but expected us to perform for his guests all the same.'

He gave a small bitter smile to Sue. 'He liked to put on these…posh dinners and we all had to be there. The number of times I dressed like a penguin to please him…show off the pretty family.'

Sue gave him a sympathetic look. The hurts of the past were still there even though well hidden.

'Still never mind that now,' Jonah said turning back to face the front, 'we're at Jenny's.'

Stuart drove past the house and turned the car around at the end of the lane before stopping outside Jenny's cottage.

'Do you know what her dress is like yet?' Sue asked Jonah as he opened the car door.

'Nope! If she hasn't told you, why would she tell me? I'm only the bloke who's taking her there.' Jonah got out of the car and walked around to the driver's door, Stuart wound down the window and handed him what looked to Sue like a small box.

'What's that?' Sue whispered to Jason as they watched Jonah walk up to the door.

'How should I know?' Jason sounded surprised.

'I thought he might have said something.'

He gave her a 'why should he look'. 'No, never said anything to me about a box.'

'Blokes! I'm not interested in the box. I want to know what's in it.'

'You'll just have to wait, Miss nosey.' Jason teased.

Jonah rang the doorbell and waited. After a few moments, the cottage door opened but they were unable to see who was there. He held out the box and Sue saw a hand which she assumed was Jenny's take it. She craned her neck trying to see what Jenny's dress was like, but having caught Stuart watching her in the rear view mirror with a wry smile on his face, she looked away trying to feign disinterest, but could not resist a quick peek out of the corner of her eye to see what was going on. Jason and Stuart were now grinning at each other via the mirror, amused by her impatience. After what seemed like ages to Sue, Jonah held out his left hand and assisted Jenny down the step as she hitched up the long skirt of her sea-blue dress that complemented her colouring perfectly. Her pale

128

blonde hair was down but at each side, at points below, centre and above the tips of her ears, her hair was twined into fine plaits softly tied at the crown and laced with tiny white jasmine flowers. She wore a little make-up. Mascara to lengthen her already long lashes, a little blusher on her cheeks to brighten her complexion and lip gloss but that was all; nothing overdone or showy. On her left wrist she wore a silver bangle entwined with small tight white rose buds, white carnations and the white jasmine that had been a happy guess on Jonah's part.

Once she had stepped down onto the path, Jonah hurriedly let go of Jenny's hand and opened the back door of the car for her. Jason and Sue moved over to let her in.

'You look lovely,' Sue told her as she settled in and tucked the long folds of her dress inside the car. 'You should wear your hair like that more often.'

'Thanks Sue, so do you, but tell Jason to close his mouth will you. It's embarrassing.'

Jason had been staring at Jenny since she appeared at the door and was still unable to take his eyes off her. He hurriedly snapped his mouth closed. 'Yeah, well…she's never looked like that before.'

'I wish I'd had that reaction when you came to meet me,' Sue said laughingly, free of any jealousy.

'I said you looked nice,' Jason defended himself.

'Nice, he said I look nice,' Sue teased. 'It's alright Jase, I don't mind. You've got plenty of time to think up some better compliments before we get to the Prom.'

The car purred slowly along the bumpy lane until it reached the road then sped off toward Wells City Hall, the venue for the school Prom. Jonah stayed facing forward for the entire trip, hardly speaking, while Jenny examined the bracelet corsage.

'That's really pretty,' Sue whispered. 'Was that what Jonah gave you?'

'Uh-huh,' Jenny whispered back, her blonde head close to Sue's auburn one. 'It's very pretty but I hope he didn't spend much. It's a bit embarrassing really.'

'Why?' Sue questioned. 'According to mum, when a fella escorts a girl to a Prom, he's supposed to give his date a corsage.' She pointed out her own lack of floral adornment. 'Not that Jason knew about that.' She ignored the 'tut' from Jason who squeezed himself even further towards the door.

'I know that, but I'm not really Jonah's date, am I?' Jenny hoped the sound of the car engine would cover their whispering.

129

'Hmmmm, suppose not, but he is *escorting* you there and he's gonna stay with you until Sam's done.' She paused. 'Of course, it may just be that he wanted to make sure you got one. It's probably only that. It's very pretty though and doesn't it smell nice?' With the windows closed so that the girls hair didn't get too blown about, the air conditioning was on to the keep the passengers cool but the air was now fragranced by jasmine.

Stuart sneezed.

'Sorry Stuart, forgot you get hay fever. Got your pills?' Jonah asked.

'No, I haven't, not on me. But we'll be there soon and I can open the window on the way back. No problem.'

Jonah turned to Jenny. 'Stuart has problems with flowers. He was OK while they were in the box but now they're out...'

'I'll put them away in the boot for now if you want, Stuart,' Jenny offered.

'No, miss, it's fine. Only five minutes to go. Thanks all the same.'

Shortly afterwards as they pulled into the car park at the back of City Hall, they could hear music coming from inside.

'That'll be Sam and the others,' Jenny said. 'Do I look alright?' she asked Sue.

'You look fine, don't worry.'

They waved to Stuart as he drove away then walked around to the front steps of the building. With a flamboyant gesture Jonah tucked Jenny's hand under his arm and led her through the double doors into City Hall. Jason crooked his elbow for Sue to put her hand through and they followed their friends into the noisy reception area where they pushed their way through groups of friends milling around waiting for those still to arrive, comparing dresses and shoes or just seeing who they fancied chatting up.

Miss Earnshaw, the school secretary, looked very bizarre in an extremely unpleasant lilac coloured lace two piece outfit with a matching lilac fluffy cardigan as she stood next to Mr Davies, the Head Teacher and his wife, Muriel. She sniffed loudly into a large white handkerchief as the students shuffled past, many of them trying not to giggle.

The band was already playing in the main hall. Jenny stopped to listen before she went in.

'Not bad,' she commented to Jonah. 'At least he's keeping in time. Come on, they're almost at the end of this one.'

Sam had just taken a swig from a bottle of water he had placed within reach, when he looked up and saw Jenny and Jonah watching him close to the front of the stage. She looked beautiful. The stage lights reflecting on her pale blonde hair gave her a luminous quality, almost like a halo and her

simple gold hoop earrings and plain gold necklace glinted in the reflected mirror ball lights. As she smiled up at him he felt proud to be her boyfriend. Her hair and dress suited her, nothing was overdone; she was just perfect.

Jenny waved and he caught sight of a flowery bracelet on her wrist and it was then he noticed most of the girls had flowers of some sort, some pinned to their dresses and a couple of girls had them tied to their waists. There were very few without at least one flower.

He then remembered his mother had mentioned he should get Jenny a corsage, but he'd forgotten all about it. Had she brought her own or did Jonah do something he should have done? He mentally kicked himself for being an idiot.

Richie signalled the next number was about to start and Sam watched Jonah pull Jenny away from the stage towards the middle of the floor. A group of girls turned to watch them, some looking at her enviously. He heard one of them mention Jonah's name. It wasn't Jenny they were looking at, they were all watching Jonah. It was only then that he really looked at Jonah. Looking very cool in his tuxedo, he stood out from the crowd and was attracting very admiring glances from girls around the room, even those with boyfriends or dates for the evening. Jenny saw it too and Sam misread the grin she gave Jonah. He felt an intense pang of jealousy.

'OK Sam, next number,' Richie said. 'Sam, Sam!'

Sam jerked back to reality. 'Yeah, OK. Sorry.' But he had trouble keeping in time with the Green Day cover they were playing, his concentration was off, but thankfully no-one seemed to have noticed and soon after they began playing Jason and Sue joined Jenny and Jonah in the middle of the floor.

Sam could not take his eyes off them as they danced and laughed, laughed and danced with a growing feeling of anger building in his chest. With the band playing loudly, hearing conversation was difficult and Jonah had to lean close to Jenny for her to hear. He must have said something funny because she threw back her head and laughed.

Sam's jealous eyes spotted Ian Brooks and his girlfriend, Pam, watching Jenny and Jonah. Ian threw a quick glance in Sam's direction and said something to Pam. She nodded and they sniggered.

'Sam, slow down.' Preoccupied with what he thought was happening on the dance floor, Sam had been unaware of Richie moving alongside. 'What's going on? You're screwing up.'

131

Jenny must have felt the force of his gaze because she looked up at him and waved. Her smile calmed him. Jed, on bass guitar, glared at him and gesticulated rudely but Mike, the keyboard player continued to play as if there was no problem.

'Sorry, Rich,' Sam said nodding his head to show he understood. He slowed down, remembering where he was. 'Get a grip!' he ordered himself to control his uncharacteristic anger. What was the matter with him? Why was he so jealous? They were both there. He could see them…they were only talking after all. Telling himself he was being stupid, he continued to play the rest of the set as he should but was relieved when their time on stage finished and he could get back to *his* girlfriend.

Jenny, all innocent smile and unsuspecting, walked over to join him as he jumped down from the stage but her happy expression was soon replaced by one of injured astonishment.

'Enjoying yourself, were you?' he blurted out before he could stop himself, cursing himself for the hurt he had so obviously caused judging by the look of surprised pain in her brown eyes. He was determined not to stir anything up and then dived right in like a complete idiot. His guilt made him angry with himself and that just fuelled his temper even more.

'What's the matter with you, Sam?' she said turning her back so that the approaching Jonah could not see the tears brimming in her eyes.

'Nothing,' Sam lied putting on a deceptively cheerful face for Jonah while Jenny remained tight-lipped and silent. Just at that moment the DJ put on 'Teenagers' by 'My Chemical Romance'. Girls dragged reluctant boyfriends onto the dance floor to mingle with those still there after Sam and the others had finished their set.

Sue had just grabbed Jason and was pulling him to a clear space in the crowd when she noticed Jenny's stance and rigid body language. It only took her a moment to realise something was very wrong. Not understanding what was going on, Jason was totally confused when she asked him to get her a drink. He had thought she wanted to dance but, as she seemed very insistent, he did not argue. As he left, she pushed through the other dancers, took Jenny's arm and led her outside to the open air seating leaving Sam open-mouthed and speechless, and Jonah wondering what he had missed.

Sam felt a bit embarrassed and a little ashamed of himself but thankfully no-one else seemed to have noticed anything was wrong. Jason approached, struggling to get through the energetic dancers without slopping too much cola over his hands or losing grip of the white plastic cups.

'Seen Sue?' he shouted over the loud music, keeping his eyes firmly fixed on the drinks and trying to avoid getting bumped by the enthusiastic pair jumping about behind him.

'Yeah, she's gone outside with Jenny,' Sam replied glumly.

'*What?*'

'*I said she's gone outside.*'

'Bloody hell! She asks me to get this for her then runs off! Typical woman! S'cuse me, I said *s'cuse!*' Sam almost managed a smile as Jason backed his way through the dancers holding the cups tightly.

'Jenny alright?' Jonah leaned in so Sam could hear him.

'Why ask me? You've been with her all this time. I've been up there.' He replied unable to stop himself again and nodded towards the stage.

'Ah...I wondered if this would happen,' Jonah frowned

'*What?*' Sam shouted just as the track stopped. Several pairs of eyes turned to look at him. He wished the floor would swallow him up.

'Come on, outside,' Jonah said, pushing Sam ahead of him towards the front doors. 'We need to talk.'

Cars drove slowly along the busy streets, their drivers looking for parking places and crowds of people out for the evening populated the square in front of City Hall. A group of laughing girls dressed in summery going-out tops and skirts or pretty dresses walked by. Two of them called out to Jonah. He waved back.

'That's Sharon and Debbie from the stables.'

Sam made no comment. He sat down on the top step, miserably staring at his feet and ignoring the girls. Without intending to he had somehow managed to ruin what should have been a good evening and it was still early. Jonah sat down beside him. Without speaking to Sam, he watched the groups of people or couples out for the evening as they paraded past the steps, waiting for Sam to say something. But Sam did not speak. He was too busy trying to make sense of how he was feeling and why his temper had got the better of him. He knew Jonah was waiting for him to say something but he could not think of the right way to start the conversation.

'You know I like Richards, don't you?' Jonah decided to break the silence.

'Yes,' Sam growled without turning round.

'But she likes you, Sam. She's your girlfriend...she's not interested in me. To be honest, if she was I'd be chuffed to take her out but...'

'I just bet you would.'

133

Jonah turned to look at his friend. 'You asked me to collect her tonight and look after her until you'd finished. That's what I did. Nothing else...and now you don't like it.' Jonah was beginning to get angry as well.

'No, I don't.' Sam swung around to face a confused Jonah. 'You didn't look like you were just looking after her. I saw you...could you have got any closer to her?'

'Now you're being stupid! Did you realise how loud it was in there. Didn't you see everyone else doing the same thing?'

'Well...'

'Well, yeah, of course they were!' Jonah's jaw was set in a very rigid line. He took a deep breath and turned to face Sam, who was now not quite so confident. 'You know how things used to be. I used to tell everyone she was my girlfriend. She's fun, pretty, clever all that kind of stuff and...yeah, well don't forget I owned everyone didn't I.' He gave a sad little chuckle. 'But you're an idiot to treat her like that or to think she'd *ever* go out with me.' Jonah looked away. 'After the way I behaved I'm lucky she even speaks to me, there's not many people who would. I wouldn't speak to me if I was her.'

Sam looked unsure of himself. 'Yeah, maybe...'

'Maybe nothing!' Jonah stood up. 'You could really screw this up, you plonker! Get back in there and sort things out before she dumps you. No-one would blame her if she did the way you've been tonight. I'm going home.'

'But...'

'No, we'll talk tomorrow. Maybe. You get back in there and sort it out.' Jonah walked down the steps and left in the direction they had seen Sharon and Debbie going, leaving Sam alone and miserable. But Jonah had only gone a short way before he remembered something and turned back.

'Stuart's coming back for you at 10.30. Be ready,' he shouted.

'But where are you going?'

'Dunno. Might go home, might go to the movies. Iron Man's on. Dunno. Probably not really dressed for the movies.'

Sam watched until Jonah vanished among the mass of people milling around the square before heading back through the main doors to look for Jenny. He did not have to go far. She was waiting for him in the now almost deserted lobby leaning against the wall close to the doors into the hall. She was not smiling.

'Where's Jonah?' she asked as Sam sheepishly approached.

'He's gone.' Sam reached out to take her hand.

'Gone where?' She did not pull away.

'We had a bit of an…'

'Argument,' she finished his sentence.

Sam looked down at his feet. 'Yeah. No, not really. We talked,' he said almost inaudibly.

'You know you're wrong don't you. About Jonah and me, I mean.'

Sam looked up. 'Yeah.'

The door beside them flew open as half a dozen boys from the school's senior football team burst into the lobby.

'Hey Sam, how's it goin?' Dean Bradley called as they ran towards the main doors.

'Fine. What are you doing?'

'Not stayin' here, we're goin' bowling. You coming?'

Jenny remained silent waiting for the boys to go.

'No,' he glanced at Jenny. 'Maybe some other time.'

'OK, see yah.' Dean ran off after the others leaving the door swinging backwards and forwards in his wake.

'How were things left with Jonah?'

'I'm not sure. He said a few things that made sense though.'

'Like?'

'Just how stupid I've been and that I should sort things out with you.' He examined her face trying to read her thoughts. The way he felt earlier had made him realise just how much she meant to him and waiting for her to speak was agony.

Jenny moved away from him and walked to the big front window watching the constant stream of people in the square. Sam stood just behind her right shoulder. She did not turn round.

'What made you think I would want to go out with Jonah?' she asked in a small calm voice.

'I don't know.'

'Did I ever give you any reason to think I was interested in him?'

'No.' Sam's throat felt as though it was closing. When he spoke his voice sounded hoarse.

Jenny turned to look him in the eyes. 'Then why did you get like that?'

'I don't know. I'm sorry.'

'He was only doing what you asked him to do.'

'I know.'

They fell silent as Miss Earnshaw appeared from the Ladies toilets at the far end of the lobby, fanning herself with a handkerchief. She looked down her nose at them as she wobbled past in very high heeled shoes which she found difficult to walk in. Sam and Jenny suppressed a laugh as, with her

135

back to them, they could see her lacy skirt was caught up in her tights revealing hairy backs of thighs and big cream coloured knickers.

'She we tell her?' Jenny whispered.

'No.'

'But she's going back into the hall,'

'So?'

'But she'll be mortified.'

'But it'll give everyone a good laugh. It'll serve her right. It might teach her not to be such a cow.'

Miss Earnshaw, completely unaware of what was to come disappeared through the inner swing doors while Jenny and Sam waited. It was not a long wait. It was only a few seconds before the door burst open again and with a red-faced scowl at them both, Miss Earnshaw ran out through the main doors, straightening her skirt at the back.

Amusement having lightened their mood, Sam asked if Jenny wanted to go back into the disco. They could hear the music playing and there was still an hour or so before Stuart would be back to collect them. At the door, Jenny halted.

'You know you'll have to see Jonah and apologise don't you?'

'Yeah, I'll see him soon.'

'Do it tomorrow, Sam. Get it over with.'

'Are you two alright now,' Sue asked as she and Jason joined them. Jason's pale blue shirt had cola stains on the cuffs.

'I think so,' Jenny smiled. Sam thought she looked beautiful. 'Are we alright now, Sam?'

'We're good and I'm sorry if I messed up.'

Jason looked around. 'Where's Jonah?'

'Not sure. He said he might go home or he might go to the cinema.'

'He'll be sorry about that. There's a few of the girls here that fancy him. Katie reckoned he looked cute in his Tux. I think the new Jonah's more popular than he knows,' Sue said.

'I'll tell him tomorrow,' Sam said taking Jenny's hand. 'I'll be seeing him then.'

Chapter Twenty Five

Having spent much of her life preferring to live quietly underground, and never really being interested in life above ground, Ellien now realised that her experience and knowledge of the Upper World needed to be extended.

'Halmar,' she asked as they walked along the transit cave walkway on their way back to the Scroll room, 'is it too late to re-arrange the venue for our wedding vows?'

He stopped. 'Why?' He smiled at her indulgently. 'What do you have in mind?'

'I'd like to get married at night, in the moonlight in the glade. Can we do that?'

He took her hand and she waited patiently, walking beside him quietly while he thought the matter over. 'It would mean a lot of upheaval. Do you want the feast up there as well?'

'Oh, yes, that would be lovely.'

He thought she looked just like an excited elfling on a feast day. 'My father will complain about it, you know that. He'll say it will be too much work, too difficult to organise…the usual thing. He likes to have something to moan about,' Halmar grinned. A wicked thought crossed his mind. 'Yes, we'll do it.'

Her eyes lit up. 'Are you sure?'

'Of course I'm sure. And anyway you're Queen…you can do anything you want.'

Ellien stopped smiling. 'But that's not the point, Halmar. I don't want it just because I can order it.'

'I know that. It's not your way and I was only pulling your leg as the humans say. Come on, we'd better get back. If we're changing the arrangements, there are things to do.'

The elves in the cavern heard their happy laughter ringing through the tunnels before they saw them. Piggybait winked at Clap-trap. 'Let's see what they're up to now,' he said.

The couple halted at the entrance of the cavern and looked around at the lights and garlands that Piggybait and his team had taken great pains to put up.

'Perhaps we shouldn't,' Ellien said feeling a little guilty about how much time and effort had been taken.

'Piggy won't mind. He adores you and he'll want you to have whatever makes you happy,' Halmar reassured her, 'as do I. What happened with Avaroc was horrible for you. You looked so happy to find your uncle but to have him turn on us...on you, like that, I know it hurt you.'

Ellien smiled at him gratefully. 'Thank the Lords of Alfheim that I have you beside me.'

'You have far more than me to rely on. The Winterne clan will always be with you, Radocas, Kaellec and the other clans support you too. Your claim to the throne is just.' He spotted Piggybait sitting cross-legged in an armchair, taking a relaxing break over a tankard of beer. 'Come on Piggybait's over there. He looks as if he's had enough rest and Primola's with him. You get them round a table while I look for my father.'

Ellien looked a little nervous about the idea of upsetting all the plans but she nodded, took a deep breath, held her head high and kissed Halmar on the cheek. 'Don't worry. It'll be alright,' she said as she strode off to break the news to the jolly pair who were enjoying their well-earned break.

And so on the day of the wedding, Piggybait, Clap-trap and a large group of elves expanded the tunnels to move Halmar's arch, tables and benches to a small glade in the centre of the wood unknown to humans. As expected, there had been a few complaints, mainly from Jerrill, when the change of venue was proposed. As Halmar had rightly said, he had brought up every reason why it could not be done but surprisingly, it had been Primola who had persuaded him they could do anything if they worked together, and that there was still plenty of time.

It did no harm either when Ellien flattered him by saying that, as her father's oldest friend and as an elder of the clan, she would be relying on his experience and wisdom to help her. Halmar suppressed a smile as she cajoled his overly cautious father into agreeing to their new plans.

And so, close to eleven thirty that evening, the clan and their invited guests, who were now minus Tarryn and Tildor's families; they had left the day before, gathered in the moon and lantern lit glade for the wedding of their Queen and her future consort.

Aelfrar sat to one side of Halmar's carved arch, a small harp-like instrument on his lap. White clothed tables were laden with food and drink and benches had been arranged in rows to accommodate the assembled guests.

After the Prom, Sam had taken Jenny home, then met up with Charlie and they slipped out the back door to walk to the wedding together. At the edge of the glade, they separated; Charlie to wait at the arch for Ellien and Halmar, and Sam to stand at the edge of the gathering leaning against the solid trunk of a spreading chestnut tree, the only other human guest. He had expected Armistice to be there but Charlie told him that, with Tanith staying, she thought it would be too awkward to get away without having to go into elaborate excuses for her absence. She also said, to Charlie's surprise, that she had been feeling unwell at times of late. Charlie wondered at this. Armistice was rarely unwell. Could it be that she was so taken with her newly-found relative that she had to some extent forsaken her old friends?

A movement at the edge of the trees to his side caught Sam's attention but by the time he looked whatever it was had gone. Something rustled the ferns behind him. Rondina emerged from between the trees and she was not alone.

Jenny! Trying not to attract too much attention he rushed over to where she was about to take a seat beside Rondina on the stump of a felled tree. She showed no surprise at seeing him there.

'Hello Sam,' Rondina said as if sitting next to his girlfriend was the most natural thing in the world.

Jenny gave a sheepish grin. 'Hi Sam.'

'*What*?' he lowered his voice, 'I mean how did you get here?'

'Rondina invited me,' Jenny said casually, turning away to see what was happening in the glade. 'I wonder what Ellien will be wearing,' she asked Rondina, ignoring Sam's bemused expression.

Sam could hardly believe how composed they both were when his insides were churning. 'OK. Enough! Explain please,' he demanded.

Jenny turned to him with a look she would give when indulging a naughty child. He'd seen that expression before. It was exactly the same look she had given him at Easter when he, in all innocence, had asked her to go out with him and she told him they had been a couple for months and everyone except him already knew. Rondina giggled.

'Likewise! How long have you been here now, Sam? Seven months?' Jenny asked in a matter-of-fact voice. 'And I've lived next door to your uncle for years. It didn't take you long to realise something was going on,

what with those night-time lights in the trees and him going out late at night. What makes you think you were the only one who figured it out? I've followed him too and I've spent time in the wood. Rondina and I have known each other for ages.'

Sam was completely gobsmacked. 'But why didn't you say?'

'It's been much more fun this way. Rondina's kept me up with everything that's been going on. I know all about the tunnel into Winterne Manor and how you got out of the cave-in at Christmas. So, now, let me ask you the same thing, why didn't you tell me?'

Sam struggled for words. 'Yeah, but it wasn't that easy. Charlie wanted it kept quiet,'

'But who did you think I was going to tell?' There was an accusatory edge to her voice. Rondina sensed that this was not a good time to be watching them and turned away. 'Didn't you think I could be trusted?' Jenny went on.

'No.'

'No?'

'No, I mean it wasn't like that. Charlie asked me not to say anything to anyone because it could spoil everything.' He took her hand. 'I think I'm relieved, you know, it makes things easier.'

Jenny snatched her hand away. 'Oh good, I'm glad it makes things easier for you.'

Sam grabbed her hand again. 'Don't be like that,' he pleaded somehow feeling as though he was completely in the wrong. 'It's just that it means we can come here together, that we can talk about this instead of me having to keep it all quiet from you.'

Jenny giggled. 'Do you remember Easter Sunday when we went for a walk with the dogs? You thought you were so clever trying to hide Claptrap and Piggybait from me.'

'I've just been thinking about that. I must have looked like a complete idiot. I bet you were laughing at me.'

'No I wasn't, not really. I thought it was quite sweet, watching you struggle to find a reason for not keeping up with me and the dogs,' she kissed his cheek.

But Sam was not to be so easily put off. 'You know, thinking about it, here's me feeling I'm in the wrong but what else are you keeping from me. How many other secrets have you got?'

Even in the dim light he could see Jenny's face had paled. 'What d'you mean?'

'First Karate, now this and you're accusing me of keeping secrets but what about you?' He was beginning to feel a little annoyed again.

Rondina shushed him. 'They'll hear you.' She pointed to the congregated elves, some of whom were looking their way.

'I don't care,' Sam snapped back.

'Yes you do,' Rondina replied. 'Look Ellien and Halmar have arrived. Oh, she's not wearing her crown.' She sounded disappointed.

Both dressed in silvery-white, they appeared luminescent in the darkness of the wood. Ellien's hair hung loose in shimmering tresses that fell to just below her knees and, as was her habit, her feet were bare. They were greeted by gasps of admiration from their guests. Sam and Jenny both stood up and Rondina stood on the tree stump to get a better view.

'She's beautiful,' Jenny whispered.

'And he's so handsome,' Rondina sighed.

Charlie stepped forward as Ellien and Halmar took their positions under the carved arch and held out their right hands for him to wind a length of shimmering silver twine around them. Charlie held his right hand over theirs and said some words that, even with his loud voice, from that distance Sam and Jenny were unable to make out. Minutes later the ceremony was over and everyone was gathering around the couple to wish them well. Jenny took Sam's hand this time.

'There's nothing else, Sam. I had reasons for keeping the Karate quiet. You know that. And I had reasons for keeping this from you, but there's nothing else.'

In the moonlight he could see her eyes sparkling and glistening. He put his arms around her and kissed her. 'It's OK. I'm sorry. I guess it was just a bit of a shock and I was just annoyed you were having a go at me. Alright now?'

She nodded. Rondina sighed.

'Come on, I'll introduce to you to Ellien,' Sam suggested, but Jenny held back.

'I don't know if I should.'

'You're here now. Do you think they won't know? Come on. It'll be fine.'

Jenny allowed Sam to lead her through the celebrating elves who showed no surprise or animosity at her being there.

Charlie headed towards them, laughing loudly. 'I wondered how long it would take before you turned up, young lady.'

'You knew?' Sam and Jenny said in unison. 'But why didn't you tell me?' Sam wanted to know.

'It was much more fun waiting to see how long it would take before you found out,' he chuckled. 'But I've seen you watching from your window and I know you've followed me,' he said to an open-mouthed Jenny.

Sam was astounded. 'But you said no-one should know. That it could threaten everything if anyone else found out.'

Charlie stood between them, put a hand on each of their shoulders and guided them to where they could talk more easily away from the noise of the crowd.

At the edge of the glade he sat on a felled tree so he could look them both in the eyes. 'You're both very young and it may seem a little unfair to put this on your shoulders so soon. You have your whole lives ahead of you after all. But I know something about destiny, Sam. You're very special and so is Jenny. I've mentioned fate to you before. It brought you together for a reason. What that reason is I still don't know. Maybe you are meant to accomplish something in the future that can only be achieved if you are together. That secret has still to be revealed. In all the years I have lived here, and elsewhere, no couple have both been privileged to know our secret world, but it has been revealed to you both. Coincidence? I don't think so. Fate has a strange way of dealing its hand. Not even Cathy knows about what I do…'

'I wouldn't bet on it,' Sam muttered. If Charlie heard he ignored it, but Jenny tugged Sam's hand.

'Come on, let's join the festivities,' Charlie said, getting to is feet. 'Come and meet Queen Ellien and Halmar.'

'Is Halmar King now,' Jenny asked.

'No. He will be Prince Consort. Ellien is Queen in her own right because of her bloodline.'

Sam congratulated the very happy couple. Ellien radiated so much joy she seemed to have a golden halo around her. She and Halmar greeted Jenny warmly and invited her to stay for the banquet. Jenny delightedly accepted.

It was then that Jerrill approached Halmar and Sam heard him ask if he had a few minutes to talk but Halmar put him off. 'Sorry, Father. We can talk in the morning, but tonight I need to stay with Ellien. We have so many people to see, still so much to do. I'll see you tomorrow. But tonight, Father, enjoy yourself, relax, have a little fun.'

Jerrill looked a little disappointed. 'I understand. Tonight is the wrong time. Tomorrow will do very well.' He turned to walk away, his hand finding the small carved wooden image of Halmar and Halmia he kept on a chain round his neck. It was rarely seen. He turned back. 'But I have been

142

remiss and must apologise for not having yet congratulated you both, but I do so now. You have my blessings for a marvellous life together.'

Halmar thanked him before returning to Ellien, leaving his father looking a little dejected, alone.

Four hours later, after dancing, feasting and emptying countless flagons of mead, dandelion beer and acorn wine, the elves cleared the glade of any sign of having been there. Charlie, Jenny and Sam had left two hours before, shortly after Ellien and Halmar had said their goodbyes. As they made their way out of the glade Sam had taken a last look at the partying elves.

'Hey, look, Jerrill's actually having fun. He's enjoying himself.'

Jerrill was huddling with a laughing Primola between the tables and twirling her around and around until she was dizzy.

Chapter Twenty Six

Sam still had to make things up with Jonah. After all, Jonah had only been doing him a favour and there really had been nothing in his behaviour to make Sam jealous; it had all been in his own mind.

While his mother washed up the breakfast things, Sam sat at the table staring vacantly, deep in thought, out of the window into the sunlit garden.

'Penny for 'em,' she said cheerfully, but received no response. Putting down the tea-towel on the sink unit she pulled out a chair and sat opposite Sam; still no response. 'Sam? What's the matter?'

'Huh? Sorry? I was miles away.'

'I can see that. Is there something wrong? Is it Jenny? Anything I can help with?'

Sam rested his chin on his upturned palms. 'No, not really, Mum. More like problems with me.'

Portia, their plump, fluffy and very spoiled black and white cat, jumped onto the table and demanded to be made a fuss of while kneading the tablecloth with her front paws and using her forehead to nudge first Sam, then Jane, rubbing her head against their hands as they stroked her.

'How d'you mean?' She looked at him, really seeing him for the first time in a long time. He was no longer her little boy. He was now a young man, starting to go through all the teenage anxieties that he would have to face alone.

He pushed Portia's very thick tail away from his face. 'Oh, it's OK, Mum. I just made myself look stupid last night. I got mardy and had a go at Jonah.'

'Why? I thought you two were friends.'

'We are…at least we were,' he sighed. 'I hope we still are.'

'But what happened?'

Sam stood up, stroked the purring Portia once more and headed for the backdoor leaving a bewildered Jane staring after him. He stood in the open

doorway and looked back at her. 'Nothing serious, I hope. Anyway I'll see you later.'

'Are you going to see Jonah?'

'Yeah, it's time I apologised.'

He walked up the dusty lane towards the stables wondering if Jonah would be there or if it was too early for him. It was only just after nine o'clock but it was already very warm. Flies buzzed in the long grass verge, colourful butterflies darted between wildflowers but Sam had too much on his mind to take in the wildlife teeming around him as he made his way along the lane.

At the stables, he spotted Kelly Jones hosing down one of the stalls and asked her if Jonah was around. She pointed to stable number five where Celeste and her foal were kept. Like most of the stalls, the top half of the door was open but the lower half closed. Angelo, the foal's sire and Jonah's sister's favourite horse, put his handsome head over the door of his stall and whinnied to Celeste.

'He's over there. Do you want me to come with you?' Kelly smiled flirtatiously.

'No, there's no need. I can find my way,' Sam tried to stay polite.

He felt her eyes on him as he walked away. He was almost at the stable when Jonah came out pushing a wheelbarrow of soiled hay. To Sam's surprise he grinned at him.

'You alright Sam? Didn't think you'd be up this early?'

After building himself up for his apology, Sam was taken aback by Jonah's easy manner. He had expected him to still be hacked off with him but there was certainly no sign of it. 'I thought I'd better apologise for last night. I shouldn't have had a go at you.'

Jonah lowered the wheelbarrow and walked over, he was still smiling. 'Not a problem mate.' Jonah took off his rubber gloves, threw them on the ground and put a hand on Sam's shoulder. 'Look I screwed up loads of times and anyway I owe you. It didn't bother me, but are you and Jenny OK?'

Sam grinned. 'Yeah, we're fine. I sorted everything out with her last night and said I was going to see you this morning. Before she told me too, that is.'

They looked up as a silver coloured Honda Civic pulled into the yard.

'John's here again,' Jonah remarked. 'He's back to see Alison, his beloved.' He patted his chest around the heart area, and then nudged Sam. 'Here, look at Kelly,' he nodded in her direction.

Kelly was leaning on her broom, gazing adoringly at the good-looking detective. Jonah rolled his eyes. 'She's always like that when he's here. She's the same with you.'

'What? Me? You're joking!'

'She's always after one bloke or the other; always got a 'thing' about someone. It's usually only one at a time but it looks like she's made an exception for you,' he winked, wickedly enjoying his teasing, 'but I guess there's no accounting for taste.'

The office door opened as John got out of his car and Briar, Alison's German shepherd dog, darted out to greet him. He ruffled her neck affectionately as they headed to the office where Alison waited for them at the door.

'I'm sure you can smell coffee from miles away,' the boys heard her laughingly call out to John.

John walked to the office with Briar closely following, while Jonah and Sam watched Kelly despondently return to her duties in the nearby stable as they disappeared inside.

'So Whadd'ya doing now?' Jonah asked. 'How about getting down and dirty with a shovel and wheelbarrow?' He picked up his rubber gloves and offered them to Sam.

'No thanks mate. I'd feel really bad if I got in the way of you doing your job and anyway, I didn't bring my wellies,' he pointed to his recently bought and very much prized basketball boots. Black and white Converse boots with flame patterns on the sides and white laces, his treasures were now covered in muddy bits of hay.

'Hmm, not exactly the best footgear to wear around here,' Jonah said with a grin. 'Still I guess they've probably clean up OK.'

'Think so?' Sam looked at him hopefully.

'No. I lied.'

As they walked back towards the gates, Jonah hinted that Kelly was watching Sam from behind a stable door which made him very uncomfortable. 'I wish she'd pack it in,' Sam whispered.

'It's love, Sam old mate. Want me to fix up a date for you?' Jonah was clearly having a great time; thoroughly enjoying Sam's unease, especially when Sam quickened his pace.

'No, thanks, I've got a girlfriend and I've been in enough trouble lately, remember?'

Jonah tried not to laugh out loud, but gave in and chuckled when he saw Sharon Bartle and Sophie Dennett, two of the other stable girls observing Kelly and giggling.

The boys had to pass the office to get to the gate and the office door had swung open again. Briar was lying on the ground just outside in the shade. She looked up as the boys approached.

'How is she now?' Sam asked, referring to the injuries the dog had sustained a few months before.

'Yeah, she's OK. Got quite a scar on her nose and she still limps a bit but…yeah…she's going OK. Aren't you girl?'

Briar beat her tail against the ground, thought about getting up, but decided against it. 'The heat's getting to her a bit though, what with that thick coat of hers.'

'Surely Alison should keep her inside,' Sam commented.

'S'pose so, but the door's open, she can go inside if she wants. She's got a bowl of water, fresh air, shade and out here she can keep an eye on what's going on.'

As they passed the office, Sam stopped. He had heard Mrs Jenks name crop up in conversation.

'…it looked like she didn't want her to go inside,' John said as Alison handed him a glass of cold lemonade, 'In fact Izz said, she refused point blank to let her in.'

Jonah had walked on a few steps but Sam stopped to eavesdrop. Suddenly aware Sam was no longer beside him, he turned back and was about to say something when Sam held a finger to his mouth to shush him.

'…so she didn't see Mrs Jenks at all?' Alison asked.

'Well, yes, but not to speak to. Izz said she saw her for a second or two behind this great-niece, or whoever she is. She didn't look herself apparently. She seemed to be talking to the wall.'

'To the wall?'

'Uh-huh. Izz said she's sure Mrs Jenks saw her but there was no recognition. Her eyes were completely blank, almost as if she'd been hypnotised or something.'

'Or drugged?' Alison added.

Jonah had joined Sam in time to hear most of the conversation and looked at him enquiringly.

'Or drugged,' John agreed gravely.

'I've never particularly liked Mrs Jenks. I have to be honest about that,' Alison went on. 'She's a bit…odd for my liking,' Alison admitted.

John smiled. 'Not many people do. There's a few of the lads at the station who grew up terrified of her. Rumour has it she's a witch, you know.'

Sam suppressed a smile.

Jonah whispered. 'He's right. That is what they say about her.'

Sam nodded quickly. 'I know.' John was speaking again and he did not want to miss anything important.

'Yeah, but witch or not, she's very clever, very experienced. She's probably forgotten more about veterinary medicine than Dan Hedges has ever learnt. Amazing skills…a couple of the Police dogs were taken to her when the vets gave up on them, but she pulled them through. She knows an awful lot about medicinal plants for humans as well as animals…got quite a reputation as a healer. I know quite a few people who've gone to her when the vets haven't been able to do any more.'

'So what's Isabel going to do?' Alison was now sitting on the chair behind the desk. She took a sip from her glass.

'I've told her to be careful but she's going back. She's convinced this…niece, relative, whatever, is up to something.'

'But what did the girl say was wrong?'

'Izz didn't say. But I know she and Mrs Jenks are very old friends and trying to keep Izz away from her is like a red rag to a bull. She won't leave it there. She wants to know what's wrong and knowing her, she'll get to the bottom of it.'

Sam listened for a few minutes more but as the conversation turned to an equestrian event being held next week that Alison was competing at, he knew he was unlikely to hear anything further about Mrs Jenks and her situation. He needed to speak to Charlie. He looked at his watch.

'Gotta go, Jonah, sorry.'

'OK, but what do I tell Kelly?'

'Just don't go there…alright. I'm off, see you later.' Sam was in a hurry to get away.

'Yeah, see you later,' Jonah laughed and returned to his wheelbarrow while Kelly alternately stared at Sam and Jonah as they walked away in opposite directions.

Chapter Twenty Seven

Sam knocked on the front door of Charlie's cottage, trying to catch his breath, having run all the way from the stables. He hoped it would be Charlie who answered the door, but it was Cathy who let him in. As they walked through the hallway, she told him Charlie was in the garden shed and then began making small talk about the weather, his parents and school.

Trying not to be impolite, Sam curbed his impatience and answered his aunt's questions as fully as he could, hoping all the time that the trivial conversation would quickly come to an end. Not a moment too soon, Cathy ran out of questions and he was able to make his escape to the garden shed where Charlie was happily whistling away to himself, re-potting his geraniums. He looked around as the shed door creaked open.

'Sam my lad, what are you doing here? Wasn't exp...' He saw the look on Sam's face and his beaming smile vanished, replaced by a deep wrinkled frown before he turned back to his plants. 'What's wrong?'

Sam told him about the conversation he and Jonah had just overheard at the stables. Charlie made no comment, allowing Sam to continue while he tidied away the unused pots and brushed down the worktop. There was nothing Sam could actually put a finger on but he sensed a subtle change in Charlie's stance. His shoulders seemed a little more rigid; his beard a little more bristled. When Sam finished, Charlie remained staring out of the window. The only sign of emotion being his whitening knuckles as they gripped the worktop.

'Charlie?' Sam said quietly. There was no response.

'Char...'

'It's OK, Sam.' He wiped his hands on a cloth hanging on a hook, his expression dark and furious. 'She didn't waste much time, did she?'

'What? Who?'

Charlie shot him an incredulous look.

'Oh you mean that great-niece of hers.'

'Come on,' Charlie ordered.

'Where're we going?'

'Where d'you think? We're going to see Armistice.' Charlie pushed Sam out of the shed ahead of him then closed and padlocked the door behind them.

'But what if that…that…um…whatever her name is…'

'Tanith…maybe.'

'…won't let us in?' Sam asked as he tried to keep up.

'…Well that's what she calls herself anyway,' Charlie said. 'Not let us in!' he growled. 'She won't have a bloody chance of keeping us out. I'll be damned if I'm going to ask.'

'But aren't we going the wrong way,' Sam asked at the end of lane, and pointed towards the road they usually took.

'*No*!'

Sam had never seen his uncle in such a ferocious mood.

'We're going this way to get round the back without being seen. If we cut across the road at the end of the village and through the other side of the wood, we can get into the back garden without her knowing we're there, unless she's at the kitchen window of course. Let's hope she's not, but I'll worry about that when we get there.'

Charlie swore and muttered curses under his breath while Sam ran alongside attempting to keep up with his uncle's long angry strides. He had thought he knew Charlie well but this side of his personality was a complete revelation. Indeed, as Charlie forged ahead through the wood, his language was appalling and definitely nothing like Sam had known him use before, but then neither had he seen him so furious or troubled.

Baron and his family of deer grazed contentedly in a small clearing. The stag raised his head as they passed by but on this occasion Charlie ignored them. This, to Sam, was a measure of just how seriously Charlie was taking the threat to Armistice. Where the path they were on came to an end, Charlie barged through the undergrowth, with an out-of-breath Sam running a metre or so behind him. On a small rise, under a cluster of larch trees, Sam saw Rondina and two elf companions gathering wild mushrooms. He knew he had seen the others before but could not recall their names. Rondina saw them and called out in greeting. Sam tugged at Charlie' sleeve to indicate their presence, but Charlie merely waved and moved on. Sam halted long enough to give her a sympathetic shrug before dashing after Charlie.

150

At the edge of the trees they could see the back of the cottage and Charlie halted looking for signs of movement at the window. This gave Sam a chance to catch up and he bent over to ease the stitch in his ribs.

'What do we do now?' Sam wheezed, pushing aside the low branches of a tree.

'We're going to get into the garden and in through the backdoor before she knows we're there.' He pointed out the way. 'I'll need to crouch down. I'm too tall and she might see me over the hedge. I want to make sure we're a surprise.'

Sam nodded.

'I think…what's that?' Charlie pointed towards the garden shed. 'Oh, it's only Bandit. That's OK.'

Sam saw Bandit climb up to the apex of the shed roof staring at the kitchen window. 'What's he doing?' he asked.

Charlie shaded his eyes with a shovel-sized hand. 'D'you know…I'm not sure but it looks to me like he's watching the house too.'

Bandit lowered himself until he was flat against the roof; his eyes firmly fixed on the cottage, his ears back and his tail switched angrily from side to side.

'Come on,' Charlie bent low and ran from the cover of the trees to the hedge surrounding the garden. At the gate, he reached over carefully and lifted the latch. Thankfully, the potted bay trees situated on either side of the gate did exactly what he had hoped and concealed him from the house. Sam joined him and together they crept through the gate and into the garden. Bandit lifted his head, observing their approach, his eyes widened.

'He's pleased to see us anyway,' Charlie whispered from their hiding place under the kitchen window. As Charlie crouched towards the door, Bandit ran between him and Sam, rubbing his head against their legs and purring loudly. Charlie picked him up. 'Don't you fret, my boy. We'll sort this out.'

Bandit's jade coloured eyes narrowed as he stared into Charlie's periwinkle blue ones and he purred loudly for a second before clambering up onto his shoulder and sprawling, scarf-like across them. His claws dug into Charlie's shirt. He had no intention of moving until he was ready. 'Don't get yourself too comfortable, we're going inside now to see how Armistice is and you're going to have to get down.'

Bandit's claws dug in deeper as Charlie tried to extricate him from his shirt but eventually he had to let go and was gently set down, protesting, onto the ground.

'Ready, Sam?' Sam nodded nervously, took a deep breath, wondered just how ready he was then, without a further pause, pushed open the back door into the scullery. Charlie moved in front of him and opened the second door into the kitchen just as Bandit darted through his legs and made a bee-line for Armistice who was sitting on the sofa. Her eyes lit up joyously when she saw him.

'Bandit, my sweetheart! Where have you been?' She wrapped her arms around him lovingly and looked up to see who her visitors were. 'Charlie! Sam! How lovely to see you and you've brought my boy back in with you. How are you both?'

Charlie was looking round for Tanith. There was no sign of her. He hoped she was out but then they heard hurried footsteps on the stairs. Charlie looked at Sam and nodded. The door opened and a grim-faced Tanith entered the room. She was obviously not delighted to see them. A frozen smile appeared on her face as she walked towards the sofa.

'Look Tanith, not only do we have visitors, but Bandit's come back. Isn't that wonderful?'

'I'm so pleased, Auntie. You've really missed him.' She held out a hand to stroke Bandit. 'Perhaps we can be friends now,' she cooed.

But Bandit was not having any of it. With a shrill hiss, his hackles rose and he spat viciously at her before dropping to the floor and vanishing under the tablecloth where Merlin now spent most of his time.

'Oh, that's a shame,' Armistice sighed. 'I had hoped this meant everything would be alright again. It would be so nice for us all to be a family. Let's hope it's not too long before they take to you, dear.'

Sam felt sorry for her. Having been alone for so long and then to find her only relative detested by the animals who had been her closest companions for so long, would be hard to take.

'Tanith, could you make Charlie and Sam some tea, please?' Armistice asked.

'Of course,' Tanith replied sweetly.

'I'd make it myself, Charlie, but I've not been too well over the last few days,' Armistice explained. 'Not really like me at all is it? But then I suppose I'm getting on a bit and it comes to us all.' Charlie noted the strange look in her eyes as Armistice looked towards where Tanith was standing. 'And Tanith's already made me one.'

Charlie saw the steaming cup of tea, seemingly untouched, on the small table beside his friend.

'No, it's alright Tanith. Don't worry making tea for us, Sam and I have just had one.' He flashed a warning look at Sam who remained quietly

152

leaning against the sink unit, his back to the window, observing Tanith and hopefully not letting her realise it. He thought that when she had come into the room, there had been a look of fear in her eyes, but it had only been there fleetingly and it occurred to him that he may have been mistaken. But there was something about her; she seemed edgy, definitely uncomfortable with their visit.

Initially he had thought Charlie had over-reacted to the information he had picked up at the stables, but now he was not so sure. Perhaps he was right to be worried.

Armistice looked very pale and had dark circles under her eyes that made her look very much older than she did before. This change had been sudden, too sudden, and had only come about only since Tanith's arrival. He was even more worried now that he had seen her than he was before, and he knew he had been right to tell him what he hard heard and they were right to force this visit.

Armistice sipped her tea. 'How're Cathy and the boys, Charlie?' Charlie knew she meant Clap-trap and Piggybait.

'They're fine, everyone's fine, Armie. But how are you?'

'Oh, Charlie, you don't need to worry about me...' she lifted her cup and took another sip of the hot tea. 'I'm just getting old. You can see for yourself, I'm fine...a couple of times I've forgotten things lately...can't seem to remember what I was doing...a bit tired, but I'm fine, aren't I Tanith?'

Tanith managed a stiff nod. 'Yes, she's fine.'

'So what are you doing with yourself, Sam? And how's young Jenny?'

While Armistice drank her tea, Sam told her how things were going at school, how Jenny was, how he had fallen out with her and Jonah at the Prom and why, and then explained how he had made it right with them both, all this while keeping half an eye on Tanith, who was showing signs of becoming more twitchy the longer they were there.

Armistice continued sipping her tea while Charlie sat back and watched both Armistice and Tanith very closely while their attention was on Sam. Bandit peaked out from under the tablecloth; his eyes followed Tanith as she moved around the room. Merlin remained concealed. Sam could just see the tip of his tail sticking out from under the tablecloth and wondered how this friendly, boisterous and loving dog had become so reserved. It just wasn't normal.

It seemed to Charlie that while Sam was talking, something in Armistice changed. Her eyes dulled and she appeared to have stopped paying any attention to what Sam was saying. Her gaze flickered around the room,

153

unfocussed and unseeing. Charlie turned to Tanith who would not meet his eyes. Sam noticed it too and looked at Charlie questioningly. Charlie gave him a slight shake of the head. Sam took this as an indication not to react.

Armistice stood up and went to the table.

'Mother, my dress is very pretty,' she said, lifting up an imaginary garment. 'Do you think Edward will like it?' She looked hopefully towards where Sam was standing, but he felt she was looking straight through him. 'Yes, so do I?'

Charlie sat motionless, watching Tanith, watching Armistice.

'Yes, he's calling for me at six-thirty. We're having dinner with his parents this evening.' She set down the imagined dress and tottered over to the sofa where she sat down again, unaware of the company around her.

'You had better go,' Tanith said, quickly hurrying over to where Armistice was trying to poke holes in the sofa's covering with her finger. 'Now perhaps you believe she's ill.'

'Is Edward here, Mother?' Armistice asked, as Tanith reached across her. 'No, not yet,' Tanith answered her gently, 'but he'll be here soon.' But instead of helping her up, Tanith picked up the tea cup from the small table and hurried over to the sink with it, hastily running it under the tap until it was rinsed clean. It was only then that she returned to the confused Armistice who had suddenly started talking to Mélusine, the raven, who was not there.

'I'll take her to her room,' Tanith said, helping the bemused Armistice to her feet. 'You'd better go. I'll see to her from now on.'

'Has she seen a doctor?' Charlie asked.

'No, she refused to see him.'

'But surely…'

'I think you'd better just go,' Tanith ordered as she led Armistice toward the stairs.

Sam followed Charlie to the back door with Bandit close behind them. Charlie turned just as Armistice put her foot on the bottom step. 'You know I'll be back, don't you.'

Tanith blanched. 'I'd rather you didn't. I'm looking after her now, she doesn't need anyone else.'

'Oh, I think she does,' Charlie replied darkly.

Outside, Charlie turned to Sam. 'I need you to get to the cavern. There's something going on in that house…she's putting something in the tea I'm sure of it.'

'But what's at the cavern?'

154

'Piggybait and Clap-trap of course,' Charlie snapped. 'I need them to get inside the house and investigate. I want to know what that girl is giving her and why. They have ways of getting into places unheard and unseen. They're far better at being devious than we would be.'

'But what do you think she's up to, Charlie?'

'I think Armie's being poisoned...drugged anyway. But for the life of me I can't think why. She's got nothing of value...not monetary value anyway. Not now.'

'Maybe Tanith...' Sam began but Charlie interrupted.

'That's another thing. Something tells me she's not Tanith. I don't know who she is but I'll find out...I have my ways and my contacts.'

Chapter Twenty Eight

Somehow Piggybait and Clap-trap had sensed Sam was looking for them and were on their way to find him when they met up on the wood path. Sam explained what had happened, how worried Charlie was about Armistice and what he wanted them to do. Thirty minutes later the pair climbed through an open upstairs window of the cottage and found themselves in Tanith's bedroom. They were watched by Mélusine from the roof of the garden shed. Clap-trap stood guard at the top of the stairs listening for any movement below while Piggybait began a search. He could hear footsteps and crockery being used but the women did not seem to be talking very much.

Piggybait emerged from the bedroom. 'Nothing. The drawers and wardrobe are all clean but the Chief's right, she's up to something.' He showed Clap-trap a narrow, black leather bag he had found stuffed between the wall and the wardrobe. 'Look what I've found.' He pulled out two passports and two cheque books, bank notes in various currencies and a small wallet containing several bank cards. 'This passport's in her name…if it is her name,' he said handing over the first passport. 'And this one's got her picture in it but she's called herself something completely different.'

Clap-trap took the passports, opened them at the back page and compared the details on both. Puckering his lips he took a deep intake of breath and shook his head. 'I don't understand this at all.'

Piggybait had been searching the wallet. 'Then there's all this money, and only one of the bank cards is in her name.'

Clap-trap handed the papers back to Piggybait who returned them to the bag and put them back where he had found them. 'There's something very, very odd going on here,' he frowned as he returned to his friend on the landing.

'Try Armie's room,' Clap-trap suggested. 'See if there's anything there. I'd help but I think I should keep a lookout.'

Piggybait agreed and disappeared into Armistice's bedroom which he searched thoroughly. Ten minutes later he emerged shaking his head.

'Nothing.'

Sam had told them Charlie was convinced Tanith was drugging Armistice. They had to find proof but both bedrooms had been searched with no result.

'The Chief's convinced there's something here but could it be downstairs?' Piggybait asked his friend.

'If it is, we'll probably have to wait until tonight...after they've gone to bed,'

Piggybait took off his cap and scratched his head. 'That's what I thought you'd say.'

They jumped as Bandit appeared at the window. He had bounded onto the porch roof from the fence, crept along the tiles and up onto the window ledge. He mewed softly, dropped onto the carpet and skulked, low to the floor, to the top of the stairs where he hissed spitefully at the sound of Tanith's voice.

'Someone else doesn't like the visitor,' Clap-trap said.

'Can't say I blame him, but we'd better get on,' Piggybait pointed to the bathroom.

Bandit shook his head and headed for the airing cupboard. He scratched at the door.

'He knows up here better than we do,' Piggybait suggested, opening the door. The warmth of the cupboard increased the pungency of the herbs drying in there. Bandit purred and licked a paw with a satisfied, almost smug expression.

'So we have fifty or so identical brown paper bags that are all full of herbs. If the Chief thinks it's an herb or plant she's using, this would a great place to hide it...among lots of others,' Clap-trap said. He sounded quite impressed.

'Especially if Armie's not well enough to use them regularly like she used to,' Piggybait added.

'Let's get on with it.' Clap-trap lifted a handful of bags off their hooks and opened one of them. He emptied a couple of leaves out onto his hand. 'Sage,' he said, putting the leaves back and laying the bag on the floor of the cupboard. Bandit walked back to the top of the stairs and crouched low.

'Look at him, he's keeping guard,' Piggybait said, following Clap-trap's lead with the bags. His bag contained Lemon Verbena, its strong citrus smell made his nose tingle.

'Rosemary,' Clap-trap put his second bag on top of Piggybait's. They would hang them back on the hooks later.

'Mint.' Piggybait said.

'This one's Borage. It might have been helpful if Armie had labelled them.'

'And Thyme. She probably knew which was which. Probably hung them in some kind of order.'

Clap-trap opened another bag. 'Feverfew.'

Bandit hissed at the sound of talking downstairs but he had not moved. His tail swished from side to side angrily but his lack of movement reassured them no-one was about to come up the stairs.

'Parsley.'

'And Marjoram. Right, let's have the next lot.' Clap-trap hung the bags they had checked back on their hooks and took down another batch from the second shelf. 'Here.' He handed a number of the bags to Piggybait.

'Basil!' Piggybait said putting the leaves back and tying the string.

'This one's interesting,' Clap-trap said sniffing the leaves in his palm.

'What's that you've got?' Piggybait asked looking over at his friend's hand.

'If I'm right, this is Diviner's Sage or Mexican Mint,' Clap-trap looked up. 'I'm sure this is it, Piggy. Not only does it make whoever uses it imagine they see some really horrible things for about an hour or so, but afterwards they can't remember anything about what happened to them. They only know that there are blanks in their memory.'

Bandit rejoined them and purred around their legs.

'And, funnily enough, Piggy, it was originally found in Mexico. How's that for a coincidence?'

Bandit jumped onto the window ledge and mewed at them before disappearing the way he had come; his job done. 'He's obviously convinced. Time to do what he's just done and disappear,' Piggybait suggested. 'Take a couple of those leaves with you to show the Chief.'

Chapter Twenty Nine

The cavern was still busy with guests but now many of them were packing up to leave for which Primola was very grateful. Tired and aching after far too much dancing at the wedding feast she flopped down next to Aelfrar at the nearest wooden table to the kitchen for a well-earned rest. Taking a wooden cup from the stack, she poured out what was left of a flagon of apple juice.

'I shall be glad when things get back to normal,' she said, resting her elbows on the table and rolling the cool cup against her aching forehead.

'I'm sure you will,' he replied with a smile. 'At least with the wedding over, everyone will be gone soon and by tomorrow we'll be back to normal.' He sucked on his pipe. Unfortunately sitting by the air vent, the smoke blew back in her direction.

'That's a disgusting habit. Isn't it time you packed it up.'

By response, Aelfar blew a perfect smoke ring straight at her. 'Just because you're upset about Saldor, and you're aching from last night, don't take it out on me.'

'I know, I'm sorry. I am worried about him, but…oh, I don't know. One minute I'm furious with him for having run off leaving me to cope with all the extra guests and the next I'm worried witless about him,' she said as she sipped sparingly at her apple juice. 'I've got a terrible headache. It's all the stress,' she grumbled.

'Not possible,' the old elf replied with a chuckle. 'We don't get headaches. That's a human condition.'

'Well I can imagine one can't I?' she snapped.

'No-one's stopping you, but what's the point?' The smoke blew towards her and she waved it away with a look of disgust.

'I know he's run off a couple of times before when he's been scolded for something, but this time it feels different. Something's wrong. I can't shake off the feeling that he's hiding from something.'

Aelfrar just nodded his old head sagely.

At a table not far away, Piggybait flicked through of the latest edition of the Elfland Chronicle, twirling Clap-trap's monocle cord around his fingers, having found them lying on a chair after lunch. It amused him when Clap-trap gave himself airs and wore the monocle; his eyesight was excellent and he had no need of the single eye-glass, but the pretentious elf thought it made him look sophisticated. Leaving it behind showed just how little he needed it.

Turning the pages, not really concentrating on any of the articles, Piggybait's thoughts were elsewhere. Images of Saldor, Diviner's Sage and Armistice, all spun around his head while he tried to make sense of the series of events over the last few days. Looking over, but not really seeing the contents of the newspaper columns, he fleetingly wondered if Avaroc had done anything else of note that would give him a mention in the paper, but then thought it unlikely. Elves like Avaroc would conceal their avaricious intentions and not attract attention until they thought they were safe to do so and he'd already made that mistake once. He chuckled remembering Avaroc's humiliated and outraged expression on hearing Halmar's revelation. Chew the bones out of that Avaroc!

His thoughts turned again to Armistice and the Chief's reaction to the result of their furtive investigations. When they handed him the Diviner's Sage and told him of the money and passports, his usually ruddy complexion drained to a pasty white before he went away to ponder their next move. Now Piggybait was whiling away the time until mid-day when he and Clap-trap were to meet the Chief for his guidance. By then he might have formulated some strategy for stopping the girl's wicked plans. His stomach twisted as he prayed to Alfheim they would not be too late for Armistice or Saldor.

A light touch on his shoulder made him turn to find an unsmiling Aerynne standing behind him. Her limpid grey eyes made him think of diamonds; clear, brilliant and strong but, surprisingly, strength was a characteristic he had never applied to her before.

'Sir?'

'What? Umm...no, no please don't call me sir,' he spluttered awkwardly, but she was kind enough to ignore it. His cheeks burned. He was blushing. He never blushed. 'Umm...no, my name's Baymar but

everyone…er…calls me Piggybait.' For the first time ever he realised just how silly the name sounded.

She smiled sweetly, looking at him through long dark eyelashes. 'Very well, I shall call you Piggybait. I think it's a lovely name.'

His toes curled in delight and it took a few seconds of smiling silence before he realised he was staring at her. 'Ahem, hmmm,' he cleared his throat, took a deep breath and recovered enough control to speak coherently.

'Here, have a seat.' He indicated the space on the bench beside him. 'What can I do for you?'

She sat beside him with her back to the table. 'I think it's more what I may be able to do for you,' she replied. 'You may have heard that I have the gift of Sight.'

He nodded.

She threw a quick, nervous glance towards Primola who, having finished her conversation with Aelfrar, had turned her attention to them. Lommie too, was keeping an eye on them from his chair in the television room, but they were not aware of him.

'I don't think she likes me,' Aerynne said quietly, leaning in towards Piggybait.

'Prim? No that's just her manner. She likes you well enough, especially after you chose to stay. If you'd gone away with Avaroc, or later with Tarryn, she would have thought you were like them but now she knows you're not.' He gave her a reassuring pat on the hand. 'You have to understand, Prim mothers us.' They watched as Primola turned away and headed back into the kitchen. 'She sees all of us as her children. It's our own fault,' he chuckled, 'we've let her do it for years.' His eyes narrowed in a frown, 'and she's upset about Saldor, we all are. He really was,' he realised what he had said and corrected himself, 'I should say is like a son to her. She may sound more cross than concerned but don't let that fool you. It's just how she deals with worry. I suppose we should really have sent out a search party before now but with the wedding preparations and the fact that he obviously took enough with him to get through a few days, I don't think any of us took his disappearance as seriously as we should have done. I honestly thought he would be back in time for the wedding. '

'It's Saldor I want to speak to you about. I think I've seen him.'

'Seen him! Where?' Piggybait jumped up from the bench but Aerynne gently pushed him back down.

'No. I have seen him, in my mind. You know, the Sight,' she explained.

'Do you know where he is? Is he well?'

'I get the impression he is well...but he's frightened. He's hiding. I do not know for certain what frightened him, I have not been able to see what happened, but I believe it has something to do with Tarryn and Tildor.' Her rain-cloud eyes became glazed as if seeing something way off into the distance.

'What is it, Aerynne? What do you see?' he asked as Lommie joined them at the table and sat opposite him, nodding at Piggybait's signal to stay silent, as Aerynne described her vision. 'The place where he hides makes him feel safe. It is very safe, a sanctuary. In there he is content but will not leave. I think he wants someone to find him, someone he trusts.'

'Can you see anything of this place, Aerynne? Can you describe it?'

'I see a long shaft going upwards. There is light...a bright light at the top and water in darkness at the bottom,' she hesitated. 'It's a well. I don't know where, but I'm sure it's a well. I see plants and other greenery.'

Piggybait looked towards the entrance of the cave. Where was Clap-trap? He could not be much longer surely.

Aerynne continued, her voice sing-song and dreamy. 'The well is not outside but within walls that are protected somehow. I think there is some kind of protective spell or influence that screens anything,' she turned to Piggybait, her forehead puckered in a puzzled frown, 'or anyone within its shelter. I think that is why your friend has gone there. He feels secure, free from danger.' She turned away again, her eyes still focused somewhere in the distance. 'This place feel's light, it is airy. There's plenty of fresh air but...I do not think...it is not an open courtyard.'

By now a small group of elves had gathered, their murmuring annoyed Piggybait and he angrily hushed them before they distracted Aerynne.

'Do not concern yourself, Piggybait. Their voices will not break my vision.' Her voice sounded small and distant.

At that point, Clap-trap appeared, pushed through the surrounding elves, and stood behind Piggybait who had not seen his arrival. He had heard a little of what Aerynne had said as he approached. 'A well?' he questioned quietly, almost to himself. 'Inside walls. I'm sure I know somewhere like that but I can't think where it is.'

Piggybait spun round. 'Thank Alfheim you're here at last.'

'Saldor is safe there. He is somewhere he feels completely secure...but he's lonely and wants to come home,' Aerynne continued. 'He wants his friends to find him.'

Piggybait tried to visualise a well within walls. 'I've got it!' He grabbed Clap-trap by the arm, kissed a startled Aerynne on the top of her

head before shoving his bemused friend ahead of him through the assembled group. Primola had heard his shout and flew out of the kitchen to see what was going on.

'What's the noise about?' she called.

'We're going to get Saldor?' Piggbait replied laughingly. 'You'd better get baking Prim, he'll be hungry.' With a joyous scream Primola ran back to the kitchen and began digging out all the ingredients she needed to make Saldor's favourite meal. Unheard by Piggybait and Clap-trap as they rushed off, she began singing at the top of her voice, imagined headache forgotten.

In the tunnel, Clap-trap rebelled. 'But where are we going?' He stood still, refusing to move his little booted feet from the spot. 'I want to know where you think he is before I go any further. After all,' he put his hands on his hips, 'it might be dangerous.'

Piggybait could not resist laughing. 'It's not dangerous, you idiot. It's the safest place in the world.'

'But where…'

'The Chief's cottage! Remember the well?'

Clap-trap walked towards him. 'No, that can't be right. Surely the Chief would know if he was hiding there. It's in his house.'

'But how often does he use it? How often does he go in there? Think about it. It must be years since we last used it to go and see him at the cottage. Once we found out how to expand the tunnels for him, he could come to us. We didn't need it any more.'

'And there was less chance of Cathy finding out,' Clap-trap added, realisation lighting up his face.

'Exactly! Now you see. Saldor knew the well. He used to go there all the time. He must have thought it would be a good hiding place. It would make sense for him to go somewhere that Tarryn and Tildor didn't know existed. Not far now.'

Ten metres or so further along, Piggybait located a large flat rock that looked far too heavy for anyone to lift. 'Ready?'

Clap-trap nodded.

Extending his right hand, Piggybait concentrated, willing the rock to move towards him using the power of telekinesis. The rock juddered slowly forward as Piggybait guided it to a position in the middle of the tunnel while a clearly unimpressed Clap-trap leaned against the wall, brushing dust off his newly made woollen jerkin.

Piggybait looked at his friend with a satisfied smile. 'See, it's all in the wrist action.'

'You finished?' Clap-trap rolled his eyes. 'I could've done that just as well.'

'Then why didn't you?' Piggybait bristled.

'You didn't ask,' Clap-trap sniffed. 'Come on, we've got a job to do.'

Mouth agape, Piggybait followed sulkily as Clap-trap climbed onto the rock and slithered ahead of him into the opening of another tunnel which had inexplicably appeared halfway up the wall.

'Come on,' Clap-trap urged, 'don't dawdle, it won't stay open long.'

Piggybait scrambled into the opening not a moment too soon. He had only just heaved himself to his booted feet inside the tunnel, when a deep rumbling indicated it had begun rolling to a close behind them as the rock on the tunnel floor slid, unseen, back to its original position. A few minutes later they reached a wooden door with a slightly tarnished round brass handle at the end of a tunnel.

'There's the door,' Piggybait whispered, all their bickering forgotten. 'Let's hope Cathy doesn't hear us.'

'Or the dogs.' Clap-trap replied. 'You're sure Saldor's here?'

'If Aerynne's right, he is. Come on.'

Clap-trap tugged to pull out the handle and then turned it anti-clockwise. Silently, and slowly the door swung wide, opening out close to the top of a well-shaft. The sudden daylight from above stung their eyes after the gloominess of the tunnels. A slightly frayed rope ladder hung conveniently from above, ending just below their position at the door. Piggybait had already placed his left foot on the bottom rung when Clap-trap touched his arm.

'Listen.' They could hear soft snoring from above.

'Bless her, Aerynne was right,' he smiled. 'He's here.'

Chapter Thirty

If things had gone according to plan, Stuart Seymour's visit to the cottage that night should have played right into Elêna's hands. An independent witness to Armistice's fragile state of mind could only help in her campaign. With the effects of Mexican Mint only temporary, timing had been important.

Dusk began a little after nine pm, so Elêna had given Armistice her evening cup of camomile tea at around eight-thirty and waited, watching closely for signs of the added herb taking effect. Half an hour later she led the disorientated Armistice out through the trees, where they were unlikely to bump into anyone and left her wandering aimlessly and talking to an imaginary being in a quiet back road to await whatever fate may decide for her.

If she wandered away and was found, Elêna would play the part of a frantically worried relative who would only take legal control of her 'aunt's' affairs because there was no other choice, and an accident requiring hospitalisation would have the same result.

However, if she died, perhaps a driver speeding along a dark road, that would solve all her problems. She had congratulated herself and poured a glass of wine in pre-celebration certain that it would be at least an hour before she had to telephone the Police to report Armistice missing.

The knock at the door had taken her by surprise. She switched off the Shakira CD she had been listening to, set her magazine down on the sofa and peered round the curtain of the front window. Armistice was sitting in the front seat of a dark car and a young man was standing at the door. It was too soon…but? How could she turn this to her advantage?

She knuckled roughly at her eyes to make them red, messed up her hair, checked her distraught expression looked as it should in the hall mirror, and ran to the door, breathless and tearful. As they brought Armistice into the house, she had played her part to perfection until she saw the half empty

glass of wine and open magazine. How could she have had time to relax with a glass of wine if she had been searching the village for her missing aunt? If he noticed them he would know she had been lying. She cursed her own stupidity.

She had to get him out of the house quickly. The sooner he left, the less chance he would have of seeing anything that did not add up. It was less than ten minutes later when he left without giving any indication of suspicion. It looked as if the fool had not noticed her clumsiness and, when she needed it, he would be able to confirm the condition Armistice had been in when he found her. But she was still annoyed with herself for being so lax. She could not afford to make that kind of mistake again.

For the next day or so, Elêna was on edge. Even the power she felt flow through her when she held the precious amulet was not enough to still her fears. There was still the possibility that Stuart might have thought something was amiss and mentioned it to someone, his mother perhaps? Would he have seen the doctor and talked to him about Armistice?

She had been even more concerned when, just the day before, he had driven slowly up to the cottage and stopped. She had watched him from behind the net curtains. He seemed to be trying to make up his mind whether to call in or not. At one point he got out of the car and walked as far as the gate before shaking his head and getting back in the car. She heaved a sigh of relief as he drove away but could not help wondering what he had wanted. Had he been about to visit Armistice or was it her he wanted to see?

The way he looked at her that night showed he found her attractive and she had to admit he was good looking, but she was not interested. There was nothing she wanted from this village other than the doubloons. Once she had them she would be ready to go.

She felt a slight twinge of pity for Armistice. She was a nice lady, but it was no concern of hers if people thought she was losing her mind. Elêna briefly thought about abandoning her plans and making a run for it when Stuart had brought Armistice home but the amulet had told her not to lose her courage. She still had work to do. She would not leave without the gold coins. They must be in the cottage somewhere. Tlaloc would help her in her search. He guaranteed her escape and future success. He had told her so.

She had begun to relax; convinced her concerns over Stuart's visit to the house had been unwarranted but then, Charlie and the boy had let themselves in, uninvited and unannounced, through the back door and she had been forced to think quickly. She had meant to knock over Armistice's

tea but had not been quick enough. Armistice had begun drinking it before she could stop her. But even their seeing Armistice having one of her 'turns' had produced no repercussions from the old lady's so-called caring friends and the incident appeared to have gone without consequence.

Even Charlie's threatening comments had come to nothing. As each day passed Elêna felt more secure but was growing impatient to leave. If she could just find the coins, she could be on her way never to be heard of again. Yesterday she increased the number of times she used the sage keeping Armistice either confused by her blackouts or hallucinating for most of the day. She would double the dose tomorrow.

It would only take a week of that kind of dosage before Armistice's mind would be so badly damaged she would be in a perpetual state of bewilderment and have to be put away 'for her own safety'. If, by that time, Elêna was still there, she would have access to all the personal effects, bank account, cottage deeds, everything would be hers while the old lady ended her days in a nursing home. If the coins were not in the house, she must have hidden them somewhere, possibly in a bank or with a solicitor. Wherever they were, she would find them. No-one would be able to prevent it, not even that Charlie.

She thought again about the shocked look on his face as he witnessed the change in Armistice's behaviour and realised that could turn out better for her. He and the boy, clearly saw Armistice seem perfectly normal one minute and acting so bizarrely the next. That could work in her favour as it proved how ill Armistice was and how much her poor, unwell aunt needed her. Just a little more patience and holding her nerve and she would be gone. Tanith's identity would come to an end and she would become Angelina Mattiolli from that day on.

She heard the backdoor close and looked out of her bedroom window. Armistice had a basket of clean laundry and was heading for the washing line. Bandit squeezed under the fence and ran up to her purring. Elêna saw her put down the basket and pick up the cat. That precious animal of hers would keep her busy for a while which suited Elêna very well.

She had also taken the plastic box in which she kept food for ravens. Elêna saw it balancing on top of the pile of washing. One of the ravens, she was unsure which one, flew down from one of the trees into the garden and landed on Armistice's shoulder.

Again, it was a beautifully warm sunny morning but held a warning of extreme heat later in the day. Armistice loved being in the garden at any time but tended to stay indoors in the shade when the temperature rose. But at this comfortable time of the day, she happily stayed as long as she

167

could with the ravens and now that her precious cat had joined her, she was likely to be out there for some time.

Elêna watched the huge bird pacing agitatedly, head bobbing up and down, across the woman's shoulders. She despised the ravens, hated them even more than the cat. She would be sure to smash their eggs before she left.

She watched Armistice carry Bandit to the wooden bench situated at the side of the shed and sit down, cuddling and talking to it as if it understood her. Stupid woman! But it would keep her occupied for long enough for another search for the coins. She had already had a good look in the study. They were not there and there were no documents about them in the desk or filing cabinet. They were definitely not in the spare room where she slept. She had checked every drawer, shelf and even tried testing for squeaky floorboards in case the old woman had stashed them under the floor.

There was only one room left. In Armistice's bedroom she peered out of the window to check she was still occupied with her cat. She was. There was no sign of the raven and she assumed it had returned to its nest inside the shed. Elêna opened the wardrobe door and carefully sorted through the clothes on each shelf. Nothing! She was looking for a small carved wooden chest containing the gold Spanish coins Tanith had told her of. They were worth thousands of pounds and, with the money she had already her future life of luxury was assured.

She checked the window again. Armistice had put Bandit down and was hanging out the washing with the cat rubbing around her legs. Next she would feed the birds. She would have to hurry. Feeding those damn birds would not take long. She went over to the bed, knelt down and looked underneath. There she found a box. Excitedly, she dragged it out, opened it expectantly, but was disappointed to find it full of photographs. She grabbed a handful angrily and started to flick through them. There were papers there too. Perhaps there would be something about the doubloons amongst them?

She put the photographs on the floor beside her and began scanning the papers. Engrossed in her search it took a while before she realised she was no longer alone. Bandit appeared at her side. He hissed spitefully, his hackles sprung out like brushes. She turned to shoo him away and there was Armistice.

'Are you looking for something, Tanith dear?' Armistice asked. Her voice pleasantly light, but her eyes brittle and cold. 'Did you find what you were looking for?' She moved forward, her elderly but elegant body straight and proud. She took the papers from the stunned girl.

'I…I was looking for a book to read.'

'There's plenty in the study, as you know. Why didn't you look in there instead of searching under my bed?'

Bandit spat. His hackles rose and he uttered a growling yowl.

'He really doesn't like you, does he?' she said in a matter-of-fact voice. 'I had hoped he would have got over that by now, but then he's a very good judge of character and it's quite strange you know,' Armistice said, picking Bandit up where he clambered onto her shoulder, 'he only dislikes people he doesn't trust.'

This Armistice was totally different from the friendly, silly old woman Elêna had got to know. This Armistice was strong, confident and very sure of herself. Elêna felt her own confidence ebbing.

'I don't know why he doesn't trust me. I've done nothing to hurt him…or you.'

'That's more by luck than intention, I believe.' Armistice looked down at the scattered photographs. 'Put those away please. They're my memories and private. They are nothing to do with you.'

Elêna felt the icy blast of controlled fury emanating from the older woman. She hesitated. 'Yes…I'm sorry.' She thought quickly. 'I was just trying to see if there were any pictures of my parents or grandparents. You understand,' she ended lamely.

'Of course I understand, but you could have asked. Did you think I would withhold anything of family history from a fellow family member?' There was a sharp edge to her voice.

'I…didn't really think about it,' Elêna continued her pretence. 'It was a spur of the moment thing.' Still on her knees, she picked up the photographs and returned them to the box, while Armistice stood over. For the first time, Elêna felt intimidated by this surprisingly commanding woman. When all the photographs were back in the box, Armistice handed her the papers. 'They belong in there too.'

Bandit sprang from Armistice onto the bed and glared, his claws clearly showing, very close to Elêna's face, his tail wagging furiously.

Elêna laid the papers on top of the photographs, closed the lid slowly and slid the box back to its place under the bed. She got to her feet and glared in cold hatred at Bandit who now prowled, without slipping, up and down the brass bed frame, angrily swishing his tail. 'Don't tell me your cat's distrust of me has spread to you.'

Bandit's eyes narrowed and again he spat at her viciously.

'No, it's not that my dear,' Armistice replied coolly wandering over to the window. She moved one of the curtains aside and peered down into the

garden. 'Ah…Mélusine and Taliesin. I love to see them together…such beautiful birds, don't you agree? They're very clever, you know,' Elêna wondered where this turn of conversation was leading, 'extremely effective communicators, especially Mélusine.'

Elêna said nothing. Armistice was playing with her, dragging this farce out. They both knew the score. Armistice turned back to face Elêna, her expression stony. 'Bandit's actually got nothing to do with this matter except he's quicker on the uptake than I am.' She stroked the angry cat. 'My, my, you have upset him.'

A noise at the window caught the attention of both women. Mélusine and Taliesin landed on the window ledge and paraded up and down. 'It seems all my friends feel the same way.'

Elêna opened her mouth to speak but Armistice stopped her.

'Charlie didn't trust you either, you know.'

'That stupid, interfering old man,' Elêna seethed. 'He might be big but like you, he's old and a fool and so is the boy. They can do nothing against me!'

'He didn't trust you at all,' Armistice continued, ignoring the interruption. You didn't know he has friends all over the world, did you? And you made a massive mistake in thinking he's stupid.'

Elêna paled. Armistice went on, 'He even has friends in Mexico,' she gave a hint of a smile, 'and it seems, *Elêna*,' the smile faded, 'that he knows all about you and why you're here.' She approached the astounded girl and pulled out the neck chain revealing the amulet. 'Ah, yes. Tlaloc.'

Elêna snatched the amulet from her and tucked it roughly back inside her shirt. 'Tlaloc has guided me, he has helped me. You have no power over me.'

Armistice laughed. 'You really are quite foolish aren't you? Tlaloc does not exist. Has never existed, he is born of man's superstition. His influence is all in your mind.'

Elêna sprang at her. 'That is not true! It's a lie, old woman! Tlaloc has commanded me to restore his religion. When I have…,' she hesitated, 'when I have what I am looking for, I will go to Europe and he will guide me.'

'Oh, my dear, your eyes are like those of the jaguar,' Armistice declared, unafraid. 'You really have been possessed by something, possibly insanity or possibly you have a talent for putting images in people's mind, something like hypnotism, but it is not Tlaloc.' She spoke with no anger, in a controlled sympathy which enraged Elêna all the more.

Bandit had stopped pacing and sat on the bed watching the exchange between the two women while the ravens waited, wings flapping furiously, on the window ledge.

Elêna thought quickly. This turn of events had never occurred to her. In all her scheming she had never thought of a contingency plan for what she would do if Armistice caught her out. In her mind Armistice would be in hospital or a nursing home. Now she was faced with this unpredicted situation and, Armistice, emotionally calm, had the upper hand.

'You know, I'm not as stupid as you thought,' Armistice frowned. 'I know you drugged me and left me out in the road the other night. What did you hope to gain by that? Have me run down and killed,' a thought occurred to her. 'No,' it was as if a light had gone on allowing her to see clearly for the first time. 'No, you wanted me to be found, wandering in body and in mind. You wanted a witness to the fact that I was losing my sanity. How very clever!' She moved nearer. 'But Charlie scuppered your plans, didn't he? It was not wise to dismiss him as stupid. You were so confident you became foolish, lax. Charlie found out exactly what happened to Tanith through his extraordinary contacts.' She went to the window where the ravens waited for her. 'He passed a message to me through Mélusine, didn't he my pretty?' she stroked the bird affectionately before turning back to Elêna to see what the effect of this revelation.

She leaned in towards the anxious girl and said softly, close to her face. 'Yes, we know the truth about what happened to Tanith.'

Elêna choked back a cry. 'No, no. That cannot be. I am protected by Tlaloc. He promised me the gold, that I would be free!' She wrung her hands. How could this have happened?

Armistice's dark eyes gazed down without compassion at the angry, frightened girl. 'You have committed some terrible acts in the name of Tlaloc but it was you, not Tlaloc who carried out these deeds and it is you who will pay for them. Not him. Murder, theft, forgery…poisoning, is there anything else I should add to the list? What about the terrible pain you caused your parents?'

Elêna looked away. Her hands shook and her usually olive coloured skin paled.

'What I don't understand is why you came here, why did you have to take Tanith's identity? Why couldn't you let the poor girl lie in peace?'

Elêna looked at Armistice standing so calm and unruffled, so in command, it made her angry. For a moment she thought about trying to bluff it out, but it was far too late for that. There would be no more fooling this woman.

'My name is Elêna Vasquez.' She held her head high and refused to lower her eyes.

Armistice sat down on the window seat. 'Yes, I already know that, but thank you for your honesty at last. Now, even though I have a good idea, I would like to know from you why you came here and what you hoped to achieve by your deceit.'

Trying to play down the enormity of her crimes, at first Elêna thought she would try to gain the older woman's sympathy and asked her to sit beside her on the bed, but Bandit sprang to the floor between them blocking the way. Armistice smiled lovingly at him. 'I'll stay where I am, I think.'

As Elêna began her explaining, Armistice showed great patience as she listened to the story of her poor upbringing and how she had run away to the convent to save her family the cost of having to feed and clothe her. She explained how she had met the real Tanith and learned her story. When she finished Armistice got to her feet.

'That's a very nice fairy story, but other people grow up in poverty. They do not commit murder, fraud or theft. There is nothing in your story that justifies the terrible acts you committed nor does it explain why you came here. Why did you wish to use Tanith's identity? What did you hope to achieve by it? I have nothing of monetary value. As you see, I live very simply here.' She moved towards the door and the waiting, crouching cat. 'I'd like the truth, please.'

Elêna followed her. 'It's your own fault. You were stupid enough to allow a stranger into your home, foolish enough to believe without question that a stranger was a relative. I typed the letter you received from Mother Superior…'

'Oh, I'd guessed that,' Armistice put in moving slowly away towards the stairs. 'It wasn't actually from her at all, was it?'

'It is your own fault you were deceived,' Elêna raged at her and moved closer.

'Yes, you're right,' Armistice agreed with her. 'I suppose it wasn't the convent I phoned either?' Elêna nodded. 'I had already left the convent and rented a room for a few days. The number you phoned belonged to that room. It was me you spoke to.'

'Very clever my dear. Your plans were very elaborate,' Armistice towered over her by some five inches or so, her expression sad, wistful. 'When I heard about how the flood had destroyed the clinic, that Luis and Tabitha had died and Tanith was missing, I was devastated. In one night my entire family was gone.' She looked down at Elêna. 'You cannot understand the joy, yes… pure joy when I heard Tanith was still alive but

now, you've taken it all away and it hurts more now having had that hope and seeing it dashed…but I still don't know why?'

Elêna leaned against the wall. 'The doubloons. Tanith told me about the Spanish coins your family stole and hid when they wrecked that Spanish ship.'

That provoked a peel of laughter from Armistice. 'But that was two centuries ago!' Elêna failed to see the joke. She pushed Armistice hard against the opposite wall. Armistice, although taller, was still weakened by the poisonous herbs and no match for the youthful strength of Elêna who easily overcame her. Bandit jumped, flew at her face, his claws scratched her cheek but she threw him to the floor and he scurried away down the stairs. Armistice continued chuckling. Even though she had been physical assaulted, she still found something about the situation amusing.

'Why are you laughing? What is so funny?' Elêna asked smearing blood from the scratches away with the heel of her hand, while holding Armistice with the other.

'The reason you came here. I don't have the coins any more. They're all gone. That's what's so funny. All this…masquerade, all these crimes…for nothing.' Armistice pulled away and made for the stairs as Elêna stared at her blankly.

'Gone, gone where? I don't believe you. You're lying,' she screamed, her green eyes blazed with fury as she desperately tried to understand how everything had gone so wrong.

'No,' Armistice had stopped laughing. 'I'm not lying. You see that's the funny thing. You have come all the way here, done all this for nothing. What a waste of a young life,' she pushed Elêna away. 'How do you think Luis and Tabitha got the money to set up their clinic?'

A terrible look of comprehension crept into Elêna's eyes as reality crashed in on her. The landing spun…she heard Tlaloc laughing.

'You know, this is just too ironic,' Armistice gave a sympathetic smile. '*No!*'

'Oh, yes! Luis Sanchez was an exceptionally good doctor who wanted to help his village, put something back so to speak. I had the coins kept at a bank; they meant nothing to me, ill-gotten gains as they were. It made sense to put them somewhere where they could do most good. I had them auctioned and they raised an enormous amount of money, enough to set up the clinic and maintain it for several years. It was such a tragedy that the floods ended all the good work done there and Luis and Tabitha had to die and then, of course, poor young Tanith.'

Elêna stared at her, confused, unable to take in what had happened. At the top step, Armistice turned.

'Have you ever heard of Fool's Gold, my dear? There is an ore called iron pyrites. Those who have never seen real gold often mistake it simply because they see what they want to see. You've been deceived, as they say.'

In frustration and disappointed rage Elêna threw herself at Armistice who lost her footing, struggled to grasp the banister but missed and toppled with a heartrending cry down the winding staircase. She was dead when her body hit the stone floor.

At the top of the stairs, Elêna listened for the sound of Armistice moving but it was quiet. Being unable to see around the bend in the staircase from her position, she was unable to see the result of her action. Why was there no sound of movement?

She called out. 'Armistice? *Armistice?*' There was no response. Slowly, one step at a time, she crept down the stairs to where they turned and saw the lifeless body twisted into a strange angle. *Dead.* She had not meant to kill her. She thought of Ortega. She had meant to kill him; he was a low-life and disgusting. All she had wanted was the coins. Why had everyone made it so difficult for her?

Chapter Thirty One

Armistice Jenks lay at the bottom of the staircase, her body twisted, her right leg pointing upwards on the stairs and the left twisted from the knee underneath her, her head and neck propped against the door. At the half-way bend in the stairs, Elêna looked down in horrified disbelief at the aftermath of the scuffle just a few brief seconds ago. Her palms placed on the walls either side of the staircase, her thoughts turned to escape.

Bandit crept into view. So low to the floor, his belly touching the tiles, he edged towards the body of his mistress and nuzzled her hands. Elêna could not see Merlin but she could hear him; he was somewhere out of view whimpering softly. She flopped down to sit on the stairs, her heart beating wildly. Bandit turned his hate-filled eyes in her direction. He made no sound, there was none of the usual bristling, but the look he gave her was one of pure animal detestation.

Merlin appeared. He did not look up. In his distress he did not even seem to notice her as he nudged at Armistice's face with his nose and licked her face, trying to wake her up, not understanding why she continued to lie there, not moving. Elêna stared, fascinated by the devotion of the pair, united in grief as they nudged and nuzzled at the dead woman in a vain and desperate attempt to rouse her.

Unsure how much time had passed, Elêna eventually realised that she needed to get away. The longer she stayed the greater chance of being caught. For the briefest moment she argued with herself that if she called for an ambulance, she might get away with saying Armistice had had an accident. She thought about what she would say. 'Armistice fell. I tried to save her but I was too far away', or, 'I was in the garden when I heard a noise and found her like this.' Would they work? Possibly, she reasoned, but then there was her Will. Armistice would not have had time to change it in her favour and, as the coins were gone for good, was there any point in

staying around and waiting for what might be months while Armistice's Estate was sorted out? Briefly she was tempted to brave it out but then she thought of Stuart and Charlie, and even the boy. It had been a sudden death and there would have to be an Inquiry. They would be asked questions and, if they had any doubts, it could go against her. No, she would be better to leave before Armistice was found. It could be hours before that happened and she would be well out of the area by then.

Decision made, she dashed back up to her bedroom, snatched up the slim black handbag concealed in the gap beside the wardrobe and, abandoning the rest of her belongings, ran down the stairs until she reached the last few steps. She slowed, inhaled and carefully placing her feet, stepped over the body, not looking at Armistice's face to avoid the expected look of accusation in her eyes but, no matter how hard she fought against it, she felt compelled to look, almost as if an unseen hand was forcing her head to turn towards the corpse. Curiously there was no recrimination, Armistice's open eyes held no reproach. Her warm personality was still there, even a hint of a smile played on her mouth.

It occurred to Elêna that in death Armistice was mocking her. She had expected to see accusation and condemnation. That would have been easier to deal with but instead, her expression was almost serene and that was too much to bear.

An unpleasant sensation beginning in the pit of her stomach burned upwards and rose until she felt she would retch. Why did she feel as though she wanted to cry? This old woman meant nothing to her. No-one did. And she had lied about Tlaloc; he *was* with her, he *did* guide her.

Hearing her footfalls on the stairs, Bandit and Merlin sloped away from Armistice; Merlin to hide under the table while Bandit sprang from the table to the top of a cupboard where he slunk away to a dark corner, only his angry jade-coloured eyes were visible.

Elêna paid them no attention until she drew level with the table when a deep unrelenting snarl emanating from under the tablecloth turned her blood cold. Merlin, lips curled in a vicious snarl revealing two rows of terrifyingly pointed teeth crept slowly toward her. With every step his growl grew louder, more savage, his hackles bristled upwards, his eyes narrowed. This was no longer the sociable pet. He was primeval, wolf-like, acting on a timeless instinct to protect or avenge.

Simultaneously, Bandit dropped from his place of concealment onto the table then to the floor, spitting and yowling, vicious and feral. Together they stole forward, Bandit, belly low to the floor, ready to spring at the first opportunity, Merlin, cautious and wary, both watching for any sudden

movement. They were prepared to attack but aware she was capable of defending herself.

Never taking her eyes off the vengeful pair who were clearly determined to make her pay for her crime, she inched backwards to the door casting quick glances behind to make sure her path was clear, her knuckles white with tension as she gripped her bag close to her chest. If she could just get to the door!

Merlin edged closer, a fraction ahead of Bandit, but still did not pounce. He was biding his time, toying with her fear. Level with the fireplace she grabbed a chair from under the table and wielded as a shield against the relentlessly advancing animals.

Bandit jumped on the table and sprang at her, landing on her chest and scratching her face and neck again. She threw him onto the table where he overbalanced and landed heavily on the floor. He staggered to his paws and shook his head in shock.

Merlin, using the distraction of Bandit's attack, circled around the chair and sprang forward going for her legs, but she swung the chair at him and blocked his charge. She was almost at the door when two black shapes screamed in through the open window and flew at her face. Taliesin pecked viciously at her cheek and she struck out with her bag to protect her eyes. Mélusine came at her from behind, clawing and pecking at her hair and scalp. Blood flowed from her wounds on her face and neck, but she was too busy fighting them off to worry. Taliesin swooped down for a second time but this time she was ready for him. She caught him by the neck and threw him violently onto the sink unit where he landed with a horrible thud, his neck and wing broken.

Enraged Mélusine redoubled her attack. Faced with the combined efforts of two furious animals and the outraged bird, Elêna knew she would not make it to the back door. Backing away she fled to the door leading to the hall and slammed it shut behind her, trapping them inside, scratching and pecking at the barrier between them and their enemy. Before opening the front door, she took a deep breath then, clutching her talon-damaged bag tightly, walked briskly down the path not noticing a red van parked a few yards away to the left. At the gate she looked back. She was free.

'Are you alright, dear?' A woman got out of the van and walked towards her. 'Have you had some kind of accident?' She was staring at Elêna's scratched and bloodied face and hands.

Elêna froze. In her haste she had forgotten the wounds inflicted by the ravens and Bandit. She turned to the woman, a sweet smile etched onto her

tense face. 'Er…no…not really. Auntie and I have had a problem with Bandit and I need to get the Vet…Mr Hedges, I think Auntie said.'

The woman nodded. 'Yes, Dan Hedges, that's right. But surely Armistice can deal with it. She never asks for the vet.'

'I know but he put up such struggle, Auntie said he must be in a lot of pain and because she's so close to him she's too upset to deal with him herself. She wants the Vet to take over this time.'

'Hop in,' the woman invited, opening the passenger side door. 'I'll give you a lift. It's just outside the village about half a mile away.' She gave a sympathetic smile. 'I can see he put up a fight,' she said, turning the key in the ignition.

Climbing into the passenger seat, Elêna threw a final, relieved look towards the cottage as the van pulled away. They had not been able to follow her, thank Tlaloc. She was on her way.

'I'll drop you at the surgery,' the woman continued. 'It's just a few minutes away.'

'Er…no,' Elêna snapped, to her companions surprise.

'No? But I thought you wanted the vet?'

'Sorry, I didn't mean to sound so abrupt,' she apologised. 'I guess I'm a little strung out. Auntie thinks he's been shot by an air rifle,' she said hoping that explanation sounded plausible. This close to freedom she could not afford to arouse any suspicion. 'We phoned the surgery but he's at Winterne Manor…the stables. Auntie thought it would be quicker if I went up to get him while she gets Bandit calmed.'

'Well, once you've done that you'd better see to yourself and get your face cleaned up. Bandit's usually very docile…'

Not that I've seen, thought Elêna.

'…he must be awfully sore to do that. Anyway it won't take long to get to the stables and I was heading up to the Manor anyway. Up this road, there's a wide track through the wood, it'll take about ten minutes less that way.'

Elêna pulled down the sunshade above the windscreen. There was a darker patch where a mirror had been. Her face was beginning to hurt. She would need to get herself cleaned up before the scratches became infected.

'Trying to check your wounds, eh? Sorry, the mirror fell off ages ago and we've never stuck it back on,' the woman glanced over at her with a kind smile. 'You know, one or two look deep enough to scar, but Armistice has probably got some potion to help them heal.'

Well if she does, it's too late for me to find out, Elêna thought, bitterly resigning herself to being scarred by those damned animals. 'I guess I do look a bit of a fright.'

The woman nodded. 'I'm afraid you do, dear.'

The woman's constant chatter got on her nerves as they drove along the tree lined road.

'Course, you'll be Tanith. We haven't met yet, but I've heard all about you,' she said as Elêna forced a smile. 'I'm Connie Askam. We run the Post Office and the village shop. I'm sure you'll be paying us a…'

'I'm sorry,' Elêna broke in, 'please stop. I feel unwell.'

Connie obligingly pulled over and stopped the van. No sooner had she put the brake on than Elêna got out and ran to the verge and, turning her back made horrible retching noises. Connie left the van and walked over to see if she could help.

'Is there anything I can do, dear? You look very pale.'

The words were hardly out of her mouth when Elêna thumped her violently in the chest, knocking her off her feet and taking the wind out of her lungs. As Connie lay on the grass struggling to breathe, Elêna darted back to the van, started it up and sped off erratically. Only ever having had a few driving lessons, she was not a competent driver but in her desperation to escape, she did not care if she did it correctly. She was on a quiet country road and unlikely to be meet much traffic. In a couple of miles she would dump the van. She had only gone a few metres when a car approached from the opposite direction. She put her foot down hard on the accelerator. They would find the woman and she had to put some distance between her and the village.

-o0o-

Jerrill had woken that morning to find his neck-chain missing. After a fruitless search of his sleeping quarters he decided he had time to return to the glade before his meeting with Halmar. He remembered his boisterous dancing after the wedding and thought it likely it had been broken there.

Searching around the glade, under the trees, and where the tables had been, he eventually found the precious chain, broken, just as he guessed it would be, in a clump of grass close to where he had been dancing. He picked it up and laid it on his palm, lovingly looking at the image of his twins. He would mend the chain after he had spoken to Halmar; he might even show it to him.

179

Slipping the chain into his pocket he set off towards the cavern. He had only gone a short way when he realised it was later than he thought and decided to cut across the road to save time. Under normal circumstances this would have been unthinkable; he hated the idea of being out in daylight when there was an increased chance of being seen by humans. But he was in a hurry.

-o0o-

The van was more difficult to drive than Elêna thought it would be, and she struggled to keep control of the stiff gear lever. With the road empty of traffic ahead and her heart beating a little more steadily, she felt more reassured of her safe escape. The engine raced, she needed to change gear. The lever stiffened again and stuck, she wrestled with it. With a clear road ahead, she looked down at the obstinate gearstick to release it. A thud! She looked up just as the van went out of control and skidded down the verge and into a ditch.

She was very shaken but unhurt. The driver's door was stuck fast against the grassy side of the ditch and could not be opened, so she slid across to the passenger's side and clambered out. She looked back up to the road. A small person, a child lay in the road. Whoever it was, they were very still. Reaching back into the van she grabbed her bag and not looking at the shape in the road, she took one enormous breath to compose herself, before fleeing to the cover of the trees.

Chapter Thirty Two

When Piggybait and Clap-trap climbed over the wall of the well, they found Saldor sleeping peacefully in an ivy covered corner of the room leaning against his sackcloth bag; his unkempt grey hair flopped across his face. He stirred in his sleep, stretched his skinny legs and turned in the opposite direction, still snoring through his open mouth.

'Ah…don't he look cute?' Piggybait put on a baby-ish voice.

'I'll give him cute,' Clap-trap sounded surly. 'Now that we've found him and he's alright, I'm not sure if I'm relieved or peeved.' He stood over Saldor, wondering whether to hug or kick him awake.

'Don't be like that,' Piggbyait put his arm around his friend's shoulder. 'He must have had a good reason to run off.'

Saldor shifted position and stirred at the sound of voices. He opened his eyes and stared at his friends in terror; it was as if he had no idea who they were. Backing away, he tried to hide under ivy while they looked on, appalled. What had happened to him to alarm him to such an extent he did not know old and trusted friends?

Gibbering amongst the foliage and huddling close to the wall, his hands clutched tightly to his chest, Saldor was a pitiable sight.

Clap-trap, his irritability forgotten, made to approach their friend, but Piggybait reached out to stop him, restraining him by the arm. 'We can't rush this. It looks as if he's going to need careful handling,' Piggybait shook his head sadly.

'Yes, but what in the name of Alfheim did this to him?'

'Or who?'

Piggybait sat cross-legged on the green-carpeted floor, Clap-trap sat beside him. They did not speak. Saldor sobbing eased but he flinched nervously each time he found the courage to look their way.

Piggybait smiled. 'Hello Snoredor. Remember us?' he said softly, taking off his cap. He nudged Clap-trap who followed his example allowing his long silver-blond hair to fall to his shoulders.

Saldor turned away again, making himself as small as possible, cowering as far into the corner as he could squeeze himself.

'Primola's making honey bread tonight, Clap-trap, did you know that?' Piggybait began. 'Do you think Jossamel's going to be back in time for it?' he winked at his friend, who took up his meaning.

'So *Primola*'s making honey bread is she? If *Primola's* baking you can be sure *Jossamel* will be there.'

The repeated names filtered through Saldor's tortured mind.

'P...Primla?' he stuttered.

'That's right Saldor, Primola,' Piggybait smiled gently coaxing the memories back. Clap-trap allowed himself a sigh.

'Joss?' Saldor eased himself away from the wall.

'Saldor,' Clap-trap began, feeling rather guilty for his earlier impatience, 'do you know who we are?'

Brushing aside the long lines of ivy he had been trying to hide behind, Saldor examined their faces. The voices had seemed familiar but two faces had been in the forefront of his thoughts for so many days that it was difficult for him to see beyond them. It took a few minutes of silent staring before a sparkle shone through his eyes and with an ecstatic cry he threw himself spontaneously onto his unprepared friends.

'Piggy...Cla-tra!' He screamed with laughter, rolling around with them like young children wrestling.

When the joyous reunion had calmed, Saldor seemed more rosy cheeked and animated than either of the friends could recall ever having seen before.

'Saldor, we've been worried about you. Why did you run off? Prim's been out of her mind,' Piggybait asked.

Saldor took hold of a long thin branch of ivy and, without looking up, began picking off the dead leaves. 'Tarryn...Tildor...I 'member.'

'What do you remember, Saldor?' Clap-trap asked gently, wondering if Saldor was up to facing those memories. Was he strong enough?

'Gave me seeds,' he shuddered. 'Bad pictures up here,' he pointed to his temples, '...member pixies. Twins told Saldor seeds...good,' he spoke in elfling fashion. A single tear brimmed in his right eye and trailed down his cheek. Neither of the friends spoke, leaving Saldor to say as much or as little as he wanted without prompting or distraction.

'Took me to pixies,' he trembled at the memory. 'Party…said it was a…party. They went away…left me…with pixies. Small cave…it was dark…rats…RATS!'

'If he wasn't dead I'd kill Tildor after I've finished with his brother,' Piggybait swore.

'You wouldn't be alone,' Clap-trap volunteered.

'Saldor, do you want to come home?' Clap-trap asked, not prepared for the reaction.

Saldor huddled back under the ivy again. 'NO…no, not home…twins there. They want to hurt me,' he cried.

Piggybait got up and slowly, tenderly reached out to take the emotional Saldor's hand. 'Don't be scared, you can come home, the twins have gone.'

Saldor raised his eyes to search Piggybait's face, daring to hope that he was hearing the truth. 'True?'

'True,' Clap-trap corroborated.

'Home…take me home, please.'

Collecting Saldor's bag, Clap-trap checked that nothing had been left as witness to the fact that anyone had ever been there, while Piggybait helped Saldor over the well wall and down the ladder to the tunnel. Just before clambering over the wall to join them he could not resist a smile. Saldor here in the centre of his home all the time and the Chief had no idea. He was never going to let the Chief live this down.

Chapter Thirty Three

Charlie had contacts with elf clans all over the World and had earlier spent a little over twenty-four hours, dispatching messages throughout his network of tunnels to Central America. Within an hour he had received a response from Belantor of Florida giving him all the information he needed about Elêna Vasquez.

He now knew the village she had come from, how she had left, knew about the theft of money from the convent in Alvarez City and about the murder of Ortega. This background information had proved to be far worse than he had imagined, and had sent for Mélusine to give her a warning message to pass on to Armistice, telling her everything and urging her to meet him that evening to decide on what to do next.

He looked at his watch. Mélusine had left just over half an hour ago; plenty of time to have located Armistice and pass on his message. They had to play this carefully. One false move, one silly mistake and Elêna would know she had been found out. If they weren't careful she could escape the Law and Charlie wanted justice. Elêna would pay for her crimes but, he was not ready to face her with what they knew about her yet. They needed more evidence and it had to be from a source the Police and legal system would believe; information gathered by elves was unlikely to be taken seriously. Of course they could deal with her themselves, but as her crimes had originally been committed in Mexico, the authorities there would demand human justice and it was right they should. In the meantime, he must do nothing to tip her off they were on to her.

At least Saldor's return was one worry less for Charlie even though he was mystified that Saldor could have been hiding within his home, behind the locked door in the hallway, all the time and he had not known, had not sensed his presence. He was still unsure how to handle the Elêna situation, but at least with Saldor being safely home with the clan he could relax on

that account. The only excuse he had for his lack of intuition was that he had had too many things on his mind; worry over Armistice, the wedding, Avaroc. All these things must have clouded his judgement and weakened his sense of perception.

Piggybait said Saldor had looked so relieved when they had found him, he cried. He cried even more when he was informed Tarryn and Tildor had gone but it was not because he was sorry to have missed them.

On his return to the cavern, Primola had greeted Saldor with shrieks of tearful joy, alternately hugging and scolding him for an entire hour until the poor elf said pitifully that he wanted to go back to the well. That was when it dawned on her just how tired and ill he looked. Apologising profusely to him, she shooed everyone away, made sure he had a good meal he was able to eat in peace and then hustled him off for a well-earned and comfortable rest in his own room. Tired, thinner, and even more pallid than before and seeming a little befuddled by having been alone for so long, Primola decided Saldor was in no fit state to endure any further upset or excitement and issued orders, under pain of no more honey bread, that no-one was to tell him about anything that had happened during his absence; this meant the wedding, which he had forgotten all about, Ellien's coronation or Tildor's fatal accident, saying that he needed time to convalesce and there would be plenty of time for him to find out what he had missed as he recovered. And so, at least as far as the Saldor situation was concerned, there was a good resolution.

The Avaroc situation, Charlie had decided, could wait. Although Avaroc would show his hand at some time, it could be years before he made his move, in the meantime he needed to be watched, maybe even have his clan infiltrated to make sure they knew what he was up to. Charlie made a mental note to talk to Jerrill, Clap-trap and Piggybait about asking a few trusted volunteers to leave Winterne and join Avaroc's group. But it was not a priority. Armistice was.

Busy with his thoughts and listening to the Electric Light Orchestra's, Out of the Blue, on his MP3 player, Charlie did not hear Merlin's anguished howl. Having arranged to meet Armistice later and convinced Mélusine would have carried out her mission by now, Charlie decided it was time to concentrate on his job. There was a possibility of the fungal disease, Sudden Oak Death, spreading to Winterne and he regularly examined the oak trees for the first indications, blackened sections of bark but, so far there were no signs of it for which he was very thankful. He had enough to deal with.

He was working right in the centre of the dense woodland where the sun blazed through the trees raising the temperature of the static air and a feeling of weariness came over him. It was time for a break.

Plonking himself down on a grassy mound he brushed his sweaty hair off his forehead and reached into his rucksack for his water bottle. He felt rather than heard the cries. The air pulsed with a strange vibration that tugged at his heart. What now?

Chapter Thirty Four

Enraged at Elêna having slammed the door in their faces, Bandit and Merlin scratched and pawed at the closed door, whining and yowling in frustration.

Mélusine, however, was not to be put off; she was determined to give chase. Incensed at seeing her enemy flee and, bent on revenge at the death of her mate and Armistice, she flew through the gap in the open window to the roof and watched as her quarry got into the red van and followed her from above. She saw the van stop and waited on a telegraph pole, black eyes glinting as she spied as the women talked on the grass verge.

When Elêna knocked the woman down, Mélusine bobbed her head up and down and flapped her wings furiously until Elêna got back in the van. She flew closer, observing Elêna from a nearby branch as she started up the engine and drove away leaving the woman groaning and trying to stagger to her feet. She took to the air again with Elêna wholly unaware of her presence.

From her vantage point a few feet above the vehicle, Mélusine saw a small hooded figure dart, head down, out of the trees without looking left or right. The van zigzagged and slowed. Recognising the elf, Mélusine cried out a warning. He heard and looked up, saw his danger but it was too late, he tried to move out of the path of the vehicle, but it swerved in his direction, gained speed. He fell under the wheels.

Mélusine knew instinctively he was dead. There was nothing she could do for him but she would rather die herself, abandon her brood to their fate rather than let this human escape.

The van swerved into a ditch. She saw Elêna struggle out and escape into the trees. Now they had her. She was in their territory.

Bandit, having seen Mélusine's departure, zipped through the open kitchen window and disappeared into the woods without really knowing where he was going but determined to find the murderer of his mistress.

Merlin, desperate to join in, bounded onto a chair to the sink unit and tried to squeeze through the narrow window. He watched Bandit vanish into the trees and howled in exasperation only to wag his tail wildly as Bandit re-emerged and scampered back to the cottage. He ran to the door and, standing on his hind legs, lifted the latch with his nose. Whimpering and clawing he finally got a paw far enough through to pull the door open a fraction, but his own weight worked against him and in frustration he chewed at the handle.

Then Bandit was at the door, mewing at him from the other side. Merlin stood back as Bandit pushed against the door allowing him space to get out. Together they raced into the trees after their quarry, Bandit in the lead, the back door still open. Mélusine was nowhere to be seen, nor was Elêna.

They stopped, wondering which way to go, but then Mélusine called to them. She was high above them and calling them to follow her. She descended to skim the treetops and swooped down over their heads, leading them on towards the enemy. This human had killed those she cared for most, Mrs Jenks and Taliesin. Her new brood would never know their father and she would make his killer pay.

Bandit and Merlin scampered after her, eight paws skimmed across the ground, shrinking the distance between them and their target. At this stage, Elêna was still unaware of their pursuit and confident of escape as she stayed at the edge of the wood keeping the road in sight, but concealed from anyone who might see her. It might be a long walk to the nearest bus stop but it would be worth it to escape. She may not have the money she had come for and disappointment over the coins weighed heavily on her, more heavily than the death of Armistice. That had just been an unfortunate accident and the woman with the van had been useful. She wondered about the child she had hit. It was too late to do anything about it now and they would be found soon enough. She couldn't possibly have been going fast enough to do any real damage. Could she?

As she waded through the mass of long grass and ferns, carefully avoiding clumps of stinging nettles and thistles, she clutched her bag tightly. She may not have much but she was clever enough to make her way in the world without it; she had done so before.

Not far behind her, Merlin sat down, threw his head back and howled into the air. His soul-rending cry carried beyond the wood and into the village where those who heard it stopped and shivered, wondering what pain could possibly cause such an awful sound. Within seconds Merlin's cry was answered by another. This time deeper, more throaty and mournful, the howl rang through the air, this time chilling the blood.

In a cottage at the other end of the village, Benny and Bjorn darted out of the open back door before Cathy could stop them. She shouted at them to come back but they sped around the side of the cottage and disappeared down the lane before she could stop them.

Chapter Thirty Five

Charlie tore off his headphones and heard the last strains of a terrible howl. Wolf! What could have brought him out in daylight? Something had happened, something dreadful. His stomach lurched as the sound of broad wings above made him look up. Owls! It was broad daylight and the owls were flying. Fear made his stomach heave. What were they doing? They were heading towards the river.

A disturbance to his left spun him round. Baron ignored him as he and his herd strode between the trees, the young staying close to their mothers. They usually roamed around the wood in no hurry unless they were panicked by something, then they darted between the trees to a place of safety, but this was different. They were striding purposefully along, not looking either side, heading in the same direction the owls had gone.

The ferns moved beside him and a pair of foxes followed the deer, five rabbits followed closely behind them, unafraid of their traditional enemies. The undergrowth, the paths, everywhere the wood teemed with movement, even adders and slow-worms slithered on their creamy-white bellies all moving in an unstoppable tide toward the river.

Above him the sky so darkened with flocks of birds, it could have been night-time. This was unnatural. Every kind of woodland creature was on the move, all heading in the same direction. In all his centuries of being, Charlie had never seen such a phenomenon.

His bag and MP3 player lying forgotten on the ground, music still playing, he joined the growing throng of animals, carefully placing his feet to avoid stepping on mice and the smaller animals as they broke out from the cover of the undergrowth, in every direction, to join the extraordinary, silent procession on the pathways.

An image broke into his thoughts. Armistice was falling, tumbling the length of the winding staircase and, for one awful moment, he was in her place, seeing what she had seen as a pair of cruel emerald eyes watched her rolling and twisting downwards, hurting and fearful, without compassion or care.

Tearing himself away Charlie raced through the wood to the familiar back garden of his friend. The back door was open, so was the kitchen window. There was no sign of the ravens. He stood on the threshold of the back door praying his vision had been wrong. But there was no Merlin to greet him as he entered the backdoor and no Bandit. Things were not as they should be.

He pushed open the inner door, not wanting to see what he knew he would find. His eyes first landed on the broken body of a raven lying on the draining board. It had met a violent end. The yellow leg ring meant it could only be Taliesin. Mélusine had vehemently, almost violently refused to wear one. He recalled the struggle Armistice had with the determined and obstinate bird trying to persuade her that it was for her own protection, but Mélusine would not yield.

But what he saw next stopped his breath. Armistice lay at the bottom of the stairs, one leg on the lower steps, the other under her. Apart from the strange angle of her neck and head, she looked so peaceful he could almost believe she was asleep but he knew, without touching her, she was dead.

'Oh...Armie!' he wailed, dropping to his knees beside her body. 'I'm too late. Why didn't I see this in time to stop it?'

He touched her arm. She was still warm. He lowered himself to the floor and, for a while he just sat looking down at her, heart aching, paralysed by the dreadful feeling of loss. Another of his dearest friends of so many years had gone, first Jimander, now Armistice. A terrible cry, like an animal in pain, escaped from deep inside him resounding through the room, ending in harrowing sobs. His huge shoulders stopped heaving, his weeping ceased and he reached out to close her eyelids. He thought of putting a cushion under her head to make her more comfortable or fetch a blanket to keep her warm but then remembered what was happening in the wood. He would tend to that later but, for now there were things he had to do; official things. Everything had to take its rightful course.

'I'd like to make you more comfortable, Armie, but I mustn't touch anything. David and Ernie have to see you first. Bless you.' He picked up the telephone and dialled Dr Brownlow's surgery first and then Ernie Rogers. The Police had to be informed of a sudden death.

Ten minutes later the doctor's car pulled up outside. Charlie went to let him in. 'Hello David. Looks like she fell down the stairs,' Charlie said sadly as the doctor walked by him into the hallway.

'It's very sad, Charlie. Very sad,' Dr Brownlow said spotting the dead bird at the far end of the room. 'Of course I didn't know her as well as you did, I can't remember the last time she came to see me on a professional basis. She never needed to,' he added almost as an afterthought.

Although the doctor had his job to do, he could not take his eyes away from the array of tapestries, charts and plants that hung on the walls. He stared, open-mouthed as the extraordinary spectacle. 'Remarkable woman,' he said.

Charlie coughed, reminding him of his duties. A knock at the front door signalled Ernie's arrival. Charlie let him in. He shook his head on seeing the body.

'This is rum do an' no mistake, Charlie. Any idea what happened?' Ernie asked soberly.

'Not reelly, Ernie,' Charlie answered, remembering to get into character. 'Jest looks loike she fell down stairs.' Shocked as he was, Charlie knew he had to keep his head and continue to be the person everyone thought they knew.

'Is her great-niece here? I'll need to talk to her,' Ernie said taking out his notebook.

'No she 'ent. In fac' Oi'd forgot all abou' 'er. Wi' poor Armistice loike this, she'd clean gone outta me 'ead.'

'Hiya Doc,' Ernie and the doctor were old friends. 'Accident?'

'Hello Ernie,' the doctor replied taking out a pad of forms. 'I'd say so. It certainly looks like it. But then it's your job to investigate that.'

Ernie nodded. His experienced eyes surveyed the room. 'Looks like there's been a bit of a tussle and that dead bird's a bit of a coincidence, don't you think, Charlie?'

Charlie nodded. 'Does seem a bit odd. If you don' need me fer a minute or two, Oi'll leave you both to it. Back in a minute,' Charlie said, pretending he needed the toilet. Stooping under the doorframe, he walked past Armistice's body and climbed the stairs.

Upstairs he entered the first bedroom. It was obvious from the clothes scattered around the room it was Elêna's. He opened the wardrobe door, searched under the bed and lifted the mattress; he inspected every part of the room. There were clothes, books, other things but there was no handbag, no purse, no passport, credit cards or cheque book. She had obviously left in a hurry. If a person needed to run away, as long as they

192

had enough money and a passport, they could leave the rest behind. Elêna had escaped.

His thoughts returned to the strange behaviour of the woodland animals, the missing Mélusine, Merlin and Bandit. Was it possible she had not escaped? Were the animals watching her? Once he had done everything he needed to do, he would go in search of them. If she had murdered Armie, they would know. They would know and they would not let her get away with it. Even if had been an accident, her actions had caused it. Either way she was to blame.

'Armie, my old friend, why did you trust so easily?'

Chapter Thirty Six

In the wood, Elêna, not knowing where she was going, followed the path she hoped would lead her to the nearest road and on to a town where she could mingle with other people and disappear. The sun shone in dappled light through the treetops and apart from the rustling leaves, there was no sound. Then came the howl; first one dog, then another and another. Their cries rising and surging, mingling in suffering until she clapped her hands over her ears to shut out the sound. But still she heard them.

The howl stopped. Slowly she lowered her hands and turned in a full circle searching the trees and undergrowth around her, now aware of a creeping sensation of being watched, but there was no-one about. Nothing moved, not even a butterfly, bee, nothing; not a living thing to be seen anywhere.

Fear fluttered in her heart for a moment, but it was brief. Tlaloc, her protector was with her. The silence, the stillness was strange but she would be away from this place soon. It was all over, she was free.

Putting her misgivings behind her, she slowed and began to enjoy the walk, forcing all thoughts of Armistice out of her head, seeing for the first time the beauty of the English countryside. She began dreaming of what she would do when she reached London. She was confident of the future. She still had the money in her bank accounts which would be more than enough to get her to Europe and provide for her for some time. All she had to do was find her way out of the wood and her new life could begin.

A rabbit appeared from the undergrowth on the left of the path, but instead of running away at the sight of her, it remained stubbornly staring at her. Another appeared at its side, then three more emerged from under the ferns a little further along on the right.

She wondered at this peculiar behaviour but they were only rabbits. She shrugged and walked on. The rabbits moved onto the path behind her and hopped slowly along in her wake. A few metres further along two foxes

appeared from the undergrowth. She thought it strange that they actually looked as if they were waiting for her.

A scratching noise behind made her turn. The rabbits were still there but now there were more of them; she counted quickly. There were at least twelve. She looked up as an owl flew onto a branch overhead. It stared unblinkingly at her. She shivered. An owl? In daylight? Owls meant bad luck. The rabbits and foxes were momentarily forgotten. Instinctively she crossed herself, thought about what she had done and laughed out loud. The owl flapped his wings, disturbed by the sound. She and the owl eyed each other as she passed under his branch. She moved on, the following rabbits and the pair of foxes pushed from her mind. She was not one for superstition, not like those fools at home. Home? She had no home.

Home could be wherever she chose; everything would be as she wanted from this time on.

An owl hoot broke into her thoughts. The same owl she had seen a few moments before alighted on a branch of an oak tree beside her. It was following her, so were the rabbits and, the foxes had joined them!

Another owl landed on the branch beside the first. They were joined by another and then, a little further along, a pair of magpies joined the crowd of birds and animals and they stared cruelly down at her.

Now she was afraid. She had seen an old film about birds and what they had done to a town and its people when they got together. This was bizarre! Natural enemies walking side by side!

A terrible howl startled her. The dense wood absorbed and distorted sound and she could not tell which direction it had come from, but it was close. Fear clutched at her stomach but she forced herself to move on. She had no other choice but to keep going and she quickened her pace.

'Get a grip,' she urged herself onward, 'you are being stupid!'

Above the sun blazed down from a cloudless sky and the still, trapped air was so warm she found it difficult to breathe, but she shivered as she forced one foot in front of the other, refusing to look back at the gathering animals, determined to ignore their presence. If she had looked back she would have been horrified to see the rabbits and foxes had now been joined by four badgers, several deer, mice, voles and springing along the branches, squirrels, pine martens, mink. There was now a silent, menacing host of creatures bent on justice.

Another howl! It chilled her blood. She had heard that sound before, outside her village. Her skin crawled, a cold shiver tingled her spine. No! El Lupe! A wolf? She shook her head. Her imagination was playing tricks.

No, it could not be, not here in England. There were no wolves outside of zoos. They just did not belong in quiet English villages.

But no matter how much she tried to shake off the irrational fear, the animals collecting behind her and that sound, that awful howl, made cold beads of perspiration appear on her forehead. A shadow scuttled across the path in front of her, then another, and another. She did not want to look up but could not stop herself. The raven! She had found her and she was not alone. Flying close behind Mélusine, kestrels, pigeons, blackbirds, sparrows and other birds she had not seen before. More and more birds joined this combined flock; the sky grew dark with them. What was happening?

Birds descended to nearby branches, silent, staring in an eerie threatening circle. She had to stay calm. She must not panic. Something told her they would be on her if she panicked. Keep them in vision, she told herself. Watch them. Stay calm. Make no sudden movements.

Turning slowly, she looked first one way, then another, her gaze switching from one tree to another, then down to the path where the animals still crept relentlessly forward. Wings flapped every time she changed direction; her heart beat rapidly, her breathing became shallow, fast. She could feel her pulse thumping in her head. Trying to look in all directions at the same time, she walked backwards, looking up and around, turning this way and that, terrified of the relentless army of animals and birds. She hardly dared to look up but her eyes were drawn upward to the upper branches.

Birds crammed almost every clear space looking down at her in a sinister silence. If only they would make a noise, that would be normal. She gripped the amulet. It felt cold, lifeless. Where was the warmth, the power that always flowed from it? Had Tlaloc abandoned her?

She had never been scared of anything in her life but now she understood terror. Changing direction, she sped up, broke into a run and darted down the only path clear of enemies. She could still get away. Feeling sick with fear, her breathing short and rapid, her heart thumping furiously, her attempt at escape was short-lived.

From nowhere her two main adversaries sprang onto the sandy path ahead of her and they were not alone. Merlin, teeth bared and slavering, and Bandit, fur standing on end, were accompanied by two silent but powerful large black dogs.

'*What?*' she screamed. '*What Do You Want?*' Her voice echoed back at her. She needed something to defend herself with. She looked around for something suitable. Trying to keep her eyes fixed on her enemies, she

spied a broken branch half hidden by ferns and slowly, very slowly, bent her knees to lower herself to a position where she could reach it, carefully stretching her hand out, her fingers inched their way toward the branch.

A wolf, concealed behind the dogs, sprang forward, his teeth bared and snarling, broke cover to stand between her and the branch. He made no further move as she backed away, at first crawling then scrambling to her feet, screaming hysterically as she blundered into the undergrowth.

He took his time padding after her, his mouth open in a hideous smile. He was in no hurry. She turned, running in reverse she was forced back to the path by more animals blocking her route. Rabbits hopped, in an unnatural truce, alongside foxes, owls ignored mice. Natural enemies gathered together, a temporary respite in normality allied against a common foe, forcing her to go the way they wanted. They left one path clear for her that she had no choice but to take and she ran, stumbling over roots and stones.

She looked back. They were still coming on. She tripped and fell onto the rough track, hurting her wrist and twisting her ankle; her skirt was torn and dirty. Getting back to her feet, she turned. Her pursuers had stopped. There had to be a way out of this and the path ahead was still clear.

She heard running water. The river! But the river was nowhere near the road. She had gone the wrong way. They had herded her away from her escape, lost, alone and terrified. Her mouth was dry, she could hardly breath and her pulse was thumping too rapidly in her ears.

Taking a second to hide behind a wide oak, she looked back. The dogs, wolf and cat were still there with the animal army close behind. They were close but no longer following after her. Maybe the sound of the river stopped them. She could still get away across that small bridge.

She turned to flee but an enormous stag barred her way, his head low, sharpened antlers just a few inches from her face. He was barring the way to the bridge. Now she understood why her pursuers were in no hurry. They were toying with her, steering her where they wanted her to go.

Trapped within a half-circle of vengeful animals and the river, she finally understood. They were going to make her pay.

'*It was an accident! She didn't need to die!*' she screamed, her hollow words rang out but were lost in the dense wood. No human would hear her. No-one would help. There would be no rescue. There was no response from those who hunted her. She fell to her knees and sobbed.

'Please, please forgive me. I did not mean to kill her, she fell. I'm sorry, so sorry,' she pleaded hopelessly. She felt the mood around her change,

become more menacing, sinister. In a moment of foreboding she sensed her death. Any moment, they would be on her.

She backed away, trying to watch all sides at once waiting for the first attack. The sound of the river broke into her conscious mind. The river! She couldn't get to the bridge but if she could just get to the bank, she may yet be safe. Her mind raced. She could swim across. Few animals liked to swim. The birds could fly but she could take her chance against them. Dogs could swim but they would be slowed by the current if they swam after her. She was a strong swimmer. It was her only chance!

Watching the wolf closely, she pushed through the bushes to the river bank. On the other side the bank was thickly bordered by rushes and water grasses and sloped sharply down to the water but, on her side it was edged with shrubs and fell away more gently to the water.

Slowly Wolf, Bandit, Merlin, Benny, Bjorn and Baron the stag approached, the other animals held back. They watched her pacing up and down the bank searching for a shallow or narrower place to cross, but the river was too fast. She hesitated weighing up the risks. In the water at least she stood a chance of safety. On land, the vengeful animals would show no mercy, she knew that, but in the river she could drown.

Seeing her hesitation, they closed in to just a few intimidating feet away. If she stayed she would die, if she jumped she might live. Using the bushes for support, she struggled to keep her balance, keeping one eye on the ever approaching animals, she slipped on the dry grass and slid down the bank almost to the water line but caught hold of the branch of a weeping willow and held on, trying to muster the courage to wade into the rushing water.

She was about to risk the icy water when a family of otters rushed at her from the river's edge. They were followed by six more. She fell back. The otters would not let her cross the river. They would attack if she tried. Perhaps if she could keep her feet on the bank without slipping, she could still get to the bridge. Then she looked up. Some children were watching her from the bridge.

They were dressed alike in deep blue hooded cloaks. She called out for help but they appeared not to have heard her. She called again. This time they responded and moved to her side of the bridge where she was able to see them more clearly. They were not children! They were small like children, but their faces were older, ageless.

'Please, please help me. The animals are trying to kill me! There's a wolf!'

One of the figures nodded but made no attempt to come to her rescue. The wolf separated himself from the other animals, circled around a clump

of bushes and padded, tongue lolling out of the side of his mouth, teeth bared in a vicious smile, toward the bridge, never once taking his eyes away from her face.

'The wolf! It's a wolf! Run!' she screamed a warning at them.

But the 'child' who had nodded at her walked towards the snarling wolf showing no fear. He actually stroked the wolf's head. Her last hope of rescue was shattered. These people and the animals were in league with each other.

Desperately seeking a way to escape, she spotted a small cave, almost concealed by scrubby bushes, where the river disappeared into the hillside. There was little light inside, but it could give her somewhere to hide from the animals. Wolf's eyes narrowed. He saw what she saw. He knew this cave; Jeremiah Atkins had holed up here. Wolf knew it led to one of the biggest caverns in the Mendip Hills and he knew the width and algae covered condition of the ledge inside it. He was also aware that once inside one slip into the fast-flowing icy waters could mean death.

He turned as Benny and Bjorn came to stand beside him. Merlin and Bandit made no move. Although they were closer to Mrs Jenks than the others, they too looked to the wolf for leadership.

Clap-trap, Jossamel, Halmar and Ellien dressed in the Elves funereal colour of dark blue, joined Wolf and Piggybait on the bank. Silent communication passed between Wolf and Piggybait until after a grave nod from Piggybait, Wolf broke away and rejoined the other animals. Some unseen signal passed between Wolf and Baron. The stag raised his head and gave a snorting bellow before returning to his hinds and slipping back into the wood, their part in this episode finished.

'Elêna.' A female voice called her name, her own name. Who were these people? They knew she was not Tanith! A small figure separated from the others and walked along the bridge towards to her. As the creature advanced, the hood was lowered revealing long shimmering golden hair and Elêna was aware of a sensation of serenity as she approached. A clear, bell-like voice echoed in her head but the creature had not opened her mouth. Somehow her voice was in Elêna's head.

'Elêna.' This elegant being knew all there was to know about her. 'You have abused hospitality and kindness,' the voice was musical and beautiful. Elêna wanted to keep listening, it mattered not what was being said. 'You have killed our friends and you have killed before. These acts shall not go unpunished.' Then the voice changed. It was no longer melodious and sweet, it had a harsh merciless quality. 'You have acted contrary to our Laws, shown no respect for the Earth or its children, be they human or

animal.' The female creature raised her hood again, turned her back on Elêna and started to walk away.

'No! Wait!' Elêna cried out. 'I'm sorry. Armistice did not have to die, it was an accident. So was the bird,' she pleaded, falling to her knees. 'Help me! Help me make it right,' her voice tailed off as the elf continued to walk away. 'The child...on the road. I'm sorry...he needs help. That was an accident too.'

'Accidents can be prevented,' the voice said. 'You created a chain of events that led to these deaths, accident, murder, call it what you will. You are culpable.' As the tiny being returned to her companions on the bridge, she turned back to Elêna. 'I know nothing of a child on the road and this will be investigated. For the other matters, there is no reprieve. Natural Justice will prevail.'

Wolf had waited patiently during this discussion. Now he moved forward. Bandit and Merlin made to go with him but his growled warning made it perfectly clear they were not to follow. Benny and Bjorn lay down on their stomachs to wait. The Elves turned their backs. They would not interfere. Whatever was to be would be.

Chapter Thirty Seven

Elêna, backed away trying to keep her footing on the gentle slope of the riverbank. At the cave entrance, the rushing water slapped over the rocky side making the grass verge and stones slippery. She clung to branches of the bush as her feet slithered on the wet bank. She fell to her knees, her bag flew out of her grasp landing a few feet away and, still gripping the branch with one hand, she stretched out for it.

A throaty growl made her look up. The wolf! Slowly, she backed away on all fours from his ice blue merciless eyes and the bared teeth, white and vicious. He watched her without moving closer, biding his time. Taunting.

Backing towards the cave mouth, her hands groped for somewhere to grip the rock wall for support as she hauled herself to her feet. Her legs felt weak and shaky. All the while she kept her eyes on the wolf's terrible face. Turning, she stepped onto the gloomy cave's slimy ledge and took a deep breath steeling herself for the precarious path ahead.

For the first few metres of the tunnel, she had the benefit of the sunlight streaming in from the entrance to show her where to place her feet. She looked back. The wolf had not followed her. More confident, she carefully turned again, almost slipped but regained her balance, steadied herself, took a deep breath and moved further into the tunnel. She had no choice but to go on, there was only death behind her.

Step by cautious step, she inched her way further along the uneven, wet ledge, sometimes having to hunch down where the roof was too low for her to stand straight. Left hand against the wall and her right steadying her against the low ceiling, she stayed as close to the wall as she could while her mind wandered a little trying to understand how it had come to this. She realised she had lost her bag. Her passports and cards to prove her identity were gone. How would she gain access to all that money in the banks she had committed murder and theft for? Had all that been for

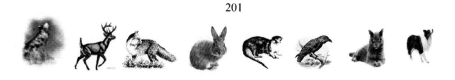

nothing? She could not turn back and retrieve the bag with those awful animals out there, they hated her. What power of communication did they have? How did they all know Mrs Jenks was dead and why would they join forces to avenge a human?

Her foot slipped on an algae covered rock. Concentrate or die! Now was not the time for thinking about anything other than survival. Straining to see in the dim light, she placed her feet carefully, horribly aware of her situation. One slip could mean a cold, watery death.

The sound of the rushing water echoed inside the tunnel so loudly she could barely hear her own rapid heartbeat. This was not how things were meant to be. She was young, good looking, beautiful she had been told. She was meant to be happy, living somewhere luxuriously expensive with lots of friends. Why had it gone so wrong? That old man was to blame! If he hadn't got suspicious, none of this would have happened, Armistice would still be alive. It was all his fault!

The tunnel took a slight turn. Until then, the further she had ventured in, the darker it had become but turning the corner, she thought it seemed a little lighter in the distance. Her eyes adjusted to the gloom, the ledge seemed a bit wider and she realised her right arm was now fully extended to reach the ceiling. Just a few metres more and she would be at the end of the ledge but into what? Where did this lead? Did safety lie at the end of the tunnel? She prayed to Tlaloc that it did. Perhaps soon she would be safe. She looked back to where just a little of the sunlight filtered around the turn. There was still no sign of the animals. Her right foot skidded on algae, she lost her balance, threw herself toward the wall and groped for something to hold on to.

Terrifying seconds passed as she as steadied herself, regained her footing and leaned against the wall, watching the swift, icy current rushing by just inches away, swallowing hard and waiting for her heart to stop racing. Something moved to her right. The wolf! He had followed her, just as she thought she had escaped him. She felt his warm breath and her blood froze. He growled low and throaty, lips turned back in a snarl, teeth glowing white and deadly in the murky light. Slowly, holding on to the wall, she stood up, edging sideways away from him.

'Get away from me! *Get away!*' she screamed, her voice echoed over the din of the river. She gripped the amulet.

'Ahh. Now I understand,' the wolf hissed between clenched teeth.

'You...you can speak!' Elêna blanched.

'Only to those I allow to hear me,' the wolf grinned coldly. 'I see you have the amulet of Tlaloc.'

She looked down, two buttons were missing from her shirt. That must have happened during one of her falls and the amulet was now in clear view.

'You...know about...Tlaloc!' She took a step back.

'Ha! Humans never cease to amaze me. Why does your race always think you are superior to us? Do you really think we're stupid?' He shook his head in disbelief and drops of saliva flew in all directions. 'It's no wonder I don't like humans very much.' He sat down on his haunches and licked his lips. 'I am wolf-kind. We have inherited memory. Did you know that?' There was no response. 'No I don't suppose you did.'

His ice-blue eyes bore into her soul promising nothing but death.

'But Tlaloc will protect me,' she yelled defiantly over the river's din, the amulet cold in her hand. Why had Tlaloc deserted her?

'Ha! You really believe that don't you?' the wolf mocked. 'You're a fool. Tlaloc doesn't exist. He never did. He's just another false deity invented by man.'

'That's what *she* said!' Elêna chanced a brief glance to the ledge, checking where to put her feet. She had to get away from the wolf. If she could get to the end of the tunnel, she might have a chance to get away from him, maybe climb high up.

'Armistice?' he asked and then answered his own question. 'Yes, she would. She was pagan too you know but her beliefs helped human and animal. *She* was loved...and you took her away from us.' He watched as she backed away half step by half step. It amused him to allow her the false hope of escape.

'You lie!'

'No, no I don't. I can't. I don't know how to. In my veins flows the blood of both Timberwolves and Gray. The history of man is remembered within my genetic makeup. There are many false gods and believe me Tlaloc will not protect you.' He slowly stood up, padded forward a little then sat down again, eyes trained on something ahead of him, something far away.

'I can see you now. You're in a temple. Ahh...you've found the amulet. There's a bright light. You've fainted. Now I understand.' His eyes locked on hers. 'Well something happened, I can see that but it's not what you want to believe, there was no god-like visitation...merely some sort of self-hypnotic trance. You excused your own greed, your own desire for wealth on a non-existent ancient god.'

'No! *No!* That's not true!' She would not believe his words. If she did it meant she was nothing more than a murderer. There was no power,

nothing guiding her to a new life other than her own greed. But the amulet was cold. There was no pulsing life force in it. Had it all been in her mind? Was she insane as Armistice had suggested? The image of Armistice falling seemed to be on replay in her head and she saw the scene over and over again.

Just a few metres away from her the wolf waited, eyes narrowed, mouth open, patiently biding his time and watching the conflicting emotions etched on her face.

Her expressions changed, he saw doubt, uncertainty revealed in her eyes for the first time, then tears fell and, finally, acceptance as the appalling truth sunk in.

A fluttering of wings behind him made them both look. Mélusine flew into the cave and landed beside the wolf on the ledge. She appeared bedraggled, had lost her healthy blue-black sheen, some of her feathers were loose. She stared at Elêna with obvious hatred. Both raven and wolf waited.

Now Elêna had two vengeful enemies glaring at her. Reaching down she felt around, located a rock and threw it toward them hitting the wolf hard on the mouth. Mélusine, flew to a large rock in the middle of the stream but, hurt, wolf yelped as the rock connected with his top lip and his teeth sliced into his tongue. Blood seeped from the wound and dripped from his jaws onto his chest and front legs. For one brief moment, she thought his yelp meant he had been frightened and would run away, that she had triumphed.

But she was wrong. In pain and now enraged, he sprang at her, pinning her against the wall, his blood dripped on her shirt. She turned her face from his, screwed her eyes tightly closed shutting out the face of her would-be assassin just inches away.

But he did not kill her. Instead he tore the chain away from her neck with his teeth, waited until she opened her eyes and spat the amulet into the river wanting her to watch it being swallowed by the river. He had thought about killing her; an eye for an eye. But an image of Armistice and her kindness drifted into his mind. She would not want that. No, she should be taken back to the humans and made to pay for her crimes under human law. It was his turn not to be prepared for what happened next.

But that was not the end of the amulet. A large dog-otter surfaced from the water with it hanging from his mouth. He swam close to where Elêna paced up and down on the ledge, furious and tearful. Wolf forgot his pain vexed that it looked as though she would have the amulet returned to her.

But, the otter had other ideas. He rolled over on to his back, the amulet on his stomach and floated close to where Elêna stood.

'Here, bring it here, do you understand?' If the wolf could talk, then perhaps the otter could too. But the otter ignored her, just staying out of her reach, teasing her. If she could just reach him, she might be able to retrieve the precious talisman. It was all she had left.

Aware of how risky any movement was on the ledge, she found a handhold on the cave wall and lowered herself onto her knees but just as she reached out, Mélusine fluttered from the rock, snatched the amulet from the otter's belly and flew towards her.

In a futile attempt to catch the amulet from the bird, Elêna, momentarily having forgotten how slippery the rocky shelf was, wriggled to her feet, skidded on algae and was thrown off-balance. She missed her footing and toppled over the ledge arms flailing as she desperately tried to clutch at the algae-covered rocky edge but could not get a grip.

In a frantic effort to save herself she reached out and grabbed the thick hair around the wolf's leg. He stood firm, allowing her a handhold but did nothing to help her and her hand slipped on his bloodied paw. Her fate was inescapable.

'*NO! Help me!* Madre de Dios!' she fell, screaming for help as the fast flowing icy water weighed down her clothes and the powerful current dragged her under.

Wolf could do nothing to help. In truth, he felt that this end was probably cleaner, more fitting, and wondered whether if he had been able to prevent her death, would he? A gurgling scream echoed through the tunnel as she broke the surface of the water just a few metres further away from where he stood for one last time, her body would find a watery grave somewhere deep within the river that networked the caves.

Wolf's eyes gleamed unpityingly. 'Justice has been done. I am satisfied.'

Outside the narrow cave, Bandit and the three dogs waited patiently. They had heard the scream. In the wood Baron had heard it too and bellowed in response. Having taken his family away, he did not see Wolf emerge from the tunnel, his mouth, chin and legs splattered with blood and wet.

Benny moved forward but Wolf growled moodily at him. The others thought it best to leave him alone as he walked up the bank to where Piggybait stood silently waiting to take him, head down and padding along in silence, home to the cave he shared with the reindeer.

205

Ellien and the other elves slipped back into the hidden paths within the wood. The owls and other birds flew off to wherever they had come from as, from all around the riverbank the animals and birds returned to their dreys, setts, nests and earths, their one-time only amnesty now over.

Only Bandit and the three dogs remained. Benny and Bjorn nuzzled Merlin and, with a last look at Bandit, turned away to take the path home. Merlin and Bandit headed wearily home to the cottage with Mélusine flying, from this time on forever alone, high above them. The river bank would never give up its secret; nothing out of the ordinary had happened there.

At the cottage, Merlin and Bandit nuzzled each other before Merlin sank miserably to the ground outside the back door, laid his chin on his paws and whimpered. Inside, Charlie was still standing over Armistice's body. Ernie Rogers was on his radio and Dr Brownlow was sitting in the armchair filling in paperwork.

'It's a sad business, Charlie,' the doctor said quietly. 'You knew her well didn't you?'

'Known 'er a long toime,' Charlie nodded. 'Strange thing, 'er niece disappearin'. Can' 'elp but think she 'ad somethin' ter do wi' this.' He broke off as Bandit entered the room and stepped slowly over to Armistice. He ignored the men, even Charlie, and snuggled into her lifeless neck, purring softly.

Charlie looked at Ernie and shook his head. 'Poor little fella's gonna miss 'er.'

But, after one long, shuddering breath, the purring stopped.

Charlie bent down to pick Bandit up to offer his comfort, but it was too late. ''E's gone,' Charlie sighed.

'What?' Ernie stopped writing.

''E's died,' Charlie said quietly without looking up. He stroked the beautiful cat who had loved his mistress, so faithfully, right to the end.

'Oi s'pose it were to be expected. 'E wouldn' wanna be 'ere wi'out 'er,'

'Can't say I blame him Charlie,' the doctor replied sadly. 'They've been together a long time. But what about Merlin? D'you think the Dog's Home will take him?'

'*Dog's 'Ome!*' Charlie spluttered. ''E ain't goin' to no Dog's 'Ome. She were my frien' an' Merlin' comes to Cathy an' me. We'll look arter 'im. Oi'll bury Taliesin, poor thing, and keep and eye on Mélusine, she'll be lonely now. Especially when her chicks leave 'ome, they'll hatch soon.'

Dr Brownlow put his papers into a briefcase just as a siren sounded outside.

'That's the ambulance, Charlie. They'll be taking her away now.' He looked down at the dead cat.

'What about Bandit?'

Charlie peered down into Bandit's serene face. 'Don' you worry 'bout 'im,' he said softly. 'Oi'll tek care o' him too.'

Chapter Thirty Eight

Charlie, his wife Cathy, Sam and Jenny followed a very hot and abnormally thin-lipped Reverend Driver to the graveside. His official robes weighed heavily and his bad mood showed in his scowling face.

From choice, the Vicar would not have performed this service. Armistice Jenks was at best a non-believer, probably pagan and, if her reputation as a witch had any foundation, she had no business being buried in his Churchyard. It had taken his friend David Brownlow to remind him in his usual gently persuasive manner, that it was his Christian duty to officiate at her funeral as she was a member of the Parish.

Even though not very popular, she was the oldest person in the village and deserving of respect for that if nothing else. The Doctor was waiting for them at the open graveside talking to Sid Foulks, the gravedigger, his yellow nicotine-stained fingers gripping the handle of his shovel. He threw the remains of a rolled up cigarette onto the gravel and stepped on it to make sure it was out before kicking it out of sight when the Vicar came into view.

There were few mourners at the graveside. Charlie, having been a close friend of Armistice, found the turnout disappointing but he was not really surprised. The villagers had never really known her, not like he and Sam did and he stared down at the open grave sadly waiting for the coffin, which was already in position, to be lowered into the ground. Reverend Driver's voice broke into his thoughts. *'Jesus said I am the resurrection, and I am the life; he who believes in me, though he dies, yet he will live, and whoever believes in me shall never die.'* The Vicar's sniffy attitude and the irony of the phrase made Charlie want to giggle. Cathy elbowed him in the ribs. He grinned down at her.

'Shhh, Charlie. *Behave!* Remember where you are,' she whispered.

Footsteps crunched on the gravel path behind them. A large middle-aged, grey-haired woman, dressed in a navy trouser suit and white blouse

walked towards them carrying a small wreath with no flowers, just green leaves and, as she got closer, Charlie saw it was entirely made up of herbs.

His sparkling blue eyes crinkled as the woman drew closer. She nodded to him and Cathy. Armistice would have liked that wreath, Charlie thought smiling warmly at the newcomer.

'*Ashes to ashes,*' Reverend Driver droned on.

The coffin was lowered on straps into the grave and Charlie stepped forward to throw the first handful of earth. From behind him, Sam produced a pure white Arum lily and let it drop onto the coffin. Charlie wiped the earth from his hands while Jenny sobbed silently. 'I wish I'd known her better. Now it's too late.'

'It's never too late, Jenny,' Charlie told her, patting her shoulder.

The Vicar, having finished his part in the proceedings said his goodbyes and headed back to the cool air of the Vestry, making no pretence of staying to pay his respects to the Departed.

The newcomer suppressed a sob, holding a white handkerchief to her nose as she let her wreath drop gently onto the coffin.

'Yeh wair ma pal. Ah'll no ferget yeh,' she said softly.

Charlie reached out to shake her hand. 'It were good o' you ter come. As yer can see, Armie didn' 'ave too many friends.'

'Aye. 'Tis a sad thing tae lose a frien', especially one like Armie. D'ye ken what happened tae the girl? Wicked wee mare!'

Charlie shook his head. 'No, not reelly. As far as we know she disappeared into that cave down by the river where 'er bag were foun'. Not 'eard nuthin' since, 'ave we Cathy? Could've drowned fer all we know.'

Cathy shook her head. 'Charlie said he thought something was wrong about her right from the start.' She reached out to shake the other woman's hand. 'Did you know Armistice well?'

'Aye. We'd bin pals fair some years. Ah'm Isabel Mackenzie by the way, an ah'm fair pleased tae meet yeh. Ah tek it yeh'll be Charlie Nowell. She tell't me all aboot yeh an' ah ken tha' wee man's Sam. It fair breks ma hairt tha' we meet fer the fairst time a' the send off. Och, ah should'na say it, but ah hope the wee bizum did droon.'

Cathy motioned for Sam and Jenny to join them but Sam was staring at a point high up on the church tower where a raven looked down at them.

''I know…I saw her earlier,' Charlie said, as Sam drew his attention to her.

'Tha pair wee baird. Ah hear her mate was killed too,' Isabel shook her head sadly. 'All o' it. It doesn'ae bare thinking aboot.'

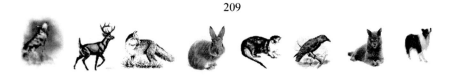

'Oi buried Taliesin in the garden close to the shed. Didn' wan' 'im far from Mélusine. T'wouldn'a bin fair, they bin together so long.'

The mourners walked away from the graveside discussing various memories of Armistice until they reached the gate. Mélusine flew over their heads returning to her newly hatched brood in the garden shed. At least she has company, he thought.

'This is where ah tek mah leave. Ah'm fair sorry we had tae meet like this,' Isabel said, heading back to her car. Waving goodbye, the group walked away in the opposite direction. 'Wha' happened tae Bandit and Mairlin?' Isabel called out.

'Bandit died wi' Armie but we took Merlin,' Charlie replied. ''E weren't goin' to no strangers.'

'Aye, tha's as it should be. If yeh'd no got him Ah'da teken him.' She waved goodbye, started up the car and drove away.

'Nice woman,' Cathy said. She looked at her watch. 'I've got to go Charlie. I'm due at the Art Centre in Wells in half an hour. You OK?' She laid a gentle hand on his whiskery cheek fondly.

'Yeah, O'im foine. We'll be OK won' we?' he said looking at Jenny and Sam. They nodded.

'OK see you at home later,' Cathy hurried off.

'Good. I'm glad she's gone. You two are coming with me,' Charlie beamed broadly, his accent having slipped.

Sam and Jenny were astounded at his sudden change of humour. 'What's going off?' Sam asked.

Charlie tapped the side of his nose. 'You know how I told you things were not always as they seemed to be.'

Sam nodded. Jenny looked perplexed.

'We have another little service to go to. Come on, they're waiting for us.' He strode off towards the wood with Sam and Jenny running after him to keep up. Soon Sam lost his bearings. He had never been in this part of the wood before.

'Where are we going?' he asked

'Not far now, Sam. Everyone's going to be there.'

Jenny, out of breath and equally bewildered, trudged alongside, very hot and sticky from their efforts. But Charlie was right. Soon the trees began to thin out and a short while later they entered a small clearing. Jenny gasped. Sam walked forward very slowly, completely awestruck.

The air in the glade was crystal clear and cool, unlike the humid part of the wood they had just left. Here the trees were bedecked with fire-fly lanterns and garlands of beautiful flowers, shimmering in a wide shaft of

sunlight that shone directly on to two simple wooden coffins, placed on a grassy mound in the centre of the glade.

Sam's quick estimation was there must have been upwards of a hundred elves, all in their finest dark blue clothing, dark blue caps in hand, gathered silently around the garland draped coffins. Charlie had walked ahead to take up a position at the head of the coffins. Ellien and Halmar, dressed alike in shimmering dark blue cloaks, emerged from the trees and joined them. Ellien wore her crown.

Movement at the edge of the glade caught Jenny's attention. She nudged Sam. Deer, foxes, rabbits, mice, weasels, badgers and otters, every sort of wild animal that lived in the woodland habitat had gathered at the edge of the clearing and moved forward to join with the reindeer and wolf already there.

Jenny shuddered on seeing the wolf, never having actually laid eyes on him before. Rondina had told her about him so she was aware of his existence but to see him 'in the flesh' so to speak, was an altogether different matter.

Sam squeezed her hand. 'He's OK. Honest. Don't be scared. Look up.'

Owls, buzzards, blackbirds, birds of every kind had flocked to the treetops where they gazed down at the mingled elves and humans in respectful silence. A raven swooped low into the glade flying directly at Charlie. She landed on his shoulder. He summoned Sam and Jenny to stand beside him.

'Whose coffins are they, Charlie?' Sam whispered from the side of his mouth and more and more elves emerged from the trees to swell the muted throng.

'Can't you guess who one of them is for?' Charlie smiled gently.

'Armistice would never have wanted to lie in the churchyard, Sam.' Ellien appeared beside them. Her clear, soft voice answered his question. 'The woodland was her love and this is where her body will remain, this time.'

'She's in there? But what? Why did we go to the cemetery? What was that all about?'

'We had to go through the motions Sam, it was expected of us.' Charlie answered.

'And why two?' Jenny added.

Halmar stepped forward just as Piggybait and Clap-trap appeared at Sam's side. 'The other is for my father,' he answered solemnly.

'Jerrill! But what happened?' Sam was dumbfounded. 'I'm so sorry, Halmar. I didn't know.'

'The same person who killed Armistice killed my father. I really believe they were both accidents but her actions were the cause. She stole a vehicle and ran him down trying to escape.' He took a small wooden disc from his pocket and held it tenderly in the palm of hand. 'From what we understand he lost this at our wedding and had gone to the glade to look for it. We were going to meet up to talk and he thought he was late. He was hurrying to get back when she ran him down.

Mélusine saw what happened but was pre-occupied with avenging the death of Armistice. She found me shortly after Elêna died to tell me.'

Ellien slipped her arm through his. 'Jerrill is a terrible loss to the clan and to us personally. He will be greatly missed, but fate played its part and natural justice has prevailed.'

'I thought it better not to mention Jerrill at the cemetery, Sam, with the others being there. But this is our way of saying goodbye to three good friends.' Huge tears welled in Charlie's eyes, brimmed over and ran down his round cheeks into his bushy moustache.

'Three?' Jenny asked.

'Bandit is with Armistice. He makes three.'

'But what was in the other coffin, Charlie?' Sam persisted, 'the one in the cemetery?'

Charlie's looked at Piggybait, who blushed and looked down at his feet. He cleared his throat.

'Umm. Armistice and Bandit in this one,' he said evading the question. 'Jerrill is in the other.'

'Yes, but what's in the one we buried earlier?' Sam repeated the question. 'It was heavy. There must have been something in it.'

'We moved Armie and Bandit last night and brought them here,' Claptrap stepped in. 'The other coffin, the one you've just buried was full of...' he looked up at Charlie, '...full of...well, you remember all the flagons of mead and cider at Ellien and Halmar's wedding?'

'We had to get rid of the empties somewhere,' Piggybait finally joined in.

'You didn't!' Jenny thought how mortified the Vicar would have been had he known.

Ellien glided to a spot between the coffins. Looking up into the clear blue sky she began to sing, her usually soft voice now strong and perfect. At once the glade rang with a requiem for the departed, sung in a language that neither Sam nor Jenny understood but its meaning was clearly

understood. Jenny shivered with emotion. Sam took her hand in comfort. Wolf howled, joining in with the lament.

'What if someone hears this?' Sam asked Charlie.

'No-one will,' he whispered. 'This glade is Elven and protected from human eyes and ears. No-one, other than both of you now, knows of its existence. No sound escapes beyond the surrounding trees and...' he lowered his voice to a whisper, 'even Jenny will forget it on her return.'

Piggybait and Clap-trap left them to take up positions on either side of the coffins and still chanting, raised their arms over them. The ground between the coffins separated and the two sections moved aside underneath but they hovered in place as a deep cavity appeared below.

Sam heard Jenny's sharp intake of breath. 'But there's nothing to hold them up!' she gasped.

Slowly and steadily the coffins descended into the hollow until they came to rest several feet below the surface. The elven crowd stopped singing. Only Ellien continued her song while Piggybait and Clap-trap chanted. Both completely different types of music blended together and were heartbreakingly beautiful and poignant to those listening. Jenny sobbed. Sam felt his throat burn with the effort not to cry.

Slowly the ground moved back with a quiet rumble as the two sides slid back into place concealing the coffins forever. Ellien's song ended. Piggybait and Clap-trap lowered their arms and ceased their incantation just as the two sides met.

Sam was cheered when he saw Aerynne slip out of the crowd and walk towards Piggybait. He turned at her approach and the smile lit his face as she took his hand. Wolf joined them and sat by Aerynne's side, leaning slightly against her, while they waited for a few more moments in respectful silence until Ellien spoke to the assembly.

'Jerrill is now with Hallane,' her crystal clear voice rang out. 'Armistice and Bandit have left us, for this life. Justice has been done. May they be at peace until we see them again.'

Halmar, the wooden disc still in his left hand, took Ellien's hand with his right and nodded farewell to the gathered elves and humans, then he and Ellien vanished into the wood. The animals slunk back into the undergrowth and the treetops cleared of birds.

Arm in arm with Piggybait, Aerynne and Wolf returned to the waiting reindeer to escort them home. Nimbus, now accepted by the small herd, walked close to Donner and Rudolph, their previous animosity a thing of the past. Within a few minutes the entire gathering had dispersed into the

darkness of the trees.   Now only Sam, Jenny, Charlie and Clap-trap remained in the glade.

Sam walked to the mound.   There were no tell-tale cracks in the grass left as evidence of movement.   No-one would ever know the earth had moved.

'No-one would know anyway, Sam.' Clap-trap had read his thoughts. 'Humans never come here.   This is our place, our above-ground sanctuary. This is what Armistice would have wanted.'

'I know.   It feels right,' Sam agreed.   Jenny joined them.   'It's time to go,' she said.

Clap-trap agreed, 'It's time I returned home.   Everyone else has already gone.   I will see you all soon, I hope.'

On the route back through the warm wood, Jenny remarked that, after Armistice's burial, it had been cheered her to go on such a lively walk through the woods.   Charlie winked at Sam.   Jenny had forgotten the second funeral just as Charlie had said she would.

They emerged from the trees at the far end of the village and walked back towards the green but waited on the kerb as a police car drove past, two police officers in the front and Stuart Seymour in the back.   He waved. His wrists were handcuffed.   Beside him was a man in military uniform.

'That's Stuart Seymour,' Sam said in surprise.   'What's all that about?'

'He's given himself up, Sam,' Charlie said.   'Cathy bumped into Dorothy earlier this morning outside the Post Office.   It seems young Stuart went AWOL…'

'AWOL?' Jenny asked.

'Absent without leave,' Charlie explained.   'Something happened during his posting in Basra that he could not live with.   He deserted, hiding out on the streets around Taunton and Wells for a while until he felt it was safe to go home.   Marj let everyone think they'd bought him out.'

'But why give himself up now?' Sam asked.

'It seems he found Armistice behaving strangely in the road one night and saw enough to convince him something was wrong, but didn't do anything about it.   Then, when he found out she'd died, his conscience got the better of him, he blames himself for not doing something sooner.' Charlie paused.   'I suppose we all have that on our hands too.   I should've done something about it myself but I left it too late as well.   I'm just as guilty as that poor lad.'

They watched the Police car drive away and out of sight around the corner before moving on.   'Still he's given himself up so let's hope they won't be too hard on him.   Come on, let's go home.'

Five Years Later

Born the youngest of seven children, life had never held any great promise for Rita Landers, no dreams of university, no glittering career, nothing beyond leaving school at sixteen and getting a job to help her pay her way. All through her deprived childhood, the only thing she ever had any expectations of was hand-me-downs from her older siblings. Her farm labourer father, the third child of a family of ten and her mother, the seventh of nine daughters, loved their children and did their best to care for them, but the efforts just to get by on a day to day basis, left them little time for any individual affection.

Sadly, life took an even more dramatic downturn when her father died in an accident involving farm machinery and the family lost their cottage shortly after. Having no home, their mother was forced to depend on the goodwill of relatives and the family was separated into two groups. Their mother and the three younger children stayed with Rita's paternal grandmother, while the four older siblings moved in with an aunt and uncle miles away near to Exeter. Rita met Sid Landers shortly after leaving school.

As the only child of a factory supervisor, Sid was spoiled by his doting mother and had grown up confident, but lazy. Romantically swept off her feet and excited at the prospect of having her own home, Rita accepted Sid's proposal of marriage anticipating their rosy future as a way out of her miserable family life.

But, once again, life disappointed her. Her dream of a happy future foundered when Sid was made redundant from his job at the soft drinks factory in Shepton Mallet two years after they married. Unhappily for Rita, Sid took to being unemployed like a duck to water, convinced that there was no reason why the State shouldn't keep him when it was keeping so many others. Four sons in quick succession meant that, with Sid not working, Rita had to earn enough to keep a family of six. While Sid watched television, spent hours at the pub or hung around the race tracks and betting shops getting fatter and lazier every day, Rita took on three cleaning jobs, sometimes taking the boys with her before they were old enough to attend school.

With Sid setting such a poor example for the boys, Eric, Sid Junior, Ryan and Shane, Rita endured rather than lived her life. The boys were at best lazy and slovenly and at worst their behaviour bordered on the criminal. Alternately spending nights at police stations or hospitals and

215

days slaving at work or at home or fending off neighbours complaints about her boys' unruly behaviour, Rita grew thinner and more wretched with every year that passed, until she became nothing more than a grey bird-like shadow of her former self.

But five years ago, at the age of forty, to her horror, Rita found she was pregnant again. The thought of yet another child, especially so many years after Shane was born, filled her with dread, after all Shane had just had his fifteenth birthday. But, strangely, things began getting better and, as the months passed, Rita's general health and attitude to life improved. It was almost as if the unborn child was breathing new energy into her and she was jubilant when the hospital scan revealed the child was a girl.

Even more unusual was Sid's uncharacteristic change of outlook. After refusing to consider even looking for a job, Sid began scouring the classified advertisements in the local newspapers and no longer frequented the Dog and Partridge Public House and betting shops.

Even the boys, without being nagged, saw where improvements were needed around the house, started decorating and took on various chores allowing her to rest more often. Shane even stopped playing truant and regularly did his homework.

On the seventh day of May, their daughter was born and Sid arrived at the hospital having shaved, washed his hair and wearing a shirt and tie. He looked smarter than Rita could ever remember since the day they married. He even brought her flowers and soon her tears flowed in delight watching her husband cooing with enchantment as he looked down into the remarkably dark blue eyes of his baby daughter.

'What yer gonna call 'er?' he asked, smiling proudly at his astonished wife. Rita tried to recall the last time she had seen him smile.

'But…iss you what names 'em, Sid!' she exclaimed with surprise. He had named the boys without any consultation with her.

'Not this toime m'dear. This littl'uns gonna 'ave your choice.'

'Oh, I dunno, Sid. I ain't gi'en any thought.'

After Sid had gone, Rita cradled her contentedly gurgling daughter, considering names. The baby did not cry, seeming perfectly happy in her mother's arms as she tried to focus her eyes on the face close to hers.

'Mebbe yer name's Hope. What you think o' that?'

The following morning, as the nurse carried the baby to the car, a very small man carrying an oversized plastic carrier bag, walked across the corridor in front of Rita, as she left the hospital, leaning on Sid's arm. He bowed to her and blew a kiss to the baby, doffing his cap as he walked

across the corridor in front of them. Strands of long brown curly hair tumbled across his eyes and he brushed them away with a grin at her.

Rita returned his smile, amused by him and by the full bag he carried which was far too big considering his size. The name emblazoned on the side of the bag caught her attention. It suggested the magical nature of the locality and Arthurian legends and how her life had mystifyingly changed. 'Morgan, it is,' she sighed.

Strangely, Sid had no memory of the encounter in the hospital corridor, but was happy with the name and made no complaint when Rita added 'Hope' as Morgan's middle name.

On a beautiful day, exactly five years later, as she made the finishing touches to Morgan's birthday cake, Rita now knew what it was to be happy and fulfilled. Life had changed very much for the better. Sid had a steady job at the Winterne Manor Fish Farm and the boys had turned their lives around. Eric was in the Navy, Ryan was doing well at college and young Sid had even joined the Police. Rita knew, beyond any doubt, that all this had come from this fairylike little girl.

Morgan was playing in their hedge-bordered garden with Shane who loved her beyond anyone else. He held a variety of flowers and was holding them up one by one for Morgan to name. She never made a mistake. The warm breeze ruffled her long white blonde hair and she giggled adorably as Bruce, one of the three enormous German Shepherds laid a paw on her lap.

During Morgan's first few weeks, Sid had enlisted the help of the boys to clear away the rubbish in the back garden to surprise Rita. What had looked like a scrap-yard was given a complete make-over that included a small raised pond with fish, a fountain and a pergola with climbing flowers and decking underneath. The herb garden was added last year when Morgan, taking everyone by surprise requested it. She loved the smell of herbs, knew they could be used in cooking and some had medicinal properties. Morgan loved being in the garden surrounded by plants but her first love was animals, with whom she had a remarkable empathy. The dogs loved her.

Sly, the oldest, black and tan in colouring, and larger than the other two, rarely left her side and was now rolling in the grass on his back behind her. Arnie was similar in size to Sly but a lighter colour and much lazier. He sat in the shade of the beech tree idly observing Morgan and Shane, his head resting on his paws.

The third dog, Bruce, who was slightly smaller than the other two and a creamy white, dozed on the shaded decking, glad to get out of the bright sunlight.

A knock at the door provoked loud barking followed by Bruce and Arnie, curiosity getting the better of them, charging from the garden through to the front door, but Sly remained where he was. Sid left his newspaper and went to answer it.

'Rita, iss Charlie. 'E's brought summat for our Morgan fer 'er birthday.'

Charlie Nowell stooped under the door frame his huge bulk entered the kitchen. 'Allo Rita. 'Ope yer don' moind but Oi jest couldn' not turn up terday, wi' it bein' Morgan's birthday,' his bright blue eyes crinkled.

'Yer always welcome, Charlie. You know tha' and Morgan'll be glad ter see yer, present or no present.'

He stood away slightly as Rita gave him a hug while Bruce and Arnie, having discovered the visitor had brought nothing for them returned to the garden and flopped down, panting, beside the little girl.

'Come on through to the garden, Charlie. Morgan'll be 'appy yer 'ere,' Sid led the way. 'Morgan, look who's come ter see yer, me little luv.'

Morgan put down her flowers and ran laughingly towards the huge man who picked her up and carefully swung her onto his left side.

'Have you brought me something Charlie? It's my birthday,' she lisped prettily.

'Morgan!' Rita looked embarrassed at her daughter's forward behaviour. 'You shouldn' ask loike that. It ain't nice. Where's yer manners?'

But Charlie only laughed. 'Don' tell 'er off, Rita. Iss 'er birthday.'

'But you should a' least call 'im Uncle Charlie, my girl. Don' ferget wha' Oi said abou' respeck.'

Morgan smiled at her mother through extraordinarily mature eyes. 'But we're old friends aren't we Charlie?' Morgan threw her little arms around his big neck, 'and have you brought me anything?'

'Certainly 'ave but you'll 'ave ter get down agen while I 'ave a fish aroun' in me jacket pocket an' see what Oi can find fer yer.'

Lowering Morgan gently to the ground, Charlie winked at Rita and Sid. From a huge pocket on the right side of his jacket, he produced something very small, furry and grey.

'E's all yourn Morgan. Mek sure yer look arter 'im proper, won' yer? 'Is name's Bandit.'

A tiny kitten with enormous jade coloured eyes sat confidently on Charlie bear-paw like hand. Morgan reached out to take him. She made no excited squealing noises, did not reach out suddenly to grab like many small children would. Taking the kitten tenderly she cradled him in her arms. The kitten snuggled up to her neck and purred before climbing on to her shoulder where he settled down immediately looking very much at home there.

'Oh, Charlie, Oi'm not sure thass a good idea. Not wi' the dogs,' Sid frowned. 'Poor li'l thing's too small to defend 'imself agenst them brutes.'

'Don' fret abou' that, Sid. Look.'

Morgan had taken Bandit to show her brother. She lifted him down from her shoulder and placed him on the ground. The kitten toddled off towards Sly who watched his approach and made no protest as the kitten stepped between his huge paws and rubbed his face against the huge dog's chest. Bruce and Arnie watched, wagging their tails showing no animosity or even curiosity at the new arrival.

'See Sid. Bandit's roight at 'ome.'

Sid and Rita looked at each with obvious concern, neither of them quite as assured as Charlie seemed to be, but he chuckled away their doubts. 'You mark my words. Tha' li'l cat'll be more'n a match fer the dogs. Anyway, iss toime Oi got goin',' he said heading back to the kitchen.

Rita and Sid followed him into the house. 'Mus' you go, Charlie? Can't yer stay fer a bi' o' birthday cake? Morgan's got a few frien's comin' soon an' she'd be real pleased if ya could stay,' Sid asked.

'No. Sorry Sid, Oi can't this toime, got too much on.' He shook his head and reached for the handle of the front door. 'We got a party ter go to. Me nephew, Sam an' 'is girlfrien' Jenny are back from their universities fer the weekend. It were 'is twentieth birthday yesterdee an' they're gettin' engaged terday. They're not getting' married yet though, Jenny's gotta another year to do for her Sports Science degree an' o' course Sam's gotta finish 'is Civil Engineerin', then 'e's loikely ter go fer 'is Masters.'

'Expensive business, gettin' wed, these days,' Sid commented.

'Yeah, but it'll be a couple 'o years yet,' he added. 'Harriet Atkins is throwin' 'em a bit of a do at the Manor tonight,' he beamed broadly. 'Trouble is they've got some o' their student mates comin' an Cathy wants me ter scrub up, wear a shirt n tie loike,' he chuckled, ' but Oi s'pose Oi'll do as Oi'm told seein' as it's at the Manor. Anyway gotta go.'

He opened the front door then turned back into the hallway for a last look at Morgan and the kitten. He bellowed a goodbye. Morgan picked up

the kitten and cuddled him closely as she walked up the garden with him in her arms. In the hallway she put Bandit back on her shoulder and Charlie hunkered down to let her hug his neck.

'Thank you for bringing him back to me, Charlie,' she lisped. Rita turned to Sid, a puzzled expression in her eyes. He frowned and shrugged.

Charlie stood up. 'You jest look arter 'im, alroight?'

The little girl nodded up at him and trotted, kitten still clinging to her shoulder, back to her brother and dogs in the garden. Rita too, said her goodbyes and Sid walked Charlie back to his jeep.

'Wha' she mean about bringing 'im back, Charlie?' Sid asked.

Charlie opened the jeep door and climbed into the driver's seat. 'Not a clue, Sid. But you know kids, they sez the strangest things.'

'Speakin' o' kids, Charlie' Sid continued, his foot on the step of the jeep. ''Ow's tha' Jonah gettin' on. Don' see 'im much at the Manor bu' I do 'ear things're goin' quite well for 'im at Medical School. I see Miz Atkins from toime ter toime at the lake and that Stuart. I see 'im about. 'E seems to 'ave done alroigh' fer 'imself since 'e served 'is toime.'

Charlie closed the jeep door and leaned out of the open window. 'Yeh, 'es due ter get married next year an' all. Marryin' that Rachel Askam.'

Sid gave him a questioning frown.

'You know, the family tha' owns the shop and Post office.'

'Oh, yeh, o' course I know 'em,' Sid took his foot off the step. 'Oi dunno, Charlie, iss all change ennit? Kids, growin' up, ol' Arthur Sykes dying sudden loike that, Ernie retirin' an im' an' 'is missus Dorothy movin' away to Spain. All different now, ennit?'

In his rear view mirror Charlie saw Piggybait and Clap-trap looking bored in the back of the jeep and started up the loudly rattling engine.

'Something's do Sid, but some stay just as they've always bin.'

Acknowledgements

Acknowledgements in this third book, will not vary a great deal from those in 'Silver Linings' and 'Queen of Diamonds' because I am still so very grateful for the continued support that highly acclaimed historical author Helen Hollick, Cathy Helms of Avalon Graphics, Daniel Cooke, the Managing Director of New Generation Publishing and his team, my daughter, Rachel Littlewood of AuthorPress Editing, Jeremy Lewis and Dawn Bond, both experienced and popular Nottinghamshire journalists who have given my books tremendous reviews and Daniel Medley, Director of Wookey Hole Caves and his team. All these wonderful people have done so much for me over the years. Their continued support is very welcome and much appreciated.

In addition, I would like to thank Steve Bowkett, prolific children's author, teacher of teachers and Educationalist who has also supported me in my writing and given amazing reviews to my books. I am delighted to have his endorsement of my writing; it means a tremendous amount to me.

Again, my thanks go to my son, Greg and his fiancée, Kaylie Hawksworth – who is incidentally a terrific singer and does a great Katy Perry tribute. Greg and Kaylie have been a tremendous help over the last year or so with the technical side of the events I organise for New Writers UK. It's wonderful to have their know-how when staging the book festivals.

Special thanks go to my husband, David, who not only spots all my typos, but continues to support me in so many ways with everything I do. Thank you for everything, my darling, and I know you'll be delighted to hear that I'll be working on the next book very soon.

Jae was born in Isleworth, West London then lived in Essex and Suffolk before spending the rest of her childhood in Sherborne, Dorset, close to the Somerset border. During those happy years, a visit to Wookey Hole caves and an inspiring History teacher at her school, Gerald Pitman, sparked her interest in the facts and myths that surrounded the Mendip Hills. Another teacher, Anne Osmond, was equally inspiring with her love of literature and encouraged Jae in her first attempts at writing.

In her early teens Jae moved back to London and began writing her first book – a story set in Ancient Egypt based on the life of Queen Hatshepsut – it was never finished!

As the years went on and career, marriage and children became her priorities, Jae forgot her writing but never her love of reading and almost always had at least one good book on the go; in particular, historical or fantasy novels.

Years later she moved back to the West Country to the village of Butleigh in Somerset, just four miles from Glastonbury and seven from Wells and fell in love with the area all over again, but this was to be a short stay.

Later, Jae met and married her second husband, David, and lived in Dumfries for six years. Then in 1996, the family moved back to England settling in Nottingham where they have lived ever since. Jae's children, Rachel and Greg, are now grown up and she has two grandchildren, Erin and Finn.

Having originally written 'Silver Linings' in 2005 and self-published in 2006, Jae met two other self-published authors and together they attended book festivals and other literary events and met a number of other self-published authors, all trying to find their way through the world of bookstores, journalists, publishers and agents.

In 2006 she founded not-for-profit New Writers UK and organised their first book festival in November that year. Participating were just eight very local authors. Having invited the Lord Mayor of Nottingham the Chairman of Nottinghamshire County Council, the Mayor of Gedling and a number of local journalists, New Writers UK was on its way.

NWUK now has well over one hundred members throughout the UK and overseas, runs an annual Creative Writing Competition for Children and Young People of Nottinghamshire and last year created a 'Silver Scribes' short story competition for people aged fifty-five. Both competitions are entirely free to enter.

Since writing her books and the formation of New Writers UK, Jae (under her given name of Julie Malone), is a regular on local radio, writes articles for newspapers and magazines in the Nottinghamshire area and for the New Writers UK quarterly newsletter.

In February 2015, Jae (as Julie) was thrilled to be presented with the 'Pride of Gedling' Award in the Public Servant category in recognition of all her hard work in running creative writing classes, creative writing competitions and organising the Gedling Borough Council Book Festivals.

For more information on New Writers UK please visit www.newwritersuk.co.uk.

'Fool's Gold' is the third book of the Winterne Series. The first and second volumes are 'Silver Linings' and 'Queen of Diamonds', all three were originally written under the pen-name, Karen Wright, and received excellent reviews. The fourth book, working title 'Avaroc Returns', is well underway and will be available early summer 2016.

For further information about Jae please email her at jaemalone.author@gmail.com, visit her website www.jaemalone.co.uk or contact her through Facebook or Twitter

Earlier volumes in the Winterne series

Volume 1   'Silver Linings'

At fourteen years old, Sam Johnson has a fairly peaceful way of life; he has the company of life-long friends and lives in a pleasant house on the outskirts of Nottingham. He even finds school hassle-free, usually.   In fact, there is only one thing that spoils Sam's life; for the last five months his father has been working in South Africa and Sam misses him, a lot. Thankfully with Christmas in a few weeks, Steve Johnson is due to come home for the holidays. But an unkind twist of fate changes Sam's life, literally overnight.   He has to leave his comfortable surroundings and friends behind, and move to a quiet country village, to stay with an aunt he hardly knows, and an uncle he has never met before. Within a very short time Sam discovers life in the picturesque village hides a darker side and his uncle has a secret. Over the next few weeks Sam makes both enemies and friends, and he discovers childhood fantasies can turn into reality.

Volume 2 'Queen of Diamonds'

Sam Johnson's first weeks in Winterne, just before Christmas were exciting, dangerous and magical. Four months later, he is settled and has made friends. Now all he wants is a quiet life to prepare for GCSE's. But knowing some of Sam's new friends, how likely is that? Jonah Atkins is now a reformed character since Sam saved his life during a cave-in, and the boys form an unlikely friendship. Harriet Atkins, Jonah's mother, deeply regretting everything Sam and his friend, Jenny, have suffered at the hands of the Atkins family, invites them both to choose a reward from a range of gifts.

Fate, again intervenes when their choices bring them renewed danger and Sam, Jenny and Jonah find themselves involved in someone's scheme to find hidden diamonds. Ghosts disappearing into bedrooms walls and mysterious figures in the wood are all part of this dangerous puzzle.

Once again, Sam needs the assistance of Charlie and his extraordinary friends, including the local witch, in the second instalment of the Winterne trilogy.

Volume 4 'Avaroc's Return'

As if the Winterne Clan haven't had enough to contend with over the last few years, Avaroc finally begins his campaign to seize power from Ellien, the rightful monarch of the British elves. He begins by turning clan against clan creating mistrust, betrayal and eventually war. But can he really trust his accomplice Tarryn? Who is Jericha and how is she involved? And what can Charlie and his friends do to stop Avaroc?

Anticipated launch early Summer 2016

Avaroc Returns

Chapter One

As a hint of dawn appeared on the skyline, flushed with success after their first night-time farm raid, five young elves, under the watchful eye of their tutor Piggybait, sang and laughed their way through the forest to their cavern home.

The older elf, tired of all their nonsense, strode ahead stabbing his carved wooden staff irritably into the frost-covered ground with every disapproving stride. Muttering under his breath at the foolishness of elven youth, he increased his pace until he had turned a corner in the tree-lined path, leaving his students some way behind.

Having been out with the hot-headed youngsters since the early hours of the morning, he found their stupidity astounding. The raids may have been successful, but their risk taking had almost caused the death of two of them.

It had not taken long before the headstrong twins, Piras and Ciran, had ignored his advice to stay away from Bragg's barn and recklessly slipped away from the group, eager to prove how brave and clever they were. Yes, they had got away with jugs of cider but, even though they knew how dangerous Bragg and his dogs could be, they had slipped away into the barn. Completely forgetting to check where the dogs were. Unfortunately, on this night they were not chained up.

Having reached the cider barn and busy with self-congratulation, Ciran made a whooping noise, startled some sleeping hens and their noise awoke the dogs. What followed was a confusion of barking dogs, lights, shouts, cries, clucking hens and feathers.

Piggybait, having heard the disturbance rushed in front of the two loose, slavering Mastiffs acting as a decoy. He was surprisingly agile for one of his age – even an elf. Distracting the dogs from the now terrified twins, Piggybait fled into the surroundings trees with the snarling dogs following him. He did not see the back door open, light flood out into the backyard or see the pellets being loaded into the shotgun. A gunshot rang out! Bragg!

Convinced Bragg would see him easily on such a crystal clear winter night when the moon was full and the sky teeming with silver, glittering stars, Piggybait fled the sound of swearing that followed him, and the

pursuing dogs, teeth bared and terrifyingly fast, Piggybait led them away to where he knew there was a small gap in the fence. He prayed the twins had got away.

Wriggling through the fence, expecting to be safe on the other side, he stopped to draw breath but the dogs, pure vicious solid muscle barged through as though the fence were made of matchsticks. Shattering the panels into splinters, the dogs charged but Piggybait was already speeding away towards the one place he knew would stop them. The river! Too wide for the dogs to jump, and slow for them to swim, Piggybait knew he could lose them there.

While he sprinted along the riverbank searching for the right tree, they almost caught him; they were so close he could smell their hot, foul-smelling breath. Finding a suitable, large tree with an overhanging branch, he sprang up the thick, gnarled trunk to the higher branches wishing it was summer and there were more leaves to hide in. But no matter, he was safe enough, dogs could not climb trees!

He rested, watching the frustrated beasts below desperately leaping high enough to snatch their quarry from his refuge. He was beyond capture but he had no doubt what they would do if they caught him.

A shout caught his attention. There was Bragg, gasping for breath, stumbling through the fence and bellowing furiously at the dogs. Piggybait chuckled. Bragg was panting hard as he stumbled up to the dogs.

Obviously disturbed from his sleep, Bragg had slipped a coat over his string vest and faded blue-striped pyjamas trousers, pulled on wellington boots and rushed out of the house having grabbed his shotgun, which he kept by the front door, on the way.

He looked around but saw nothing and, luckily for Piggybait, unable to see anyone hiding in the branches of the tree above him, he ignored the dog's furious activity around it.

'Come away, you stoopid pair,' he shouted at the dogs, 'there b'aint be nuthin there.'

Soon Piggybait had caught up with the elflings and, after scolding Piras and Ciran, ordered the sniggering band home.

Initially shame-faced and silent, it only took a short while before Piras began explaining to the others what had happened in the barn. Ciran giggled and soon the twins were noisily showing off their stolen prizes.

Annoyed at their lack of respect, Piggybait stormed off ahead leaving them to their nonsense, eager to get home to his comfortable armchair and the hearty breakfast Primola would have waiting for him.

Within the trees, hidden by the dense foliage on either side of the wide, grassy path, dark clad figures stalked their jubilant young prey. The January rising sun cast red streaks across the purple-blue sky but the crimson in the heavens would be mirrored on the ground before many more minutes had passed.

All unknowing, lugging the jam-packed cloth bags over their shoulders, the unwary elflings carried cheeses, eggs, bread, jugs of home-made cider and ale; a good haul for such young novices on their maiden raid.

One, Dastra, with pale blond hair shoulder length hair and a wide grin, toyed with the pair of boys trainers that dangled either side of his green-woollen clad chest, the laces tied in a knot at the back of his neck. Having found them in a rubbish bin, he could hardly believe his luck at the good condition they were in. Piggybait told him human children grew so quickly they rarely wore anything for long before it became too small for them.

The ambush came silently and swiftly. Silent assassins struck the young elves from behind, their small knives expertly wielded, silenced the laughter and song. These young sons of Winterne were caught unawares as six assailants sprang from hiding amongst the bushes and attacked them from behind in the dim light of dawn. There was never stood a chance of defending themselves.

Already having rounded a bend and no longer able to see the elflings, Piggybait became aware of the silence. The laughter had stopped. 'By the Lords of Alfheim!' he muttered in frustration. What were they messing about at now? He waited a few seconds before heading back to chivvy the youngsters on. Then his ears began tingling and he felt a sense of alarm. Something in the atmosphere warned him of tragedy.

On turning the corner, he fell to his knees. The elflings lay face down on the grass, their bags and contents strewn around, blood, egg yolks and milk blending before oozing into the earth.

Unable to stand, the old elf crawled, his vision blurred by horrified tears, towards the five lifeless bodies, struggling to make some sense of what had happened when his back was turned.

Dastra, the treasured trainers still around his neck, lay face downturned on one of them, a trickle of blood seeping from his mouth staining the white and blue canvas.

Just a few minutes before, these high-spirited elflings had been full of life, excitedly congratulating themselves on their haul of milk, eggs and cheese. They had been getting on his nerves; he was annoyed with them and had lost patience but how he regretted the scolding, how he wished he could go back to just a short while before and laugh with them. He would

228

forgive them anything if only he could bring them back to life. But who had done this? Why?

Even though he had sensed something dreadful had or was about to happen, he was taken by surprise at the speed, stealthy nature and ferocity of the attack. There was nothing he could do but despair at the loss of his young protégés.

Dressed entirely in dark forest green, their faces hidden behind masks, the strangers advanced on him and he knew his time had come. They could not let him live. There could be no witnesses to their appalling deeds.

'Why?' was all he asked as he backed away from them, desperately searching for something with which to defend himself. The six masked strangers encircled him.

'Remove your masks!' the old elf ordered bravely.

The one he took to be the leader shook his head. 'No Elder. You do not need to know who deals your death. Our Leader wants no-one left to tell what happened here.' He looked down at the young bodies sprawled on the ground among the broken eggs and spilled milk that was soaking away into the ground. 'No-one shall know who we are. It is our job to sow discord amongst the clans. Friends will become enemies. Brothers will turn against each other. That is his wish. It is time for his return and it shall be done his way.

Piggybait, showing courage he had not known he possessed, thought quickly. Was there a way out of this? He doubted it. He would die here. Perhaps that was not so bad. After what he had seen here, he felt he had lived far too long. Would Aerynne really miss him? Yes, she would. Their life together over the last few years had been good. She had made him happy and he thought she had been content with him. He pictured her kind face, her rain-coloured eyes. Then he remembered her warning. She had begged him not to take the elflings on this raid but he had ignored her. He should have known better. How many other times had her prophecies been disregarded but had been correct? Well, she was right and he was wrong. Would that be any comfort when she heard what had happened to him and the elflings?

More importantly right now though, how could he ensure his clan were told the truth? Looking up he wished hard; sent up a silent appeal for help.

'No good looking up there for help,' the leader of the group told him with an unpleasant smile.

But Piggybait knew better. He knew someone had heard his call. Backing further away, playing for time, Piggybait prayed she would get there in time.

And then, there she was, flying high above them, watching. Piggybait smiled. Mélusine, the Raven. She would be his witness. She would take the truth back to the Chief and the Clan. His death and that of the young elves in his charge would not be a mystery. They would discover who was behind this sickening act.

Close to the treeline, he stopped in his retreat and looked around him. Just a metre away from where he stood, he spied a large stick close to the edge of the path and bent to pick it up. His tormentors laughed.

Standing straight and pulling himself up to his full height, his years seemed to fall away as courage and faith buoyed him up. 'Come and get me!'

Lightning Source UK Ltd.
Milton Keynes UK
UKOW04f0349300915

259535UK00002B/58/P